Old Powder Man

Also by Joan Williams

The Morning and the Evening

HARCOURT, BRACE & WORLD, INC.

New York

Joan Williams

Old Powder Man

Do not go gentle into that good night,

. . . .

Rage, rage against the dying of the light.

—DYLAN THOMAS

In memory of my father, P. H. Williams
And for my mother, Maude

Old Powder Man

FRANK WYNN NEVER SPOKE MUCH OF HIS EARLY LIFE BUT could have told you in detail of the vivid afternoon it was decided they would move to Mill's Landing. He and Poppa were in the store late when Cally came in, her hat on, her face flushed and alive, having just gotten off the train from Delton, where she had been to see a new doctor. "Mill's Landing," she had said, coming in, and the door jangled its bell closing behind her. "How do you like the sound of that?"

They should have known what would happen next, they said later. But Poppa, seeing her happy face, said his first thought was, That doctor found something the matter with her.

Her eyes, like the rock candy in a big jar on the counter, glistened, pale and crystal-colored, and she clutched in one hand a paper sack with the name of a pharmacy on it they could only half-read.

"Mill's Landing?" Poppa said.

"The saw mill town on the river old Jeff Rankin started," she said. "Son's heard of it, haven't you?" She turned from Poppa to Frank.

Son answered, "The family owns all that other land over in East Arkansas?"

"Yes. For miles today we passed land with sharecroppers' cabins painted with blue roofs, Rankin land." She repeated in a soft, pretty way, "Mill's Landing. They need somebody to manage the commissary at the mill."

Poppa, understanding at last, said, "Now, Cally!"

"The ad in the paper said 'a qualified person,' and I said to myself, Henry is. You know the dry goods and the grocery and the meat business now." She held up three fingers to prove it.

I don't know anything about shoes or ready-made clothes, Poppa thought. But it was no excuse to offer Cally. Her mind was made up, he saw, and he had never once in thirty years changed it.

Son, astonished, said, "Mammy, are you talking about going? We just got here."

Cally said, "Poppa's not going to do a thing in this world running a grocery in this little crossroads, and it's my fault. I never should have moved us here from Cotton Plant without coming to see it first. It sounded like a whole lot more than it is. But you can't mistake working for the Rankins. I phoned the manager, a Mr. De Witt, and made an appointment at three o'clock tomorrow, Henry, and he said don't be late. There's a bus you can take in the morning." From the sack she took an oversized bottle of cherry-colored liquid and held it to the light. "Three good tablespoons a day!" she said, and they told by the clinking in the sack there were more bottles in it. Returning the bottle, she stood looking into the sack like a child into its Christmas stocking before twisting it closed. "This new doctor says it is my gall bladder. I knew it was."

"I thought the man last month said there wasn't anything the matter with it," Poppa said.

"He didn't know anything. A woman I met in the post office told me about him, and they were both of them old as Methuselah. You all close up and come on. I'm going to cook supper." She went out to the small house next door that came along for little rent to whoever leased the store.

Son said, "How many's this?" and counted them: "Jackson,

Brownsville, Dyersburg, Tennessee, Magnolia, Parkin, Cotton Plant, Arkansas, and here."

"It's a whole lot for a country boy that didn't intend to move any more than five miles from where he was born," Poppa said and looked back there: a wide place in the road, he called it. His family still lived in the insubstantial house next to the country church where his father had been and his brother now was the pastor. House and church stood in an old field, remnants of a corn crop growing up to the front steps, not a tree near for three acres. Having moved the five miles to town, Vicksville, Tennessee, Poppa claimed to have left home in search of shade. He was seventeen and soon employed in the dry goods store of a man not rich, but educated for the time and place, who sent two daughters to boarding school in Nashville to learn more thoroughly than in a country school. His third daughter, Cally, was only fourteen. The next year, she and Henry quietly married.

As her family had cautioned, Cally realized shortly to forego education for early marriage was a mistake. Her sisters married well. Suffering from a feeling of inferiority, Cally determined to live her own life beyond that with which Henry would have been content. Mild, meek, totally sweet, he was satisfied with not getting ahead. Every position Cally heard of she thought was better and took for Henry, who never ceased wondering what made her so restless, what made her think by changing her address, by making him change not only jobs but professions, she would change anything else. She had not. After the dry goods business, she had him manage a meat market; he was just catching on when she switched him to the grocery business. They moved first to places larger than Vicksville, then to places smaller. Criticized, and rightly, Cally also was admired for her determination and willingness to work. Bringing up two children, Frank and Cecilia, she had, when there had been no extra money, which was frequently, turned to catering and brought the family past many bad times. She loved Henry and his devotion was steadfast. He only sighed that afternoon in the store, thinking of the alien sound of Mill's

Landing, as he had sighed the other times thinking of the alien sounds, and having counted the cash and closed the store, told Son to look on the bright side. Maybe in the new place he would make enough to go on and on paying for Cally's medicines and for her doctor's bills.

Three years later, Son and Poppa could agree Mill's Landing was the best place they had ever lived. Poppa was doing better than he ever had before. He told Son he dared even feel roots, for Cally seemed pleased—dared even hope Mill's Landing was where his bones would rest. This morning, waking, he looked again with satisfaction at what he could see of the small, sound house; it seemed to be sleeping too, dark green shades drawn all around shut, like eyelids, its essence into darkness. Knowing autumn sparkled, Poppa got up and had almost finished shaving when he heard Cally get out of bed. Hurrying, he nicked his chin, opened the door and stood aside as she came toward it. "Morning, Boss," he said, prepared to ask for witch hazel, with the cut oozing blood, but she turned toward him a face of pain, real or imagined no one ever knew, and he saw her mouth was already full of pills. Dressed, he went to the kitchen and began breakfast, but soon Cally was there, surveyed her domain and said, "You wake Son."

Poppa would have knocked on the door had his daughter-in-law been at home, but since Son's marriage a year ago, Lillian had spent as much time with her mother as she spent here. The Lord knew, Poppa excused her, entering, there was not much for a young woman to do in Mill's Landing. Lillian, at seventeen, was five years younger than Son, and only slightly older than Cecilia who, at Cally's insistence, had been sent to boarding school in Delton, the nearest city. To Poppa's astonishment, money for the tuition had appeared ever since when a bill did, as Cally had promised. There was no high school in Mill's Landing. Children of the twelve other white families in town went by train twenty miles to Marystown, Lillian's hometown, where Son had met her. Until he brought Lillian home his bride, the family had never heard of her. They knew only Betty Sue who lived three miles away. Two springs and summers, with the evenings so long, Son had taken the buggy and gone to visit Betty Sue after the commissary closed, a rough, hard trip over a deeply rutted road. On Sundays he brought her back to Mill's Landing. They had gone through town and on down to the river where young people came from the countryside around to barbecue; or they swam in the bayou at the edge of town, behind the commissary, just opposite the mill, where old, twisted, grey-brown, sometimes topless cypresses provided spring boards from which to dive, seats on which to rest. Poppa remembered Betty Sue as bony, redheaded, laughing, with unsmoothed edges, a country girl, pure and simple. Son had met Lillian on a Saturday night in Marystown, where everyone went for the nearest fun; had seen her on frequent steamboat parties the young people took; going up river to a pavilion in Caruthersville, they danced until daylight to a band imported from one of the Virginia universities, and returned on a steamer for New Orleans, which let them off at Mill's Landing. Son did not know how to dance and not to know meant not to learn. Cecilia had offered to teach him and sensed he was too shy.

In Marystown, Lillian's mother ran a genteel tearoom on Main Street, tucked between the post office and bank, patronized at lunchtime by merchants and planters who on Thursdays, when the tea room was kept open until eight, brought in their families for supper at five. The men gave her their business because they admired a "widow woman" who had gone out in the world to make her own way. Lillian had grown up helping her mother after school but a year short of graduating gave it up, seeing no earthly good an education could do her. It certainly was not leading toward the early marriage her mother urged. Afterward she worked in the tea room full time, only refusing to wear a pink uniform and frilly apron like the other girl her mother employed.

What part of the two years Son took out Betty Sue, he also took out Lillian, the family never knew. But one Saturday evening, closing up the store, a year ago, Poppa had looked up to find that fall had come. The sun had gone. He was counting cash in almost total darkness where a few weeks before at that hour the store had been flooded with a dying daylight. Beyond the houses across the road, the cotton fields lay dark and gloomy, and while he watched, they had disappeared altogether, and he had looked at a night sky. Chill enveloped him and at the same moment, the doctor's boy had passed in shirtsleeves, pedalling his bike, and Mrs. Owens opening her front door, had pitched him a jacket, which he caught with one hand and put on, pedalling still. It caught more'n me by surprise, Poppa had thought, and the summer's death had touched him with shock, like the death of someone he knew.

He had had a similar shock on another morning when, shaving, he had looked at himself in the mirror and his instinct had said, quite calmly, You don't have much longer. Maybe two years, maybe more.

His razor halfway to his face, Poppa had looked at himself in surprise. But why? There's nothing the matter with me.

I know it. I don't know why. I just know.

Poppa, furious, had argued a few mornings, declared he did not believe it, had been defeated, and now almost accepted the defeat.

That Saturday, discovering himself in early fall darkness, he had reached overhead, pulled a string, and turned on the unshaded bulb hanging from the ceiling over the register, and was counting cash again when Son suddenly stepped into the circle of light, dressed in his best navy blue suit, the high collar of his stiff white shirt already making a red circle about his neck, his black shoes polished to a silvery sheen. He had been carrying a light topcoat and Poppa had seen it with approval thinking, the boy might need it.

"Poppa."

Poppa had looked quickly at Son, knowing it was something important.

"I'm going to get married. After I'm gone, tell Mammy. Would you lend me some money?"

Poppa had handed him a roll of bills, noting half-conclusively it was two hundred dollars.

With thanks, Son had gone to the door and looked back grin-

ning, a cockeyed, crooked sort of grin, handsome, somehow fool-
ish-looking, and yet brazen. Out of incredible blue eyes, health
and youth and hope and promise had looked at Poppa. Why
couldn't it be me? he had thought with a startled, jealous twinge
and said, "You're making an old man out of me, boy," and forgave him.

"I'll be here when the store opens Monday, Poppa," Son had
said.

When the train had left town, Poppa went down the one short
block home, having decided to tell Cally at supper. Cecilia was
home for the week-end. After grace she had said, "Where was
Brother going so spruced up?"

"To get married." Having poured thick gravy onto a slice of
white bread, Poppa had watched the bread soften until it was almost nothing. It took Cally that long to find her breath. It seemed
she could have died breathless it took so long. She even half rose
out of her chair then sat down again with an audible plop and
said, "Get married! He doesn't have any money. How can he get
married?"

"I gave him money," Poppa had said.

The women had begun to cry. Poppa guessed partly because
they had not been told, had been left out, but he saw, too, and
somewhat to his surprise, it had not occurred to Cally she was going to lose him. Her face had turned a very red color, except in
its wrinkles, and they had turned intensely white. Her colorless
eyes were cold steel grey and tears the same no color had run
one after another down her cheeks. Suddenly she had banged her
fist to the table and Poppa could tell she had wanted to cry more
than anything, But I didn't want him to get married! and that her
practical mind told her she had no right to. She did say, "He's too
young!"

It was Cally they consoled but Cecilia who had felt abandoned.
A tall, plain girl, she did not begrudge her brother's looks but
loved him. She had tried to be a good sister; why hadn't he told
her? she had thought mournfully.

9

Poppa had said, at least Betty Sue hadn't made Cally's mistake; she was as old as Son. Cally had said, "Yes, but she's . . . He could have done so much better."

Poppa had felt relieved. It was the first remark she had ever made concerning the boy's appearance and he had wondered if she were blind to it and why. "Well," he had said, and picking up his knife, had held a crust and with his fork pulled away bread and begun to eat. Cecilia, excited, had said, "Where will they live?" And they had discussed the practical aspects of what they thought of as reality, knowing if Son had said he was going to get married, he would, just as Poppa had known when Son asked to be lent money he would pay it back. Some of the money he had given Son had not been his own and Poppa would think about it later.

Son and Lillian had come in a buggy on Monday in time for Son to go to work. Cally and Poppa, knowing Betty Sue, had made no preparations for a new daughter-in-law. When Son opened the door, closed it, and said, "Here's Lillian, my wife," they had stared in embarrassment. Cecilia, waiting for the noon train, had seen a contemporary, felt foolish in her schoolgirl clothes, and knew her first fear of being an old maid. Laughing, Son had pushed Lillian into the room, and the family had come one by one to hug her.

Beautiful, with a round face and an enormous dimple in each cheek, when she smiled, which she did frequently and spontaneously, Lillian showed perfect, even teeth and the dimples spread and deepened in a way no one could find anything but enchanting. Her hair was brown and close to her face she had made several locks lighter, almost blonde, but even Cally, won over, never complained. Cecilia, her hair similar, began immediately to experiment with her own color.

In the next few days, Son and Lillian had turned the spare bedroom into a sitting room and had exchanged his single bed for Cecilia's double one, arrangements which seemed to content Lillian. Her background made her fit in well; she had known only moderate means, grace at the table, and had never seen anything but her mother's muscatel wine drunk at home. She had spent her time in the kitchen with Cally, learning to cook. On Saturday nights, Son took her back to Marystown. In Mill's Landing, the only entertainment white people had was to enjoy vicariously fun the Negroes had in their cafe. On warm evenings, sitting on front porches, white people listened to their laughing, yelling, and loud thumping music; the sounds came down the path, past the mill, down the road of town, high and low, like sounds being manipulated, all night, into Sunday. It would seem to be a high laughing voice and the next moment a roomful of voices high with glee, with music always as an undertone: passionate, sensual music that made Son's heart and blood beat with its beat.

When spring came the young people went again to the river and on steamboat parties, though Son said he was tired of watching people dance and would seldom go, despite Lillian's pleading. In summer, people came from everywhere to swim in the bayou and Son finally had persuaded Lillian into the water, though she feared snakes and the water's muddiness. It was only Mill's Landing to which she could not seem to reconcile: their first and continuing argument had been over the place. "But you knew I lived in Mill's Landing," Son had said in despair. Hadn't she accepted him knowing it?

"But I didn't know it was *nothing*," Lillian would say and begin to cry. Rather than wanting to comfort her, Son had to get away, crashed out of the house to pace the porch or the road, while a temper he had no idea how to direct flailed in all directions. Nor could he rationalize the reason her words so angered him was because they expressed his own feelings. What, after all, was Mill's Landing? What could he succeed at, here? His torment was relieved only by temper and his reputation for having one had begun to grow. He had had several slight skirmishes at the Marystown Tavern and was increasingly short-tempered with Lillian and Cally. Once, in a fit of frustration, he had kicked at Cecilia. He excused his attitude toward Cally; she always found a doctor to agree with her diagnosis of a new illness, leaving the family nothing to say, and he resented the way she kept Poppa's nose to

---

11

the grindstone, paying medical bills. Except for them, he believed Poppa could have gotten a little ahead in this world.

Poppa, having come farther into the room to wake Son, thought a second time, No, there was not much for a young woman to do in Mill's Landing; still, Lillian should have stayed here this past year more than she had. Now, he stood close to the bed and looked at Son. To Poppa, he seemed always a small child in sleep. His face against the pillow was dark; he tanned at the first appearance of the spring sun and kept the color until November. His hair was dark blonde, not particularly thick but it lay close, emphasizing high cheekbones and a narrow, well-shaped head. His eyes were amazingly blue, his nose prominent and strong-looking but slender at the tip. Above each nostril were indentations Cally enraged Son by calling dimples, and since he had been thirteen no female of comparable age or older had looked at him without reacting to such a degree that Poppa always had to laugh, to tease him too.

Having waked Son, Poppa went to the living room to read the morning paper, opened it as quietly as he could, had it hardly opened, when Cally's voice came as he had known it would: "Henry."

"I'm coming," he said. He edged forward, reading quickly.

Cally cocked her head around the kitchen door and called down the hall: "Henry."

"Coming," he said.

"You've got to help me," she said. "You've got to help me."

She did not need help, was quick as lightning in the kitchen; but she could not abide Poppa's sitting to read the paper. To her, it was doing nothing at all. Poppa entered the kitchen as Son did and when grace had been said, Cally put before Son the plate he had used the night before. Her rule had always been he and Cecilia had to eat first anything left at a previous meal. On the plate was a small amount of mashed potatoes, congealed gravy and half a biscuit. When in the world was the last time this happened? Poppa wondered. His mind, running backward, could not remember. He had assumed the practice long forgotten and could tell from Son's face he had thought so too. Last night, Son had received a telephone call from Lillian. By the time it was over, Cally and Poppa had left the table. Son did not return either, having so little left. So little, Poppa wanted to say.

Son stared at Cally; his eyes, white with anger, were as colorless as hers. Poppa saw something else in Son's eyes, alien to himself, and was not sure he wanted the boy to feel it either. Son's manner partly apologized for a look of determination tinged with mockery and a certain sadness, making Poppa feel unworldly. Looking down at his plate, Poppa pondered again his own life and its end, wondering if he had done anything at all. Unexpectedly, Son ate, and Poppa, relieved, did not think about the same half-foolish, brazen, cocked grin he had seen again. He said, "Is Lillian coming today?"

"Noon train," Son said. In the silence afterward, they thought of her frequent absences. "If I can have extra time, I'm going to take her to the river for lunch."

Poppa nodded. Cally said, "It's cool at the river."

"Not too cool," Son said. "We can go one more time. Old Deal got me to caring about that river, maybe Lillian will too."

"It's men love the river," Cally said.

Son said, "Speak of the devil, yonder's the old man now."

"Uh, oh," Poppa said, glancing out. Standing, he put on the black coat hanging on back of his chair.

At that moment, the mill whistle, punctual as Deal, blew a long shrill time. Son watched the old Negro take elaborately from his pocket a large, gold watch, smooth and slim as a full moon, and thought of all the times he had heard its story: the watch had belonged to old Mister Jeff, the mill's original owner, and had been willed at his death to the oldest employee; along with it went a job as long as Deal lived. Standing on the porch, Son watched the ice man come up the walk, carrying with dull tongs a large block. Behind him, its dusty length, the main road of town was pocked by a trail of water from his wagon and children on their way to school followed, begging ice in chips and pieces. Ice boxes were kept on the back porch where holes in the floor allowed water to drain under the house. People were furnished ice boxes, and ice, like everything, was charged to them by the year. Poppa came out. Going down the walk, he and Son faced Negroes coming from their houses to join Deal, forming their daily procession from the part of Mill's Landing called Niggertown. Some Negroes were headed toward the mill, others toward the river and the woods. Son watched them all with envy, thinking restlessly of his day in the store. He saw a man stop Deal; the old man started then on his first trip of the day to the commissary. Son mimicked to Poppa what Deal would say: he was a trapped rat, running from one place to another, the others crying in his ears all day: Deal! get us boys some cold lemonade. Old Deal! you not doing nothing run mail me this letter. Deal's job was to check on the Dutch ovens beneath the mill, ordinarily done by someone in a few spare moments; sawdust, the refuse, fell into the ovens and burned. Poppa said, "You enjoyed the old man's stories at first, learned all about this countryside from him. You can't just cast him off. We're the only ones not too busy for him to talk to."

Son said, "Yeah, I guess so," and watched Deal settle himself onto a bench at the commissary; this, the only two-story building in Mill's Landing, had two doors fronting the road; the largest led into the commissary proper and was flanked on either side by plate glass windows with benches beneath. The smaller door, to the left, led to a hotel upstairs where migrant and unmarried mill hands lived or those who had left their families elsewhere, sometimes temporarily, sometimes not. Behind the stairway to the hotel, adjacent to the commissary, was the hotel's dining room, a spacious, bare-looking room with a table in the center long enough to seat twenty people. Every effort was made to make eating there homey, and it was. At every meal the table was covered with a heavy white cloth. Every regular diner had his own napkin ring and a good large napkin, regularly washed. Three times a day the table was obscured by dishes. The men always had a choice of light bread, corn bread or biscuits and for breakfast there was bacon or smoked sausage and in season quail, not a luxury in those days. Early enough in the morning to clean them before breakfast, the two cooks went out and tramped the frosty woods some several hundred feet from the kitchen door. Through the quiet, still morning, the mill people would hear occasional shots, and the cooks always came back with enough of the frail little birds. In summer, when corn was fresh, it would be on the table in three different ways, on the cob, scraped from the cob and fried, or creamed, and there were black-eyed, crowder, field and tiny lady peas; tomatoes, fresh from vines near the back door, seemed bloody and ready to burst, a bite of one disappeared in your mouth. Son and Poppa, coming up the commissary steps, smelled ham and red-eye gravy, lifted their noses like hounds to sniff. Men in various attitudes of having just eaten, inserting or removing toothpicks, lighting or rolling cigarettes came from the dining room and spoke.

A corrugated tin awning jutted from the building over the sidewalk, its length supported by thin iron poles. Often when Son and Poppa arrived Deal was there, sitting on a bench, waiting for the store to open. Recently he had taken to carrying a cane and walked tap, tapping it like a blind man, though his eyesight was as good as when he was twenty; he carried it to lean on when he sat, feet pointed out, cane between them, his hands clamped one over another on its silver head. His wife worried about his forgetting to button up. He couldn't help being old, Pearl had said, but was not going to be one of those old men. She wiped his chin, kept him shaved, made him change his underwear every day. Sparse as a bird, Deal gave the appearance of roundness: had a round head full of thick curly white hair and his pants, too big as he shrank with age, tightly tied at the waist with clothesline, bagged out around his legs, balloon-like. At night, he was kept awake by the straws of their worn old mattress. But Pearl was big. He stuck a straw in her, it broke off, and she never knew the difference, he told Son. Her side of the bed had sagged long ago. In sleep, he braced himself. Times Pearl turned over he was lifted from the bed: bounce bounce bounce. When she was settled at last, he was. She called him Birdy: Birdy man! at their best times. Little or no, he always had done the job. But that had been over with some years now and to his surprise it had been something of a relief when it had gone, so intense had it been. It had tapered off, gone gradually, and left him with a kind of peace afterward. Pearl, younger, had not been ready. He had watched something in her wilt that brought a certain grumpiness, though she never said a thing. He had wanted to say, Girl, go and get it someplace else; he would not have minded that so much as the others knowing Birdy man had dried up. She lay beside him hoping, waiting, remembering. For a long time, out of a desire to please, he had tried to arouse the feeling again but it wasn't there; it wasn't anywhere. Son had said, "You're lucky anyway, old man. You got a good woman who don't complain."

Poppa unlocked the store. Son wondered if Deal were asleep. Sometimes the old man pretended to be, so people passing would not bother him with talk of the weather—what it was like today and expected to be like tomorrow—or of crops or the mill. He had told Son none of it mattered: one of the advantages of old age. Rid of the world about him he thought of the past and the future when he would know what the reason for the past had been. One thing Son had found working in a little country store was you had time on your hands; lumped together, the times would add up to hours he and Poppa stood, staring into the road. That first year if Deal had not come in to talk, Son did not think he would have made it. But now he had heard all the old man's stories over and over. In each of the other little towns they had lived, he had hung about Poppa's store. But here Deal's stories had taught him to care about the outdoors. This minute, Son drew in the dusty sweet smell of freshly cut wood Mill's Landing was always full of: one of the few things Deal said was the same. Inside the mill, the smell floated about like the sawdust glittering there; early, Son had learned to hold his hand into the semi-dark and bring it down covered with a thin fine gold film. Reluctantly, he left the porch to follow Poppa inside.

Never before had he had patience with old people; in fact, Son knew he did not have much patience at all. But since living in Mill's Landing he had listened for hours to Deal talk about the past. Deal had been a roustabout on lumber barges, had sat at docks until a barge came in going someplace he wanted to go.

Many times Deal came into Mill's Landing and saw Mister Jeff, a barrel-chested man who always rode a big white horse. One day Mister Jeff had offered him a job at the mill; without knowing why, Deal took it. Pearl, eleven years old, was cooking for Mister Jeff then; that was when Deal met her. All around Mill's Landing there had been one great world of trees. Taller than the highest building Deal had ever seen, trees had grown up as far as he could see. In those days, no one knew about draining land. In the swamps that stood, cypress and willow flourished in bent, scrawny, strange positions, like things from a world that had been and gone. And moccasins! Deal told how when you blew their heads off, they went on moving, headless, until they slid from wherever they had been sunning, back into the ugly, brown-green water. Whong. Deal's hands would clutch his cane; he would pull the trigger again. But swamps were disappearing; these past few years people had begun to drain land, to farm. And cotton, Mr. De Witt, the mill's manager, said, was going to be king. Acres of trees had been felled and tree stumps stood in rows as even as a crop. The sky where they had been, suddenly revealed, looked awkward, too bare and big, empty of tree tops.

Deal had taught Son to chew the sweet gum's sap, taught him to cover its sticky balls with tin foil, decorations for the Christmas tree he cut in the woods. Sometimes they repeated the names of trees wondering which they liked best: Sweet Gum. Maple. Sycamore. Oak. Pecan. Cottonwood. Hackberry: they liked them all. Deal told often a repeated dream: all the trees floated away toward heaven, dirt falling like brown rain from their roots; he called, Where are you going? but they were gone, gone with old Mister Jeff and the world to which he and Deal had belonged.

Now the sun blazed on Mill's Landing all day long if it wanted; in the summer evenings, twilight lingered till almost bedtime. But in Deal's time, trees had been so thick that dark came early. Hunters, deep in the woods, would stop and listen in the late afternoon and way back home, down by the bayou, the womenfolk, taking turns, would ring a great iron bell. Clang clang clang through the still cold silence, through the dark the sound came, and shouldering their guns, calling the dogs, the hunters followed the sound home. Not until the last man was safe, walking the town's road, would it cease. Those were the days of the Lord's plenty, Deal said. He told about the men bringing home full-breasted turkey, their wattles red as fire even in the pale flickering light of a lamp one of the women would bring on the porch to see. Squatting on their haunches the men would compare their birds: quail, duck, geese. There would be rabbits, frozen with legs extended as if they were still running, and squirrels, their little legs lost altogether in a limp lump of fur and tail. Many nights, with the moon high, there were fox hunts, just to run the dogs. In Niggertown, they sat on their porches and listened to that far-off baying. Sometimes it came with a pressing urgency, with a sound more ghostly than real, that sent a chill down a Negro's spine. In those days, even the river had been a half-mile further east. Like the rest of the world Old Deal had known, it had refused to remain unchanged. In sleep now, before the commissary, he dreamed and called, River, I know you! It seemed he stood on the bank this side, shaking his cane. Go back where you belong, case Mister Jeff come! Deal opened his eyes into blue ones. Son, having watched from inside the commissary, had come out to wake him. "Hey, Old Deal," he said. "You must have been chasing a rabbit. You were setting here just a going."

The old man got up slowly and came through the door Son held open. "I come after something, Mister Son. But it slip my remembers."

"Sit down," Son said. "You'll remember after awhile." They went to the dry goods counter, Son's part of the store. Deal sat on a nail keg, and Son began to dust shelves almost to the ceiling lined with bolts of cloth. Later, he would set out boxes for the women to poke in, full of socks, thread, buttons. Above the shelves, two narrow windows admitted almost the only light; the plate glass ones were shaded by the tin awning. Through the small windows two shafts of sunlight, alive with motes, fell in unspectacular ways, making the commissary gloomy. On the opposite side, Poppa dusted equally tall shelves full of canned goods. On the floor were small bins of potatoes and onions, fruit and a few other vegetables; people ate food from their own gardens. The store sold flour, meal, lard. Shoes and boots hung from the rafters; down the center of the room a waist-high counter was full of heavy work clothes and underwear. About the room were racks of the shapeless, flowered cotton dresses the women wore year after year. Presently, Deal remembered it was tobacco he wanted and went to buy it from Poppa. It was only such small items the Negroes came in for regularly, candy, gum, cold drinks. Unexpectedly a child, shot up like a bean pole, had to be brought in for shoes or pants; a woman might run short of something inexplicably, for the Negroes shopped twice a year, spring and fall, bought their families clothes and supplies for six months of either cold or warm weather. In summer they might buy side meat or baloney, but in winter ate their own meat, kept in smoke houses. Everyone raised hogs and chickens, hunted, kept cows. The Negroes were encouraged to charge in the commissary and at the year's end always owed money. For many years, few of them could read and it was true, as they suspected, that if they ever got out of debt, their accounts were juggled until they were back in it. Now, many had been to school and checked their accounts or paid cash. But Mr. De Witt, the manager, was a step ahead; he had their medical bills juggled; who could estimate what a doctor's time or medicines were worth? No one was ever free enough of debt to quit the mill. A few men had run away.

Deal left the store and several ladies came in to spend the morning talking to Poppa and looking at patterns. Son went out for air once, looked past the houses opposite, beyond cotton fields and toward the river where on clear, still days he could hear the Negroes yelling and cursing as they cut and loaded logs; they were put on the Rankin freight train that ran twice a day from Marystown to the river and back. Coming into town, the train stopped to unload mail and supplies for the commissary, then ran on to the river to be loaded with lumber for the mill. Extra logs were dumped into the bayou where they floated all winter long like somnolent brown alligators, bumping each other slightly. Loaded with cut lumber the train returned to Marystown; connections could be made from there anywhere, via Memphis, Delton or St. Louis. One year, the train was made up of a hundred flatcars, half loaded with sixty bales of cotton each, the rest with lumber. Between Marystown and the river were eight little villages; at all of them people came out to see the hundred flatcar train, to wave and yell.

Two slow passenger trains a day ran the same route, the only ones in this part of Arkansas. Begun by old Mister Jeff, the trains belonged to the Rankins too. Before them, people and logs travelled on the river. Today Son heard only lumber being stacked at the mill with a sound like, Clam. Clam: one plank being stacked on another.

Throwing away his cigarette, turning back to the store, he glimpsed Cally in their yard. Stooped, she coaxed a fire under the black iron pot where clothes boiled and bubbled like a witch's brew. As Son watched, she stuck a heavy, black cast iron skillet into the fire, squatted, balancing it. As long as the fire burned, the skillet would stay and by degrees its crinkled stubborn black crust would melt into the fire. Removed finally, the skillet would have the same shiny, blue-black look like coal it had had the day Cally bought it. She recoiled from a sudden spurt of coals, shielded her face, and standing, eased her back by pressing her hands into its center. She went inside and Son jerked open the commissary door, slammed it, and went angrily behind the counter, his face burning as if it had been thrust near the fire. That's not going to be Lillian, he swore. It's not going to be Lillian or any kids we ever have. Somehow, things had to be different.

Like Cally, the knowledge had come too late he should not have quit school when he did. He had quit when he was fourteen years old, after the eighth grade, to run away from home: had done it to spite Cally, he guessed. She had drummed into him from the time he could remember that he had to finish high school. When he got ready to spite her that was the only way he knew how. From the time he was twelve, he worked every summer and Christmas vacation, earning his own way, and she took away most of his pay. One Christmas he had worked for a jewelry store, famous for finding old silver, that had a large mail order business; he worked in the receiving office and felt important because most of the business was with a dealer in San Francisco. At Christmastime the store was so busy he often worked till midnight, spent the night on a little cot the manager set up. At five-thirty he was up again; he was making ten dollars a week, adequate then. Cally said he was a young boy, liable to be reckless with the money; she took it to keep him from spending it. He believed her reason but one day knew she was not going to take his pay anymore. After work he went down to the south part of town and got on a freight train going to Kansas City, where he changed onto another going out West. It had been his dream as long as he could remember, and don't ask him why, because he didn't know, to go to Colorado and to climb Pike's Peak. And he did.

In Colorado he worked for a timber outfit, a long way out from nowhere, and part of his job was to get on a handcar and pump it to the nearest little old town and collect the outfit's mail, then pump on back to the lumber camp. It was hard work, and in the summertime, the sun beat on his head as if it were a drum inside and sweat poured down over him like a bucket of water tossed. But if you didn't think that was a time for a kid, fourteen years old, flying along the railroad track, pumping that handcar, you had another thought coming, Jesus!

He stayed two years, with no one knowing where he was until he walked in home again, a day he would never forget. Cally was fixing for some big fancy society party and had baked two dozen or more angel food cakes, the thing she was famous for. She had them all over the house, on every flat place she could find, on every stick of furniture, cooling. He never had seen so many cakes in his life; the smell in the house was sweeter than a garden. Walking in, he had said, "Well, Mammy, I'm back."

She had turned around. In her hand was a big spoon coated with white icing just come to the right stage. "So I see," she had said.

He did not know why he had come back, except that it was home. He sure had liked it out West. He wished he had been born a cowboy instead of where he was. Nobody knew what had hap-

pened out there, though he had had it on his mind to tell Poppa.
He had seen him bursting with questions. Coming back into the
store, he decided to do it now.

"Poppa," he said across the empty store. Poppa stood at the
front window, looking out. "You know when I was out West? Was
there anything you ever wanted to ask me about it?"

Poppa, having turned, held back the interest in his face. "Was
there something you wanted to tell me?" he said.

So Son told him the whole thing, climbed up on a stool, hooked
his feet into the rungs, and Poppa sat on the nail keg. Son told
about the freight to Kansas City and the train out West from there,
about all the jobs he had applied for and the one he finally got,
about the lumber camp and the handcar. He told about the man
and his wife who had run the camp and how they had liked him
so much they had wanted to adopt him. It was not until then they
knew he had run away from home. Perhaps that was when he had
decided to come back, when he had thought of never coming again.

"What was the country like, Son?" Poppa said, unable to wait
any longer.

Son looked a moment out through the plate glass window at the
town's dusty road, past the little houses, and at the dark green
cotton field. All around its edges trees grew up as tall as you could
want, but they did not seem as tall as the trees out West. Nothing
here seemed as big or as wide or as beautiful. To gaze upon the
flat land here for miles gave you the feeling there was nothing
else, only the flat land going on without end, always the same. But
in the West the mountains, like kaleidoscopes, continually changed,
burst red with sunset, changed slowly into deep purple and disappeared altogether with night, all unexpectedly reappearing capped
with snow. Son's mouth fell open and he was about to say how it
was nothing like this flat muggy country. It was air you could
breathe. He was going to tell about the mountains, purple at dusk,
circled with clouds like rings of smoke, about snow falls, and the
opportunity there for a man even if you were not so young.
Poppa's face was closer now, waiting to hear, and instead of telling, Son shrugged. "It wasn't so much," he said. "The mountains

---

22

were pretty, but there was nothing to do with them. Just look. After awhile you forget they're there."

Poppa said, "But what about Pike's Peak? What about when you climbed there?"

"Poppa, shoot. You couldn't have breathed halfway to the top. I thought I was going to give out. It's just a country some folks like to talk about. It's not much."

Son had averted his eyes lying but now looked back. He saw he had not fooled Poppa. On his face was a look of wonder mingled with longing and excitement, then Poppa said, "I got to go get up a canned goods inventory."

Half a mile away the noon train whistled. Son went out and stood on the front steps. Glancing to his right, he saw Sudie Baker, the postmistress, putting up mail that had come on the morning freight. He called back, "Mail's puttin' up."

Poppa came more hurriedly than usual and went next door. Mrs. Owens, having crossed the road, caught up with him on the post office porch. "Henry, you look like you're expecting some big something."

"No mam." Standing aside, Poppa held the door for her. "I don't get no kind of mail but doctor's bills."

Down the road others were coming, and down the road at the elementary school, the doors opened, and children, pouring homeward for lunch, slivered the country stillness with high-pitched thin voices, startling birds from trees. Old people sitting on their porches turned expectant faces toward the sounds, speaking in their faded voices when the children came up the walk to home. Jumping on and off the post office porch, Sudie Baker's children cried, "Ma, we're here! We're here!"

"Coming," she called from inside and came out shooing mail readers before her and locked the door. Those who had not made it in time turned away disappointed until one o'clock.

Poppa, looking pleased, stood a moment finding gum in his pockets for the Baker children. Son, whistling, went down the steps, his hands in his pockets; he started to the station as the mill's noon whistle split the world in two. It caught Mrs. Owens with her mouth open; she stood so while it blew, then finished telling Sudie what she had been telling. Son ceased whistling, the sound by contrast small and useless. An old man who had shouted through the whistle, not realizing it had stopped, kept on shouting to another man as Son passed. The train's noise seemed like a toy's by comparison. Son saw Lillian through the window an instant before she waved and came, a small person, down the train steps. She held up her face to be kissed. "Is everything all right?" she said.

"Sure. Everything's the same. How's your Mammy?"

"Don't call her . . ." she said, but her eyes grew round, and she stared past him in surprise.

Turning, he stared in surprise too. Cally, dressed for travelling, came toward them carrying a needlepoint shopping bag, black with a cluster of red cabbage roses. As if everything were ordinary, she kissed Lillian, then went on past to the train's steps, turned and called, "Tell Poppa I'll be home for supper. It's already cooked. I'll be here to put it on the table."

She was wearing, Son saw, not just better than everyday clothes, but her very best clothes, a heavy black crepe dress, black oxfords, a wide black hat, the severity relieved only slightly at the V-neck of the dress by a large cameo set in a heavy gold mounting. Cally had been pretty, and could have been still with any effort; but she wore her hair pulled straight back, "skinned" Lillian called it, from her face and twisted into a tight knot. Her hair had been dark auburn but greying was the color of sand and with her colorless skin made her nondescript. She would hear nothing of applying artificial coloring; though on Sundays she powdered her face heavily with corn starch. Lillian, gathering courage, once suggested she wore too much. Cally had shrugged saying, Oh it'll blow off by the time I get to church.

"Mammy, where on earth are you going?" Son said.

"Marystown to get the train for Delton," she said, pulling herself up the steps. Son and Lillian glanced at one another; he reached the train as she started into the coach. "How are you getting back from Delton tonight?" he said.

_____

24

"With the people of one of the girls at Cecilia's school," she said. "They're driving me to Marystown, and I'll get the evening train home."

He stepped back, not needing to ask, but Lillian came forward to say, "Why are you going to Delton, Mammy?"

"To get my gall bladder drained," Cally said and entered the coach.

The train, like some medieval dragon, snorted, sending puffs of steam from its undersides; Son and Lillian, stepping back, could not see Cally through the steam-obscured window. "Do you think she's really going to get her gall bladder drained?" Lillian said.

"Jesus if I know," he said. "Let's go to the river. I got the buggy all spruced up. It's over to Old Pete's."

All around them mill hands, white and Negro, who had stayed to watch the train, were moving on home for noon dinner, now that the train was going. In the hotel's old wooden dining room lights were on and several men were going in the side door. A cluster of Negroes passed close, laughing, jostling one another, and Son took Lillian's arm and held her close. They went the length of the mill to the blacksmith's, a dark little shop, where Old Pete, sitting up on a buggy, waved a sandwich and said, "It's out yonder, ready."

The horse, tied in the shade of a great maple, had its head sorrowfully hung. "What's the matter, old lady?" Son said, swatting the animal's rump. He untied it and Lillian, twitching her nose in distaste, climbed with difficulty into the buggy, clutching, pulling at her tight skirt. Son got in and Ruby, the horse, deliberately mischievous, set out at a pace too fast.

"Frank!" Lillian cried, clutching his arm, but he grinned mischievously too and let the horse run on, its ears flat back, eyes walled till nothing showed but their whites. "What's the matter?" he said. In a burst of hilarity, he laughed until tears came.

Her voice shaken by the buggy's bouncing, Lillian called, "I haven't been in a buggy since I left. Automobiles . . ." but she gave up; it was too hard.

"We'll have us one," he said shortly and stared ahead, letting

Ruby continue in her headstrong way. Hearing the commotion, several women came to their front windows, peeked at them passing, and confirmed to themselves what they had already suspected: the Wynn boy was a wild young buck.

Going down the main road they passed between two rows of cottonwoods. In the latter part of summer and all through the fall, the trees dropped a white lint that scudded in fluffs when the wind blew and lay otherwise like a light snow over the ground. They met Negro children going home from school, the smallest being pulled in rusted wagons, their short legs stuck out before them. Little girls wore enormous hairbows like magnificent butterflies atop heads that seemed hairless, so tightly was the hair drawn in three places into plaits that stood out from their scalps. With the sun behind them, the little faces looked darker, the clearest feature the whites of their eyes. Their teacher, in a buggy, touched the whip to his hat and Son called, "Brother Roy!" in acknowledgement. The children had gone to school two months of the hot summer, July and August, and now were released to pick cotton until Christmas. Those passing in the buggy chanted, "No more lessons, no more books, no more teacher's dirty looks," and Lillian saw several pairs of eyes peeping at them, the children, like small wild animals, thinking because of their own stillness, they were not being seen.

Ruby went now at a genial trot. They watched in silence the road ahead, so bright beneath the sun as to make them squint. Occasionally the road swung one way or another into a curve so wide it was almost unnoticeable, but it never altered direction, went always straight ahead, sometimes between dense woods, sometimes between woods which had been thinned and had sunlight entering them, sometimes between fields thick now with cotton bloom. The land visible between the rows was black as coffee, alluvium-rich, virgin still to farming. Above them, the sky hung with that suddenly vacated, almost surprised look. Negroes in relief against it, bent-backed, with slow rocking motions chopped and pulled back, chopped and pulled back, straightened altogether and stood leaning on their hoes to watch the buggy as it passed. A half-mile from the river the land rose once naturally and from the crest of the slight hill they glimpsed the river, looking as blue and as sparkling as the ocean. Ruby, hurrying despite herself, ran down the slope on the other side, had hardly time to catch herself up again before they arrived at the river's bank. "Back yonder," Son said, "is where a levee ought to be." He half-turned and waved slightly at the rise behind them.

"But why would you want another levee?" Lillian said, staring at the bank before them; it was matted heavily with willow branches for protection.

"Shoot, what about '12 and '13?" Son said. "We get another flood like those, the willows won't do any more good than a feather in a fire. You need a secondline levee. Something between here and town." Once he had said as much to Mr. De Witt and could tell by the way Mr. De Witt answered too loudly he saw the validity of the idea. It's all we can do to keep up the damn levee we got, he had said. There lay the problem: money. You get the s-o-b Federal Government to do something. Get it to build and maintain the levees instead of every man for hisself, and we'll build another one. Mr. De Witt had cursed more vividly the Federal Government and sent Poppa, with a scarlet face, to the back of the store. But Son had only stood watching him in admiration, laughing. Mr. De Witt was prosperous and determined; they seemed to Son the marks of success. Mr. De Witt had gone onto the porch, spit through a space in his teeth, and said, When the water rises, we'll put down more willow mattresses. We'll hold the Goddamned river! His boots were a mahogany-colored leather, so fine, so mellowed, so polished, they flashed, reflecting the sun. He had mounted, putting the crop to his horse's rear with such force it would seem he hated it, though he loved it more than anything in the world. Cantering off, he had scattered small children playing in the soft dust drifted to the center of the road. When he was gone, everything had seemed quieter, the commissary darker and smaller, and Poppa, standing in the store, seemed smaller too,

27

his black, flowered galluses seeming to slice into his thin shoulders. Hell, Son had said that day, having to go behind the dry goods counter.

At the river, Ruby snorted and shuddered all over, as if shaking from memory her recent run. Son sat forward and held the reins loosely. Ruby, taking them one turn of the wheels forward, bent to nibble at dry grass around the clearing where they had stopped, her upper lip, soft as moss, lifted delicately. Mesmerized, Son and Lillian stared down silently at the great rushing river, at the wide unbroken view of its sweep above and below them. The distance across was such that while they could see quite clearly the white sand bar that was Tennessee, it was only indistinctly they could see three Negroes stretched out on it fishing. When they spoke at last, it was to guess whether it was three men or two and one woman. Close up, the water held no hint of blue as it had from a distance and flowed swiftly; when clouds parted, the water was colorless-looking beneath the sun's bleaching, but moving slowly, the clouds came together and the water, shaded, took on its true color and swept on past them southward, a light, watery-looking brown. The water would seem suddenly to overtake itself and instead of flowing would come in a series of foamy ripples like miniature breakers, then again would flow smoothly, carrying with it sometimes a log or a branch and once some indistinguishable whiteness that, speculating, Son and Lillian decided was cotton lint. Above them the river came in one straight course, curving only slightly around the end of the sand bar, but below them, having altered its once straight flow, it curved now toward the bank opposite, eating away again year after year the levee it had formed depositing sediment to pile up in the years of its unconfined overflow. The river made no sound; all around them was silence. The Negroes stood up and moved about, threw in their lines or pulled them out; labelless tin cans in which they had their bait sometimes caught the sun and shone out like signals from the opposite bank, but their voices were lost in the distance between. Cows grazed nearby, lifted their heads to chew, chewed silently and looked at them with seeming depth in their dark eyes. Trees behind the sand bar screened from view the farmland beyond, but they heard shots there now, short, dull, muffled sounds lingering after themselves like thunder rumbling harmlessly across a humid summer night's sky. Then crows, scattered from corn, flew up, something moving and black above the tree tops, against the shining sky, and one of the Negroes, leaping up, ran after them a long way down the white sand waving his hat while their deep-throated, jeering, raucous cries filled the countryside.

Ruby lifted her head and started forward, but Son caught the reins and held her back. "Whoa, girl," he said softly. The crows having hushed or gone, the silence had returned, but it was not the same, having been broken.

Lillian shifted about several times. "Shall we go back? What about your lunch?"

"Got it with us." Son leapt from the buggy and took a brown paper sack from beneath the seat. Poppa had made them baloney sandwiches, filled a jar with ice and lemonade. Lillian got down and followed Son across the clearing toward a shade tree, watching in dismay as dust clung to her recently polished new kid shoes. "Watch that," Son said as she almost sat; he drew from beneath her a branch broken from a thorn tree, the thorns as large and as thick as his fingers. He started to toss it away, but Lillian took it and said, "I'll give it to Mammy. She uses these thorns as stilettos for her punch work."

Son passed her the lemonade jar; she drank from it and gave it back to him. They ate the sandwiches in silence. She was beginning to find that he never talked much. He found they had less to say after her trips home. It caught him back from what he was going to say when he saw her look around as if, all over again, she could not believe she lived in Mill's Landing. He had told her repeatedly, and was beginning to see she did not believe it, that even if they stayed in Mill's Landing, he would save her from Mammy's, even from her own mother's way of life: no wife of his would ever have to work.

Lillian laid her hand lightly on his leg, but only a moment; as she began to speak, he drew it away. Her hand remained, unsupported, not much larger than a child's. She returned it to her lap. "Mr. Warren ate at Momma's again this week, visiting back home too."

"Yeah. How's he getting along with his work." It was an expression, not a question. Son, leaning against the tree, finished the lemonade, let ice fall into his mouth, then spit it repeatedly back into the jar. He did not want to hear what she was going to say. Lillian carefully tore bread crusts into small pieces and tossed them away; on nearby tree branches birds hopped excitedly, indecisively.

"He's doing good," Lillian said.

"Keeping somebody else's books?" Son said; spitting ice, he wiped furiously at his chin.

"What's wrong with that?" She turned, arched, looked at him for the first time.

"I'll tell you what's the damn-hell wrong with it."

"Don't cuss."

"I'm not. Keep your mouth shut and I'll tell you what's the damn-hell wrong with it. I'm not going to spend my life working for some other son-of-a-bitch."

She put her hands to her mouth. "I don't want to listen to all that."

"You'll listen." He emptied the ice, clapped the top on the jar, and said, "Come on."

She followed him saying, "But Mr. Warren likes keeping books in Delton. He likes it a whole lot. He's already had a raise, and his company has a big picnic every year."

Son was already in the buggy and because of it, Ruby began to move. Lillian, tugging at her scant skirt, climbed up, half hobbling. Son flapped the reins across Ruby's back in a way almost mean. Surprised, the horse's ears stiffened and, with a look of listening, Ruby set off at a gait that bounced them unmercifully. They flew with a great rattling over the natural rise in the road, down the other side, past the shuttered little Negro school, on down the dusty, seldom-curving road. "Son-of-a-bitch," Son said, his teeth clamped together.

"Ruby! Whoa! Whoa!" Lillian called.

The horse was exceeding itself and Son drew in on the reins. Ruby, snorting indignantly, rippled her sides and slowed immediately; foam, flying from her mouth, caught in her mane. At a walk they passed the elementary school where children with bland faces were returning from lunch and a pumpkin with a grinning jack o'lantern face watched them from a window with empty eyes. Again they faced the shadowed main road where the cottonwoods dropped their soft lint. And this was Mill's Landing: the elementary school and twelve white houses with blue roofs, six on one side of the road and six on the other, the commissary-hotel building, a two-room building set aside for the doctor's office, and another two-room building housing the post office and drug store: the clerks in one doubled as clerks in the other. On the opposite side of the road leading from the far-away highway into town was the mill, the blacksmith shop, an ice house, and beyond them, Niggertown. Everything the Rankins owned, from here to Delton, from the largest bank down to the smallest sharecropper cabin, was painted the same, white with a blue roof; recently, Mr. De Witt built his own mansion several miles away and painted it similarly. It was said those with Rankin blood did not like it, but there it stood, like a small castle, with a moat and drawbridge. Geese strolled the lawn, keeping the grass neatly clipped; the rumor was their heads were to be painted blue, also. Going along the road, between the houses, beneath the cottonwoods, Lillian stared ahead miserably. The mill blew its returning whistle, shorter, not so loud. The last returning mill hand left the commissary, the yellow string of a tobacco sack in his mouth while he rolled a cigarette. In a cackling frenzy, a chicken flew away from Ruby's hoofs, leaving a feather in the road. Far, far away, Lillian heard the world. Feeling Son might lash her with the buggy whip when she spoke, she said nevertheless, "They're still looking for a salesman at that company Mr. Warren told us about. The one in the building where he works. He still says he'd recommend you. Frank, we'd have to move to Delton." Lillian had a momentary hallucination: an old story book had a beautifully colored picture of the Prince offering

---

31

Cinderella the glass slipper; she erased the figures, saw not one castle but a city full, pastel-colored, with turrets of gold gleaming in the sun.

Son, tying Ruby to the commissary's hitching rail, said, "Lillian, I don't want anybody trying to tell me what to do."

Poppa, in a white shirt, appeared like an apparition behind the dark screened door, until he pushed it open, saying, "Come here, children." His face was flushed with excitement; his cheeks were two red spots.

Making his second trip, Deal came from the store with a can of Prince Albert tobacco and said, "How do, Missus"; having touched his forehead with his cane, he hung it in his shirt pocket, where it swung.

"How you, Old Deal?" Lillian said.

"Too good. Overstayed my time," he said.

Son said, "Shoot, Old Deal. You telling me all those stories about when you was a roustabout, you better be glad you're here, stead of where you might be going."

"Naw suh, I repented," Deal said. "The Lord allows young folks a little something, don't you think, Mister Henry?"

"I don't know, Deal," Poppa said. "It seems to me like I never was young." Just then Son came up the steps looking at him, laughing, his eyes as blue as the sky behind him. He stood out as if the sun struck only him, so alive, so strong and tan, it made Poppa want to gasp; hearing the echo of his own words he suddenly wanted to bring the boy to his breast hard and hold him, as if by treating him as a child he could give him the childhood he had never had. The boy had known too early about work. Twelve years old, he should not have been out having the part-time jobs; all the things that had been wrong for Son came back to Poppa now, turned inward, and he felt everything had been his fault: his fault Cally had to work, his fault she had to scrimp along and teach the boy too young the world was hard, that if you left a bite on your plate, you ate it cold before anything else, that you could work your tuckus off and somebody bigger could take your pay; and what kind of things had the boy learned out there in the busi-

32

ness world, twelve years old? All he had known to do to fight back was run away, Poppa thought, wanting to bang his fist against the store post thinking of those people offering to adopt his son, *his* son; and he wanted to cry thinking of the better life they could have given him. They might have sent him back to school, helped him make something of himself. But what made Poppa suffer most was knowing they could not have given him a childhood he had never had. Before he was twelve years old, Son had helped in the store, helped Cally deliver cakes, scrubbed and waxed the kitchen floor on Saturdays. Poppa could not remember him ever having a time of doing nothing, like a boy ought to have.

"Poppa, you got your gas pain?" Lillian said.

"No, I feel fine, daughter." With a stricken face, he had tried to figure how to give childhood to this twenty-two-year-old boy, with a wife.

Deal said, "I got to make tracks. Take care," and waved the tobacco can. For an instant the austere bearded face on it looked at them behind the old Negro's back. Deal's cane went tap, tapping, poking at whatever came within reach, turned a leaf over, struck a cigarette butt in two, sent some cottonwood lint flying. Mr. De Witt, passing on his great clomping horse, looked at him out of the corner of an eye, and Deal slowed his way to work.

The three on the steps, laughing, turned into the store. "What is on your mind, Poppa?" Son said, wiping his face; the store was a relief like evening after a hot day.

Poppa took an envelope from his pocket and seemed as if he would dance a jig, he turned about so excitedly. "Listen!" Then too excited to remember what he wanted to say, he said, "Look!" From the envelope he took a printed circular and unfolded it; the words that leapt at them were FORD MODEL-T. There was a picture of it, black as and looking no more substantial than their buggy, with a canvas top folded back. The three bent over it exclaiming, seeing themselves up on those seats riding through the golden autumn afternoons.

"Poppa!" Lillian squealed like a banshee. "Are you getting one?"

Poppa, extending his chest, drew in breath, then let it out. "Well,

---

33

I've been saving toward it a long time. Son, when you made payments on the two hundred dollars, I said, 'Henry, pretend the money that belongs to you is extra.' I put it away. Sometimes I had to take a little out again if there was, well, too many doctor's bills. But I've kept on putting away here and there without its hurting anybody. I don't think?" He looked at them questioningly, half-afraid; quickly, they shook their heads, and Lillian said softly, "Oh, no": they had not been deprived. "Sometimes I didn't bring home the best cut of meat, you know. Little ways like that I saved. Cut down on tobacco. Didn't hurt me any either," Poppa said.

Well, I'll be damned, Son thought. He held the paper between his great thick hands, feeling a sudden strange sense of power. Never before had he been interested in mechanical things, but he peered at the automobile as if he could dissect it with his eyes, wanting to know every intricate piece of it, down to the last nut and bolt. He pondered the tires, the steering wheel, the brass horns on either fender, knowing he would polish them until his hands dropped off. He could not wait to get Lillian and go shooting off down the main street of Marystown. If they wouldn't be something! It had gotten so he was embarrassed to take her in the buggy, so many people had autos: it had marked him as, made him feel like a country boy.

Lillian with her mind on the same trip was deciding what to wear. An automobile at hand lessened immediately her pressing desire to move to Delton.

Poppa showed them a letter, neatly typed, business-looking. "I been in touch with the agency in Delton handling the cars. Now the man says he'll have one all gasolined up and ready to go next Saturday. I thought that would be the best day for you to take off and go get it. Then we can spend all Sunday riding. I haven't told Cally. Do you think I ought to tell her, or let you come driving up in it?" At the mention of her name, Poppa felt as if his stomach had dropped down a well. His excitement had been so tremendous, he had not stopped to wonder about Cally. She would not take even the buggy reins into her hands, would certainly not drive the car, but surely it would please her. She had worked all these years to set them up a little, to get the extras he could not provide; now he was providing a big one: for her, for his whole family. He would not tell even Son he did not have all the money. Because of amicable relations with the auditor, and without Mr. De Witt's knowledge, he had borrowed a little ahead on his salary; but he and the auditor had agreed his job here was money in the bank, so successful had he been at running the commissary, at pleasing Mr. De Witt, who liked a man no match for him.

"Surprise her," Lillian said.

For another reason, Son agreed. He did not want Cally to mar ahead Poppa's pleasure if she did not take to the idea.

Carrying the thorn branch, Lillian went home. The dining room table was set and in the oven supper was ready. She unpacked and kept busy straightening their two rooms. Once she came again to look at her mother-in-law's orderly quiet house, wondering if it had any physical appearance to explain a lady going alone to Delton to have her gall bladder drained.

When Lillian left the store, Son told Poppa of Cally's expedition. Poppa at noon had found his dinner set out on the kitchen table and thought Cally was at the drug store, at Mrs. Owens', anywhere about. He said, "Gone to Delton to get her gall bladder drained? Do you think the woman means it?"

"You got me," Son said.

"I guess we'll see," Poppa said, feeling cold all the way to his fingertips and toes wondering how much it would cost, this time.

At closing, he found on the counter a small can of snuff Deal had bought and forgotten to take. Would Son run to the mill with it? When Son went out it was almost sundown, the sky brilliantly pink, touched with yellow. Deal was on a campstool outside the oven room and as Son came up, a man appeared in a window above, spit, and said, "Shorty says you bringing his snuff or not?"

Deal looked up in surprise. Son, waving the can, said, "The old man forgot it. I'll bring it."

"I sho thought I took that, Mister Son," Deal said. "I sho did."

"It don't make any difference. He got along without it," Son said and went up the steps expectantly, glad of a reason to go; the mill, a busy shrill place, gave him a feeling of excitement the commissary never did. It was a place for men to work. Faces of the Negroes shone with sweat; muscles were apparent on their backs and arms. Son regretted again the hours he stood in the store. The mill had few windows but opposite the door he had entered was another and between the two was an alleyway of light alive with sawdust motes. Even when the day was dark and grey with rain the motes were alive there, dancing. Steel blades catching the remote light shone evil as shark's teeth, devouring trees as if they were no more than kindling. Son gave the snuff to Shorty who quickly returned to work; it was dangerous to look up for long; Shorty's hands directed logs to the lathe: swoop and swoop, the bark fell away as easily as an apple or a peach being peeled, fell to the floor in strips having exposed clean, sweet, surprisingly white wood. Son drew in again that familiar smell and went down the mill's steps wondering what it would be like in an office in Delton.

He stopped and spoke to Deal who was poking drifted sawdust to the rear of the ovens; it was safer there for the spitting, popping piles to burn. In the low room even Deal had to stoop; the ceiling was reinforced with railroad ties to support the mill's floor above. Forgetting, standing erect, Deal bumped his head; he came out, showing his hand bloody from the cut he had touched. Dr. Owens was away; Son took Deal to the store. When the cut was bandaged, Poppa gave Deal a good drink of whisky from the bottle kept beneath the counter for emergencies and Christmastime and said Son better walk the old man home. He could close up alone.

On the way, Son and Deal passed Mr. De Witt. For the hundredth time, Son listened to Deal say the reason Mr. De Witt rode that big white horse was because of old Mister Jeff riding Dixie Belle. They went on through Niggertown, between the rows of little houses that were all the same, with a privy in the back. Son, still restless, did not want to hear about Dixie Belle again. But Deal told again how when the horse died, he and Mister Jeff had eased her way on out, how she had shuddered her way out of life as she shuddered when she had eaten her full of oats. Son only half-listened and Deal told how that was the first time he had ever seen a white man cry, how he and Mister Jeff had spent the night, let dawn find them there, crying and talking about the horse, times they remembered this with Dixie Belle and that. Mister Jeff had said it was his time next and Deal had said, When the roll is called, ain't you afred to go? Mister Jeff had said, No. For, then I will know what's on the other side.

As Son and Deal reached the house, Pearl came to the door. She had been straightening her hair and it glistened as if full of rain-drops, just new. Inside, her jar of pomade was the brightest thing in the room: Miss Peacock: on the label was a tailspread bird, gaudy blue green gold. Excited, Pearl made Deal go right to bed. But before Son could leave, Deal had looked up from his pillow to continue his story: Mister Jeff had stood up on his old man's thin shaky legs. A rooster crowed and dawn had come. There was a musky, dark smell in the barn; the horse lay on her great side as they had never seen her, still, and flies had already begun to gather. The other horses stood silent in their stalls, their heads hung, as if mourning too. Then Deal had found courage to ask the question always on his mind: Mister Jeff, when I get to heaven, will I be white?

Son had moved toward the door; but he asked, as always, "What'd the old man say then?"

"If I wanted to be," Deal said.

The knowledge had comforted Deal through life; he was not afraid to die. Son knew the old man wanted to teach him not to fear the hereafter either; but Son never thought about dying. In this room, caught up with old gone sorry things, he felt more than ever his life was just beginning. He said, "Well, take care, old man. I got to hep Poppa."

Pearl opened the door and shooed away a porchful of chickens. "We both too old to be fooling with chickens," she said. "How else you going to eat? Mister De Witt has things higher at that comm'ssary than they are in Marystown."

Son shrugged and was sorry, knowing she was right; but he wanted to get away from people being poor: something he was al-ways surrounded by. He said, "I'll be seeing you."

Pearl said, "Tell Old Miss and Miss Lillian hello."

Son went away, neither answering nor looking back. All the way down the hill, passing again between the identical little houses, he remembered the dark eyes watching him. Callous and young and knowing he was too, he put them from his mind. Ever since he had been in Mill's Landing he had heard about Old Deal's life. Now, he wanted to concentrate on his own.

When steam obscured the train's window and Son and Lillian could not see Cally, she could still see them. Their images remained in her mind all the way to Delton. She was glad a nice girl had married Son; there was a roughness about him Cally did not understand at all. But she had not wanted him to marry so young. Why did he keep making her mistakes when she had tried so hard to keep him from making just those mistakes? It was the curse of motherhood, she believed; it was what kept the tight hard lines she knew perfectly well were there about her mouth, made the wrinkles in her forehead, kept her awake at night. Thinking of insomnia, Cally added to her shopping list a large supply of aspirin.

In Delton, she hurried through the station smelling in its various dark corners like urine, and took a street car to the doctor's. She told how she felt, dizzy upon arising, better after hot water and lemon juice, was going full strength by noon but had a decided letdown after that. The gall bladder draining was postponed, new medicine prescribed, more visits appointed, and Cally left happy. She rode another street car through weed-filled countryside to the end of the line and got off. All around as far as she could see, land was divided by strings and stobs into squares; in their midst was a wooden hut out of which smoke came. She went toward it on narrow planks, balancing one foot before the other. A man, coming out to meet her, said, "Good afternoon, Missus."

"Afternoon. Mr. Bianco?"

"That's right. Careful." With a strong square hand, he caught her elbow as she stumbled. Cally held toward him a newspaper taken from her shopping bag. "I saw your ad about the houses you're building for only a small down payment."

"All over here, there," Mr. Bianco said, taking a cigar from his mouth. He pointed and the lit end glowed and darkened, circumscribing air. "You pick which lot you want. I build the house. The road will run along here." Having stepped off the planks, they walked along a swath cut through the field and stood where Mr. Bianco said a sidewalk would be, looking up and down at two rows of foundations. Mr. Bianco told which plots, all one-fourth of an acre, were already sold and which of those left he thought most desirable. If you were going to use the street car line, why build at the other end of the block?

Cally saw the logic in that. She did not want Henry walking any farther than necessary, having noticed a certain slowing down in him. Yet you did not want to be too close, she said, to hear the noise, or have folks taking a short cut over your property.

Mr. Bianco saw the sense in that and sized Cally up as a practical woman, with a level head.

She asked about the occupants of the houses he had sold. Not having small children, she did not want to plop herself in the midst of too many.

Mr. Bianco took out a list on yellow paper and with a contractor's loving eyes looked up and down the street, describing the people. In one house was a Baptist minister and his wife, older, quiet people. The ends of Mr. Bianco's heavy, muddy boots turned straight up into the air; Cally wondered if his toes went with them. Perhaps his stomach balanced him, sitting over his toes, his belt beneath. Under his coat he wore only a thin undershirt; his stomach and chest were covered with hair. When he spoke, a dark gold tooth caught the sun and gleamed.

"What about just this side of the pastor's?" she said.

"Perfect!" He threw out his hands lavishly, delighted.

"We're Methodists but they ought to be nice people. And it's not too far from the street car."

"Lady, I wish all my customers could know their mind like you. Two or three bedrooms?"

"Two."

"Brick? A nice red brick. I got a whole car load of new brick."

"Stucco."

"Stucco." He threw his hands higher. It made no difference.

"Yellow," Cally sighed. "It's going to be the first house we've ever owned. I've always wanted a yellow stucco house. With brown trim."

"Brown trim." Mr. Bianco seemed to be making a mental note.

Cally was smiling. "Oh, I can see it. I want a screen porch across the back. Awnings on the windows where the sun comes in. And lots of shrubbery." Her mind held all together, separate and distinct, in one flash, every house they had ever lived in. They had come along rent free like the one they lived in now, or at a nominal rent because they went with the business. There had been rooms over stores, or houses they rented only because they were nearby. Never had there been money to buy a house they wanted, and she was determined not to die in a rented house. "Well, I'm ready to put down a down payment."

"How much?"

"Twenty-five dollars."

"Twenty-five dollars!" Mr. Bianco's gold tooth glinted dully a long time before he closed his mouth.

"It's all the money I've got. I've saved it. It's all the money I've got," Cally said.

"But, lady, how do I know you'll ever get the rest? Where are you going to get the rest?"

"I'll get it. If I miss one payment, you can take the house back. You can put it in the contract. I'll never miss a payment. I'm a cateress and I can work even harder. I plan to take in a boarder too."

Mr. Bianco threw his cigar to the ground and spit after it, shook his head from side to side a long time, as if the wrath of the Bianco clan, all connected with him in business, had already descended on him, then looked her straight in the eye. "Lady, if you got the nerve to come here with twenty-five dollars and ast me to build you a house, I got the nerve to do it."

He stuck out his hand, and Cally, having reached into her bag, put the twenty-five dollars, neatly folded, into it.

They returned across the grassy field and signed the necessary papers. Cally went alone over the plank walk to the street car line, hearing the street car in the distance, whining along the tracks a long way off, a thin, high sound. All around above the vacant fields, the sky seemed far away. The sun, not yet down, glowed behind a bank of clouds, turning them yellow-pink; the glow fell on the earth, touched the ugly empty fields, lit the windows of the little houses in the distance, fell full on her face, and gave her a sense of peace: God was in heaven, it seemed to say, and with a full heart, Cally thanked Him for the house they would have at last.

At Cecilia's school, she consulted the newspaper again, made a telephone call and was driven away as all brilliance left the sky. Through the grey evening, she went with Cecilia's friends along a dingy street where the shops were still open; secondhand clothes strung outside them on clothesline danced in the air like frenzied things as people stopped to stare, and pulled. At a traffic light, a vendor in a sidewalk stand tilted forward in a cane chair to say, "Fresh fruit?" Cally stared past him at a small shop on Main Street, then was driven on between closed cotton warehouses where cotton, laid out on sampling tables, looked, in its amazing whiteness, phosphorescent in the darkened rooms. The car rattled over cobblestone pavement to the crest of the natural bluff on which the city was set. Below, placid and muddy, the Mississippi stretched as far as they could see. As they descended, Cally looked at the waterfront full of colorless barges and tiny boats bobbing like toys; a paddlewheel steamer lit up, looked garish, for here at the foot of the street, beyond the river, the last of the pink and yellow sunset stretched, blindingly. They travelled a road paralleling the river, on one side the waterfront and the failing sunlight, on the other the dark high bluff where night had already come. Feeling tiny, insignificant against the sky's panorama, the great river beneath them, they crossed the bridge, feeling one moment airborne, the next, going again over flat land at the car's top speed between marshy fields that were Arkansas now. Cally looked back with a new feeling of kinship at the city.

.   .   .

Poppa met her at the Mill's Landing train and listened intently, walking her home. She told first news of Cecilia, then of her doctor's visit. He was relieved at first the draining had not taken place; then hearing of the planned future treatments, wished it had; the gall bladder phase might have ended.

When Cally was not home, no one remembered to turn off lights. Approaching, she said, "It looks to me like every light in the place is on."

"Boss, don't fuss," Poppa said. "We've got a surprise."

"So have I," she said.

They entered the house among a quick exchange of greetings and Poppa let the words go by; but while Cally and Lillian warmed supper, he and Son sat in the living room and the words came back ominously. Poppa wondered why he had not given them more thought. On legs slightly trembling he went to the table, lost in thought, did not even hear Son return grace, had his head still bowed, his eyes closed, until Cally said, "Henry, you can carve the ham."

He carved, watching the opposite end of the table. "You're hacking," Cally said.

He tried to focus but his mind dwelt on the other end of the table; at her place Cally had a small, cut-glass decanter full of her blackberry wine. Four small matching glasses beside it reflected like diamonds in the dull-orange light from the ceiling fixture. The bottle with its dark, still wine seemed foreboding, and made Poppa feel melancholy. Having poured the wine, Cally passed the glasses; they sat, their full plates before them, looking at the glasses apprehensively. She served wine only on occasions and what could this one be?

"I bought a house today," she said.

Poppa jumped as if someone had slapped him on the back, his glass in mid-air; wine splashed out, warm and sticky, dripped over his fingers, one by one, encircling the glass, fell onto the white tablecloth which drank it like a blotter, leaving a shocking stain. Lillian, glad to escape, went to the kitchen for a wet rag and took her time coming back. She washed at the tablecloth almost viciously, until the stain was as gone as possible, and left the towel beneath like some terrible malformation. Poppa, gone white, sat and stared as if the stain were his own blood, drained away; he felt weak and helpless and wiped his fingers with a napkin, but the stickiness would not leave.

"In Delton," Cally said. Her cheeks took on a becoming redness; even her lips were red and her eyes shone like a young woman's. The orangey light reflected smoothly on her hair, giving it its original color.

"In Delton? What the hell you going to do with a house in Delton?" Son said. The light dealt harshly with him, heightened his face with shadows out of which his eyes stared pale and furious.

"Don't curse at your Mammy," Poppa said.

Cally said, "We're going to live in it, that's what. If Poppa and I don't get out of this little country place now, we never will. He's got to get a job some place better before he gets too old. I've answered a very fine ad in the Delton paper. The people were ready to take Poppa as soon as I told them all his experience. You don't realize, Henry, you've got a very fine experience. It's a shoe store off Main Street, one of those chain stores selling a good, low-priced shoe. You'll have a big business at that location. Colored and white. Just think, right near Main Street, downtown in Delton." She drank wine and it seemed to flood her cheeks; they flushed and were redder. "You'll have to go for an interview."

"Shoes?" Henry said, as if the word were foreign.

"Shoes!" Son said, his teeth clenched; he held the sound a long time, gave it a final hiss before letting it go, without saying the other word on the tip of his tongue.

"What about us if Poppa leaves?" Lillian said. She was ready to switch; they would not have the automobile, but they would be moving to Delton.

"What if Poppa doesn't leave?" Son said. His huge hands tightened on either side of his plate, his knuckles whitened. "Listen, Poppa has a surprise too. He's bought a Ford."

43

"A Ford?" For a moment, they saw everything Cally was eating, then she swallowed with difficulty and said, "A Ford automobile? Why, Henry."

He gave a little desultory wave with his fork. "It was a little surprise. If I'm going to change jobs, though, we'll have to let the automobile go, Son."

"Well, we don't need a automobile in Delton," Cally said. "The house is right near the street car line. But I declare." She sat back with a pleased look. They had to smile back at her expression: Obviously she pictured herself as they had—riding down the road. "Wouldn't it kill Sudie Baker and Thelma Owens?" she said. They heard a slight hesitancy, then it was gone. "We need a house more than we need a automobile. Have you given them any money?"

"Not yet," Henry said.

"I've made a down payment on the house."

Lillian said again, "What's going to happen to us when you all move?"

"The house has two bedrooms," Cally said. "You can rent one."

"If we go, we'll get our own place," Son said. "It's time Lillian had her own kitchen. Maybe we won't go. Maybe we'll stay. I could run the commissary and we'd have this whole house."

A whole house, Lillian thought, looking at him affectionately; but he looked back with hard eyes. She knew he wanted to go—the success he talked of by implication meant leaving Mill's Landing —but he did not want to be told when to go. Suddenly, Lillian feared ending up with neither the car nor Delton.

Everyone in Mill's Landing went to work at the same time, and everyone went to bed soon after dark. Supper went on longer than usual. By the time Lillian and Cally had washed dishes, swept up, set the breakfast table, the town was in almost total darkness, and it was nine o'clock. In the railroad station a light was on. A bare bulb burned over the entranceway to the mill; Poppa had left on the one hanging over the cash register. At the drug store a small blue night light burned, but there were no street lights.

After the Wynns settled into bed, the house was silent. Son

thought Lillian was asleep but could not tell; she breathed as unnoticeably in sleep as when she was awake; to have her beside him was like having a small warm animal—perhaps a rabbit—asleep there. Down the hall he could hear Poppa snoring faintly, with the regularity of a pump running; once he stopped, cried out, "Huh?" then was quiet again. Son knew Cally had pushed him until he turned over.

He thought of Betty Sue and how she had slept, as roughly as she lived, thrashed about, flailed her arms, kicked. It was a workout to have slept beside her; the times they had managed it, he had waked exhausted, but she woke as lively as ever. She had been coarse and too much like him; that was why, he guessed, he had not married her. When she ate, if she spilled, she did not even look down, just kept on eating. Lillian was dainty and yet, of the two, he sometimes thought Betty Sue had been more like a woman. She had plowed in the fields beside her Daddy, helped her Momma wipe the noses and bottoms of eight at home, kept her Daddy's grocery going when he was lying up in bed with a jug of whisky. She could hold her own whisky, too. Lillian had worked—but not really *worked*, not broken her back or gotten her fingernails dirty. It made a difference about what a woman expected, he was beginning to see. To make the money he wanted, he was going to have to leave Mill's Landing, but he was afraid of Delton, the place itself. It was so big. He was afraid of the men he would find there, educated men; they were all going to know a lot more than he. But he had a system he did not think could be beat. Going over it in his mind, he fell asleep.

In sleep he had the job. He was selling dynamite for the Delton company, the way Lillian wanted. Only he was out West doing it, pumping a handcar along a railroad track with the boxes of dynamite stacked up behind him. Wind rushed back against his face and pine trees whispered all around him, the ground beneath them brown and soft with dropped needles. He flew along the track until he came to its end and a great, faceless man said, But you brought the dynamite with you. You were supposed to have sold it along the way.

Cursing himself, he stood, wanting to hide. Then a white fury took hold of him and he cried out, Son-of-a-bitch! They would not beat him. He would make it. Country boy or not. Schooling or not. He would make it.

He fought back the only way he knew how, with his two great fists, beating the featureless face. Two things in the whole world he had no fear of, fighting and work. He would bet you right now it was the right system. All you had to do to make it was work.

He cried out telling it and woke to find Lillian bending over him. "Wake up, Frank," she said. "You're having one of those dreams again."

He was soaking wet as well as the pillow beneath him and the tangled sheets. Trailing a blanket behind her, Lillian went toward the sitting room to sleep on the couch. Hell, let her go, he thought, and it was the first time he had not called her back.

He lay back, his breath coming short, thinking now he would sleep with everything against him thought out, whipped. But suddenly he sat up, crying out to Poppa, to Cally, to Lillian, to the whole vast dark Goddamned world: "Listen! There's got to be a place in the world for a man as willing to work as me."

There was silence before Lillian's voice came back. "Oh, go to sleep, Frank," she said.

D ESPITE THE RAINIEST WINTER ANYONE COULD REMEM-
ber, Cally and Poppa moved after New Year's. Cecilia would continue at boarding school, and Son and Lillian moved into the tiny
second bedroom. As always, the southern winter alternated with
spring; one day it would be thirty degrees, the next seventy-five.
Cally and Poppa sat on the new front steps warming themselves
beneath the sun as beneath something furry, though the steps, being concrete, held winter still, were cold. Cally, busy settling the
house, did not think about weather but talked continually of
needing a back porch. Where would she put the daily things no
kitchen could hold, newspapers, gardening shoes, canning jars
empty and filled, the bushels of vegetables and fruits themselves, a
churn she might someday use again? Quick, she caught in their
faces a hint of acquiescence and repeated often, as if it were beyond
belief, A house with*out* a back porch, making the family feel she
bore the lack alone; aging, she must wash, cook, clean, cater
handicapped. The matter, taking root as she had intended, was
settled at the suppertable. Son swallowed and something difficult
went down. He said, "Mammy, make your plans. I'll pay what
Poppa can't to put the porch on."

Poppa would not be able to pay anything; they knew that. He

47

looked away a moment and the room's objects seemed colorless, almost indistinguishable. He assumed embarrassment caused it. Lillian's napkin fell to the table like something unbillowed and she thought how satisfaction became Cally. Her eyes and face had a new luster. Her smile, turned inward, seemed it would be enigmatic, then was not. It said she had won and they could understand winning. But they could not forgive the smile's briefness or their helplessness watching as her eyes turned thoughtfully to something else she wanted. She passed salad in a cut glass bowl to Son and he shoved the bowl past him hard, into Lillian's hands, as if the poked out edges of ornate glass could cut and hurt, it did not matter who.

In late spring, he and Lillian moved to a bungalow of their own, in an established neighborhood: the acme for most of its residents, the unsuspected end for many yet to experience the Depression. To Lillian, it was a stepping stone. The houses were the same, like giant turtles, she said: their roofs humped and overhung, their interiors were always dark. Oaks and maples lined the street. Beneath them were the favorite playgrounds of children; grassless plots were filled with toys, corroded or in the process, and old bent tablespoons, the implements for digging. Lillian longed for someone to fill the holes but, permanently, they provided mud pies and scratching places for dogs, frantic on a scent. In houses without grass there were few rugs and dark furniture with sagging springs. But Son, in a brief afternoon, scattered seed, raked, watered and soon had a lawn. He hired a Negro boy to cut the grass. Along with Lillian's aloofness, it set them apart. On the porch, in concrete urns shaped like Grecian vases, she put cannas, red and yellow. Every morning, watering them, she listened to traffic, a muted sound some distance away. Only the milk truck, the ice wagon, the laundry man travelled the street children deserted for school. Gladly, Lillian listened to the garbage truck break the morning's silence; it ground down wild sunflowers that sprang up large as saucers, taller than the back fence, and added a festive note to the Negro men doing their job. She watched them toss garbage cans lightly as balls and toss them back again—empty, joking, complaining of one an-

other in a dialect so rapid it was unintelligible to any but of their
own race. Summer induced the most intense smell of everything
in the alley, weeds, grass, splintery unpainted fences, dirt road and
spurious flowers, but the smell of garbage overlay it, and Lillian
seldom went near. Imbedded in the dirt were countless pieces of
broken glass, red blue green and plain-colored for diamonds; following the jewelled road, children peered into the privacy of otherwise unseen backyards: ran through Lillian's bushes in fits of laughter, having glimpsed her neighbor, Mr. Woolford, in his B.V.D.'s.
Hanging up wash one morning, Lillian drew back a sheet and
caught a covey of little faces watching her; then, beyond the
morning glory vine twisted into the wire fence, she saw them go.
Later, with candy and cakes, she tempted them, close, closer and
finally every day, the children alleviating her loneliness as Son
worked longer and later. Often Lillian roamed the small, dark,
cleaned house and cleaned it again, twitching aimlessly with a dust
cloth about the spotless rooms. Despite Son's continual proclama-
tion that he would "defeat the s-o-b's," uttered now frequently on a breath smelling of liquor, to which she listened
as though attentively, her baby-soft eyes turned up to him,
she began not to believe it. He had a steady job; the salary
seemed adequate to start; but would it lift them, ever, beyond this street where the breadwinners came from the car
line, slapping evening papers against their thighs, to enter the bungalows whose dark interiors were darkened more by black window
guards and green awnings and already smelled of supper at five?
Lillian's dreams were of a large house, of knowing the right people,
her own car, and at their ultimate of membership in the Country
Club. Her fear of never having any of them grew worse as Son continued to bring home men she had never expected to know, rough,
uncouth, usually half-drunk, and twice his age. Disarranging the
living room they spread on the floor to shoot craps the entire night.
The Sunrise Club, they called themselves: noon Sad'dy to Sunday morning, Son said. To avoid them, Lillian went to bed early,
stuffed her ears with cotton, but it was dawn, the last door slammed
and the last car driven away before she ceased hearing their loud

abandoned laughter and vile words. Coming in the morning to clean, she was sickened by the old odors, smoke and whisky and sweat, by a cigarette ground out on the floor, glasses scattered, and ties draped everywhere, forgotten. She saw herself middle-aged and gross like so many on the block, facing the morning eternally in a faded wrap-around, facing it even like the carpenter's wife next door, with a permanently shamefaced smile for the husband who lurched home every evening bringing, like an obedient school child, his empty tin lunchbox. Her heart felt for the woman in the kitchen early to make him another sandwich, pour his thermos full of milk, when on the previous evening the whole neighborhood had heard her scream in agony as he hit her. Didn't the woman wonder how her life had turned out this way, who once had been young and pretty? Don't let it happen to me, Lillian prayed. Why hadn't she told Son the second time not to bring those men home, told him not even to see them? And asking herself, she wondered why she bothered, already knowing the answer: she had no wile that worked. He did exactly as he pleased, always.

When she did mention the men, he said, "What's the matter with those boys? Not a thing in this world's the matter with those boys."

And she said, "Boys! They're old enough to be your Daddy, that's partly what's the matter with them. And they're too rough, and they make you drink too much."

"They're my customers," he said. "I have to do what they want. Shoot some craps, drink some whisky. There's nothing wrong with that. That's the first thing I've learned, do what your customers want."

"Well, I'd get me some new customers," she said.

"Get me some new customers!" he said. "I'm damn lucky to have the ones I got. You know how many people there are in this town selling dynamite? You know how many people there are who want to buy any?"

If he told her again, she'd croak, she thought, and was about to tell him so when she saw Mr. Woolford, starting down the walk with his lunchbox, stop and look at their window, and she saw Mrs.

Woolford, behind the screen, watching. The two houses were about an arm's length from one another, and she shut up.

Get me some new customers, Jesus Christ, he thought. All the way to his office, on the street car, the wheels on the tracks seemed to say the same, Get some new customers. That's all Lillian knew about it: just line up some folks on the sidewalk and say, You want to buy some dynamite? and pick out some new customers. Jesus Christ. You had to talk people into using dynamite and you had to do some talking. He'd found that out in a few months. Shoot, you had to win 'em: eat, drink, play some cards, stay with them. Now when he called Lillian from downtown and said he had to take folks out to dinner, for her to come on down, she would say no, she was too tired. Too tired to help him entertain his customers? Cally had stood on her feet all day to help out Poppa in the store when he needed it. He told Lillian she'd still be there waiting on tables in her Mammy's tea shop if it wasn't for him, and was this how she showed gratitude? It was something he couldn't understand for a woman to act like that. His friends, she had said, were too common for her to eat with.

Common? he had said.

From the street car, he stared at the grey, winterized city. Everything beneath the bleak winter sky blended into the greyness. Everything seemed drawn in, closer, smaller. People, colorless in dark heavy clothes, huddled, their faces nipped-looking. Telephone poles stood out more starkly against a leafless background, and all the trees looked fire-burnt, charcoal-colored, withered and old. Sparrows, secured to telephone wires that seemed too thin to hold them, black string stretched across a grey and gigantic world, surveyed everything from above, loftily, motionless and fluffed.

He had ridden the street car a full circle of seasons and this was the second winter. At a junction where car tracks fanned to all parts of the city like bicycle spokes, silvery in the sun, Poppa transferred to Son's car. They rode mostly in silence, upright against the stiff seats, jounced one way and another, toward the window and toward the aisle, until the little blunt-nosed car, screeching in flight, deposited them finally, feeling as if they had been on a small ship, in the wake of a larger. They alighted at Mississippi Street just up the bluff from the river where, no matter the season and dependent on the wind's direction, they smelled one of two things, the unbearable stench of sewage or a smell of vegetation, hay, grass, marsh, with a hint of vapor lifted from the river, so that country people who had never seen one, passing there, thought of the ocean.

The first six months, Son and Poppa separated to remeet for lunch. Poppa brought his in a brown paper sack and only Son's most violent refusal prevented Cally from sending him one too. By noon the pendulant bottom of Poppa's sack was a circle of grease and the longer they were in the city, the more that circle irritated Son. Poppa carried the sack even into cafes Son selected, ordering only buttermilk. When they did not meet, Poppa ate in back of his store, for gradually Son went to lunch with friends and was learning to share their favorite tables and places and waitresses. But one day recently, meeting Poppa, Son watched him come slowly, the greasy sack bumping his thigh, and his irritation was such that when Poppa reached him, he grabbed the sack and squashed it into the nearest trash can, to Poppa's total astonishment, who in all the years of his life had never seen food wasted and had not recovered from the incident the day he died. It was a story Son would tell a long time; eventually all up and down the river, men would want to know the story of his throwing away his old man's dinner, how the old man had stood, and looked and never got over it. The river men would laugh hard anticipating the end as Son would laugh telling it, being men who had grown up on the same thing as Poppa, hard times, and who had Poppas who would have reacted the same. Son had afterward ushered Poppa into a restaurant and told the waitress, "Bring this old man the best T-bone steak you got, well-done," over Poppa's protests, who knew neither his stomach nor his teeth could handle it. Poppa, hiding steak pieces beneath his napkin, longed for Cally's homemade biscuits drowned in sorghum wasting in the trash outside.

Afterward when they met, Son bought Poppa's lunch, though

Poppa brought his sack. Cally would not hear of his leaving home to buy food when she had food in the ice box he could take. Poppa gave the lunch to his Negro stock boy or any Negro lounging about behind the store, and they were always glad to get it. Today, having eaten, Son and Poppa came out of the cafe to a rain the grey morning had promised, Son wearing a heavy raincoat, just warm enough with winter on the verge of giving up. But within a block Poppa was wet as a soaked dog, rain having matted his slick old wool coat. Son was about to ask if he didn't have a raincoat and realized suddenly he never had had one. Jesus, he thought, he'd buy the old man at least a two dollar slicker to pull on over that old coat, and telling Poppa so, huddling against buildings, hurried him to the best men's store on Main, where instead of a slicker, he bought him a coat like his own.

"It's the best we carry," the salesman said, a tape measure slung like a snake about his neck. "It'll last a lifetime."

Poppa wondered, Whose? He had no lifetime left. Who would they give the coat to when he was gone?

Wearing the coat he said, "Thank you," and Son, holding him back from crossing the street, said, "Hell, old man, I'd rather buy you a coat now than pay for you to have pew-monia later on."

To Poppa, the light turned green, that funny milky green it turned, like green in a marble; but when he started forward, Son held him back speaking roughly. But why? Because he had started to cross the street, or because Son truly did not want to pay if he was sick? Son cursed too much these days, Poppa thought, like those friends of his he had met. Now people who had stood impatiently on the curb, smelling as bad in their steamy wet clothes as wet dogs, crossed; but, to Poppa, the light looked the same. And crossing catty-cornered at Main and First, he admitted finally there was nothing the matter with the lights; it was him. Too many times recently he had started to cross wrongly and been pulled back by strangers or his own instinct. His eyes had been checked and were in order. He promised himself to see a doctor.

Poppa returned to his failing store and his need for sleep was something he could not shake off. He lay on a cot in the back, telling himself if anyone came, Willie, the stock boy, would wake him. But the store contained a golden burst of late afternoon sun when he woke. The day had cleared, the streets were drying. Dragging himself into the store, Poppa saw several displays of shoes badly disarranged by people he had not heard. Willie, sitting on top of a ladder, picking his teeth, stopped doing it to say, "I tried to waken you up, Mr. Wynn, I couldn't."

Poppa walked straight toward that golden burst of afternoon sun, his bones gathering warmth as he went, and confided to the Negro what he could not to his family: "Willie, I just can't stop sleeping. Whew."

"Naw sir," Willie said who already knew it, who had already told his young wife, Mr. Wynn was one of the sweetest white persons he had ever known; he sure hated for anything to happen.

But not only Poppa's physical disability was causing the store to fail; he did not understand big city selling, did not know how to bargain, haggle or outwit. If a customer said he could get shoes elsewhere for a certain price, Poppa would lower his. It was only when he strolled down the street, he would learn from the other merchants, you could not sell for that price without losing money. Invariably, he would fall into the trap again. Everyone seemed honest to Poppa and he was sorry for people buying shoes that were not going to last and for kids brought in with toes so scrunched up in old shoes they could hardly walk. Anybody with a quarter he let put something in the Lay-Away. It was Willie who once pointed out they had as much in the Lay-Away as they had out to sell. Poppa would always believe people were coming back to get what they had started paying on. Too late, the merchandise, out of season or out of style, would be returned to the selling counter. Facing the brilliant after-rain sunlight, Poppa watched people emerge from a movie and glance about happily, glad to have escaped a few hours not only their troubles but a rain storm as well. The gutters rushed, full. The sun had brought spring after a winter morning. Poppa pulled his coat close and went out for air. Feeling directionless, he directed himself to the corner and bought an apple from the Italian vendor. He returned eating it, looking at prices in other shops, patting the heads of children who passed, speaking if spoken to, but turned even into his own store without seeing any of it. He saw only the fine white fall of lint from two rows of cottonwoods, dark green fields with cotton buds turning pink at evening, a storm heralded by a rise of yellow dust and the rain itself pocking the soft yellow road outside the commissary door. Closing his own door, he told Willie they would leave early; he had a doctor's appointment.

Son thought about Poppa a short while after lunch, then, picking his teeth, went down Main toward his office, thinking about business. He was happy, even in rain, to brush through crowds on a city street. Thank the Lord he was out of that hick place that hadn't even been a town, just a mill and a store at the end of a country road. But entering the small marble lobby of his office building, he did not fool himself any. He was tired of hard floors and a desk and of air coming mostly through windows. His stomach, unexercised, was beginning to push his belt and he did not like the feeling at all.

A pretty little girl ran the cigar stand in the lobby. He tried usually to buy something from her. "You doin' any good?" he said.

"Hel-lo!" she said. "Folks crowd in on rainy days. Good business today."

He bought cigarettes and a pack of mints; giving his change, she looked at him obviously. She had a pretty face; that was all his interest. He said, "Well, don't take any wooden nickels," and went to the elevator where the white-gloved operator held the door. The cigar stand girl sighed, wishing he would take her out. She, her replacement, the cleaning women, the elevator operators all long ago agreed Mr. Wynn, on twelve, was the handsomest man in the whole building.

Down the beige marble corridor, quiet as a hospital's, every office door was shut, keeping in heat. Son missed the easy cordiality of warm weather when doors stood open, fans whirred, and shirt-sleeved men visited back and forth. On twelve, they sat above the city with nothing between them and the river; sometimes only their floor, out of the entire city, had a breeze. Behind the opaque glass door panel of his office, a shadow crossed; knowing Scottie was back from lunch, he opened the door, having touched once briefly, for fear they would not be intact, the gold letters that read,

American Powder Co.
Frank Wynn, Representative.

In the lower right hand corner was the office telephone number, with Day written after, and his home number, with Night. His predecessor had not allowed the latter; Scottie, whom he inherited along with the office, had said, "You're crazy to put that on. Some bozo, with a load on, will call you up in the middle of the night."

Son had swung his feet to his desk, stared at the river as he spent too much time doing, and said, "If it gets us some business, it's all right with me."

Scottie had grown up around river people and was as tough as you needed to be in this business. She used curse words even Son did not, and though he would not have wanted Lillian to know them, he admired Scottie for it. Often he and Scottie held a cussing contest. One after another, they said every word they could think of. In visiting weather, people on their floor dropped in to listen; the contest was considered a draw. Scottie had made her way since she was sixteen, and at thirty-five still was, because of a husband who alternately had a job or did not. Her dark hair curled tightly to her head and her legs were large. Son thought she was a good woman who worked hard and never shot off her mouth unnecessarily. It was long after their lives had gone divergent ways, he learned how Scottie had loved him.

Today as he came in, she said, "A Mr. Rollins called. His number's by the phone."

"Sho nuff," he said. "What'd he want?"

"Wants to buy some dynamite is all I know," she said.

"Hell, that's all we need to know isn't it?" he said. Having given the number, he glanced out at the sky which seemed it would clear and at a pigeon sitting on the window sill looking in. Then he sat forward seriously when a voice said, "Wildwood Country Club."

"Frank Wynn, American Powder Company, calling Mr. Rollins," he said. "Hell, I don't know which Mr. Rollins, he called me." A door closed on a room noisy with the partying of women, then a voice said, "Mr. Wynn, Carl Rollins. I'm head of a committee for building a golf course out here, beautiful eighteen holes." Mr. Rollins' voice rose, swelled with pride. "We've got some rough acres to clear first though. I wonder if you'd like to give me an estimate on the work? The other three dynamite representatives have been out and are turning in one next week."

"I'm always interested in selling some dynamite," Son said. "I'll come on out now if nothing else's going on."

"It's mighty wet," Mr. Rollins said.

"Hell, I've never known the rain to hurt me yet," Son said.

"Well, come on then," Mr. Rollins said.

Son had a secondhand company car to use for business. He drove it to the club, where Mr. Rollins met him on the porch: to Lillian's consternation when she heard, perishing to know what the club was like inside. They rounded the building to woods behind it, Mr. Rollins going ahead, his rubbers squeaking and squishing in and out of the soggy ground. Following, Son felt dampness penetrate the soles of his shoes.

"I'm told any method but dynamite clearing will cost me more money," Mr. Rollins said.

"It'll cost a whole lot more if you got to pay men to dig up trees, break up stumps and haul them away too," Son said. "And it'll take you three times as long."

Mr. Rollins said, "Suppose the windows in the club all get blown out, or something like that? The woods seem awfully close to me."

Son, looking back, suddenly felt exhilarated wondering about it himself and laughed beyond what the moment called for. "I can't guarantee it, but I don't expect to blast out any windows. Might shake you up a little now, though," he said.

"I guess we can stand that," Mr. Rollins said. "How long do you think the work will take?"

Son had no idea and guessed: "Two weeks." He saw by the

quick surprise on Mr. Rollins' face he had said a time shorter than the others. "Of course, I'll have to let you know definite when I've thought about it a little more," he said.

But Mr. Rollins was saying, "Two weeks." He looked at the old woods in surprise as if, if they could disappear in two weeks, they could disappear instantly.

"I'll blow you those stumps into nice sized little pieces," Son said. "Hauling them away will be as easy as feeding candy to a little boy."

"Dynamite's the ticket, I guess," Mr. Rollins said, and waving his hands in all directions like birds taking flight, he talked of fairways and hazards and greens. Coming out of the woods, he said, "You ever play golf, Mr. Wynn?"

Son stopped in surprise, trying to imagine himself doing it. "Naw sir," he said. "I guess I never have had time to play any games, except some craps."

"That's something I've never tried," Mr. Rollins said. "I understand there's an agreement about the price of dynamite."

"Yes sir, the dynamite companies have always agreed to sell at the same price," Son said.

"I guess the estimates will differ in the amount of dynamite to be used and the time the work will take," Mr. Rollins said. "I'll look forward to your estimate next week with the others." At Son's car they shook hands, "I sure do appreciate your calling me," Son said. "I'm going around the block and look at the woods from the other side. Don't get anybody after me for trespassing now."

Mr. Rollins laughed and waved him on, surprised. He had decided against Son before he ever saw him, the other representatives having singly dropped a word of warning against him: he was too young and had no experience. But once Mr. Rollins had decided on a way of doing things, he could not change; having made a list of all the dynamite representatives in town, he could not rest until he had called them. He read over the list: Du Pont, Hercules, Michigan, American. Checking off the final name, he found he could not put it out of his mind as he intended. The young man had seemed too interested.

Driving off, Son thought, Son-of-a-bitch, he couldn't do it; he didn't know how to do all the figuring involved. All his previous business had been men calling and telling him how much dynamite they wanted, not him telling them how much they needed. He turned the corner and drove close to the curb, peering into the woods. Behind him a driver came close, blew his horn and drove irritably around him. Another car stopped, the driver peered at the woods too, and finally drove on. Unaware of either, Son inched along, turned another corner, finally got out of the car and went up a rise and into the woods. His feet sank immediately into mud and he pulled them out one by one, with a noise like sinks being drained; he sought higher ground, tree roots, piles of dead foliage, though unavoidably he continued to slip into mud. For an hour the sun had been a bright cloud in a day full of grey ones. Now it came out and shone. Son was aware of the sun beyond the tree tops but in the woods it was a grey day still. He leaned against a tree, its bark crinkled, running in all directions like the lines in old ladies' faces, and said, Pheww, telling himself he had to do it.

He did not think about mud, knelt in it until dampness penetrated his heavy wool suit. Still, he remained, one knee delving further into the ground, his arm across the other, holding in his cupped hand a scoop of dirt. Balanced against his youth were the woods which had been here longer than he had the knowledge to dream of. He compared himself against the other men he knew; he was just a boy in the business compared to them, but he was willing to learn. He realized now that all the time he thought he had been just playing cards and shooting craps and drinking some whisky with those men he knew, he had been learning from their experiences, which was where they had gotten all their education, in the school of hard knocks. To the levee contractors, ditch and road builders, equipment salesmen he knew, dirt was more than something you walked on. It was something you depended on for your livelihood, the same as the weather and seasons. He had to know the kind of dirt he was dealing with, the same as in a business deal he had to know the kind of man he was dealing with: Tennessee and yellow clay shot easy, they told him, the same as black, rich gumbo; for crumbly, "crawfish" land, you figured in extra dynamite; if soil had too much sand, you couldn't use dynamite at all.

He stood, cleaning his hand against the wide flare of his pants, and began to walk as if he could learn dirt through the soles of his shoes; silently, the trees dripped rain. The oldest river man he knew, old Red Johnson, who had made more money than the rest of the fellows put together, claimed to have learned about levees by walking them, St. Louis to New Orleans, and most people believed him. Shoot by the lay of the land, Red had told him. Son remembered it, studying the trees. On some, buds were tightly furled and bright green, and he was sorry the little buds were never going to open, never going to be leaves, that the old trees would never know another spring.

Mr. Rollins wanted clumps of trees left, harder than blowing the whole eighty acres sky high. Several times Son sifted dirt, wondering if it were light or heavy, sandy or clay and silt; he thought desperately of *The Blaster's Guide* back in his office. "Blaster's Bible would be a better title," his predecessor had said, pointing it out. It was a small book with not much information; but it was the only book there was. Son had tried to commit parts of it to memory over the resistance of his untrained mind:

Stumps in loose soil must be loaded more heavily than in stiff soil.

A smaller quantity of explosives is required to blast a stump in soil of fine clay and silt material.

Which was it? Son, walking to the car through a mist that had settled heavily with evening, realized for the first time how cold he was. The mist, touching him, turned wet; but on each cheek was the track of a single tear he had been unable to hold back. At the edge of the woods he picked up several rocks and chunked them at a far tree—chunked and chunked and chunked—cursing himself every time: "In sandy soil it pays to blast when the soil is wet." Or was it dry?

In the car, he turned on the heater but could not stop shaking. He drove away toward a pink tinge in the sky promising a clear day tomorrow. But it was almost dark when he parked at his office building. The building was deserted except for the cleaning women and Ulysses, the janitor, who took him up in the elevator. "Where you been?" Ulysses said. "You soakin' wet."

"Hell, everywhere," Son said.

Ulysses opened the door, "I wait right here for you," he said. "Take your time."

"I don't know how long I'll be. I'll ring you up."

"Naw sir, I wait," Ulysses said, settling down with a secret smile and later, below, the women had to fan out to include his job in theirs.

Almost before the light was on, he had the right page:

Stumps in loose, sandy soil must be loaded more heavily than those in firm, stiff soil.

Twice, he banged his fist sharply on the wooden desk, "Don't you ever forget it either, you s-o-b!" he said. Reading on, he underlined in red pencil much that had been underlined before, only now he was determined never to forget it and was so absorbed that when the telephone rang, he jumped.

Lillian said, "I've called everywhere for you. Why didn't you say you wouldn't be home to supper?"

"Who said I won't be?" he said.

"Are you crazy? It's eight-thirty at night. I've had supper ready since six o'clock."

"Eight-thirty?" he said, astonished; not knowing how to apologize, he said it was business he was attending to and she ought to understand that.

"How am I supposed to know?" she said. "I never know where you are. Who else's there? Is that woman Scottie?"

"Not anybody else is here. I don't mix up any women with my business," he said. "I'm doing some business," and forgetting even who he was talking to, he hung up. He read on, but it suddenly seemed too cold in the office to stay. He was shivering and opened a drawer to take out a bottle of something to warm him up when he realized he could take the book home and read and he shut the drawer. He would not let anything interfere with his work.

Going down, Ulysses said, "Something sure got you in a sweat tonight."

"Sweat?" Son said, and put up his freezing hand to discover his forehead was hot. He sure felt limp as a dishrag, was not even sure he would make it; maybe he should have had a little juice to fix him up after all, he thought, driving.

Lillian was too startled by his appearance to complain further; she said, "Are you drunk?" came close to sniff, and said, "You must be sick."

He sat down and said, "There's sure something got hold of me."

He went to bed and she brought him pork chops warmed, but the thought made him sick and she brought him soup which he ate, and later lost. His fever was high but he would not call the doctor, and to avoid contagion Lillian slept in the living room. It was late when she woke abruptly and even while she ran to his room, something else crashed over. He stood in the bed, rumpled as a child, one corner of the mattress pulled toward him. Pillows without cases were flung about the room; he jumped to the floor, pulling the mattress after him, saying, "Where is it?"

"What, Frank?" Lillian said and stepped backward to the living room as he came forward, it seemed menacingly, but he said, "The book, the book." He found it and went back to lie on the mattress, the book beneath him.

Lillian said, "Frank, get up and help me put the mattress on the bed. You'll freeze down there. You'll die," but he would not budge; at last, she brought blankets and covered him.

He said, "I'm too tough to die," and fell asleep, heavily, until morning.

"Flu," the doctor said. "Like everybody else in town." The newspapers had warned for days the city seemed to have an epidemic. The doctor prescribed medicine, rest and fluids. "Stay in bed now, boy," he said. "You got a case."

"Hell, flu," Son said: anybody could beat that. But the amount of phlegm in his chest surprised him and shooting pains came and went. He slept, dreaming he had lost; the others were running through the woods, laughing back at him. He got up, took a slug of whisky before breakfast and another one afterward and said, Hell, he had that bug beat. It was the only way.

He put aside pride and got out books he had kept hidden even from Lillian; he had felt silly, like a schoolboy, reading them; he spread them on the dining room table centered beneath a light fixture that seemed far away it was so small and flat against the ceiling, three pronged unshaded bulbs, similar to a pawnbroker's insignia. He had two nickel school tablets and three books, *Perfect Penmanship, The Salesman,* and *Modern Merchandising.* They had been his texts in a night course he took in business school when they moved to Delton. He was proud to have taken it but not anxious to tell anyone; inevitably, it led to a discussion of what other education he had had. In the course a month had been devoted to each of six topics: "Building A Selling Personality," "Aspects of the Selling Talk," "Increasing the Average Sale," "Making and Holding Customers," "The Joy of Creative Selling," and "Vital Sales Statistics"; the latter instructed him how to figure percentages, keep records, figure profits. One of the first problems had been: If Mr. A waits on 30,000 customers a year and sells $15,000 worth of merchandise and gets a salary of $1,500 a year what is his average sale? his cost per customer?

In despair, the first night, he had written on his paper, I don't know. But he had learned. Business and selling came to him naturally, making him regret more the education he had not had.

Lillian hovered wonderingly about the table all day as he read, underlined, and wrote, mumbling to himself. He went to bed exhausted as soon as it was dark; afraid to touch the papers, Lillian bent over them to read headings; Trees Acres Sticks Per Stump; questions were beneath them: How many sticks of dynamite do I need? How many lengths of god dam fuse?

In the morning, he began again. Lillian was washing lunch dishes and heard him take a drink. She saw him in the dining room, his clasped hands gripping his head, his head bent between his knees. She thought he was in pain and ran toward him. He raised his head and she saw the pain was in his eyes. Bound briefly together by mutual ignorance, they looked at one another as they seldom had. Lillian thought with regret there was nothing in the world she could give him. He did not need encouragement, sympathy or even love and did not lack courage. He needed someone to tell him how.

"Frank," she said. "You've got to get somebody to help you." He rose in a fury. "If I weren't the stupidest Goddamn son-of-a-bitch that ever . . . !" he said.

She said, "Frank, I'm going to get somebody."

He said, "Who?"

She was silent, unable to think of anyone; no one in the family knew any more than they. She thought of the bank teller who lived on the street. He would know figuring, but how could she invite him over to help her husband with his arithmetic? His wife would tell everybody on the block. Out of a reluctant mouth, she said, "What about one of your friends? That old man Johnson you think a lot of?"

He went out and down the hall to the bathroom, banging on the walls saying, "Hell, oh hell." But she had known by his face he had been considering it too. His fever was gone, and she slept in the room again. Long after he lay asleep, snoring, Lillian stared into the dark wishing she could change everything about them, past, present and future.

Early, she was awakened by birds, returned for spring, making too much noise beyond the window; the bed was empty and light shone around the closed door to the dining room. Tiptoeing, she went to it quietly and opened it and he did not hear. He was sur-rounded by discarded paper, ashes and ash trays that were full. She looked at him helplessly, and suddenly he snapped his pencil in two, turned around and saw her. "Frank," she said, "you've got to get somebody." He cursed himself violently and after a moment, Lillian went back to bed.

The second time she woke, he stood in the doorway. "Lillian, I've got to have something to eat," he said. She got up thinking, I know how he'll look when he's old. Pale and tired, he stood caught in sunlight and bleached. He was pale and his hair looked white and he walked like an old man too, shambling, to the bathroom. On her way to the kitchen, Lillian looked at his meaningless papers, struck by the way he wrote, beautifully, in ornate, bold, slanting letters. On impulse, she opened *Perfect Penmanship,* and saw how meticulously he had learned. She did not feel compassion but pity and, afterward, told herself that had been the turning point: nobody could love a husband they pitied like that.

After breakfast, he said in a half-shout, "Old man Red Johnson's coming over here!" as if she might argue.

From behind organdy curtains they watched the old man arrive, in a black Cadillac with a Negro chauffeur. On the sidewalk Red stood as frail, as brittle, as thin all over as a grasshopper. The old man was eighty and had made a million dollars twice, Son said, having lost it the first time. He had been to school only three days in his life and said those were to answer "present" for his brother when he was home with mumps. Most of his adult life had been lived in a tent on the levee; he had brought his wife to it and raised three children there. But when he made money, his wife wanted a house. He bought one of the city's finest and she furnished it with authentic and spindly antiques. Red had to use the back door and could not put his feet on the footstools. One afternoon, looking out the window, Mrs. Johnson saw two Negro men erecting the old levee camp tent in the back yard. At that moment Red passed her carrying a few possessions and did not return to the house for ten years, except at Thanksgiving and Christmas.

"Come on in, old man," Son said, opening the door. "You want Shut-eye to put you on the couch?"

The old man looked down at it, his eyes brimmed with tears as he laughed. "I wouldn't never get up off of there," he said. Shut-eye helped him into a chair instead. Red walked leaning against Shut-eye's shoulder, his feet coming ahead first.

"Shut-eye, you want you a little something in the kitchen?" Son said.

"Naw suh, I got to shine the car," Shut-eye said. When he had gone, the old man laughed and again cried. "I just keep that car for Shut-eye," he said.

Son fixed Red a toddy, corn whisky and Coke; then Red said, "What kind of dirt you got, Frank?"

"That's what I'm damned if I know," Son said. "There's maples and poplars and oaks in it . . ."

"Don't worry," Red said. "You got oaks, you got good dirt. It'll behave for you."

Instantly, Son felt himself in those woods again, knew the look, feel, smell of that dirt was with him forever now. He would always know good dirt and he imagined it already swooshing up, a beautiful brown blast.

Red's hand trembled toward his whisky glass; he picked it up between unbent fingers, as if he were not holding it at all, yet brought it to his lips, drank and lowered the glass; whisky remained on his lips an instant, glistening, before he licked them dry. "Frank, you got to play it a lot by ear," he said. "There's not so many set rules. That's what makes it hard. A man's experience and judgment, alone, will determine how much dynamite he should use for any given stump. Write this down. If the diameter of a stump one foot above ground is six inches, you use two cartridges of dynamite for green wood, one and a half for old wood, and one for wood that's partly rotted. If it's twelve inches, double it and so on. Take that as a little guide, but there'll be times when it don't work that way."

Son looked up from his paper. "I'm much obliged," he said.

Red spoke again about the lay of the land; after blasting you had to be sure the rain ran off. "Now that little table I told you, is if you got firm soil. You got light soil you use you about one-fifth less dynamite . . ."

"One-fifth?" Son said.

Red leaned carefully forward and took Son's pencil. Over and over that afternoon, he showed Son how to use simple fractions. Once he laughed. "This may not be the way they teach you if you

---

66

go to school, though," he said. "It's my own way of figuring, but the answer comes the same."

"Then it's good enough for me," Son said. Learning to go your own way was something he'd have to learn, he thought.

Red told how much dynamite he had seen shot in a day and how long he had seen a good man work; Son mentally added on to both for his estimates. Then he sprang on Red the idea that had come to him in the two nights of his feverish dreams. He was going to shoot the dynamite himself, something no other salesman had ever done: they hired professional handlers of explosives. Son said, "That's the only way I see I can be sure I'm low man. I'll do the shooting free, myself, and save him the price of hiring somebody; those fellows get a lots of money for shooting dynamite."

Red said he could do it; Shut-eye had learned, had shot off dynamite on several small jobs.

"Well, by God," Son said, laughing. "If that boy can learn to shoot dynamite, I can."

Red, sipping his whisky, thought Son would do all right. He had already become a favorite of several contractors, because he did not act like a big shot, the way most salesmen did. He tried to accommodate his customers. Son, when they had finished work, said, "Old man, you realize when I come over here to Delton to start working for American, I never had seen a stick of dynamite."

He and Red sat back, laughing. Red said, "How'd you come to know it?"

Son said he had asked his predecessor where he could see dynamite and the man had told him to phone Mr. Ryder. Mr. Ryder drove the dynamite truck and was also the warehouseman, shipper and receiver for all the four dynamite companies in the mid-south area. In his house were four telephones, a private line for the salesman of each company. Mr. Ryder had sounded a little surprised at Son's request, as if it might be a joke; but he had said he would pick Son up at the end of the Carolina Street car line at two o'clock on the following Sunday. When Son got off the street car, Mr. Ryder met him with a wagon and team. They headed south out of the city at the mules' slow plod. Son had asked Mr. Ryder if he shot dynamite and Mr. Ryder had said only when he had to, though it paid twenty-five dollars a day. Blasting gave him too bad a headache.

"Headache?" Son had said.

"Dynamite headache," Mr. Ryder had said. "Worse kind there is."

Well, that was something he didn't have to worry about, Son had thought; he'd never had a headache in his life.

Mr. Ryder, in dusty overalls, had been gardening and said when he got too old to haul dynamite, he was going to haul vegetables. As they left the city behind, Son removed his tie and high-crowned felt hat and sat back, glad to listen again to the hollow clop clop of slow mules, to smell cityless air. They had turned off the highway into back country, down a road that was two tracks through weeds which, bent by the on-coming of the wagon, sprang up after them with little pings against the wheels. Sometimes the mules shook themselves and their harness jangled, their hooves plodded on the ground; the only other sounds were that of the countryside in any warm season, insects in the grass, the occasional bellow of a cow starting on a low note and ending on a high waver causing its bell to clunk, and a dog's barking: so much a part of the landscape that if asked, the men in the wagon would have said everything about them was quiet. They passed no houses until Mr. Ryder turned down a lane and stopped at a Negro's cabin. From its dark interior a little boy came, stretched his legs to their utmost, and climbed by way of the wagon's wheel into its bed, grinning in delight, though too shy to answer when Mr. Ryder said, "Hey, boy, what you been doing?"

Shortly he had stopped before the wooden gate of a barbed wire fence leading away in either direction as far as Son could see. Jumping down the little boy ran to open it, climbed one slat up, slid the bolt, and swung wide and free to the gate's full opening. He had returned to collect the nickel Mr. Ryder handed down and when Son looked back had already closed the gate and was running home. The wagon had seemed to tilt dangerously toward a valley as they followed countryside as hilly and wild as it had always been, except for the barely visible road and the barbed wire providing boundaries. When they passed two small brick buildings set close to the road, Mr. Ryder said, "Those there are the detonator magazines where the caps and fuse is kept."

At last they were in the valley they had overhung so long, having descended bracing their feet, the mules shifting their weight backwards to brace themselves too; at the road's dead-end Son saw a larger building like the small ones they had passed, red brick with a corrugated tin roof. When they stopped, a mule had reached up to scratch its nose against the blue-looking steel door, set dead-center in the otherwise totally unadorned building. In the wagon, they had been only slightly higher than the bottom of the door; up to it from the ground was the full stretch of a man's leg. Mr. Ryder, standing in the wagon bed, had unlocked two heavy padlocks and stepped into the single room that was the magazine, with Son following. The only light came through the propped-open door and air vents set close to the ceiling. Son's first impression had been of the darkness, but his second was of two things he could not have separated, the coolness, as if he had been in a springhouse or a cave, and the sweet scent of freshly shaved pine from which the boxes were made, so simply as to be splintery. The boxes were in stacks. Lifting one, Mr. Ryder had held it against him and was turning when Son had called, "Hey!" Turning back, Mr. Ryder said he had known what he would see and saw the silent disappearance of a snake's tail. "Should I kill him?" Son said.

"Might's well let him go," Mr. Ryder had said. "They're always in here. Come in out of the woods to the cool. I kill the bad ones but that's just a little old black." He had brought the box to the light by the door and from his back pocket took a small claw hammer and pried up a corner of the box saying, "There's your dynamite, Mr. Wynn."

His hands in his pockets, Son had come forward as if it might be a box of black snakes as well as anything else and having seen still did not know what to say. In a box full of sawdust he had seen, individually wrapped in brown paraffin paper, perhaps a hundred sticks of what Mr. Ryder said was dynamite. Lifting out a stick, he had judged it to be about eight inches long and said, "What is it, a inch thick?"

Avoiding the wagon, Mr. Ryder had spit out the door and said, "Inch and a quarter."

Son had turned it between his fingers like a man judging a good cigar, then because he had no other ideas had put it back, carefully, where it had been. With two swift blows, Mr. Ryder hammered the top down and returned the box to the stack. "I wouldn't slide a box about now," he had said. "But you don't have to ever be afraid of dynamite. Just respect it."

Standing in the doorway, Son had surveyed the rocky path down which they had come, wondering how those mules were going to make it up again and had looked at the surrounding woods out of which repeatedly at measured times a bobwhite called his own name, wondering how a man went about learning all he needed to know. Would time answer everything? He hadn't known you had to keep dynamite cool. Mr. Ryder had told him the attic of the magazine was insulated. When they were in the wagon again, the door padlocked twice behind them, Mr. Ryder had urged the mules on to crest the hill; afterward, he had turned them in the direction from which they had come, saying of the other way, "Down yonder's where the other three dynamite magazines are. I got in all now about a hun'dert and eighty thousand pounds of explosives."

"Jesus Christ," Son had said. "One of us boys better start selling some powder."

The little boy had been at the gate. "He always hears me coming," Mr. Ryder said. They passed through and when the boy had climbed into the wagon, Son paid him the nickel. It took as long as it was to his cabin for the little boy to gather courage to say, "Thank you," then he had gotten down and run.

Inside the rusty screen door of the cabin, visible only because of her light-colored cotton dress, his mother had stood, staring.

"How do," Mr. Ryder had said, whipping the mules on.

"How do," Son had called back.

"All right," she had said.

Son told Red the story as it had happened. Only he did not tell all the questions he had asked Mr. Ryder the long slow way back to the street car. "One cap will shoot . . ."

"A couple tons," Mr. Ryder had answered. "One stick is a half pound. One stick'll shoot about a thousand pounds."

Drawing on his memory of *The Blaster's Guide* and the diagram in it of how to shoot a stump, Son had questioned Mr. Ryder closely: a man who'd shot a stump himself, he believed, had a whole lot more to tell him than any book stuck under his nose. Mr. Ryder had verified it, just as Red had today. "You can read all you want about blowing up a stump," Mr. Ryder had said, "and you might get your stump blowed, don't you know what I mean? But the thing is there's always one way that's the best that day. You got your different conditions each time, don't you know what I mean?" He had spit carefully to the side of a mule's rump and said, "Course that's not your worry. You just got to sell the dynamite. If a stump don't get blowed right, it's not the fault of the dynamite now."

Sit and wait, Son had been told. Business would come to him. One of the country's oldest manufacturers of explosives, American's name brought customers. Business was all right, but Son wanted more. He had asked his predecessor if he ever went out looking for business. The man had said, Why, that little Ford coupe's in as good condition as the day I got it! and handed over the keys, proudly.

When Son finished telling Red the story, he said, "Mister Red, I got it in mind just to get in that little car and hit the road, looking for business." Red said, "It wouldn't be no bad idea, Frank. Things aren't going to stay the way they are now forever. Farmers are already hurting, have been for some time." Thoughtfully, Son sucked on a back tooth and poured in ginger ale to help the taste of the bootleg whisky. Red said he had to go and Son called Shut-eye who came in through the back way. Son said, "Shut-eye, don't you want you a little something to drive home on?" Shut-eye accepted half a glass of whisky and Son said, "Don't you want you a little chaser?"

Shut-eye said, "Naw suh, I don't see no sense starting a fire, then putting it out." He drank the whisky straight and Son said, "Phew," making a face for him.

When Red was sitting in the car, he was like a bent straw, as long and thin from his hips up as from his hips out to his knees. He looked out at Son, into the dying daylight, which made his eyes water, and said, "Days are getting longer." His old hands with brown spots as large as dimes trembled on the half-raised window. Son covered them with his own, verifying what the old man wanted to hear. "Spring's almost here," Son said, and if it were that close, maybe the old man would see it.

About them was sundown, golden-orange; dusk was an instant away. "Shut-eye," Son said, "you take this old man on home and don't let him get in no trouble, hear."

Red's eyes watered, his lips trembled. "Shut-eye can't keep me from doing nothing I want to."

"Oh, does this old man still think he's tough?" Son said.

"Yes suh, he still gives us a powerful lot of trouble," Shut-eye said.

"Well, you get him home fore dark then," Son said. "So long."

As they drove away, the old man's voice fell back softly on the night, "We'll see you."

Son had never taken a walk just to be walking but he did not want to go back into the house. It was as clouded with cigarette smoke as his head felt. He sat down on the front steps and suddenly dark came. The street lights came on as unobtrusively as if they had been on all the time, had become visible only with night. And he thought, Hell, he had some row to hoe.

When supper was ready, Lillian called and he came inside and she put the food on the table. But he went to the telephone and did not return for ten minutes. When they were eating, he said, "This damn food's cold."

She said, "It's been on the table ten minutes. I thought you were coming right to supper."

"I'll do the thinking around here," he said. "You're not supposed to do any thinking. I had to call a man on the telephone. Now get this food on the stove and get it hot. Jesus Christ." When they were eating again he said, "I don't want to eat any more warmed-up food, either."

After supper, she said, "Can we go to the picture show?"

"I have to go out yonder to Mr. Ryder's and to the dynamite magazine," he said. But he came back from the bedroom with his coat, into the kitchen where she was washing dishes, and said, "If you want to ride out yonder with me, we can go to the picture show afterward."

He would not keep the man waiting though, he said, and Lillian had to come on, leaving the pans, her hands barely dried. In the car, she cried and said she couldn't stand to live with him anymore, the way he was.

He said, "Go to hell then."

They continued in silence to Mr. Ryder's which was beyond the city limits where there were no street lights. Son left Lillian waiting in the dark for twenty minutes, with her feet cold. Finally he came out on the porch, the Ryders with him. Son took off his hat and shook Mrs. Ryder's hand. Mr. Ryder, pulling on his jacket just then, stopped and looked and then resumed. Mrs. Ryder, catching sight of Lillian's pale face peering out at them, came down to the car and said, "Lord have mercy. You must be cold. Mr. Wynn, why didn't you bring your wife inside. He didn't even tell us you was waiting."

Some day, with easy grace, she would kill him, Lillian thought. The legs of Mr. Ryder's brand-new, as yet unwashed overalls swooshed together as he got in beside her, smelling of sweat and tobacco. Mrs. Ryder said, "You all come back to see us," and Lillian, who had determined never again to shake the dry, rough hand of the woman who had come out in her old, felt bedroom slippers with one big toe cut out, said nothing. Son sped them to the highway and slowed only on the side road when they passed the

Negro's cabin; inside, a man pulled back a torn lace curtain to watch them pass. They saw the mother and little boy at a table holding the cabin's only light, a coal oil lamp. A cow, disturbed by their noise, made a low soft sound into the night, then the only sound was rocks hitting beneath them, until they stopped and the headlights were on the blue-looking door. How funny, Lillian thought, to come up on a brick building out in the middle of nowhere. The men went inside and returned shortly with something that Son put on the shelf behind the seat. They stopped once again, short of the gate, and Mr. Ryder went into one of the smaller buildings and returned with something he put on the shelf too. They drove him home and Lillian waited expectantly for the lights and excitement of downtown to change her mood. At last she was standing happily on the pavement waiting for Son to lock the car. She smelled ribs being barbecued nearby and caramelized popcorn in a shop next to the movie. Music came from a radio somewhere and she felt like dancing. If only Son would take her dancing sometime, she thought: something pent-up might be gone. She saw his hand remove things from the car's shelf to the darkness of the seat. But at that moment, glancing across at Poppa's shuttered store, she remembered Cally's telephoning and told Son they had to go to dinner with her on Sunday.

It was not until he was buying tickets Lillian thought to say, "What were those things in the car?"

"Dynamite and some caps and fuse," he said.

Her hands flew straight against her breasts. "Are you *crazy*?" she said.

People coming from the movie stared, and the ticket-seller pretended not to. "I'm not going home in that car," she said.

"I don't want to get blowed up any more than you," he said. "But Mr. Ryder says it's all right. He carries them together all the time."

Absorbed in the picture, Lillian told herself not to think about it. At least she was here, in Delton, not stuck up in the country anymore.

But wouldn't it be better if you were here with someone else? Reason asked. Lillian thought, I can't think about that now. You'd have to have somebody else before you left him, though, or go back to your Mother.

Just then, Son leaned forward and then back, crossed and recrossed his legs and said, "Whew! I didn't know this was about love and ro-mance. I thought it was a shoot-'em-up."

Lillian turned on him, furiously, in the dark and whispered, "I'm not going to leave," but the picture was ruined. He squirmed until its end.

The next morning, wearing a leather jacket instead of his suit coat, he went out to the garage. Lillian thought he had gone to work on the car and was scrubbing the sink with bleach when she heard a thud, a slight boom, and the house shook. Thinking the furnace had exploded she was about to scream, realizing the next moment the house was not only intact but totally silent. Out the back window she saw a little cloud of smoke dispersing into nothing, dirt splattered around a large hole in the ground, and Son just coming around a corner of the garage, a smile turned up like a quarter moon across his face. Going down the back steps, she saw the Woolfords peering from a window and over the back fence the top of the orange garbage truck, the collector standing in it, a large garbage can in his hands, his mouth dropped into a perfect O. Seeing her, the Negro instantly disappeared and she thought, I can't even face the garbage man again.

Gleeful as a child, Son cried, "Did you see it? It went up just as pretty, just as eas-y as a airy-plane!"

She stared at the hole where the stump had been, realizing only now that it was gone, she had always set her clothes basket on it.

"Frank," she said, "somebody'll call the police on you. The windows in our house, probably everybody's, almost shook out."

"Woman, I can get new windows. And I can get out of jail," he said. "Don't you realize I just blasted out my first stump. There isn't any way now another man can beat out my estimate."

"Frank, you just can't blast off dynamite in your back yard in the middle of the city with neighbors right close up."

"Hell," he said. "I just did," and with the smile as big as ever he got in the car and drove away.

Standing alone in the back yard, Lillian felt like a fool without exactly knowing why. She told herself it was not her fault he did all these wrong things, that his people ought to know just how many wrong things he did, and that it was not her fault.

All winter it had rained frequently over the whole lower Mississippi Valley and now, with March, it rained almost every day. From Cairo, Illinois, south to the mouth of the river, below New Orleans, a flood larger than any the valley had ever known seemed imminent. The river rose enormously the valley's length, the crest not in sight. Fear mounted, like the river itself. Radio programs were continuously interrupted for bulletins about the river's stages and people stayed home to hear.

On Sunday, at Cally's and Poppa's, Son opened the door to a smell of roasting beef rushing toward them on a shimmer of heat as if he had opened the oven door instead. The little bungalow was almost exactly like their own; they stepped into the living room and beyond was a dining room exactly the same; a hall ran the length of the two and at each end was a bedroom, called the front and back; the latter Cally had recently rented to a young woman from North Carolina who was a school teacher.

Cally came down a short pantry from the kitchen toward them, and Son wondered who the little old lady was. Seeing it was Cally, he was surprised at how stooped she had become. She wore heavy black oxfords that made her feet look as clumsy as a clown's. He knew they must be the new arch supporters she had asked Lillian to take her to town to buy: that had cost ten dollars. He had said it was the last damn pair he was going to buy. Cally had decided all the pains in her back came from her feet. Poppa was asleep on the sofa and woke to say he had been listening to the news, had only just dozed.

"What is it?" Lillian said. "We haven't heard any since early morning."

Poppa looked blank and Cally said, "I could hear it all the way back in the kitchen. They don't have but one railroad to their name running up near Cairo, Illinois, and they're afraid the levee's going to break right over yonder in Wilson."

"Wilson!" Lillian said. "Frank, that's not anywhere from Mamma."

"She'll get warning in plenty time to get out," he said.

Toward the end of dinner, Poppa said he wondered what was happening in Mill's Landing, and Son laughed. "Old man De Witt'll have niggers out slapping down sand bags," he said. "I don't know how he'll do it but he'll pass that water on down to somebody else!" He stopped talking to laugh again and the others looked at him, not thinking funny all the devious ways people used to shunt high water away from themselves, to their neighbors, who in turn used any method to pass it on to those below them.

At their objections, Son said, "It's every man for hisself." He did not necessarily think it was right; but there were a lot of things in life that weren't: that didn't change them any. "It isn't right folks in Washington don't go more than fifty-fifty helping us keep the river away from our doors. Shoot, it wasn't too many years ago the government wasn't paying even half to keep up the levees. Folks had to build their own and keep them up too. The whole country drains into the Miss'sippi and it ought to be the whole country paying to keep it in its bed. If this turns out to be as bad as it looks like it is, the whole country's going to hurt though. Farmers are going to be wiped clean out and I mean clean. Folks everywhere going to be looking for food and paying the price."

After dessert, Lillian and Cally washed dishes. Son, picking at a tooth that always bothered him after eating, followed Poppa to the living room and turned on the news: Special trains, the announcer said, from the North loaded to capacity with old trench sand bags from the war were being rushed to Cairo and points south in an effort to stem the river that was at some points already overlapping the levee a foot.

"Oh hell," Son said. "We got it now."

Poppa, recalling all the floods he could, '03, '12, '13 and '22, said he did not remember such excitement, such precautions be-fore. By the time the women came from the kitchen, warming their chapped-looking hands before them, the news was worse and they all sat hushed, communicating infrequently by lifting their eyes to one another as some word or phrase struck them each differently at different times. Unfamiliar words became familiar by the time the afternoon was over and would become a large part of their daily life in the weeks to come: breaches, inundations, evacuations. Over and over that afternoon in announcing that un-told numbers of people had fled home and were either destitute or dead, that industries were paralyzed and crops flooded, what had happened to the people of the valley was declared to be a national disaster. Local authorities, losing no time, were already on the air to ask, Would the Federal Government at last commit itself to a definite program of flood control? Admit, at last, that only full Federal responsibility for building the levees would provide at least a *chance* of controlling the great river on a rampage?

It was later than usual before Cally said, "You all getting hungry again?" and she went to the kitchen, with Lillian following. By now the news was repetitive and, standing, Son turned off the radio. He had smoked all afternoon and the smoke remained, push-ing against the ceiling. Poppa, as he had since noon dinner, was dozing. Shortly he would wake. Son went to the front door and opened it to the wet March night. Far off, farther away sounding than it really was, he heard a train and thought of it rushing away through the night, a sliver of dark patched with yellow. He was thinking how glimpsing the people and having them quickly gone made you feel left behind when Poppa said, "Son."

As Poppa had known the night Son spoke his name before tell-ing he was going to get married that it was going to be something important, Son knew it now.

"Close the door," Poppa said.

That's not it, Son thought, closing it; he came back into a room as cool as the night now.

Poppa clasped his hands and said, "Boy, the store's not doing so good."

Son ran his tongue around his gums looking for a fleck of tobacco that had been worrying him. Finding it, he stuck out his tongue, removed the fleck, and said, "Is that so?"

Other times Poppa lost businesses he had not told until it was too late; Son knew it would be too late now. If he asked why Poppa had not spoken earlier, he would say what he always did: he hadn't wanted to be a bother.

Son said, "What are you going to do now, old man?"

Poppa looked around as if he might find the answer in the confusion of yellow on white that was the wall paper, and his eyes grew moist. Son said quickly, "I can hep you out some. Hep you find something else."

"I thought maybe a little grocery," Poppa said. "If I could just work in a little grocery somewhere, I believe I could do all right." Medicine was helping a kidney infection the doctor had found, had lessened both his dizziness and his sleepiness. Poppa considered himself on the road to recovery, but the doctor held back. Something in his hesitancy, in the set of his mouth, had kept Poppa from telling he had even been to a doctor. Only noticing that he had a little more get-up-and-go, Cally had told him so.

Son asked if he had told Mammy about the store. By a slight lift of one shoulder, Poppa indicated he had. Cally called them to supper and the new boarder was with her. Kate Jefferson, Cally said, and was happy introducing Son, sensing he and Poppa had been talking about what she had wanted them to. When Son came forward to shake hands, to hear Kate had come all the way from North Carolina to teach school, Cally, looking at him, thanked him silently for help. Kate said she had heard a lot about Son; she was glad to meet him. He did not notice too much about her, except that she was tall.

In the next few days Son, like everyone, thought only about the flood and not once about the golf course job. Daily, he and Scottie watched from the office window as the river rose, and finally crested close to fifty feet. From the Delta and as far away as Kentucky, refugees who had been plucked from tree tops, roof tops and the highest windows of buildings, were brought into the city.

Son watched as bus loads of people stared at him with faces acknowledging their homelessness and sometimes hunger, holding in little bundles all they now possessed. It sure looked, he said, like the Government was going to have to take over flood control; levees people had now just couldn't do the job. Always, people living in the lower valley had had a solitary struggle to protect themselves and their settled land from high water. Unbelievably long, flood control had been left to chance and isolated local effort.

And always there had been floods, old Red Johnson said; he spent much of his time now reading the valley's history. He told that De Soto, searching for gold in 1543, had been delayed by a flood lasting forty days, and La Salle, exploring for the French, had found much of the valley under water. Both men had noted mounds the Indians lived on in spring when the river annually overflowed. Everyone stayed at the Army Engineers office, talking. Red said one afternoon as bad as this flood was, it didn't represent the old river's full flood potential. "Someday," he said, "all the rivers going to flood at the same time, you watch." Terrible as that day would be, he could not help a look of amusement. He called the names of the rivers, relishing them: O-hio, Red, White, the Mo, Tenny-see, Cumberland, Arkansas, upper too.

"Jesus," Son said, unable to picture anything that bad happening, yet knowing it could. He drove into the Delta with Red and Shut-eye to view damage. Shut-eye called the river hongry. "That river's hongry," he said. "Always going to be." The land would not drain even in time to plant ridges, higher ground; a year's worth of crops were lost. Red said, "Before levee days, the river's natural flow-way was forty miles wide. It overflowed and met all the other rivers overflowed and it was all high water then, just high water five or six months out of the year."

"Naw," Son said, not skeptically but in astonishment. Then Red went on to tell about the first levees, how the French built them after settling New Orleans in 1717. (Son never had thought about any Frenchmen having to do with anything he had to do with.) In the Delta, where now they stood, the first levees had been built by slaves after a war with Mexico when the cotton plantations were beginning to flourish; afterward slaves were too valuable to risk in malarial swamps beneath the broiling Delta sun. Irish were imported from ports, New Orleans, Cairo, St. Louis, and continued the work using wheelbarrows, the slaves' only implements. Muckers, Son said. By 1890, yellow fever had driven them from the Delta forever: the unmarked graves of those left behind made clear the early railroad and levee lines.

Shut-eye drove them back home. Son settled in the living room with a snack of cheese and crackers and opened the afternoon paper to read that if the flood had been confined, water would have reached almost sixty feet everywhere, nearly seventy in some places. Existing levees had not even been designed to hold such water. Water in such volume had not even been thought of. The newspaper printed a chart, a brief flood history. Having listened to Red so much, Son read it with unusual attention:

1844: one of the valley's worst floods; the following year, at a convention in Memphis, John C. Calhoun termed the Mississippi River an "inland sea" and claimed it a proper object of Federal interest. Abraham Lincoln, Horace Greeley, Thomas H. Benton advocated Federal flood control. But aid for navigation would come sooner.

1849 and *1850:* the valley was hit by severe spring storms causing numerous levee crevasses. The Government showed a slight awareness of its suffering: passed a Swamp Act granting states unsold swamp land within their borders, funds from sales to be used for flood control projects. But lack of cooperation between states and levee districts involved caused the plan to fail.

1851–1858: prosperous years for the Delta; but in the latter year and in 1859 floods severely damage the levees, now a straggling and broken line from New Orleans to Memphis. Delta people clamored for one unbroken line from the Chickasaw Bluffs of Memphis to Vicksburg, but the Civil War halted all progress.

1862: levees were damaged by military operations and a flood; no men remained at home to repair them. The following February, Grant, to reach Vicksburg, ordered a mine exploded in the Yazoo Pass levee. Additional levees were cut to overflow Confederate guns on low embankments. Toward the war's end a flood severe and remarkable in duration caused more than a mile of levee to cave into the river. After the war communities struggled to rebuild but by 1878 hundreds of miles of main line levees had disappeared or were worthless because of crevasses.

1879: Congress established a Mississippi River Commission to mature plans and estimates that would correct and permanently locate, deepen the channel, and protect the banks of the river. "To improve and give safety and ease to the navigation thereof; prevent destructive floods; promote and facilitate commerce, trade, and the postal service . . ."

1880: the Commission submitted its first report. Congress has appropriated a million dollars for the construction of improvement works under the Commission's jurisdiction; the bill states specifically that funds are to be spent only for deepening or improving the river's channel. This marks the begining of a coordinated levee system for the lower Mississippi. However, expenses are limited to levee construction as part of navigation. This will hold true for thirty-five more years.

1882–1903: seven major floods inundate the lowlands. Levee work begun in 1882 under the Commission marks the beginning of actual construction of a coordinated levee system.

1912–1913: severe floods in both years, the former causing $40,000,-000 worth of property damage. The President requests from the Commission a report on methods of flood prevention; levees, reservoirs, cutoffs, outlets, diversion channels and reforestation are to be considered. Despite the report, Congress took no action toward authorizing a flood control plan for the entire alluvial valley. The Commission's work continued to be limited to repairing levees and keeping the navigation channel open.

1916: another severe flood results in the first Federal Flood Control Act.

1917: on March 1, the Act is approved. The control of levees for flood becomes by law a definite part of the Commission's work and responsibility. The Act authorizes the construction of levees for the control of floods but affirms the policy of local cooperation; local interest should contribute not less than one-half the construction cost, in addition to furnishing rights-of-way. Local interest was charged with the maintenance of levees once the work was completed. The Commission was allowed to spend Federal funds for work on tributaries as necessary to protect the upper limits of any alluvial basin from flooding. Under this act many miles of levees were constructed, but the end result was unsatisfactory. Local interests could not meet the responsibilities; a fifty-fifty split with the Government of the costs of flood control was more than the local districts could handle.

1922: during March and April almost every stream east of the Rockies is in flood. Inundation into the Mississippi Valley continued into May and June.

1923: a second Flood Control Act is passed further clarifying the River Commission's jurisdiction.

1927: the valley has suffered the most disastrous flood in its history.

Son, having finished the chart, sucked at crackers caught in his back tooth and glanced at the rest of the front page; all articles had to do with the flood. Physical loss had been estimated at $236,000,000 read one headline and another that such disparate groups as the American Investment Bankers and the American Legion had taken up the clamor for the Government to accept flood responsibility. Advocates of Federal flood control argue that waters from as far east as New York and as far west as Montana contribute toward floods in the valley. Only the might and wealth of the whole country can attempt to hold back the Mississippi, they say. The flood has shown that a levee system as the only method of flood control is inadequate. The curving channels of the river increase flood in high water. The river does not stay in a fixed channel; it meanders. Those for Federal control argue further that national benefits will come from it; it will add to overall prosperity. They say that the Government has accepted responsibility for navigation, built revetments to restrain low water so ships can move on the river always. Why does it not maintain levees which restrain high water? Those opposed, sectional-minded men, claim that once the Federal Government assumes all financial burden, a maximum demand for flood protection will result. Local adjustment will reduce itself to a minimum.

Son folded the paper and stood up. Lillian had called him to dinner but he stopped to answer the telephone. Buzz was calling with news he had just heard on the radio: the President was sending a Cabinet member to take direct part in rescue and rehabilitation, an act without precedent.

Several days later, having surveyed the area, Secretary of Commerce Hoover declared it to be the worst disaster of peacetime. Water had breached the levee in two hundred places and had inundated approximately twenty thousand square miles of Mississippi River bottomland. Still, the major cost of the flood was to be borne by the citizens. But Son, Red, most of the Engineers now thought that feeling was running so high the Government would have to recognize the unfairness of the valley spending its own millions to hold back the floodwaters of a nation and would relieve it of its long burden, at last.

Son always told that he certainly thought that was the extent of his interest, that he never had any more idea than a flea the flood would touch him personally. When the entire city of New Orleans was threatened, he was mostly interested because the Engineers wanted to blast a levee below it to draw away water. The blast would wipe out entirely one small country parish. There, a great protest went up from the farmers and fishermen, declaring it unfair they be ruined to save the city and its people. Let the city go under, they said. But permission came from Washington for the blast and the papers were full of pictures of angry farmers leaving their homes forever, carrying their most valuable possessions; these were cabbages and heads of lettuce for some, hastily pulled, loaded into bushel market baskets. Levee work for Son took on a scope and feeling it had not had before.

The first attempt at blasting the levee was unsuccessful. Only a small amount of water was forced through. Son went to bed that night after the radio announced the Engineers planned to try again. Much later, he answered the telephone to hear a voice, with an unfamiliar drawl, telling him something he could not follow until suddenly, understanding, he knew he had heard it all. The second attempt at blasting the levee had failed. The Engineers were desperate for dynamite to attempt a third time, and they needed it by morning. Delton was the closest source of supply and Son the only man they could reach at night; the voice, belonging to a Major General in the Corps of Engineers, apologized for the time of night. "Hell," Son said. "I'm in business. How much powder you want? What train you want it on?"

"Thousand pounds," the Major said, having no idea of the astonishment that filled Son. He was already out of bed and had removed his pajamas and telephoned Mr. Ryder as soon as the Major hung up, not even wondering whether Mr. Ryder would go to the magazine at this hour of the night. He heard surprise in Mr. Ryder's voice and thought, Hell, he had to sell that dynamite and the man was working for him. "It's Frank Wynn," he said.

Mr. Ryder always spoke in a soft, faint voice; now it seemed fainter. "Mr. Wynn?" he said.

Son said, "Mr. Ryder, those folks down in New Orleans need some dynamite bad. The Army's arranging for me to put it on the five o'clock train. They want a thousand pounds and, Mr. Ryder, I need to sell that dynamite. If I meet you out to the magazine, can we load the truck, can you take it to the depot? Hell, if you can't, I will!"

They both laughed, Mr. Ryder removing his pajamas, neither having any idea the other stood naked, shivering, dreading entry into the cold pre-dawn and already on the way. Picking up his pants, Mr. Ryder said, "Yes sir, I'll carry your dynamite," and what propelled him forward without coffee, through the truck's slow starting, into the night, and over the unlit and bumpy road was the boy's calling him Mister. The others called him simply, Ryder. He was almost fifty years old, a country boy who had gone to work driving a dynamite truck because it paid more than he had ever dreamed of making and he thought of himself as just a truck driver because that was the way the other salesmen treated him. He had not thought Mr. Wynn any different the day Son leapt down off the street car; Mr. Ryder only thought him one of the handsomest men he had ever seen. The difference had come when Mr. Wynn came to his house. Not only had he lifted his hat to shake Mrs. Ryder's hand but had come into their living room as if it were any place he was glad to be. And there was the boy's urgency, like his had been. Over and over, driving, Mr. Ryder heard the boy's voice say, Mr. Ryder, I need to sell that dynamite, and heard himself, Poppa, I'm not going to be no sharecropper.

At the magazine, Son had worked beside him for hours; like a nigger, like himself, Mr. Ryder thought: had loaded the truck and followed him to the depot too. Not, Mr. Ryder knew, because Mr. Wynn thought he might not get there. Mistrust had been done away with, leapt over, in the long two hours they had worked toward a dawn that broke wet and without sound, except for the steady thumps of the boxes being set into the truck and their struggle for breath which, when they found it, remained close, white puffs against the still grey morning until, starting their motors, they drove away, breaking the silence before them and restoring it behind.

The levee broke, the parish was gone and New Orleans saved. The next day, the paper told that the explosives had been rushed from Delton and gave Son's name as distributor for American; as if American had had something to do with it, Son thought. But it tickled him to see his name in the paper; he bought all the copies the cigar stand had, then did not know what to do with them. He sent one to American and kept the rest on the car shelf until the day he threw them all away, except one. He received a nice letter from the head of American, congratulating him on the sale. He was pleased but disappointed more was not made of the personal aspect. American's concern was the largeness of the order; he might as well have sent a thousand pounds of dynamite next door on a pretty afternoon. Strangely, he had the urge to sit down and write the man about how it had been, to tell about the dark and the day slowly growing light as he and the old man who had been a stranger before worked side by side, the old man like a horse though he must be fifty years old, and how afterward they had not been strangers, though they had hardly said a word. Son felt as if he had been part of something big. History was not a word that would ever have come to him and he never found the right one.

One day he started to write the letter, then decided it was silly, and threw the blank paper away, causing Scottie to look at him in surprise. At the month's end, he received a commission; fat and juicy, he said. He bought the first stock he had ever owned, stock in American. He sat a long time looking at the paper with the fancy sort of pretty writing on it thinking, Damned if he hadn't come already a long way from being a country boy.

At lunchtime, he went to the bank and for the first time, entering it, did not feel dwarfed by the marble colonnades, lofty domed ceiling, and palehanded men in dark suits who, sitting at desks in the lobby, watched when they were idle, everyone who entered.

Passing between them, he spoke to a woman in the rear who was more than pleased to rent him a lock box. It was like initiation into some long-sought fraternity as she led him down carpeted dark stairs and up to an iron door which, when it was opened, he passed through to be locked in with the same sense of elation a prisoner, barred, might feel passing out the other way, into freedom. Yes mam, he was glad to sign, to give her all the information and a check for rental; he had a great desire to confide to the woman not only that it was his first lock box but exactly what he was going to put in it: his share in American and the newspaper clipping with his name in it.

Coming late to the office, he shoved his hat to the back of his head and said, "Whoo-whoo, let's ride the train!"

"I've already had a drink," Scottie said and flung a letter on his desk, turning to the window while he read.

He said words shocking even to them which they could never remember afterward, though they tried, able to laugh finally over the afternoon the golf job went to A. W. Woods and Sons, representatives for Michigan Powder.

Son said nothing else; he was quiet for several days, though he would have told you anytime something was wrong with the man's estimate; but he could not have told you when he decided to do something about it. One morning he came in looking just as he had when he returned after the flu, that white. Scottie was about to ask if he had been on a toot the night before when he leaned back and said, "I talked to the fellow, Mr. Rollins. That son-of-a-bitch cut the price of dynamite."

"Cut the price! Mr. Woods?" Scottie said and was silent. There was nothing else to say: Mr. Woods had been in the business as long as anybody, not only knew the rules, but had always obeyed them.

The southern spring had come suddenly with a force almost unbearable. Scottie closed her eyes against the windowglass, blinding, tinted by a sun too brilliant to behold; and, even above the city, the air entering through the half-open window had the sweetness of a child's touch. On the river she heard a tug, sounding lonely or fog-bound, and opened her eyes to be startled by day.

"Get me old man Woods on the phone," Son said.

It was described ever afterward as his cussing the old man up one side of the street and down the other. And if he wasn't a old man, he told him, he'd beat the hell out of him. Then he was not talking to Mr. Woods, but to one of his sons who said not to cuss his old man out that way. Son said, "I can't beat up your old man but I sure as hell can beat you up. I'm coming down there to do it."

"Come on," the boy said who had nothing to fear, having graduated two years before from the University at Sewanee, the finest full-back the school had ever had in the years of its finest teams, called Bull.

"Jesus H. God," Scottie said when Son hung up. "You know who his boy is? You ever seen him?" And trying to think of a word larger even than Bull to describe him, she followed Son, who seemed unaware of it until they were way out toward the dog pound where, despite the pallet-like colors of the day, separate, distinct blues and greens, everything seemed grey, sidewalks, small factories, Negro houses and smoke rising above a switch-yard.

"There she is," Son said. Across one of the low grey buildings they saw Mr. Woods' name in yellow. One half of his office was a warehouse for storing road-building equipment; instead of steps, a short ramp led up to the entrance. Son stopped directly in front of it. A door opened and young Woods looked out and started down the ramp. As he took two steps down, Son took two steps up. Opening his mouth, the boy drew in a breath: impossible to tell whether to speak or by instinct to receive the two blows that at that moment landed against his temple and his face, giving his nose not only the look but the feel of an overly ripe tomato, just smashed, the soft red pulp flying everywhere. Son, having drawn back his fist and shot it out, drew it back again, the three knuckles he had broken covered not with his blood but the boy's. Losing consciousness, A. W. Jr. fell backwards. Scottie, just making her way out of the car, had one foot on the running board, the other on the curb, and looked confused as if she had lost direction, then realized that what she had come to see had already taken place, returned both feet to the car and closed the door. Re-entering it, Son drove away, like an animal licking his hurt softly.

By morning the hand was twice its normal size, but he did nothing about it. "Hell, I'll put a little mentholatum on it sometime," he said.

And by morning everyone in the business knew about the incident: those in the Army Engineers office across the river, levee people, road builders and equipment people. The dynamite men telephoned and thanked him for setting Mr. Woods straight. But there was something in their voices the same as when they spoke to Mr. Ryder and, hearing it, Son cursed them silently.

Later he was having a drink in the office, lessening the throbbing in his hand, when Mr. Rollins telephoned to say Mr. Woods could not sell the dynamite at a lesser price after all. Son had the job.

He put three fifths of whisky on his desk and opened them all. Anyone passing had to have a drink. Some people had one and went on. Others, having no place special to go, stayed to be eventually obscured from one another by twilight and smoke. It was Ulysses who, having hung about the door unobserved as long as he could stand it, finally turned on the lights.

"Come on in here, boy," Son shouted and gave him not only a

drink but a fifty-cent cigar as well. "You ain't never had no ci-gar that smelled like that. It'll put hair on your chest."

It was Ulysses who, in a little while, having had a second drink, thought to say, "What you celebrating, Mr. Wynn?"

"Oh hell," Son said, displaying his swollen hand. "I just had to make a Christian out of a fellow yesterday."

M

R. WYNN, WHEN WE GOING TO GET STARTED ON THIS golf course out here?" Mr. Rollins said.

From his office, Son looked out over rooftops dried of puddles for the first time in weeks. Refugees had been bedded in the Country Club and now were gone. Rain had delayed the starting date but now the ground was just wet enough. He didn't want to make hay out of the other fellow's trouble, he told Scottie, but he was lucky to have the ground soaked like it was. The sky drifted marvellously blue toward Arkansas, so bright the clouds, banked high, reflected the color; as far as he could see, it stretched unhindered. If you lay on the river bank at Mill's Landing now, he thought, the sky would look the same.

"Monday morning," Son said. "We'll be out yonder at six o'clock."

At that hour the woods were so beautiful, so still that he and the three Negroes entering them hushed; the city around them, quiet at that hour, seemed not to exist. Beau, one of the Negroes, put a foot against a tree trunk and stood one-legged, stork-like, his face brooding; the others stood silently, leaning on implements they carried, tamping stick, augers. Dew heavy as rain lay on the leaves and the sun, making its way through them, turned the drops irides-

---

cent. A mourning dove nearby sounded far away, deep down somewhere, calling over and over in a pattern unbroken. Except he's going to get the shit scared out of him soon, Son thought; he said as much, and the Negroes laughed. Son started forward as the Negroes began to wonder about him.

After the long weeks of grey, rainy days that had seemed suffocating, threatening, like a hand at your throat, they were not used to the hot, clear May days. By ten o'clock Son and the Negroes had stopped wiping their faces, let sweat run over them, salty as tears. Laboriously, continually, like a line of ants working, the Negroes carried dynamite from the truck into the woods after Mr. Ryder's arrival. Dovetailed, the boxes stood in neat rows, smelling even in the open air cleanly of their pine scent. Beside them lay implements, punch bar, tamping stick, auger, boxes of caps and coils of orange fuse. "You got anything to crimp the fuse to the cap? A cap crimper?" Mr. Ryder said.

"Shoo," Son said. The Negroes, squatting, resting, looked at one another.

"I've always used my teeth myself," Mr. Ryder said and laughed. "You always got those with you, if you're lucky." The Negroes looked at one another in amusement, silent still, resting. "You boys got your teeth with you?" Son said.

"Yes suh," Beau said. They grinned, as if to show. Son tried to smile but his teeth ground together apprehensively.

"You ought to get you a good lift to the blast with the ground wet as it is," Mr. Ryder said.

"That's what I'm counting on," Son said. But what if he didn't? he thought. For a long time this morning he had restudied soil and stumps; *heavy,* he had said over and over under his breath, *heavy* soil; and wet as it was, he was figuring now on using even less dynamite than he had put in his estimate. The root system was shallow mostly: lateral roots. The classification of dynamite he had chosen was slower than what some might have picked; but he figured it would be better to shoot the stumps out slow, lift them up with the roots, too: not to blast them out fast, a piece here and there, maybe leaving the roots behind.

With augers, the Negroes had made bore holes beneath stumps Son had chosen: one evenly rooted stump (it was the roots going to give him trouble, not the stump, he told himself) had the pocket directly beneath it. Where the roots were heavily to one side of a tree, the bore hole was made off center. With a pocket knife, Son cut, slashing straight, several lengths of fuse approximately three feet long. He inserted them as far as possible into metal caps, until they were in contact with the explosive substance. One after another he stuck them into his mouth and crimped the two parts tightly together. Having punched a hole in two sticks of dynamite, he imbedded a cap in each, well; then laced the fuse around the stick. With a knife he slit the exposed end of the fuse and smelled the dark powder, sharply. He put dynamite into the hole beneath each stump, a hole Mr. Ryder called the "blew pocket." Into each he put twenty sticks, a short estimate. Suddenly, he knew how it would feel to be the last man alive. The others were a safe distance away, the distance he had to go while the fuse burned. Suppose he fell? Suppose some jar, some friction he didn't know anything about caused the cap to detonate too soon? His tough luck he thought, and grinned despite himself. In his mind, clear as his own name, was the information about how to light the fuse; the book had illustrations, one two three four, of hands holding matches in certain ways, holding the fuse in relation to them. At the time he had thought it was kind of silly. Now, he did not. He felt like a one-handed man with too many things to hold. Only the *initial* flare of an ordinary match is hot enough to give sure ignition; he remembered that sentence well. Hold the match head on the exposed powder in the end of the fuse with one hand and strike the match head with the box in the other hand. He did that. Immediately, as the book had said, a spit of flame shot out of the fuse; like a child's sparkler, only black, and over in a second. Next, smoke came, and the fuse was lit. He was already on his way to the other stump, had the match box and the match out ready. He struck it and as it flamed, sweat dropped from his chin, made it flutter, and its potency was gone. Instantly, he struck another match. Instead of flaming, it started as a tiny blue dot and began

93

to grow; eternity he stared at its tininess, could not wait, and threw the match away. With fingers usually clumsy, he drew a cigarette from the package in his pocket, lit it, and had it to the fuse in the time ordinarily it would have taken him to draw one cigarette from a full package. So swiftly had he drawn on the cigarette that his lungs had filled with smoke and he coughed; tears filled his eyes but through them he forced himself to see the mating of the two tiny points. In the second the fuse spit, he was already walking away. Long gone, he thought afterward, the beating in his chest so enormous he thought once it was the blast itself, behind him. The two came, seconds apart, just before safety, though he was not hurt. Rocks and dirt rained around him. Having turned his head at the moment of the first dull rumble, he saw the earth twice rupture and spray upward.

When silence came afterward, it was total; all the little sounds of the woods had hushed. Only a car horn sounded off in the city somewhere, ineffectually.

"You got you two pretty test shots, Mr. Wynn," Beau said; the other Negroes made pleased, assenting sounds: the success of a white man they worked for reflected on them.

Son smiled, thanking them. They were good boys, he thought. He and Mr. Ryder went toward the blast, overhung by black smoke. Only then did it begin to drift toward them, slowly, on the windless day. Phew, Son thought as it touched him, it even smelled black. His sinuses reacted immediately, opened and were filled.

The stumps, cleanly lifted, lay broken open, easy to remove. Mr. Ryder complimented him too. Son put his hands in his pockets and could not stop grinning. When he spoke, his pleasure spread into laughter; he moved his foot around in the evenly spread dirt and said, "Hell, is this what those birds been getting twenty-five dollars a day to do?"

"You go on a couple more, you'll have earned it," Mr. Ryder said. He had a trip to make, dynamite to deliver over into Arkansas. He left saying, he didn't think Son needed help anyway.

The rest of the morning and after lunch, Son and the Negroes

94

continued the work, though after each blast, he found he waited longer and longer to return and reload for another. But no matter how long he waited—no matter how far away the smoke had drifted —far enough to look like rain clouds overhead—the fumes remained: as potent and stinging as if manure mixed into the broken-open ground were steaming up at him; like being under water, unable to push through to the surface and breathe. He had meant to go on all day until sundown. By one o'clock he knew he could not go any longer. At two, having pushed himself that far, he suddenly sat down in the woods, pushed his hat back and said, "Jesus Christ."

Behind him, the Negroes were already sitting, having said nothing for a long time; now one answered, "Amen."

Son swung on his buttocks as if on a swivel, too tired to move any limb individually, and saw the extent of the Negroes' tiredness and was glad, realizing his was not a lack in himself; as good shape as he was in, the Negroes were in better. "You boys aren't tired, are you?" he said. He took out cigarettes and tossed them a package.

"Yes suh. I thank you," Woodrow said. He caught the package and divided the cigarettes.

"Hell," Son said. "I thought we was just getting started good. But if you boys going to give out on me, I guess we'll have to quit."

It being agreed upon, no one moved, held still by their own weight and the mugginess of the hot afternoon.

But he'd known a lot of hotter, muggier ones, Son thought, all of July and August. He wondered what made his head ache so it drooped toward his bent knee. At last, they rose and picked up what they could carry home and, reaching the car, felt alien to the peaceful mid-afternoon scene, as if the erupting earth should have changed that too, the street car following its snail-like track, a black and white dog lifting its leg against the front tire of Son's car, people passing, intent on themselves.

Rolling down the car window, Son thought, Damn if he didn't smell as bad as they did. No one spoke as he drove toward the car stop the Negroes wanted. Wind dried their sweat and smoke made curlicues through the car. Occasionally they smelled flowers, passing briefly fully blossoming lilac, wisteria, jonquils. But suddenly Son felt pervaded by that other smell, smoky, burning, black, rushing up against him like something blind. "Whew," he said, more to himself than to the others, "that stuff give me the worse damn headache I ever had."

"It sho do," Beau said, beside him.

"You won't get over with it soon either," Woodrow said. He sat on the back seat with James.

Son had not thought of Negroes getting a headache. At the car stop, he gave Beau a dollar, told him to get two bottles of aspirin in the store next to it. When Beau came back, Son said, "That going to hold you boys?"

"We thank you, Cap'n," Beau said.

Driving away, Son looked back and saw the Negroes already bent over their bottle. He opened his own and popped pills into his mouth quick as peanuts. He did not know how many aspirin he could take safely at once and, right now, did not care. In the middle of the night, he woke, nauseated, his head still throbbing and knew what Mr. Ryder had told him was true: nothing helped.

Day after day the mugginess continued, with June on them now, and heat wavered over the day, making it seem always as if they looked through something porous, like gauze.

The second morning, entering the woods, they had heard the mourning dove, which also heard them. No sooner had they arranged their tools, talking to one another, than it quit. The four of them, the original ones, were aware of its absence as long as the work continued. Son said once, "We sho scared the squeaker out of that bird," and Woodrow said, "Sho did," and the others showed by a darker look of their faces their contemplation of it. Sometimes after the cacophonous, loud, harsh sounds of their day, they unconsciously listened for the bird, knowing, with reason, it was not there, because neither were the woods. Flat, yellow-looking acres of ground had emerged to bake and dry, fallow; the little clumps of trees left seemed like people huddled together, astonished. Now, all day long tractors, their roar as monotonous and persistent as the buzz of some giant mosquito, graded and levelled, back and forth; the stumps were hauled away and burned in great piles on the far edges of the work, adding heat where it was not wanted and smoke to the already shimmering look of the day. Each day they arrived before the sun was out and each day Son thought they would work on a little longer, but they never did. Half a day was all a man could take. Every morning they had faced a new headache; yet when the work was over, when he was driving in a stream of traffic toward town, Son was sorry. He missed the Negroes. The last morning, Woodrow had said, "You got any more work around here, Mr. Wynn, we be here," and Son had said, "I'll be seeing you boys," and had driven off, thinking it was the first piece of information any of them had offered; they had spoken only when spoken to.

At the year's end his commission was far larger than the first one. Again, he bought stock in his company and would have had enough to open a little savings account, not much but something against a rainy day, except that Cally had a gall bladder operation. She had asked for the money and he had refused. She went ahead with the operation and the bills, presented, had to be paid. Months later, still weak, she leaned on an old mop to walk about the house, its sparse, tangled strands going ahead of her over the floor like drowned hair. To partly repay Son, Cally accepted the catering for a large reception in honor of a candidate for mayor, though the family tried to dissuade her. For days she worked, and Lillian and Cecilia helped when they could. On the final day, a Saturday, even the boarder, Kate, stuffed eggs and trimmed bread crusts while Cally iced cakes. Cally was to attend the reception and supervise the food; Lillian, eager to help, drove her there. All the way, Cally sat forward on the seat, more resplendent than usual, her mother's antique garnet earrings hanging like a tiny drop of blood from either ear. Rouge the same color, rubbed into a spot on each cheek, was overlaid with corn starch. Lillian hoped some would blow off before Cally arrived, hoped she did not look as obviously invited somewhere. Parking, she said, "Mammy, how do we tell from the kitchen when the platters are empty?"

"Girl, I didn't get this dressed up to stay in the kitchen," Cally said. "I hired me some waiters a long time ago."

"Hired waiters?" Lillian said. "How can you make any money if you got to pay waiters."

"Shoot, the more I charge these rich folks the better they'll think the food is," Cally said. "I'll clear close to five hundred dollars." She stood by the table all evening, only sometimes leaning slightly forward and then back as if she had forgotten the mop were not there. Lillian stood opposite and people spoke to them pleasantly, complimenting the food. One man returned repeatedly, talking to Lillian, and finding, to his relief, the food was of no more interest to her than to him, discussed the weather, his afternoon's bridge game and the political campaign. Lillian knew nothing of politics and was interested in the night's guest only because his name appeared frequently in the society columns to which she was addicted. But knowing enough to mouth clichés, she said she thought the candidate was honest and would do a lot for the city.

The man said, "Young lady, we need you down at campaign headquarters. Come on down to the Andrew Johnson and say I sent you." He handed her a business card; glancing at it, Lillian tried to show no emotion. A. G. Singer, Cotton Broker, was a sign she had seen often across a warehouse that stretched an entire block on First Street.

"I drop in headquarters every afternoon about five. Teatime, you know," Mr. Singer said, with a wink. He had a handsome face gone soft and was heavy but carried the weight awkwardly as if it were a recent acquisition; Lillian judged him to be about fifty. Saying she would try to come, she was about to summon her most engaging smile but glanced up and saw she did not need to. Bending closer than necessary to hear, he said, "What is your name?"

"Lillian," she said, and reluctantly, "Wynn."

On Monday, presenting the card, Lillian did not understand she was one in a long line of young women who had done so, and, misinterpreting the looks of the other women, felt ill at ease about her clothes. The young women of inferior background A. G. sent were tolerated by the other women because he contributed largely to the campaign. Like those before her, Lillian was assigned a telephone to answer and envelopes to address. The women did not speak to her again except about the work at hand, and she went to lunch alone. All day, her eyes seemingly on her work, Lillian studied their mannerisms and every detail of their clothes. By five, when A. G. Singer arrived, she had convinced herself he was a ridiculous old fool. But as soon as he walked comfortably into the room full of people to whom she so aspired, Lillian forgave him. He gave her a drink, drew her into the group, and several of the women managed to smile; she was not, they would say later, as bad as the others. After several drinks, A. G. offered to drive Lillian home. They went into the hall and at the elevator he said, "Say, you know what? I left my wallet back in my room. We'll just have to run up and get it."

"Your room," she said. "Do you live here?"

"I keep a room here just for convenience. I'm divorced and if I'm downtown late there's no reason to drive way out to my house." When they had gone into the room, he said, "Say, you know what? I've got a bottle of the best whisky you can buy. Why don't we have a stirrup cup right here."

He had telephoned for ice almost before Lillian could answer. She sat down. Removing his coat, he went about the room springing lightly on the balls of his feet, humming and straightening things. Passing close, he stopped and cupped his hand beneath her chin, "Oh, you're a pretty little thing, you are, you are," he said. She tried to smile and stood up in relief when the bellboy knocked. Afterward, holding the drink he fixed, she moved about the room restlessly and inevitably let him put his arms about her. Trembling, he said, "Oh darling, Oh darling!" over and over until it was all Lillian could do not to say, Hush! When they had made love, she said she had to go home. He jumped out of bed jubilantly. To escape him, she went into the bathroom. He had wanted to zip, hook, button everything. That night, Lillian lay awake remembering him bouncing about the room or hovering close as a pesky fly. She would have to take him as he was or leave him. Considering what she had and what he had to offer, she made her decision.

Lillian had not had to go home that night. Full of confidence after the golf course job, Son had announced he was going to get in that little car and go: find work; things were slowing down. Money was tight and it looked like it was going to get a lot tighter before it got any looser. If he was going to make it, he had to hustle. He had left that Monday saying not to expect him again before Friday. Lillian returned every day to campaign headquarters and every afternoon to A. G.'s room. It was Thursday before he said, "Oh darling, oh darling, if only we could stay together all night." Admitting her husband was out of town, Lillian stayed. Friday morning, A. G. said he would not be able to see her that afternoon: he needed a little rest. Lillian said it was all right. She had to go home and wash her hair. Gradually the ladies included Lillian in their lunches and in answer to questions, she made vague reference to the distant Arkansas town from which she had come, clearly implying Delton was a place she had come only recently to know.

Son set out that Monday to see Will Carrothers, an engineer repairing levees along the St. Francis River. A minimum of dynamite was used in levee work and Son had decided his future lay in convincing contractors they ought to use more. His experience was enough that he had begun to develop theories about ways to move dirt and clear land that would be easier and quicker. It seemed logical that if he were on the spot, looking at a job with a man while he explained it, he had a lot better chance of convincing the man of what he was saying, of selling him dynamite to do the job.

That was when Son packed his grip, got in his car, and set out on the journey that would last thirty years.

Leaving town before dawn, he crossed into Arkansas and was headed down the one straight road that was West Delton when daylight came. From dusty sideroads a few Negroes emerged on their way to fields and in one cafe with the lights on, a waitress looked out. He could sure stand another cup of coffee, Son thought, and drove on by at a faster rate of speed. He hadn't even taken time to go to the bathroom this morning. He had a place to go and had to get there. He held his speed for some time, the road ahead always empty; but the good time he made, he lost as the road became crowded with mule-drawn wagons and rickety trucks carrying fieldhands to the fields, white and colored, the women either thick-bodied or scarecrow-thin, wearing wide, frayed straw hats and the men handkerchiefs bound about their heads. Son had to brake continually as they pulled onto the road; no slow conveyance ever waited for him to pass first. He trailed them for hours, it seemed, while the fieldhands, jogging ahead, stared back at him fixedly, without expression.

On through several little towns just coming awake he crawled and at last was free; he sped on with nothing on either side but wild grass and trees. It was so hot by early morning that if it got hotter the rest of the day, Son never noticed, he was already so hot. Wind whipping past was arid and continually he sat forward to unstick himself from the seat. Relief came only when trees grew close over the road, casting filigreed shade. It would seem to have rained when cool came on suddenly; even the tires had a different sound after the baked road. Passing Marion, he went on into Marked Tree and had expected a little more, but as far as he could see, there wasn't a thing in the world going on in Marked Tree. He had lunch in a good cafe, Grandma's; for thirty-five cents a plate of vegetables, corn bread and iced tea; you couldn't beat it for the money. Leaving town, he left the main road and drove for some time in back country over a road that was not called one on a map. It petered out to become two tracks through a cotton field and he thought he must be lost. He saw a Negro standing in a wagon coming toward him, whipping on a mule, and wondered how they would pass when the Negro drew off into a field and stopped. Looking surprised, he took off his hat as Son got out of his car and came toward him. "Uncle," Son said, "I'm trying to get out yonder to where the work's going on on the levee. How the hell am I going to do it?"

"This here's the levee road," the Negro said. "You going out to Mister Will's job?"

"That's right," Son said.

"He out there. Keep on like you going. You be there in a half hour."

Son wiped his head with a handkerchief already soaked with perspiration, muddy with dust from his face. "Pheww," he said. For as far as even the Negro standing in the wagon could see there was nothing but flat cotton fields, not even the rows visible, like a solid dark green canvas. The sunbaked sky seemed yellow, the sun a hole in it; heat fit close like a lid. Sweat stood in blisters on the Negro's face and shone in his hair. Son got back in the car and waved. "Much obliged," he said and as he started the car, the Negro put on his hat.

Driving away, Son looked back apprehensively at the wagon disappearing in their mingled dust. If anything happened to his little old Ford, if anything happened to him, it seemed he'd be out here till they came picking in the fall. There was nothing out here, only silence and the fields where nothing moved.

What in the distance appeared to be clouds took shape gradually as the levee itself. When he came to it, his road ended and another went in either direction; which way should he go? Passing a hand over the yellow grime on his face, he left finger tracks and dust settled like fine rain as he sat, wondering. He took the direction away from the highway he had left some time ago, searching now for what Red had said he would find: some kind of track over the levee. He passed what he thought was a cow path but stopped and backed up; he had come a mile and was about to run out of levee. Cursing, he gunned the car, giving it all it had. The tires spun on the hard road and the car shot ahead; as he wheeled onto the new path, the car's rear swung wildly. Gunning it again and again, he fought his way up, thinking he would not make it; then he spun the wheels once more and was on top of the levee, going in the direction he had chosen, wondering who the hell had had the nerve to make the road. Machinery had not cut it; it had been made by the determination of people driving the same place until they had worn the two ruts he now followed. He ate dust but would suffocate with the windows up. Summoning saliva to wash the dust down, he thought, it even tasted yellow. Fine as flour it sifted over the car and slid from the fenders. A wasp buzzed about his head and threw itself against the windshield, seeking escape, but he kept his eyes on the road, his hands gripping the wheel, his foot steady on the gas, knowing any deviation from the ruts would send the light car hurtling down the embankment, on the one side into the silent green fields and on the other into high grass that led away into a mass of tree tops. Beyond them was where he wanted to go. His tires crunching rocks cast them steadily with sharp clicks against the underside of the car. Ahead he saw the place to descend and gently applied brakes. When he stopped, the silence was as if a battle had ended. Dust showered him like fireworks and lay on the windshield so thick he had to turn on the wipers. Behind him the sun was going down where smoke curled up from town. Below, birds swung on tall weeds making various cries, cheeps, twitters, squeaks. Every bug he had ever heard made its own sound in the grass, magnified by the silence, until it seemed the insects were all in the car, even in him, the way when he heard a band, the bass drum seemed to be the beat of his own heart, a thousand times louder. Now with a buzz, final and loud, the wasp flew away. He looked back once at the long way he had come, realizing he would have to retrace it to find a place to sleep tonight. Already tired, he put his foot to the gas and turned the car down the levee bank.

He went a half mile with weeds on either side and then several miles through woods where it seemed late evening. But he emerged to sunlight and barren cleared land. Borrow pits, he thought: the first he had ever seen. From them, dirt was "borrowed" to build the levee. His impression was of great activity: many mules, Negroes, wheelbarrows, wagons, and several tractors, a few white men. As hot as he was, he thought every man and mule out there looked a whole lot hotter.

Following the road to its end, he was in the middle of the levee camp before he realized it. For some time, seeing a haze of blue smoke rising above the trees, he had wondered if there were a fire in the woods. Now, stopped, everywhere he looked he saw the same smoky blue look; wood smoke, the old familiar smell, drifted to him. He was surrounded by tents of the same design and would later learn their pattern, the same in every levee camp he was ever to enter. Supported by a pole in the center, the tents had a raised wooden floor; halfway up were green wooden walls, then screening to a canvas top of the same dark green; canvas flaps to cover the screening were rolled up when occupants were at home, kept down when they were not, to suffocate mosquitoes trapped inside. Son would have asked information from two tow-headed children but they giggled and ran away. He passed a tent with a sign over the door reading Commissary, then went along a path between two rows of tents. Ahead he saw what was obviously the dining tent with a kitchen connected; the smoky look came partly from there. Behind it, on the fringes of camp, brush and garbage were being burned. He knew there were two sections of camp; clearly the dining tent was the dividing line. Beyond it, he saw only Negroes. A man was roasting something over a little fire of his own and many Negro women were boiling wash. There were always fires; the smoky blue hazy look was permanent, the first thing anyone noticed arriving in a levee camp. Son turned in surprise before reaching the dining tent as a Negro woman said from behind a screen, "Hep you?"

The tent was connected to a similar one by a screened breeze-way. He stopped and said, "I'm a dynamite man. I'm looking for Mister Will."

"He out to the job," she said.

"When does he get in?" Son said.

"He be's in about fo'," she said.

"Could I wait for him up yonder by the commissary? Is that where he comes?"

"Yes suh." She turned in answer to a query behind her and said, "It's a white man say he's a dynamite man looking for Mister

Will." She looked back at Son. "Miss Martha say come in and wait out of the heat." Two wooden steps led up to the tent and as Son started toward them, the woman pushed open the door. Quicker than a whip's lash, a black snake, uncurling from beneath the steps, threw itself at the door. "Hyar that snake!" the woman screamed. She pulled the door to sharply, knocking the snake to the ground. It disappeared beneath the tent as men who had been burning brush came running with shovels. The Negro woman said, "Gone again. You all get you some axle grease and come rub around this tent. I ain't studying that snake no more." As the men went off to obey, she opened the door and Son came up the steps. She said, "We been fighting that snake ever since the baby come. It's the determinest."

Behind her a woman who had been watching said, "I'm Martha Carrothers. You must be the new dynamite man we've heard about." She came forward, a capable-looking woman, her hair fashionably waved, much younger than Son would have expected. There was an air of serenity about her that made him know she was leading exactly the life she wanted to; she wore high heels, her nails were polished, and she surprised him. He had removed his hat and now they shook hands. "Yes mam," he said. "Frank Wynn. Pleased to meet you." His eyes had adjusted to the lesser light in the tent and he was surprised by that too; it was as if he had walked into a house in the city; on the floor was a thick rug and drawn close to a sofa with velvet throw pillows were deeply cushioned arm chairs. Brightly polished, a silver water pitcher and goblets sat on a heavy walnut sideboard the length of the tent. He would learn that people who lived in levee tents either all year or most of it usually furnished them so. In a small wicker bed he saw a baby about three months old. "Looks like you're bringing out contractors mighty young these days," he said, bending over the bed.

Martha said, "We didn't bring him. He was born here. Will went for the doctor but I couldn't wait and Carrie here did as well."

Carrie said, "Miss Martha didn't intend a doctor to deliver that baby. She knew it was almost here long befo' she told Mr. Will."

Both women laughed. Carrie said, "Ever since we been boiling milk that snake been trying to get in after it." The men had come back and she went to the screen to give directions. "Grease ever inch, all around, under the steps. No snake going to pass over no axle grease." She called back into the tent, "They starting to come now. Mister Will be along directly."

Standing, hat in hand, watching men pass behind the tent, Son felt as if he were watching a parade when the flag passed; jocular but with evidence of tiredness in the slopes of their shoulders and slowness of steps, their speech barely audible, the Negroes came, sweating still. Some, so old their hair was white, had bodies comparable to the young men's who, whether they were big men or not, gave the impression of it because of their strength. I wouldn't want to mess with none of them anyway, Son thought. Some men looked up and nodded and spoke to Carrie who said, "Afternoon," or "All right." Their eyes, passing over the strange white man, went obediently blank. They were gone, their soft voices, the shuffle of their feet, the clink of things they carried fell away into distant sounds and the two silent women waited. Martha said, "Isn't Will coming?"

Carrie turned her eyes in neither direction but spoke with certainty: "No'm."

Son knew enough to know the Negroes had been too quiet and that now the women were; he felt prickly along his hairline, as if touched by cold fingers. Carrie's eyes had been bright and clear before; but now she sat out on the breezeway and the whites looked bluish, the color of skimmed milk; she lowered her eyes, not to meet, even by chance, the white man's; her lower lip protruded. She had the look another white woman besides Martha would have called sulky. Asked anything at all now, she would have denied knowledge of it, even the time of day. But, later, she would say she had known all along there was going to be trouble. That morning, waking, a dark shadow had leaped into her breast and she had had to battle it all day.

Holding his hat tightly, Son said, "I'll run up yonder and see can I find him."

Martha's eyes met his. "Something's happened," she said. "He always come here directly."

He said again, "I'll see can I find him," and went out into an afternoon still hot, put on his hat and passed Carrie, who saw nothing. The women, separated now by more than rooms, dwelled on their necessarily different alliances: only to what lay in the bed were they the same, and both moved at the sound of a tiny sneeze.

All the way back up the sloping path, Son wondered how he would know Will Carrothers; there were other white men in camp. Carter, Will's cousin, managed the commissary; the head mechanic and greaser, the job foreman were always white. Coming toward him now was a man in grease-covered clothes, one of the tow-headed children on each foot squealing as he walked. "Evenin'," the man said.

"How do," Son said.

In a cleared place before the commissary, three white men stood talking. Overflowing the commissary porch, Negro men and women stood, waiting. One man towered above the others, silver-haired, straight, thin as a bamboo pole, and Son knew instinctively it was Will Carrothers. As Son came up, the man turned and said, "Yes sir?"

Pushing back his hat, Son put out his hand. "I'm Frank Wynn, Mister Will, the new dynamite man in Delton for American Powder."

"Yes sir," Will said, shaking hands.

Son, not knowing anything else to do, came to the point. "I come out here to sell you some dynamite," he said, his approach so direct, he and Will laughed. The other white men had stopped talking and shuffled their feet, waiting for Son to leave. Son said, "I'm going back to Marked Tree to look for a place to sleep. But I'd like to come out and see you first thing in the morning."

Will's hand had seemed bone barely covered with skin but it was hard, calloused, sunburned. He leaned down to talk to the average man but did it in a kindly way. Son thought he must be about Mr. Ryder's age; he spoke in the same gentle way, his voice seeming also to belong to an older man. But he ran the most successful levee camp on the river and Son knew he had his tough ways. He had always been too light to fight and had devised a way of clipping a rebellious Negro under the chin with one of his long legs; had knocked them clear off machinery and down levee banks that way. Will came from an old family, had graduated with honors from Georgia Tech, could have had an engineering job anywhere and had purposefully picked the river; Martha said it was as if he never had been to school. No matter their background almost all the levee men chose to talk much the way the Negroes did. Will said, "We usually put you peddling men up in camp. I got an equipment salesman over yonder in the guest tent. You're welcome to stay there. Take some supper with us too."

"I'm much obliged," Son said. Will turned immediately back to the others. As Son went to his car for his grip, a man came to the door of the guest tent and called, "Mister Will, Carter, anybody going to join me for a toddy before supper?"

Will said, "Yes sir, we'll be there directly. That's Frank Wynn there. American Powder. Buzz Campbell, Mid-Valley Equipment."

Son went inside and shook hands with Buzz Campbell who stood in his undershorts shaking out the dustiest pair of pants Son had ever seen. He said, "Looks to me like you've been through a Oklahoma dust storm getting here."

Buzz said, "Hell, I rode a mule out here from town. I ain't tearing up the bottom of my car getting out to these levee camps. But I'll be glad to ride with you when you go back. I'll give a boy a dollar to ride this mule back to town." He took from his pockets his overnight things, toilet articles and a fifth of whisky and put them on a small washstand beneath a flecked mirror. He said, "When Carter goes back to the commissary we can get us some Cokes."

Son, changing clothes, looked at the men still talking, all the Negroes still waiting. He said, "Who are those other fellows; what's going on?"

"That there white-haired one is Cotton Riley, the head mechanic. The one starting to the commissary now is Carter Carrothers. Some of the niggers didn't show up this morning and the others say they've run off to the Number Two job up the river aways. Charley Holt's job. One of Mister Will's boys arranged it and got them more pay."

"What'd he do that for?" Son said.

"Charley Holt paid him to send him some help."

"Hell, I thought there was enough niggers in Arkansas to go around," Son said.

"Cotton picking ones. Not levee ones." Buzz said. "And there's a world of difference between the two. The levee ones don't have nothing to do with the ones that'll pick cotton, either. They don't know who's carrying the boys off and they're worried sick about not getting the job done on time if any more leave."

When Carter went into the commissary, the Negroes crowded in. But most had left by the time Son and Buzz started there. They went out and the sun, perched like a ball on the farthest rim of trees, set as they watched. Its going cast shadows like dark paths to follow; the sun had long left the commissary and, going inside, they felt the day's first cool. Opposite the front door was a back one with a large desk in front of it and all around the room were shelves full of foodstuff. Shelves and counters were made in sections, to be folded when camp moved; then, everything went on barges—mules, people, tents, all the equipment used in building the levee. Explaining, Buzz said it was a sight to see. All that stuff floating down the river. Twenty times worse than moving a circus. Last February, he said, I was here when they brought in all this stuff and it was cold. *Cold!* The river bank here was revetted and so sloping they couldn't get the barges close enough. There was water between the barge and the bank. They threw off the bales of hay that fenced in the mules, for them to walk over. Talk about having to whup mules! Them were the worse damn mules in America. I thought they'd never get them off that barge. And they couldn't get the niggers to do nothing either. They were a dragging with the cold. Cotton said he'd get 'em started working, give him some whisky. Mister Will give him the only bottle he had at the time and Cotton got those boys in a huddle and got that bottle started around, drinking with them. They just had a couple of sips, just enough to warm 'em up and get 'em to feeling good. Then those boys got that gangplank to going, up and down, up and down, what we call the old roustabout shuffle. Tippety-tap, rippety-rap. I can hear it now, Buzz said.

Carter was standing behind the commissary's counter waiting on a Negro woman. She said, "How much your side meat?"

Carter said, "Three cents a pound."

"I'll take three pounds," she said.

"Anything else," he said.

"No suh."

Carter brought the meat, wrapped it and wrote out a ticket. The woman looked at it and said, "I'll take a quart of molasses."

"You going to want anything else?" Carter said.

"No suh," she said.

Carter brought the molasses and wrote another ticket with a new total. The woman looked at it then said, "I'll take five pounds of sugar."

"I could have put all this on one ticket, you know," Carter said.

"No suh, I never thought of that, Boss," she said.

"Now you want anything else?" he said.

"No suh," she said. She took the packages and the ticket with a new total and gave him the money. When she had gone, Carter laughed. "She does that to me every week. She knows how much money she's got to spend but she don't know how to add and she don't want me to know it."

When Son had been introduced, they talked of Charley Holt. "What's Mister Will going to do to him?" Son said.

"Nothing. He's too mean to fool with," Carter said. "Him and his wife both just as soon kill you as look at you; both of them have killed Negroes. He was the one got drunk one Saturday night and got bounced out of that showboat at Blytheville and come back with some of his Negroes early that Sunday morning, soaked it with gasoline and burned it down. Everybody knew he did it.

110

The construction company he worked for paid the showboat owner fifty thousand dollars Monday morning."

"Your good boys don't run off anyway, do they?" Buzz said.

"No, the good ones been with us since we been on the river," Carter said. He explained to Son, "During the winter lay-off, they scatter. Go to De-troit, Chicago, New Orleans, all over. But when Will gets ready to start work in the spring, he sends word and it gets carried and here they come from all over the country. They like levee life as much as we do. Camp's a good place to hide out from the law, for white and colored. We just want to know who's carrying them boys off." Son and Buzz bought Cokes. Carter was beginning to close up but said, "Here comes Cotton's wife."

Carrying the youngest of their eight children, Mrs. Riley came in, her hair as white as Cotton's. "What you got good I can fix for supper, Mr. Carrothers?" she said.

"Got some pork chops," Carter said. "Some tender greens."

Mrs. Riley shifted the baby to her other hip. "No, I don't believe so today."

"Pot roast," Carter said.

"Too late to start a roast, I reckon," she said.

"Chicken?" Carter said. "Nice fryers. Fresh garden peas."

Mrs. Riley sighed. "I reckon it's too late to start anything," she said. "Just gimme three pounds of baloney and two loaves of bread and eight sticks of this here candy."

When she had gone, Carter said, "I don't know why Cotton puts up with that. She waits to the last minute every day to shop so she can say it's too late to cook." A Negro at the screen door said, "You closed, Mr. Carter?"

"Come on in here, Tangle-eye," Carter said. "What you want?"

"I need me three-fo' mo' bottles of Dr. Tishnor's, please suh," Tangle-eye said. Coming in, he doffed his hat. "How you Mr. Campbell?"

Buzz, introducing Son, said, "You need to know anything about shooting dynamite, ask Tangle-eye. He's shot it for Mister Will."

"Well, there's sure a lot I need to know," Son said.

111

Tangle-eye said, "I be glad to hep you some." When he looked at Son, one eye momentarily went another way and was the reason for his nickname. Every Negro in camp went by a nickname given by the other Negroes.

Carter said, "Tangle-eye, you cleaned me out of Tishnor's already this week. You better lay off that stuff anyway."

"I rub it on my back. My back aching," Tangle-eye said.

"You got a hangover," Carter said. "You'll have to take vanilla."

"I'll take me the large size," Tangle-eye said. "And Greaser out in the yard wants six Co-colas." He called to a Negro waiting outside in the shade of a large maple. "Greaser, come get your Cokes."

Coming to the doorway, Greaser so filled it, the room darkened. Looking up, Son saw the largest man he had ever seen. Greaser was introduced as camp's best mechanic; he was respected not only because of his size but because he held the highest job a Negro could; he helped the white mechanic oversee the greasing and care of equipment. Almost before the introduction was over, Greaser had drunk two Cokes. In each hand he enclosed, completely, two more bottles and went out on the porch. Tangle-eye opened the vanilla and put the bottle to his mouth so eagerly, Son laughed. "Boy, it looks to me like you're in bad shape. Come on over to the tent. I'll give you a drink of some real whisky." When they went on the porch Son said, "Greaser, you want you a drink?"

Tangle-eye said, "Greaser been saved. He don't do any drinking."

Son looked again at the hands that completely enclosed two bottles of Coke and said, "I don't guess nobody messes with him no matter what he does, do they?"

Greaser said, "I don't look for no trouble."

Going down the dusty path, back to the guest tent, Tangle-eye said, "Greaser don't do nothing wrong since he been saved. Work, saves his money, that's all." When Tangle-eye had had his drink he admired the shirt Son had worn to camp; it lay over his cot. Son said, "I'll look at home. I got some shirts I can't wear anymore. I'm going to bring you some." He realized from the way

Tangle-eye left, quickly opening and closing the door, it was to keep out mosquitoes. He poured a little whisky into his hand and rubbed his ankles. He had scratched them until they were almost raw.

Carter, Buzz and Will came and while they drank, Son listened to insect sounds outside; the mingled cries were so loud that sometimes the men had to raise their voices to hear, though it was only variations in the tone they noticed. Once, they listened to a frog just beneath the tent and to a locust screaming in discord to the others. For an unaccountable moment, all the sounds ceased, the moment so strange, Mister Will started up, the others were motionless. As unaccountably, the sounds started up again and the men looked at one another with half-foolish grins and began to talk. If they lost any more boys, Will said, they could not finish on time; they would lose as much as two thousand dollars a day. Work went on seven days a week, from daylight to dark; there was no way to make up lost time. Part of a contractor's winning a job was his guarantee of when it would be finished; his bonding company guaranteed the date too. Reputations were important and had to be maintained. The Government was an exacting boss.

The supper gong called them into the warm evening. They went along the path between the rows of tents and Martha joined them as they went to eat. Families usually cooked in their own tents; only men sat at the long wooden tables. Emmie, the cook, was the only Negro who spent any time in the white's part of camp; during the winter lay-off, she cooked for the Carrothers in Delton. She looked up, her face the color of new copper, shining from the stove's heat; her grandfather, half-Indian, had operated one of the first ferries ever to cross the White River. Will said, "Emmie, here's Mr. Frank Wynn, never been to a levee camp before. What you got good to eat?"

"Got levee camp chicken tonight, Cap'n," she said, indicating a bowl of molasses and water in which pieces of salt pork had been soaking all day. As they talked, she dipped pieces into another bowl of water then dropped them into a skillet full of grease. "If I'd knowed you had company, I'd have done you some better."

Carter, passing, slapped Son on the shoulder. "This ain't no company," he said. "Just another peddler come by."

Buzz said, "Emmie, I been starving to death up and down this river. You the only one that feeds me right."

Close at hand, at supper, Son smelled the sweet-crusted smell of the fried pork and with slight variations in the evening's breeze he caught a whiff of creosote coming from the privy back of camp, but mostly he smelled mosquito spray and he could see the floor soaked with it in large greasy spots. On almost every part of him he could name, he felt welts rising and tried to scratch them unnoticed. From one table to another, they talked of who had taken the Negroes to the other camp. Full dark had come before they finished and Emmie lit the lamps. The dark enclosed them, heavy and warm, like something solid against the screens. Specks of light in the far dark told where other tents were. Somewhere in the woods, toward the river, a wolf howled and the head mechanic's dog, waiting for him outside the tent, set up such barking the man rose and yelled "Hyar!" through the screen and the dog crawled under the tent to whimper. In the kitchen tent, Emmie stopped rocking and said, "Ooo wee, I hate that sound out there," and everyone else hated it too and said nothing to comfort her. Leaving the tent, Will gave Buzz and Son flashlights and told them to play them around everywhere before they went to bed. When they set up camp, they had killed as many snakes as possible but many were still around; he told of a momma snake that had swallowed her young to move them away from a boy chopping brush; the boy had struck the momma snake a blow that killed her but she opened her mouth and released the young and they had never found a one. "Go on, Mister Will," Buzz said; but Martha, walking beside Will, promised it was the Lord's truth.

As Will did, many other whites and Negroes had two tents connected by a screened breezeway; people sat there in the dark after supper because it was cooler and not having lamps lit discouraged bugs. Son heard Negroes singing, heard a guitar. He went back up the path and insects in the grass hushed until he had gone by. Martha went into her tent, but the men went back to the guest tent to play Pitch. Entering, Carter said, "Get that damn mosquito off your cheek," and Son began to brush at it. Will said, "You can't brush 'em. Pull. Pull like a tick." Then Son was holding between his fingers a mosquito as big as a wasp, squashed into a large spot of blood that was his own. "Jesus Christ, I thought them mosquitoes were about to tote me off," he said.

Buzz gave him alcohol to rub on his itching welts and Will said, "You got to keep something on you all the time." He meant kerosene or a spray. "Clothes don't help. They bite right through."

They did not play cards long and no one drank; it was too hot and they had to get up too early, work too hard. When the others had gone, Buzz and Son used a tree outside, sprayed the tent, looked for snakes and went to bed. The moonlit trees were close and still, the night had little breeze, and beneath him Son felt the cot grow steadily wetter as he perspired. In the woods an animal called and before he could ask the question, Buzz answered it: "Wildcat." Buzz said the woods around here were so wild that earlier in the spring two salesmen coming out on mules were lost in them for three days. He fell asleep, snoring lightly, but Son lay watching the silver play of moonlight over everything, realizing how tired he was, that it had been a long day; he looked back at himself meeting the Negro in the cotton field and to the moment when he was finally shooting along the levee, saw himself dip down and struggle on out to camp. Mister Will's face freed itself of the day's other impressions and Son thought of the moonlight silver on his silver hair and the now familiar sprinkling of freckles in the corner of each eye; it seemed he had known him always. Carter, Buzz, Tangle-eye, Greaser: it seemed he had known them all a long time. What seemed strange was his life away from here. He had not thought of Lillian once. Cally was a faint, nagging worry that underlay everything. Poppa he thought of comfortably and fell asleep wishing he were there.

Morning was the sun shining through dew-wet cobwebs all around the screens and a mourning dove calling in the distance answered by another in the opposite direction; ooo-oo went one and the other responded at longer intervals, oooo-oooo: over and over, all day. The sun at a level with the screens was already hot and lay over him with the warmth of a light blanket. The first pair of eyes he met were two black ones in a pointed face. Seeing Son, the racoon, which had been on the steps eating something between front paws, put them down and went away without hurry. A thud and two groans were Buzz getting up; he stood, rubbing his buttocks, and said, "That may be the last Goddamn mule I ever ride."

In the tent nearest the tree they chose, Cotton Riley's wife fried pork rind. A child with a tangled head of hair stood in his cot and watched them with unsurprised eyes; they shot their water at a frog which belched when Buzz hit it and the child cried the news excitedly back to his family.

Behind the dining tent the path was crowded with Negroes going to work; already many were milling about the commissary. The foreman sopped his plate clean with half a biscuit and reported no more men were missing. But Will still had a look of worry that was more than usual. He said he had dirt in a borrow pit he wanted to show Buzz and Son. After breakfast, they followed him to the commissary where a Negro named Sho Nuff held mules. Like almost all the Negro men, Sho Nuff wore a large floppy straw hat and a pair of overalls pinned together at the shoulders with safety pins. His four upper front teeth were gold; his lower jaw had been knocked permanently to one side. As they went along on the mules, Will told how it had happened. Another year, on someone else's job, Sho Nuff had gotten into a fight with another Negro; when the white boss tried to break it up, Sho Nuff sassed him. Will said, "Sho Nuff had the nerve because he knew the white man was afraid of him. You can't show fear of Negroes. They can smell it every time." Then, the white man had picked up a willow root and tried to beat Sho Nuff but slipped and fell. Sho Nuff stuck into his leg the knife he had been trying to stick into the other Negro.

"How'd he get out of that?" Son said.

"Run off," Will said. "Had to. He came to me then and been with me ever since."

"You don't think he'll stick a knife in you?" Buzz said.

"No, he knows I'm not afraid of him," Will said.

The borrow pit they approached was ten acres. But before they saw it, they smelled it. First they smelled themselves, sweating, then the sticky wet hides of the mules, the customary dust and the long dry sun-browned grass before, Will having said nothing, Son and Buzz stared at one another in surprise and later told it this way: riding a old Arkansas mule down what back country Arkansas called a road, they all of a sudden smelled the sea. Salt water, Son would say, having never seen the ocean. But Buzz told, I be damned if it didn't smell just like the Gu'f Coast.

Before them a panorama of Negroes, mules and equipment laboriously moved the dirt, like ants, working steadily and small in comparison to their undertaking. Harness-worn, many of the mules, despite the good care they received, had sores, and flies and gnats followed them in swarms. The mules were worked in pairs. From a distance one seemed always a shadow of the other, stuck close. They pulled wagons and slip scrapers which were big pans on wheels, pulled by two to four mules, and slipped over the ground to fill with little more than a yard of dirt at a time. Bottom dump wagons were pulled by twelve to sixteen mules and had trip doors worked by a hand crank. On one elevating grader, dirt travelled up a belt until the wagon was full. The scraper's bottom, the mules' hooves packed the dirt once it was on the levee. But all Son and Buzz could think about was the pit. His own mouth had fallen open and Son saw Buzz had to close his before speaking; then all he could say was, "I'll be damned." The dirt, black, shone like asphalt just rained on, though there had not been rain for weeks. They sat on mules covered with dust, dust settled on everything about them, and in the borrow pit dirt was being dug, dumped, hauled and not a particle flew anywhere. Leaving the mules, they walked to the mud; close up, it had a greenish cast and steamed up at them with its thousand-year-old smell of the sea and things that had belonged to it. "The Gulf," Will said, "used to reach up here and on to Cairo. We came across this pocket by accident. Just started digging and here it was. Come here, close." The others stooped as he did, watched as he dug his hand into the dirt and broke it open. For an instant they saw tiny petrified sea fossils, little shells, but as soon as the air touched them they were gone, turned to dust, and all Will held was the dirt smelling as if it had come from an outhouse, inescapably around them. "It's the most wonderful dirt to move I've ever seen," he said. "The quickest moving and it don't stick to anything."

Borrow pit land was abandoned once the dirt was removed, left to fill with rain water and eventually form another of the numerous muddy fishing ponds dotting the Southern landscape. "Liable to be good cat fishing here someday," Will said, and they all wondered if they would see.

Buzz spoke to Will about buying equipment. Son tried to sell Will dynamite, said he would do all the blasting free. "Yourself?" Will said in surprise. All morning they followed Will who oversaw everything, even a mule the head skinner reported sick, and Son talked about his theories of using dynamite in levee work, about all the ways he thought dynamite could be used in swamps, for clearing, to make drainage ditches, ways it had not been used before. And he began immediately to learn from Mr. Will. He said, "Frank, I'll tell you something that's my system. The other contractors don't use it, but I think it's the best way." Son knew then he would try it. "I only have the trees cleared as far ahead as I'm going to work that day. Because the trees drink the water. If you do it that way, you'll have a better job." At noon, work ceased as abruptly as if a signal had been given though none was: fill, dump, back and forth, the pattern was broken; the jangle of mule harness ceased, the rattle of wagons, the roar of tractors, dust settled. Those who had not worked Will's black mud were covered with dust; white and Negro, they trooped back to camp for noon dinner, sweating and smelling and baked by the sun. Son had kept on his hat but knew his eyes were bloodshot; he entered the shelter of the tent and had a moment of adjusting; things flashed in yellow, like sparklers against night; for one instant he saw the whole levee panorama as if it were on the head of a pin and himself there too. Walking in, sitting on a bench at one of the long tables, opposite Will, he looked about at the grimy, burned, uncomplaining faces of the men who were laughing and talking quietly, as if purposefully guarding their strength to go again into the blazing afternoon, to the work as backbreaking as any Son had ever seen a Negro do. At that moment, he realized he had found his life's work and it was something he liked to do. If there was anything else in the world a man could be luckier about, he didn't know what it was.

Will drank his iced tea and said, "Frank, I been thinking about what you been saying about dynamite. I don't know whether your ideas are right or not. But if I win any big work when we have another letting, I'd be willing to experiment with you just a little."

Son said, "Mister Will, just let me try. Just let me show you. I know I'm right."

Will said, "Well, if you're going to do all my shooting free, I ain't got nothing to lose."

Buzz looked at Son. "Boy," he said, "you might as well get you a old floppy straw and a pair of pinned-together overalls."

Will's eyes met Son's. He said, "Yes sir, I believe Frank's a good one. He's like the rest of us, not afraid to work."

Son had been going to say he never had been afraid to work, had always had to; his nose was enclosed in his glass of tea and he was draining the last sweeter gulp at the bottom, had been about to lower the glass when Will, standing abruptly, almost knocked it from his hand. At the same moment, Emmie came screaming from the kitchen, "Greaser gone crazy. Fixing to kill us!"

Everyone stood. From behind the screen, they looked out at Greaser who had run up from the Negro section and stood outside, looking crazy. Enraged, he struggled to speak and only saliva slid from his lips. Veins stood on his forehead prominently, knotted as rope; his hands swung, back and forth, open, itching to take hold of something. Will opened the door and went out and Son heard Martha call him back softly.

Will stood perfectly still and said, "What's the trouble, Greaser?"

Watching, Son could only think of Greaser's enormous body sustained by the tiny thing beating within it. Greaser sucked powerfully, found breath and said, "I'm going to kill him."

Other Negroes, having followed, stood in a semicircle behind camp's invisible dividing line, looking scared. Will said, "What's happened?"

"Gone. Gone. Carried my money. Carried my gun." Greaser's voice broke with rage and grief.

"Who done?" Emmie said, before anyone else could. Her own money was hidden in a dark corner of the kitchen; she went to check it.

"Booker T.," someone said. The name echoed around the semi-circle; Greaser's breath still came in a spasm. Son saw his arms were so long, his hands were just short of his calves; still they swung, back and forth, back and forth.

Tangle-eye, holding his hat against his chest, stepped forward. "Doll seen Booker T. slipping around Greaser's tent this morning. Greaser come in and found his mattress cut up, his money he had inside gone. A gun too."

"Loaded," someone else said. "Booker T. knowed it too."

"I'm going to kill him," Greaser said.

"There ain't going to be no killing," Will said. "He's gone, Greaser. You might as well forget your money."

"I'm going to kill him," Greaser said. His face set, he turned and started up the path out of camp. Martha had come down the steps to Will. She said, "He is going to kill him, Will. We've got to do something."

Hell, let him kill him, Will thought. He said, "He'll be all right."

She said, "He won't. He's going to kill him. Let me ride him to town and try to help."

"You can't go to town alone and there's no men can leave work," he said. Already, the others were starting back to the levee.

Son said, "I'll drive him," and when Martha said she was going too, Will only shrugged and went back to work wishing she did not care. They found Greaser not long out of camp. He got into the back seat. All the way to town, Son felt it was Greaser's impetus driving the car forward. Martha had told him she did not think it was just the gun and money; it was Doll too. Long ago, Doll had been Greaser's girl. One day Booker T. treated her to a Coke at the commissary. Greaser saw them, picked up Booker T. and simply pitched him over into the woods and that had been the end of it, until now. Martha said the changing of partners in camp was of constant interest, she could not wait to get back every year and see who was paired off; couples who had lived side by side in tents one year, the next had changed partners and again set up tents side by side. Son drove fast, down the great dip to ascend the levee, then horizontally across it as if across the world, on through brooding green fields and to the edge of town, wondering what to do if they saw Booker T., how to keep Greaser out of trouble. He remembered Greaser had recently been saved, remembered all Old Deal had told about salvation. He said, "Greaser, you have saved your soul. It's not worth losing it over Booker T."

Greaser said, "I'm going to kill him."

As they drew close to town, to the Negro section, the road was lined with small cypress cabins, the wood shaggy, splintery, silver-grey in the sun's glance; old women rocked on the porches in straight chairs watching traffic pass; the cabins gave way to small paint-peeling houses whose yards were full of flowers and to neat, well-kept frame and brick houses. At the end of the road there were cafes and a pool hall, their interiors as dark as night; pencil-printed placards in the windows told the price of fried fresh cat and that smell hung deliciously over the windless afternoon. Except for Greaser, Booker T. would be the biggest man anyone had seen but no one had seen him any of the places Greaser asked. As Greaser emerged from each dark place, frowning into the sun, Son and Martha, waiting in the car, would hear music behind him insinuating something that belonged to night too. They waited outside a house where only women peeped from behind curtains and Martha asked no questions. They went on to a tent show at the edge of town and waited at the door in case Greaser flushed Booker T. They climbed wearily back into the car and Son tried again. He said, "Greaser, are you going to turn against your Lord this way?"

Greaser said, "I'm going to kill him," but Son thought he heard the first hesitancy. Glancing into the rearview mirror, he saw Greaser had leaned back against the seat; the hands that had been

121

at all times ready to choke Booker T.'s neck rested on his knees. He stared ahead instead of searching by-ways. Son said, "Let the law take care of it, Greaser."

Martha said, "That's right, Greaser. You listen now."

They drove up to camp just before full dark; Son parked where the car would be shaded from even the early morning sun. Greaser had said nothing else all the way, though Son and Martha had continued to talk about keeping his saved soul. When he got out of the car, Greaser turned as if he were going to speak. Instead, he smiled. Forever afterward, telling the story, Martha would say it had been a smile just like an angel's, lit up, beautiful, gigantic, before he disappeared into the dark.

Son and Martha started toward the center of camp, tired and silent. Then Son gripped Martha's arm and they were still; still, they were not noticeable among the shadows. They looked at one another in instant understanding, peering toward the rustling bushes; talking softly, men crept there; they stood when they were out of camp and hurried down the road. One remained, in silhouette only the floppy straw and the sagging pinned-together overalls. Turning, he crept back to camp. From their vantage point, Son and Martha glimpsed, in disbelief, Sho Nuff.

"Sho Nuff!" Will said. Suddenly his chin stuck out and he straightened. Martha saw it hurt him as much as it had her, the difference being that Will would try not to show it. He told Son his father had taught him from the time he could remember a nigger is a nigger and he had never believed it until now, forty-odd years later, Sho Nuff had put him in the position of having to; he had to teach him a lesson because of the others. Son saw it was as if Will were at the top of a carefully built pyramid, and Sho Nuff was loosening a bottom block; to reprimand or fire him was not enough. Though, Will said, he only went so far. He had to laugh, repeating what one of the Negroes had told Carter: they liked working for Mister Will because "he'll whup us but he won't kill us."

Carter said too, in disbelief and sorrow, "Sho Nuff!" then his lips set too. The next afternoon Martha went into the tent, held the baby, and did not look at Carrie. Son and Buzz went for their evening drink, drank up almost a fifth and never found anything funny. The Negroes left work silently. In the way that always happened, word had spread without anybody knowing who had known it first, and with Sho Nuff the last to know.

The day ended and Sho Nuff stopped work; suddenly Carter and Will were beside him. Will nodded, once, in the direction of the mule corral. Sho Nuff said, "Cap'n," and Will's lips set and he nodded again. Sho Nuff started walking and they came behind. Skinner, in the corral, took one look, threw down a bucket, and ran. Inside the shed, in the close, hot, mule and hay-smelling place, Sho Nuff said, "Please, Cap'n."

Will said, "Take off your pants."

"Naw sir, Cap'n," Sho Nuff said.

"Take off your pants," Will said.

Sho Nuff let down the pinned-together straps and having on nothing underneath, stood naked.

Will said, "See that bale of hay? Lie down."

Sho Nuff went to the bale and lay across it. From nails on the wall, Carter had taken down two mule belly straps. He gave one to Will and they began to strike him: struck him twenty times, ten times each, alternately, until it was twenty. Then it was done. Will said, "Put on your pants," and Sho Nuff did. He picked up the straw hat from the floor where it had fallen, put it on his head, and went out and out of the corral, closing the gate behind him. Will and Carter came the same way and saw him, still walking; they stood and watched and he went on as far as the levee in the distance, clambered up the bank and was still going, across the top of the levee. Once he took off his hat and wiped his forehead, then put back on the old floppy straw and that was the last they saw of him, against the setting sun.

The next morning, hung-over, Son and Buzz went back to Marked Tree. At his car, Buzz said, "Where you going now?"

Son said, "Up the road, to hit every camp between here and Cape Girardeau."

In Cape Girardeau, he ran into Buzz again who introduced him to a blonde-headed woman and they got drunk together and had a time, all night. That week he kept in touch with the office by telephone and once Scottie said Lillian had been trying to reach him. "What's the matter?" he said.

"Nothing," Scottie said. "She just said she wanted to talk to you."

"Oh hell," he said. He certainly did not see any reason to run up your phone bill talking to your wife. He received only a few small orders. But he accomplished something of what he set out to do. People who had not known him before, did now. He was not just another voice on the telephone. Day after day he was on the levees, exposed beneath a wide sky to the sun from which there was no hiding place. He gave a man an estimate right there, looking over the work with him, tried to convince people of using more dynamite, in different ways. A few times he shot dynamite Mr. Ryder delivered. At night, he fell into bed as grimy, sunburned, exhausted as the workers themselves and believed those birds had some respect for him because of it. He saw his road ahead, a long way, a repetition of these days without let-up. But he would bet his bottom dollar, now, someday he would have run every bit of his competition out of this territory, Arkansas, Mississippi, Tennessee and Missouri. He suddenly determined to do it, sitting one night in a little fleabag hotel. One of the first things he had learned about this travelling life was you got lonesome. He had had some drinks and he was tired and tight. He got up and looked at himself in the bureau mirror, his eyes pale and his grin cockeyed, two things that always happened when he was tight. He swore at that moment, Someday I'm going to run ever one of those birds right straight plumb clean out of this territory.

He had another drink and got into bed thinking about how he would do it. There was only one way, to offer better service; dynamite was all the same. He would build his reputation on service. The day would come when nobody would think of dynamite without thinking of Frank Wynn and he'd tell those other peckerwoods if they wanted to sell any dynamite in this territory they better go up and down the levee the day before him, because it sure wasn't going to do any good if they went the day afterward.

He stretched his feet toward the end of the bed and planned his retirement. He set the age at sixty. Then, he would like to travel and see some of those places nobody but he knew he ever thought about seeing, some of those foreign places. He would not get up in the morning until he wanted, something he had not been able to do even as a boy. He would have time just to do nothing, maybe even play some games.

It was a set pattern. He left at dawn every Monday and returned at evening every Friday. He told Lillian to have his supper on the table when he drove in the driveway; he would be ready to eat. All Saturday and Sunday the house was full of his friends; sometimes the Sunrise Club met, sometimes the men brought their wives or women who were not; at night they went out, always a crowd, to eat and drink, gamble, sometimes to dance; whatever they did ended on a wild note, with a fight or a prank, always with everyone drunk. Lillian complained that she had been home all week and he came home and went to bed. On Fridays, at least, she wanted to go out with her friends, to some place that was quiet and nice. He said, "Woman, I been out beating my tail all week, I got to rest sometime. Seeing those customers helps get our groceries on the table so keep your mouth shut."

It was getting harder and harder to find those groceries too, he would tell you. And not only did he have to worry about business for himself, he had to worry about Poppa's too. He had borrowed money to set Poppa up in a little hole-in-the-wall store, barely getting along, but it was what Poppa wanted, close enough to home to walk, with a room in the back where he could nap. Poppa sold some groceries but it seemed to Son he had it mostly stocked with candy; cases were full and barrels of it sat on the floor. One barrel, particularly, brought children to the store. It was full of chocolates with different colored centers; even Poppa did not understand how, but he could guess accurately the color inside. If a child asked for a nickel's worth of greens, his sack contained them when he bit into the candies one by one to see.

One Saturday morning, Son went to the store to talk to Poppa; Lillian had reported the night before Cally had a tumor which had to be removed. Son entered the store as children, taking candy, left pennies on the counter; no one had seen Poppa. Hell of a way to run a business, Son thought, leave in the middle of the morning. He went to the back, pulled aside the curtain separating the two rooms and could no longer be annoyed, looking at Poppa asleep there; easy to see he had not sought sleep but that sleep itself had been the aggressor. Poppa lay as if flung back, his hands trailing off the cot on either side, his mouth open, and was captive still when Son had waked him: groggy and pale. He sat up, reached for a glass of water and took several pills. "How you getting along? Your kidneys acting up again?" Son said.

"I'm not worth killing around here," Poppa said. "How you getting along?"

"Just scratching around trying to make a living," Son said.

Poppa confirmed what Lillian had said; Cally had been truly in pain and the doctor was reliable. The operation had to be immediate and was set for Monday morning. Son said, "Well, I'll give you whatever your in-surance don't cover."

Poppa said, "Son, it's going to be all right after this. She was still too weak to even want this operation. She had gotten so she just wanted to feel good." They went out into the store and a customer came asking for a small checker set; Poppa looked high and low but could not find them. "My wife was in here last week helping me unpack a new shipment," Poppa said. "I don't see how in the world I sold them all that fast." Son told the man they would keep looking if he would drop in again. He left the store and drove to see Cally.

Since graduating from high school, Cecilia had lived at home, sleeping on a cot in the living room, her feet hanging off the end; anyone but Cecilia would have complained. Her time was taken up mostly with Cally and the house but she taught Sunday School and went to prayer meetings on Wednesday nights. She did a little bookkeeping for the church, was not paid very much, but the compensation was that she could do the work at home. She came out on the porch to meet Son and said the doctor had just left; he felt Cally was weak for an operation but that the operation was necessary; it was the one before she should not have had. And, Cecilia said, Kate had confided that one reason she was moving was because when she read late at night Cally took the fuses out of the box in the basement, said Kate wasted electricity sitting up at night reading. Son and Cecilia had to laugh though neither one of them understood why Kate was always going to the library and coming home with an armload of novels. Going inside, they stopped at her door. She was bent over, fastening her suitcases, and when she looked up her face, usually pale, flushed bright red; her hair, cropped short, just covered her ears and she pushed back the waves on either side of her face, leaving streaks of dirt; but she looked pretty just the same, Son thought. She said, "There's one big carton in the closet I'm leaving on purpose. It's something of your momma's she asked me to store."

"Well I certainly can't imagine what," Cecilia said. She went into the closet and came out, perplexed. "You know what's in there? A whole lot of checker sets."

"Sam Hill," Son said. He went into Cally's room and asked why in the world she had taken them from the store. Cally sat up as if with all her old strength and said, "Foolishness! Grown-up people playing games. It wastes time. I don't want Poppa having any part of it." Without saying anything, Son took the sets back to the store when he left. On Monday he waited until the operation was over and declared a success, then set out again.

During the week he called Mr. Ryder one night but he was not at home; he called Lillian to ask her to deliver the message early the next morning but she was not at home either. He wondered where she could be that time of night, but had forgotten about it by the time he drove home on Friday. Then, before he even had supper, Lillian said, "Frank, I'm going to leave you. I want to have some children, but I'm not going to bring up any around the sort of people you bring home and with all the gambling and drinking going on here."

His first thought was, he was about to starve to death and did

127

she have supper on the table? Then he put his grip down, felt too tired even to take off his coat, looked at her and said, "Lillian, there isn't any woman going to walk out on me."

She did not say anything else; she stayed in her room all Saturday night while the poker game went on. The next afternoon they went to see Cally, then out with Buzz and others to eat steak. On Monday, he left again.

As soon as he turned onto the block that Friday, he saw the house was dark. It gave him a feeling of emptiness and fear, as if somebody had taken his house away. He came up the steps, barely able to drag his grip he was so tired, thinking maybe Cally was sick and Lillian had rushed off there. He went straight to the telephone and turned on a light as he picked up the receiver. Without its reaching his ear, he put the receiver down again. It was his house, he knew that; he had had the key and let himself in. But the living room was almost bare. Even the rug was gone. The furniture left was a few worthless pieces they had taken from Cally's attic. He went about the house and everything was the same, except that Lillian's clothes were gone. He did not know what else to do and he went about the house again. He walked through the few rooms looking at knickknacks, not seeing them any more than he ever had. He stood in the living room looking at where the rug had been, outlined by the floor waxed darker around its edges. He cursed not only Lillian but the department store and the salesman and everybody else he could think of who had had anything whatsoever to do with that rug; because it was not only gone, it was not even paid for. Son-of-a-bitch, he said again.

Lillian he thought he dismissed, if she were that kind of woman. But he only shoved the thought of her down inside himself so far it was twenty years before he could speak her name again without being flooded with all the rage and despair and disappointment and embarrassment he was flooded with now, unable to reason that if he felt that much, what he had felt for Lillian was love, though she had told him for so long he did not know anything about love that he had no longer used the word, guessing she was right.

He locked the house, went out and got in the car. As soon as he walked into the other house, he saw two things, they had a place set for him at the table and the three waiting could not look at him. "Where the hell is she?" he said.

"She said she had an apartment somewhere and you would be hearing from her lawyer," Cecilia said. "She just called a little while ago."

To the family, Son made so much money that only he wondered how Lillian would pay for an apartment; he knew one thing, she'd never get even a thin dime out of him.

Cally said, "Oh, if only you had been church folks. If only you had listened. Whom God hath . . ."

Poppa led her away, saying, "Come on, Boss. It's time for your medicine. Time for you to go to bed."

Cecilia brought Son's supper saying, "Brother, ever since that operation, Mammy's been like a child. Do you think her mind's going to be right again?"

"She's probably just got it on some other damn way for Poppa to spend money," Son said.

"Listen," Cecilia said. "Poppa never has had all that money. And wouldn't have made what he did if Mammy hadn't pushed him. What would we have now, this house? Anything? if Mammy hadn't worked. Standing over that stove like she did, to feed other folks and us too. Don't forget it." She hushed, hearing Poppa. He came in and said, "That medicine makes her sleep awhile, then she gets up and just roams around all night."

"Maybe she needs a new medicine," Cecilia said.

"Hell, let her roam," Son said harshly, his mouth full of corn bread. Suddenly, everything stuck in his throat, them, the food, Lillian and all that had happened. He wanted to be some place drinking whisky and seeing his friends; and how was he going to tell them? A moment, he closed his eyes and all around him in the dark he heard the buzz: Frank's wife's left him.

When he went out to his car he realized for the first time he had to go home alone. Kate had just gotten off the street car and was going down the block, her hair the color of sunlight. He always had liked yellow-headed gals, he thought; her hair came forward

---

in two deep waves over her cheeks. She came closer and it occurred to him that she was nearer his age than Lillian. He put his head out the car window and said, "You want to go to the picture show?"

"Me?" she said.

He said, "My wife's left me. You want to go to the picture show?"

She said, "Why, I think it would be fun." She got in the car and he smelled faintly a scent of perfume but something that was even nicer, just the smell of her skin; he thought suddenly of walking down a country road that was sun-baked; she had a line of freckles along either cheekbone and her eyes were as predominately dark as his were blue. She did not ask him any questions at all about Lillian and he was grateful. She said, "This is the latest I've ever started out to a picture show. I grew up on a tobacco farm fifteen miles from any town and daddy's a Baptist and didn't approve of picture shows. But there wasn't anybody to take me anyway. I took up teaching to get into town."

"You like teaching?" Son said. "Ain't you afraid of ending up a old maid school teacher?"

She said, "Better than ending up a farmer's wife some place the size of a cotton patch. I have twin sisters that both married tobacco farmers. But the only thing in my life I ever wanted was to get away from there. I don't know why I had to be born there."

"What difference does it make? You're away now," Son said.

"There's so much I never had a chance to learn," she said. "There's so much I'll never do or see."

He said, "Well I'll show you around Delton. Want to go down to the Andrew Johnson on Sunday and eat some lunch."

She said, "Oh but everybody goes at night, when there's candles on the tables and music. I've heard about it."

He said, "Well I go down there and eat lunch on Sunday. You want to come?"

Kate sighed and said, "Yes."

On Saturday morning, he telephoned Buzz and a couple of others he played cards with regularly and said, "We got to find some place else to play this afternoon. My wife's walked off and left me and took the furniture!"

When they got together at Buzz's several men slapped Son on the back and several kidded him; then they dropped all mention of Lillian, never letting on as long as they knew Son that they saw anything at all of the hurt in those eyes that turned from bright blue to almost white as surely and gradually as their Saturday turned into Sunday morning.

He stayed home on Monday long enough to have the locks on the doors changed; there were already window guards and he felt safe, leaving. Maybe that was why it hit him harder than ever when he drove in again Friday and found the house broken into. Lillian had taken everything worth anything except their bedroom suite which had been Cally's. He stood, unable to believe any woman would do what she had done and that it had been done to him, because that was not even all. When he went through the mail there was nothing but bills, bills she had run up the last month before leaving him, one from almost every department store in town for clothes and one for a permanent wave for twenty-five dollars: in all, a thousand dollars' worth of bills. He saw no way in the world he was ever going to be able to pay them. Mrs. Woolford was next door hanging up wash and he made himself go and ask, embarrassed as he was, if she had seen anybody moving his furniture out. She said, "Yes sir, she came; there was a white man and a couple of Negro boys in a pick-up and they moved things out. They fooled around at the back door a long time till one of those boys got the lock busted. Wednesday it was, I reckon."

He did not see Lillian again. But when the divorce came to court her lawyer asked that he pay her thirty dollars a month. Son did not even think about where he was; he just stood up and said, "Judge, it'll be a cold day in hell before I pay that woman a damn cent." He told his side: how she had broken in and taken the furniture; he showed the bills and told just about how long it was going to take him to pay them off, too. The judge decreed Son did not have to pay anything, beyond the bills. Son had the feeling everybody in court was as disgusted with Lillian as he was. When he came out of the courthouse to a cold icy day, no longer married to Lillian, he thought the sort of thing had been done to him nobody was going to do again. And never again would he be in the position he was in now, owing money to every soandso up and down Main Street; credit offices were already sending threatening letters. He had been working about as hard as he thought a man could work; but he had to work harder. His car was at the curb, his grip packed. He got in, put his foot on the gas pedal and did not take it off until he got to Vicksburg after midnight that night. He had an appointment at six o'clock the next morning with a plantation owner who was thinking of using dynamite for ditching.

He never saw Lillian again but once in his life, though they lived in the same town always; shortly after the divorce, he was walking down First Street and did not see her until she caught his arm. "What the hell you want?" he said; he thought he hated her but her face and touch made him feel the way he first had felt about her; all he wanted to say was, Lillian, come back: because he wanted her and because only that, her coming back, would heal the hurt inside that was always there, unhealed: having to face himself and others, a man whose wife had left him.

Lillian said, "You shouldn't have kept on seeing all those men and drinking so and going off with them on week-ends when you could have been home. It was you who did all the wrong things and your family thinks so too."

He had been going to go on, not even listen. He turned. "Who?" he said.

"Cecilia said you shouldn't have done all the things you did." He turned and walked off. Lillian, at that last glimpse thought, He was handsome and he had seemed so young, hurt; her heart wanted to break. She wondered if she had done the right thing. A week later she married Mr. Singer. When it was announced in the paper, Cecilia called Son. It was the first time he had spoken to her since talking to Lillian: repeating the conversation, he said, "I never did expect any member of my family to take somebody else's side against me."

132

Cecilia drew in her breath sharply. "Brother, Lillian is deliberately trying to make trouble telling you that. She called up one night and talked on and on about what you did that she didn't like. It was before the divorce. I didn't know she was even thinking about one. I was just trying to be nice, agreeing with her. She said you stayed out all the time gambling and drinking and I said, 'No, he certainly shouldn't do that.' That's all I said."

But his hurt over Lillian was so deep, he could not forgive Cecilia's saying even that. Before hanging up, she said, "Do you do all that drinking Lillian says you do?"

He said, "I have to drink with my customers. That's the kind of business it is."

She said, "Well, I'd certainly get into some other kind of business. Mammy doesn't even know you drink at all."

Hanging up, he thought that was the last he wanted of Cecilia trying to run his business. She thought just the way she would have if she were still in Mill's Landing, small town and country; he could not feel the same about Cecilia and when she told him she was going to get married all he could say was, "Is that so?" He thought it didn't matter what he said because there'd never be but one way he'd feel about somebody who wasn't one marrying a Catholic. He said to Poppa, "What in the world did she want to go and fall in love with a Catholic for?" But Cally and Poppa felt it was better than if she married someone not religious at all; and they said Joseph Kelley was a nice boy from a good home and had a good job. Next, Son heard Cecilia was going to become a Catholic and said, "Whew." He did not know a thing in the world about the Catholic religion except that you were supposed to have a lot of babies; but it was strange to him, out of the ordinary, different.

A few weeks before the wedding Cally disappeared. Son was down in Tunica doing some clearing for a man when Poppa telephoned to tell him. She had been gone when he and Cecilia woke up; it was almost suppertime and she had not come back. Son started home and walked in about eight to hear Cally had called. She had gone to Memorial Hospital for a thorough check-up and had been waiting all day for lab reports. She was ready to come home. They were all without patience and Son said, "Call her back and tell her she wanted to go to the hospital, get a room and stay there. I'm not going anywhere else in that car tonight."

Poppa phoned. Despite Cally's protest, he arranged for her to stay all night. After supper he showed Son the batch of bills she had run up going from doctor to doctor and the medicine shelves of drug stores. The only way they saw out of it was to put a notice in the paper they were no longer responsible for her debts. The next morning Son phoned the newspaper and afterward brought Cally home. Then he went on back to Tunica. He had met a gal down there named May who reminded him of Betty Sue, only she was a lot younger. She was just a little old farm gal without any kind of education at all. But she sure was sweet talking, he told Poppa. Poppa said, "What about Kate?"

"She's sweet talking too," Son said. "I been seeing her every week-end."

He had taken over the payments on Poppa's house; he would live there when he was in town and hire a good Negro woman to come by the day. He had rented his house and would move when Cecilia married. That was in spring, unbelievable May, the dogwoods starry white blossoms against the soft and bright blue sky. And something else happened then, he and others in the valley had waited for so long. During all the long months of controversy many men Son knew had been going back and forth to Washington, appearing before committees, pleading for Federal flood control. Son guessed he would never forget the date Congress passed what those along the river called "The Flood Emancipation Act of the Mississippi Valley"; in Washington, "The Jadwin Plan": May 15, 1928. The government had committed itself to a definite program; flood control now was almost entirely under the direction of the United States Engineers. That morning, Son drove across the river to the Engineers office; people would gather all day, talking. "Right here in this valley," one of the Engineers said, "they going to spend three hundred and twenty-five million dollars in ten years."

"Whew," Son said. "I ought to be able to sell somebody some powder."

"Dynamite, you going to have plenty of chances to try," an Engineer said; coming in, he brought a map. They bent over it. "The majority of the work's going to be right here where we are. They going to fix levees from Cape Girardeau down yonder to Head of Passes, Louisiana, in the old St. Francis River Valley in Missouri and Arkansas, build an emergency reservoir at the mouth of the White, dams and reservoirs to protect the Yazoo Delta in Mississippi."

"Hell, that's enough to keep you busy ten years," Son said. "What about all those floodways."

"Five in all," someone said.

An Engineer pointed on the map. "The first one's going to be up here on the west side of the river between Birds Point and New Madrid, Missouri, to protect Cairo. It'll reduce flood heights the levees in this stretch of the river are liable to be subject to. If you get a real high flood stage like we just had, the flood waters going to enter the floodway through what they call fuse plugs: and the water will go back into the river again, just here, above New Madrid."

"They figured the floodways to carry an amount of water twenty per cent greater than this flood we just had, in '27," another man said.

It sounded safe, Son thought. Everyone was satisfied; no local contribution to these projects was required; local interests were to provide the necessary rights of way and maintain the works when completed. Son drove back across the river that May day feeling a lot was about to happen. Later, he saw Buzz who said, "No stopping us now, boy." All up and down the river people talked of the work to come and of being millionaires. But Son wondered how they expected to get rich and spend the way they did too. In the Delta, even more so in the hill country, he saw farmers who were hurting: bad, he said. It was a bad year for the weevil and though poison was cheap, the farmers did not seem to be able to get ahead. People warned the construction boom was over but since it was not the kind of construction concerning Son or his friends they paid little attention. All that spring and summer Son travelled hard and was beginning to pull ahead; by the end of the summer he had the department store bills almost paid off; another six months and he would be free. Never again would anyone be able to threaten to take him to court for not paying a bill, by God. And by fall, he was lonesome. He decided to buy May a pair of teddies, all soft and shiny, you could see through; five bucks, he said; he showed them around first and took a lot of kidding, but he liked to tell afterward that they had tickled that little country gal to pieces. But somehow, afterward, he felt even more lonesome; maybe he did not want a girl he could give a pair of teddies to after all. When he was away, he had begun to think about Kate. He had gotten use to her being taller than he liked a woman to be; and he had decided she was even prettier than Lillian; the more he thought about her, he decided Kate was one of the prettiest girls he had ever known and she was thin; he never had liked a woman with too much meat on her. One thing, there wasn't any time Kate wasn't ready to pick up and go, go anywhere; though, like Lillian, she was all the time wanting to dance.

That fall, he was able to buy another little piece of stock, some A.T.&T.; it seemed like a good steady thing to him and that was what he was interested in, growth, not getting rich quick. He wanted something to retire on. Stock was expensive but everything seemed to be going nowhere but up. Other fellows kidded him about the kind of safe investments he made. Everyone else was taking flyers, held on to things about as long as a feather in a fire. Buying and selling, that was all anyone talked about, and getting rich quick. He took out waitresses in a couple of little towns and even they were talking about getting rich quick; he tried to tell them they better hold on to some of their money, but no one listened. Others traded, but he was sitting on what he had.

And then that fall day—he didn't know why it was such a pretty day but it was one of the prettiest he could ever remember—he was walking down a side street and there was an office on the ground floor of one of the buildings, the kind that had a new business located there every few months and even so, he stopped and looked at a big ad in the window about buying land down in Coral Gables, Florida, cheap. Next to it was another ad about buying shares in a gold mine in Colorado: Bull Dog Gold Mine, Handy, Colorado; he figured that probably wasn't far from where he'd worked in the timber outfit when he was a boy; maybe that was what sold him. He believed if you could get rich quick it would be through finding oil or gold. Before he could stop himself, he went in and gave the man a check for five shares, about the same as buying his two of A.T.&T. Then he walked back out into that glorious fall day, crisp as apples, and even the buildings and sidewalks shone in the sun and if he didn't feel like something, walking down Main, owning shares in a gold mine!

He went straight to the bank and put the certificate in his lock box. He wasn't even going to tell the boys; he wasn't going to tell anybody. He was just going to let his ship come in.

Later on he did something else he had never expected to do, voted for a Republican. He just could not bring himself to vote for any Catholic, even though Mr. Al Smith's running mate was from right here in this part of the country, Arkansas, and he knew some of his people. Casting his vote, he hoped this Hoover fellow knew what he was talking about. If so, it looked like gravy from here on out, all gravy. But he sure needed to hep the farmers like he promised, Son said. When the election was over he took Kate down to the Andrew Johnson for dinner, at night, so she could get it out of her system about eating by candlelight and listening to some fellow scratch around on a violin; he said he hoped her pain was easy because he couldn't see a damn thing he was eating and this was the last time he was going to eat in the dark. He travelled often to places like Vicksburg, Little Rock, Helena and he had begun to eat in the best places everywhere. He had learned when walking into these fancy ho-tel dining rooms to give the Captain a little something to get a better table. He liked to be able to order anything on the menu he wanted and to think back to the time when he couldn't. But usually he had a well-done steak and this Sunday Kate said,

"Why don't you ever order anything different? Something you can't have at home."

"I like steak," he said. "But I'm going to have to have me a dozen of these oysters on the half-shell," he told the waiter. Then he sat back, pleased; he was glad that he knew about oysters and liked to eat them; he knew by the expression on Kate's face she was not sure exactly what they were; he talked her into ordering some. He had learned about seafood on a trip with Buzz to Biloxi, "the Miss'sippi Rivy-era," Buzz called it. On the way down they had bought whisky from an old man who kept his jugs wrapped in gunny sacks and hidden in the Pearl River, and for a week that's what they had done, drunk whisky, gambled and eaten things he had never eaten before, shrimps, lobster, oysters. Unexpectedly he had sold half a car load of dynamite to the man he had gone along with Buzz to see; that topped off everything. He told Kate about it now, watching as she ate her oysters, swearing she liked them. But he could tell she did not from the way her eyes popped and turned almost the same wettish grey color as the oyster when she swallowed; she ate them because tobacco farmers she knew did not. Son said the next thing he wanted to do was drive on down the Rivy-era and see what New Orleans itself was like. Buzz had told about gal shows in the French Quarter he'd like to see himself. Suddenly he thought of doing everything alone and knew he did not want to. He said through the candlelight, "How about us getting married and going down yonder and seeing all those things on a honeymoon."

Kate's roommates thought Son the most handsome man they knew; he was wildly jealous of Kate and they had long urged her to marry him. But something in Kate held her back; perhaps because she had felt bitter so long she was not without reservation about anyone; to hide numerous fears, she stayed aloof. She had dreamed of marrying someone of a finer nature than Son but did not believe that someone ever would choose her, so recently a hick. She was twenty-seven years old and did not want to teach as a career. Having imagined every place in the world, she had been nowhere but from Bess, North Carolina, to Delton, Tennessee.

She was thrilled by the idea of going to New Orleans and thought it was over getting married. "Yes, let's do," she said.

To Son, getting married was something people just did and ought to do as early as possible. It was living together for better or worse, like the man said. He worried only about making plans and said, "Well, when?"

Kate said she had always wanted to be a spring bride. He said, "Hell, I can't leave my business in the spring. Mister Will, other folks are started back to work good. We got to do it earlier, slack time."

Kate said, "We could go for Mardi gras."

He said, "No, I got to be back earlier than that too."

They finally agreed on January. Leaving the dining room, Kate thought two things: how pretty the candlelight looked and that she had to go to New Orleans in the dead of winter when nobody else did.

Son meant to tell the news at breakfast but Cally sat alone, drinking tea. "Poppa still asleep?" he said.

"He just fell asleep about dawn," she said. "Something didn't set right. He was up all night." Son would be leaving for the week and after breakfast stopped at Poppa's door, then went all the way into the room thinking, nobody just asleep was ever that white, whiter than the sheets. He felt Poppa's breath against his cheek but barely; he could not wake him. He telephoned the doctor who sent an ambulance; Cally rode with Poppa and Son followed in the car. Cecilia had been called and met them at the hospital. Mr. Wynn was in a deep coma, the doctor said; that was all he could say for now. They had known it was coming, hadn't they? He had expected it sooner, with Mr. Wynn's condition.

"Condition? His kidneys?" Cecilia said. She and Son talked to the doctor. Cally had forgotten the cane they had substituted for the mop and was sitting on a bench down the hall. "Kidneys yes," the doctor said. "But I told Mr. Wynn some time ago he had Bright's disease, that uremic poisoning was liable to set in. Now it has. I had no idea he wouldn't have told you the seriousness."

"You didn't know Poppa," Son said.

139

"He's never wanted to be a bother," Cecilia said. "But he's going to be all right?"

"I wouldn't want to say that, young lady," the doctor said.

There was nothing to do but wait out the morning as there was nothing for Poppa to do but wait out his life. But his condition did not change. Son did not leave town, was at the office by eight o'clock every morning, kept in touch with customers by phone. Every day he went around town checking hotel registers to see if any contractors he knew were in Delton; if so, he invited them out to eat, gave them whisky, got up a card game. During visiting hours he went to see Poppa; Kate went with him regularly and willingly and Son never forgot that. Poppa regained consciousness and after a week went home but he could not work again. Son sold the store and invested the money except for what Poppa insisted on using to buy a little insurance: Cecilia's husband sold it. Beyond what he had to carry on his house and car, Son did not believe in insurance, carried none on his life; he'd rather put his money some place it was working for him, he said. Try as he would, he could not cotton up to Cecilia's husband, Joe. Besides being a Catholic and selling in-surance the man didn't touch a drop of whisky and went into the kitchen at night with an apron on and dried the dishes; whew! Son said. When he told Poppa about marrying Kate, Poppa said, "She's a sweet girl. I hope she'll do better by you than Lillian did."

"It'nt any woman going to do me that way again," Son said.

Confused, Cally had already made the substitution; Lillian seemed to have slipped from her mind. Cecilia said she was glad, but told Joe privately she wished Brother had picked somebody who didn't go along with his partying so much; and as far as she knew Kate hadn't stepped foot in a church since coming to Delton, but she was dead-set on getting married in one. She and Son couldn't afford a large wedding; her family did not have the means to come; but, clearly, Kate could not separate what her wedding would be from the vision in her head of what it ought to be. Endlessly, she thought of flowers and of what people would wear, even Joe as usher. Fearful of her decisions, she bought a blue suit to be married in then complained over and over afterward she should have chosen a beige one. When she was radiant with final plans, they could find no minister who would marry them because of Son's divorce. Kate's mouth went askew; she said, "I just give up."

They were married by a Justice of the Peace, the brightest object in the room a brass spittoon he used before the ceremony; all during it tobacco juice dangled like a dancing worm from his chin. Cecilia and Joe attended as witnesses. Afterward Son and Kate went out to the curb, got in the car, and headed for New Orleans. Kate did not complain about the honeymoon. If you were going to do something, do it right, Son felt, and for those few days was not tight with money. They ate everywhere, everything, spinach baked with oysters and fish in a paper bag. Son even drank some of the frothy concoctions Kate discovered there were to drink. They sure saw every nekkid gal there was to see in New Orleans, Son said when they got back.

Before the trip, Son's tenants had moved. He and Kate came back to the house furnished with the odds and ends Lillian had left. Son gave Kate an allowance and money to buy the furniture she could. What he couldn't afford now, they would do without until he could, he said. Kate said why couldn't they buy on credit like everybody else? Goddamn everybody else; there wasn't any store going to have him in the position of owing them money again, he said.

For a long time, when Kate's friends came in the afternoons to play bridge, she turned her eyes in despair toward vacant corners saying, "I just give up. I'll never have anything to fill them." She had a maid; at three dollars a week almost everyone did. Son would not have let her work; she did not want to. There was nothing to do but play bridge and shop. Then shortly after the honeymoon, she was pregnant. By the middle of February, Will was in camp and others were setting up. One Monday morning, Son got up, packed his grip, and said he would be back Friday. "But I'm having a baby," Kate said.

"Well, hell, you're not having it today," he said, got in the car, and was gone.

But Kate had to call him back before Friday. On Thursday

Poppa went into his final coma. By Friday afternoon, he was gone. The next day they made the long day's trip back to Vicksville: Cecilia and Joe, Son, Kate and Cally. On Sunday they laid Poppa to rest in the old churchyard next to the parsonage he had left long ago; trees, planted since, winter-stripped now, made the land look about the same as Poppa had always described it, bare, open, endless, the way Mill's Landing had looked with the trees cut, Son thought; he wished again Mammy had left the old man there, who had been doing all right.

The place from which Poppa had come received him again and Son shuddered, thinking with dread of death; fighting, work, his system wouldn't be any good then. Turning, he walked away over frozen ground to the house, thinking Poppa had come full circle: he was back where he started from, without too much to show for having been away.

Over and over they told Cally Poppa had died and thought she understood; but death seemed to have no more meaning than life. She only went to where he was laid out in the parsonage and held one of his hands a long time. Son said probably the best thing was if she didn't know what was going on; he sure didn't know what was going to become of her now.

In the way of a small country town it made no difference that Poppa, having left over thirty years ago, had hardly been back since. Everyone he had ever known came to the funeral. Afterward even the most remote member of the family gathered for home-made ice cream, cake, and the retelling of humorous incidents about the one who was gone: Remember the time Henry . . . someone would start, and someone else's old eyes would glint with memory and a soft southern voice would add another bit to what emerged finally as almost Poppa's whole life, because Uncle John went so far back as to when he and Poppa were five and were caught smoking corn silks in the barn. Now, what Poppa's life had been was what people remembered, and Uncle John laughed so hard recalling that day his poor wizened arthritic hands seemed to have life again. Aunt Sally said, Only think, if you had known that day you'd be recalling it when Henry was buried; someone else wondered if you wanted to know how important a day was to you at the time. But Uncle John fell silent, realizing how long ago it all had been. Catching the thought, Aunt Sally said what so many of the old ones in the room were thinking, How time flies! Not even John, in his pain, guessed how short a time it would be before, regathered in this room, the family would talk of him: Remember John telling about him and Henry learning to smoke in the barn? Now, they're both gone. And the day would become part of their legacy, for the youngest in the room, after the first hearing, went straight home and tried out corn silks; in turn, his sons and their children, overhearing the tale, stole matches at an early age and, learning to smoke in some secret place of their own, thought always of the two long ago boys, John and Henry. It was far more than Poppa ever dreamed of, whose fondest wish had been only to be spoken of occasionally after death. It was all he had asked of life, to be remembered.

On Monday, the five returned to Delton and on Tuesday Son took out the grip from which he had removed dirty shirts and underwear, put in clean, and as he always said, lit out again. Cally went home with Cecilia; they would decide later what to do with her. Son could think of nothing but to put her in a home and wondered about the cost: having to pay for Poppa's funeral had eaten into reserve again. Thinking of the money going out and the money coming in, he stepped on the accelerator and sped down the highway as fast as possible, into the sun just rising.

On Friday he found that Cecilia, who was pregnant, had the same idea about Cally. She had located a Catholic home, with nominal fee, and Son had to agree, though it turned his stomach to think of Mammy there with all those women in black, the Sisters; they scared him and he stayed away altogether. Cecilia brought Cally home for Sunday dinner and he and Kate were there; afterward they took Cally for a ride. All she ever wanted to do was ride, not to any place in particular, just ride. All her old restless energy having no other outlet had focused on being in motion. Soon she was not satisfied with once a week and flew into such rages a Sister had to call Cecilia to take her riding often.

Spring was busy. Gone from home, Son thought only of business, something he enjoyed. The first big work in a long time was to be let in Vicksburg, Son's first big letting. Spring was rainy and the roads so bad the railroad put on a special coach to accommodate those going to the letting. Red Johnson announced he was going; it might be his last. But he was going as he always had and invited Son, Will and Buzz to drive with him. Shut-eye put on the floor of the car a tub of crushed ice and set-ups, had plenty of the sandwiches he was famous for: Cannibal, made of raw ham and sliced onion. He went to Arkansas for two five-gallon oak kegs of his own whisky, aged in the woods a long time, drove them to Delton as fast as possible, the theory being that sloshing whisky around aged it even better; all the way to Vicksburg he kept the accelerator to the floor, though the road was like a washboard and several times the younger men, finding it hilarious, had to get out and get the car unstuck. Going on, they downed more whisky and more Cannibal sandwiches and arrived in Vicksburg, as Son said, lit up like Christmas trees.

Lights were on in every room of the hotel; the wide front verandah, the lobby were jammed with people trying to register; because of the crowd, rooms had to be shared. Shut-eye brought the second keg to Will and Red's room, broke it open, siphoned it, and the whisky was there for anyone who wanted a drink. The actual letting of the work would be held in the Army Engineers office; for the two days prior all companies, wooing those who might win work, held open house; people roamed from room to room drinking whisky, eating food provided by the various dynamite, iron, wire rope, equipment, machinery, gravel companies and others Son never even got around to visiting. On the day of the letting, the salesmen would wait in the lobby where a blackboard was set up; as work was let, the information was phoned to the hotel and written on the board; as soon as the winning contractors returned, they would be set upon again.

As Son registered, a man gripped his elbow and said, "Dynamite, remember me? Winston Taylor, Drainage Engineer, Spotsville County."

"Oh hell yeah," Son said. "You peckerwoods decided to drain out your ditches using dynamite yet?"

"There's still a lot of opposition to it, but I didn't come up to do no business with you, boy. They got my reservation lost and I'm looking for a room to get a cot set up in."

"Come on in with Buzz and me then," Son said; he introduced the two, made arrangements about the cot, said he was about to starve to death, and they started for the dining room. Just outside it, Son recognized young Bull Woods who immediately looked away; but not before Son saw to his surprise and amusement the damage he had done to the boy's nose had been permanent. Jagged as lightning a scar went across its bridge; the nose was not exactly in the center of his face.

At the door of the dining room, they waited, looking into a room which was enormous. Wall sconces with light bulbs shaped like candleflames and glass chandeliers sparkling as truly as crystal imitated the period when the hotel was built. Table linen and waiters' jackets were white and stiffly starched, the latter, cropped, fitted as skin-tight as vests. One mirrored wall reflected the diners who were in odd contrast to the furnishings, seeking to evoke the past. History held little interest for Son or these men; yet, like the rest, Son would feel compelled soon to visit the silent battlefield, study not with wonder but more with a professional interest the fertile hilly contours of land from which all vestiges of battle had disappeared except the flat markers and stripped cannon, greening, pigeon-smeared, pointing aimlessly. Scarcely seeing, Son, the other men, would pass beneath the guard on permanent and silent duty, the once white stone as greyed now as the uniform it had been fashioned to represent; the men would not mention war, would not think of it again until the next time when again instinctive duty would compel them between the iron gates; their already hot blood would be more so, momentarily, as they were forced to think of the enemy whose fault it had been: so that against the enemy's descendants who retained speech, manner, habit different from theirs, Son and his friends harbored suspicion, scorn, pity, said of them, they were such damn fools they weren't even going to tell them, would work with them thirty years or more and still sum them up, reduce them to one phrase which never changed and needed no explanation: somebody-who-thought-they-were-so-damn-smart: in short, a Yankee.

Now, Son, Buzz, Winston followed single file behind the head waiter, thinking only of food. Will and Red joined them and all the time they ate others stopped to shake hands, exchange jokes and job information. Even during prohibition, Vicksburg was a free city; liquor could be bought anywhere but each man had his bottle under the table and intended to empty it before the night was over. Few wives came to lettings but there were plenty of women: local women and those who followed lettings, by pre-arrangement or to find a good time. Son had paid no attention to any women in the room; later, he said he did not even notice the woman who passed the table and then turned back. First he saw Buzz's surprised look, then the woman who stood over him about to speak. At the moment he recognized her as Bull Woods' wife, she began to call him names he did not expect any woman to use in public, not even Scottie. It was as if he were two people, the one who knew if it had been a man talking to him he already would have killed him and the other who wondered what to do because it was a woman cussing him like he was a nigger fieldhand. Because of what he had done to her husband's face, she said.

Son had a reputation for not taking anything from anyone; men in the room were afraid of what he might do. Those close saw his face flush, fade, and his eyes turn white. He looked at her once and not again. Buzz noticed his hands for the first time and equated them to a bear's paws: clenched, they rested heavily on the table. He was sure Son would swat her, was about to get to his feet to help her, thinking somebody had to. Having finished her tirade, she hushed as abruptly as she had begun and waited for Son's reply. It seemed a long time, the room full of people waiting too. What was happening dawned on them all, and someone snickered. Mrs. Woods' neck slowly turned purple, splotchy with rage; she did not know how to go or stay. Son's grin had slipped to one side; only a line like chalk outlining his lips showed what he felt. He neither looked at her nor spoke. Bending to his plate, he began delicately to eat his apple pie.

A flapping of heelless shoes in the otherwise silent room was her leavetaking. At Son's table they sighed and Red spoke for them all: "I'm proud of you, boy." Other men leaving the dining room slapped Son on the shoulder, meaning the same. At midnight, Will and Red went to bed. Son, Winston, Buzz put on pajamas and ordered ice. Son felt so good he tipped the boy a dollar and suddenly, with a whoop, fell on the bed and they were all laughing. Winston said he didn't even know what it was all about; he just never would forget it. Buzz told the story and Winston said, Hell, Son couldn't hit anybody that hard.

"Oh yeah," Son said. "You want to find out?"

"Now wait a minute," Buzz said.

"Naw," Winston said, "but I'll wrestle you. I wrestled a bear once and won."

"Hell you say," Son said; he bent, hands before him and waited.

Winston, as if from ropes, came forward, pushing his cot aside. "Listen here," Buzz said.

"Don't worry, old man, it's just a friendly wrestle," Son said. Clutching one another, they went around, bumping furniture. As if on signal, they stopped, went to separate corners, breathing heavily, sweating. Again, by silent signal they met, locked, went around, grunting. Once they stopped for Son to tie his pajamas and started again. Taking a blanket, Buzz left to make a pallet on the floor in Will's room. Entering, he said, "Them two's crazy as coots," and needed no other explanation. He slept wondering how long they would go on and found out at breakfast the next morning when a man stopped by the table to ask Son what the hell he was doing shoving the furniture around till three o'clock in the morning.

Son spent the day visiting from room to room, meeting new people, looking at exhibits, talking about dynamite. Dynamite: he guessed he could talk about it all day. With pleasure he discussed jobs he had done and with pleasure almost as equal another fellow's job, the way the dirt had blown and what kind it was, the kind of job a man had afterward, what price he had had to pay.

How much dynamite had been used? he would ask. Son had a joking good-natured way among men but was serious saying he could save a man money by shooting dynamite himself, free. Contractors had to listen. Dynamiting, dirt, all their possible conditions were getting to be as familiar to Son as the face he shaved each morning. Just hearing about a job, he could say pretty much how it ought to be done. When he was working, he did not drink but made up for it at night. Late the second afternoon Winston, feeling no pain, insisted on going to a gambling boat tied up at the river. It was an old paddlewheeler strung with colored lights and had a machine gun mounted on the front. "Not for any joke either," Winston said, stumbling down the gangplank. Below, he went straight to a wheel Son learned was roulette; but he was not interested in any of that fancy stuff. He joined a crap table and every few minutes a waiter at his elbow asked if he wanted a drink and he bought. He got hot on those dice; then the shoe was on the other foot; the house was buying him drinks. Every time he turned around a waiter said, Compliments. It was only later he realized that when the dice got fuzzy was when he began to lose. But for a long while, he could do nothing wrong. His points turned up. The lucky streak went on so long, people came from other tables to watch. Calling his point, he stamped his foot; soon everyone about the table did the same. Six! Fifteen people stamped heavily. Ten! Stamp. His bets became heavier and wilder, the drinks came faster. He lost back all but two hundred dollars of two thousand he won. Hell, he said, he had two thousand dollars' worth of fun; quitting, he called, "Winston, let's go," and long out of money, Winston came willingly. "Come back again, Dynamite," people called. When he had been hot, he had told everybody who he was. A waiter helped him steer Winston to dry ground, then driving, Son said, "We got to get something to eat before I starve to death." He found open only a greasy spoon diner on the edge of town and the waitress said she was fixing to close. Son said, "Not till you rustle me up some ham and eggs," and Winston ordered half a dozen hard-boiled ones. Son was eating when the waitress brought Winston's eggs, cold, peeled, slithering on the plate. Picking up the nearest container, Winston poured from a great height a long stream of grainy white substance. "What the Sam Hill," Son said; turning, the waitress said, "Lord help us, he thought it was salt." A moment, Winston's face was like a child's, tricked; then he said, "I like sugar on my Goddamned eggs," and ate them every one. The next morning, hearing, he groaned, said it might not be too late to lose them eggs, but Son was still laughing.

They had entered the lobby about midnight; it was deserted, quiet, but Son knew all the way to the top floor people were carrying on various pursuits. Winston gave the elevator boy a dollar and went to meet a girl. Son, getting on, said, "Just let me off where the biggest crap game's at."

Having taken him up, the boy opened the door and said, "You can hear 'em hollering to the lobby from this flo'." Son started down the corridor and the boy called, "Need anything else, let me know," and Son called back, "I can find that anytime." Hearing the sounds he wanted, he opened the door and went into the room, feeling feverish with excitement. His fingers itched in anticipation and belief in himself rose, remembering, feeling again the uncontrollable excitement of winning. He was at home entering; games in hotels were always the same. As firm a rule as if it had been written down somewhere was that craps were shot on the bed. The roll of dice across a sheet, blanket, spread drawn tight was true; dice could not be set. The bed had been pushed into the center of the room, beneath a ceiling fixture that cast light in a spot; floor lamps had been drawn close. Men in shirt-sleeves surrounded the bed and those who through loss or choice kibitzed stood behind, two and three deep. Smoke, whisky, sweat were the smells mingled inseparably, heavily as if it were the room itself, the bare walls, the serviceable carpet, the heavy curtains that gave off the odor. When he opened the door, Son let in fresh air that tumbled smoke about like clouds on a windy day. Every man had his own bottle, in a particular place; using the radiator as landmark, Son set his beside it. Men, looking up, moved aside; someone said, "Let old Dynamite in."

Shortly, he was off. Hour after hour the game went on; the only conversation was in relation to it: exclamations, curses, coaxes to luck, expressions of sympathy or congratulations—and these given in half-yells. Men joined the game or left it and their absence or presence never changed the game's smooth flow. Give the man some room, was a repeated cry: everyone about to throw had a wind-up similar to a pitcher's, spectators went back then came forward to see and cried out grievously or gladly. Wisely, some did not drink while playing. But Son felt the need of whisky like a stoke for the fire inside him. Winning, he remembered Buzz standing close once to say, "Leave off the bug juice, old man, you might keep some of that money."

"Hell, I'll keep it," Son said.

"Yeah, yeah," Buzz said.

But he felt himself beyond mistakes. The fire inside said the world was his and if he had to choose the perfect moment to leave it, it would be now: at the height of happiness, with people his kind, winning at craps, full of bug juice. Dawn's first sign was an almost imperceptible lightening of the black past midnight sky into a grey one, growing lighter, with one whiter spot where the sun would be. No one could have said exactly when it was filled with the bright high sun; just suddenly, it was morning and its cast at the window made the men look there. There were ten still playing who for some time had been the only ones. Scratchy, dark-bearded, they rubbed faces, went to the bathroom to wash and someone ordered coffee; others celebrated morning with drink. The initial wildness had gone from the game but the intensity was still there; they spoke softly now, even less frequently. The longest sentence spoken was about eight o'clock when someone said, "Dynamite, you bout to lose everything in this game but your ding-dong." Son sat forward on a chair drawn close to the bed; he had to grin, agreeing. He ran the flat of his hand over his face and head, smelling his own all-night sour smells. He had not only lost his own money, he had borrowed from everyone there and lost that too. He said, "I'm sure in a hell of a mess," and finished a drink. Whew! he thought; that was the worst damn nigger whisky he'd ever drunk; he had to have been drunk to buy it off that elevator boy. Morning swam dizzily, yet he did not believe drinking affected his game, did not believe it would affect anything he wanted to do except shoot dynamite—and he never went near explosives when he had been drinking. He could not stop playing, lost steadily as earlier he had won. Last night he had been full of that wild free sensation and his bets had matched his spirit. Now without excitement and without money, he could only say, "You boys got me in turr-ble shape." It was the first time in a long time he had felt in such bad shape: shaky and afraid as he had in the nights of the long and terrible dreams in Mill's Landing, dreaming once he had delivered dynamite somewhere when he was supposed to have sold it along the way; he remembered that. He had thought the night's excitement would return but at noon a church bell began to ring and standing, he said, "I owe you boys a bunch of money and I'll be back with it directly."

A man said, "We'll take your I.O.U., Dynamite," and another said, hell yes, his credit was good.

"I owe you some money, I'm going to pay you," Son said.

"O.K. Keep your shirt on," the first man said; they had learned not to cross him unnecessarily. They gave no more thought to what he had said, only knew he would not welsh on paying, and went back to the game. Afterward, the only dispute was over what time he came back: some said it was past two, others said the church bell had not struck the hour. There was nothing else to disagree on; plain as day he stood there, as rumpled, hungover, unshaven as they: a look in his eyes half of amusement, half just plain cold steady look. Visible in every pocket, clutched in both fists before him was money. He knew exactly what he owed everyone, had not written it down, had it burned on his brain. He went around the circle, repaying: "Bubba, I owe you thirty dollars, Claude, I owe you sixty-five dollars and two bits, Fat Boy, I owe you fifty, Uncle Bob, I owe you . . ." until it was done. Then with a grin triumphant and slightly shy, troubled if you knew, he left them.

No one ever knew how he borrowed money that quickly from the town's largest bank, but they heard he went to every one in town until he got the best deal; they put it down finally to the fact that old Dynamite sure had done a whole lot of talking and added it to the list of tales about him. Son went straight to his room and borrowed Winston's car; he had heard of a man on the road to

Natchez who might want some dynamite; if he drove faster than the law allowed he would be back in time for the first letting at four. All he could see to do was go straight back to work, work harder, until he made back not only what he had lost but the interest he would owe the bank. The man did not want any dynamite; but Son never considered a trip a waste; he gave him a card with his name and phone number and said if he ever did want any, now he knew who to call; then he turned the car around and hit the road, lickety-split, back to Vicksburg.

Will was leaving for the letting as Son arrived at the hotel; they shook hands and Son wished him good luck, then went inside to sit in the lobby and wait. Weeks prior to a letting contractors received a mailing list from the Government, stating it would receive bids on certain work at a certain time; a form was enclosed and a brown envelope for the bid to be sealed in. When he had made his estimate, the contractor mailed his bid to the Engineers. Will had said it reminded him of school; on the designated day the contractors sat in quiet rows with expectant faces; an Engineer entered carrying the brown envelopes as if they might be exam papers just graded. The envelopes were opened, the name of the bidder and his bid read; the information written on a blackboard; quickly it could be seen who was the lowest bidder. Until ten minutes before the envelopes were to be opened, a contractor could change his bid; in a flurry of excitement telegrams often arrived. Work was let in sections called items; Will won the largest job of the afternoon, the only item he had bid on; several smaller jobs went to contractors Son barely knew and he would have to hustle. As quickly as the winners entered the lobby, he invited them to his room, to ride the train and eat a steak afterward. He set out whisky and told the men to fix their own; he didn't wait on nobody. Many men brought along women and the whisky went fast; Son said they had better go eat and no one suggested the women leave; he invited them too. When there was trouble about his expense account, Scottie said he should not have taken out all those women. Son said not to have invited them was what the other dynamite salesman would have done; what he gained buying a few more steaks was something you couldn't write down on an expense sheet and if those birds up at American Powder didn't understand that, he ought to be running the company, not them. From Milwaukee, American's head called Son, still hedging about the amount he would allow for entertainment. Nobody, he said, in the history of the company had ever spent that much on one night's entertainment.

Son said, "Hell, you better get used to it; there'll be a lot like it."

The man said, "Well, now . . ."

Son said, "Well's a deep hole in the ground. I spend the money the way it has to be spent to get the business, and I get the business. You seen the orders I sent in after that letting? I got ever damn one of the big dynamite orders at that letting, ever damn one."

Then the man could say nothing except, "All right, Mr. Wynn. But, for God's sake, next time put down 'wives' not 'women' when you fill out the sheet."

Live and learn, Son thought, hanging up. Those squareheaded Dutch Yankees might be getting a good laugh out of him, but if they looked at his orders, they couldn't laugh long.

R ED, WILL AND SHUT-EYE LEFT THE LETTING LATE IN THE day. Son went with Winston who was anxious to get to Delton and in no shape to drive; soon after leaving at daylight, he fell asleep. On either side the narrow Mississippi highway was lush with greenery and the various calls of birds. Son stuck his foot to the gas pedal thinking how long he had been travelling these roads, how much longer he would have to, and shot the car forward as if to gobble up the road were to gobble up years, plunge himself ahead in time to when he would not have to get up in the morning unless he wanted.

Only having Winston changed this spring morning from the many so sweetly come to Mississippi into which he had started out, from the hundreds into which he would. Early, mist lifted unnoticeably and the day was beautiful, startling and gentle; the pavement, everything smelled as if it had been washed. Past Negroes on their way to fields they sped and past the cabins they had left, where pot-bellied babies played wearing only little shirts that failed to cover them. Smoke from fires inside cabins and out in yards drifted toward a sky only slightly more blue. The smoke's smell gave Son a feeling the same as hearing country people in church singing old Baptist and Methodist hymns: one of sadness and yet a feeling as if he had lived a long life and found out something about it; it was rough and finding you had the stuff to make it was half the pleasure; the other half was making things better than they might have been. Sometime you just accepted it was lonely. And, Jesus, it was lonely.

He thought of a Bible he had won for never missing Sunday School all the elementary years he had gone. Probably not even Mammy remembered. Thinking of old hymns, he thought of an early favorite: What can make me white as snow? Nothing but the blood of Je——sus. What can wash away my sins? Nothing but the blood of Je——sus: he sang those lines and Winston, opening his eyes, said, "Is that the radio?"

"Naw," Son said, "that's me."

"Boy, you can't carry a tune in a bucket, can you?" Winston said and closed his eyes again. "That's what Miss Kate is always telling me," Son said, hearing her tell others: Frank doesn't know the difference between Yankee Doodle and Dixie; he guessed she was right and closing music off from himself fell silent, thinking again of Sunday School, how he had gone without urging, and never given trouble there or in school as long as he went. He had been a clean-nosed little boy; he thought of the difference now between himself and his family. The change had taken place, he guessed, as Lillian always said, because of the business he had gone into.

They rushed on past Leland, Shaw, Cleveland, Hushpuckene, morning in each of the little towns the same as the towns themselves were similar: a square or a pump the center on which the stores fronted; whoever sat on the benches before them was in the middle of town. Old men, Negro and white, came and often sat together, talking or staring out at the road. As early as the stores opened, before the sun was too high, from down every side road, they came, usually the Negroes first, wearing perforated hats, clean clothes, and carrying canes; bound about their heads to catch sweat, handkerchiefs stuck out from hat brims, giving the old men the air of soldiers bandaged haphazardly in long ago wars. Mid-morning, Son stopped at one of the Delta's numerous Chinese groceries to buy a Coke, rat-trap cheese and crackers. Hung-over, he felt empty, scooped-out, a shell to be filled. Winston woke and went to find a men's room. Coming from the store, Son stood on the sidewalk eating, listening to the Negroes; he liked their talk. One said, How you today? and another answered, All right, um-hummm, meaning the day was fine too. Stubborn, one old man said of another. That man's stubborn. Stubbornest man I've ever seen; still the old man could not let the word go. Stubborn, he said again, poking the sidewalk with his cane. Son heard one man bothered by an insurance collector: I tol' that man. He come to my house every Thursday then. I'm not afred. The others were a chorus, You right about that. That's right. That's the truth. Those who did not speak made the soft little sounds that said the same. One summed up another's problem: You don't have no trouble; you got a habit, and Son was laughing when Winston returned. "Come on," Son said, "you got to have some of the Chinaman's peanut brittle." Winston followed, thinking it easier than to argue with Dynamite. Inside the dark, sweet-smelling store, the proprietor nodded amiably. Pointing to the candy, Son said, "Gimme two bits' worth and give this soandso the same. He ain't worth a damn but I promised him some of the Chinaman's peanut brittle, the best I've ever eat."

The proprietor's golden face was even brighter, pleased; he gave Son two full bags. In the car, Winston put his away. "Old man, you better eat that candy I put out two bits for," Son said.

"I never said I wanted no damn Chinese peanut brittle," Winston said. Son cursed him, arguing. Winston laughed. "Don't everybody have to do the way Dynamite wants," he said, but only when Winston got mad too did Son stop urging. Eating his own candy in disappointed silence, he drove on through the country he loved, the Delta, where everything seemed shimmery, shiny, silver, like coins tossed into the day: roof tops, silvery bark of brooding cedars, poplar leaves and cascading willows; even the rich dark earth after its fallow winter, now being turned open to the spring sun, flashed whitely, as did bits of mules' harnesses and slick plows, seed and fertilizer, thrown as if waywardly upon the wind; only figures sowing or following in the new furrows behind the plows were dark against the bright and dancing day, going in the same slow ritualistic measured steps that men had since first they began to woo the earth. Minnows of Your Choice, read a large sign, an equal indication of spring, and keeping the pedal to the floorboard, Son sped them on wondering how you chose among the wiggly things, what standard you used. In the noon sun and after, cows sought shady places to nestle; in swamps covered with scum as bright yellow-green as moss, as thick and lush, stark grey shells of trees stood as if they were the aftermath of some terrible destruction. Clarksdale to Tunica they went and straight up the highway toward Delton, the pavement interminably ahead flat and bright, the sun reflected there reflected on the windshield too, so that Son saw three white balls yet could not look away, for his seared eyes hurt worse to turn in their sockets. And it was just spring; he thought what summer would be like; those three white balls would burn even whiter, brighter, hotter, from pavement, windshield, heaven; the hot dry air would rush past, welcome, because when the car stopped, it stopped, and there would be no air at all, just heat like a heavy, hooded coat slipped over you, the day shimmering and wavering while you stood with sweat like tears, blinking, trying to see, thinking Jesus Christ, it couldn't be like this everywhere, that if you just moved from one spot to another, got under the shade of a tree, went somewhere else it would be different; but it wasn't, it was just the same every single place. He started to mention to Winston what spring would turn into, what was ahead for at least four months, summer was always that long; did Winston remember one year to the next what it was like? Then he thought, Hell, he was making money; he couldn't complain. Kate, those women she played bridge with put a washtub with a block of ice in the room, let a fan blow across that. Kate wanted to sleep that way; he wouldn't let her, said it would do her good to sweat some. She said he just liked to be mean.

That spring he went as far north as St. Louis and south below Natchez, averaged selling about a thousand pounds of powder a month. Everywhere his reputation went ahead. He began to charge for blasting; it was on his own time and he pocketed the money, told American Powder it was his own little side business and he named it The Agricultural Blasting Company. Putting money straight into his pocket that way made him see the possibility of getting ahead, taught him one thing quick: you'd never get anywhere working for the other fellow. People said how good things were and he took some of that money out of his pocket and bought another gold mine stock. All the wild speculating going on around him went against his grain. Still he could not shake himself free of his young man's dream of finding gold. Rocky Mountain was the mine's name. That day, too, he felt like a boy with his hand in the cookie jar going to the bank to put the big gold-rimmed certificate into the lock box with his other things. At home, Kate said, "More stock! Frank, I hardly have enough clothes. The walls are bare. I need to buy some things for the baby." She named them.

"Hell, bathe the baby in a bucket. You don't need to buy a tub. If you got to have something stuck on the wall, buy it out of your savings," he said.

"What savings?" she said.

He said, "Woman, don't tell me you spend all the money I put in that account each month."

He had not told her to save. He said he thought any woman had that much sense. What had she done with all that money? She had bought a second set of dishes. They had dishes! She said these were for company. She showed him a damask tablecloth with fringe. He said it looked like something Mrs. Astor's horse ought to wear. Christ on a crutch; she wasn't going to waste any more of his money. Kate said her friends bought nice things. He said how much did they have in the bank if anything happened to them? She said, "We can't live just thinking of the future."

"I can," he said.

The next day he closed out Kate's account. Buzz said he ought to let Kate have money she could feel was her own. She had her chance, Son said. From then on, he gave her a weekly allowance.

Kate said it was embarrassing not to be able to write a check; and she had to hide the cash about the house each week. There wasn't any second time, he said, when it came to not saving money.

By summer, steel and automobiles were off; he thought maybe putting money into gold wasn't such a bad idea. Agricultural prices declined and he said again folks didn't appreciate what the farmers were up against. In July there was rain in Central Arkansas heavy enough to damage cotton and overflow the river in several places. When the river rose at all fear stood on the faces of people still trying to recover from the flood of '27. Going to levee camps in Arkansas that summer he passed through towns where men huddled on street corners discussing the weather; in every cafe he stopped, the radio was on; everyone talked about the rain and the river until the weather report came on, then they hushed. Contractors were behind because of the bad weather; farmers had no money. He drove about all summer not only trying to sell dynamite but to collect bills, soon saw people figured the dynamite man was the easiest person to avoid paying; there was nothing he could take back. Standing, they would shake their heads, saying they just didn't know when they'd be able to pay for that dynamite, as if Son had sold them smoke that had drifted off and they could not quite remember its ever having been there. He adopted then a lifetime resolution, without exception for friends, hardships, weather, any excuse ever offered. Call him hard; folks did. Words rolled off him just as easy as water off a duck's back, just as ee——sy as that, he would say. His bills got paid on time; he needed money to pay them; he wouldn't listen to any conversation. At the end of every month, his books were going to balance. He gave a man thirty days to pay his bill, then called on him. Kate said he was too rough. Rough? How else were you going to get ahead.

That was the reason, he told her, he wasn't in as bad shape as some folks when fall came and Mr. Hoover let the stock market go straight to hell. But first, Laurel was born. He had spent some time in another camp in Arkansas, near Will's, had crossed the bridge at Helena, and driven on into Mississippi, had worked his

---

way half across the state and the night Laurel was born hit Columbia City, dead-tired. That was one of the things he remembered most afterward, how tired he was. He had checked into the town's best hotel; otherwise in these little burgs you didn't put your feet on the floor, even with your socks on. In the lobby he bought several newspapers and was going up the stairs when the boy bringing his grip said, "You want to meet a girl?"

He had thought he was too tired, hadn't even been thinking about it, but having it offered, it sounded like a good idea. He said give him time to take a bath and shave. The boy said someone would knock at his door and Son gave him a dollar. First thing in the room he took off the bedcovers and spread the newspapers over the bed and put the sheets back on. He did this as a matter of course now, having inspected beds in too many little towns, seen nothing and lost sleep when newspapers would keep bed bugs away.

When the knock came, he opened the door to see a red-headed woman standing there, not half-bad. He invited her out to eat. They ran into friends of hers, got to drinking, and later thinking about those newspapers rattling, he said, Let's go to your place. He came back to the hotel at eight o'clock the next morning, packed, and was leaving when he saw the telegram beneath the rug's edge. He thought it was from the office, had not thought much about the baby. Just sometimes, driving along, he had thought how he would toughen the little sucker up. He read the telegram and sat down, hearing the newspapers rattle. It was from Cecilia, saying his daughter had been born the night before and they had tried to call him.

He had wanted a little sucker to toughen up, had not thought about a girl. He sent Kate a telegram signed, Daddy: hoped she and his baby were doing fine, then got in the car and started home, stopping to see a few customers along the way, arrived at the hospital that evening with a box of candy. First thing, Kate started out asking where he had been all night. It never occurred to him to think up an excuse. He said it was his business. She said they had called and called and left the number and when he did not call back, Cecilia sent the telegram. Kate said again, Where was he all night? He had already said it was his business, could not think of anything else to say and said nothing.

Soon after Kate came home, he saw the candy box and opened it; the candy was gone. Inside were the baby's hospital identification bracelet and his telegram. He said, "What's all this?" Kate said, "Some things to remember." He said, "What else you going to put in there?"

"Nothing so far," she said.

In another month the country went to hell in a bucket except right there along the river where he was. From everywhere, people came because of the government work: contractors, tractor drivers, ditch diggers, bondsmen, insurance salesmen, peddlers of everything connected to building with dirt, all with the same story; there was no work being let anywhere else. The Southerners never got over Yankees coming, taking away jobs; they made money, too, and never left the South again. What the Yankees never got over was the Southerners' way of doing business. Will, Son, Buzz, the men they knew, never wrote a contract on paper; to conclude a deal, they might spit together over a far crack in the road or merely shake hands.

During the Depression, Son was told to cut expenses; he needed only a telephone, someone to answer it, and moved his desk to Buzz's office; they would share Buzz's secretary, a boy named Holston. Son guessed letting Scottie go was one of the hardest things he ever had to do. Still, he had not expected her to blubber. He thought maybe she was short of money, took fifty dollars out of his own pocket to add to the company's bonus. But she shoved it back. She had another job; it was not that. He never did figure it out. Once she called up just to talk and said, "Old soandso, you got the key to the sweetest music, B natural. Always keep it."

He said, "Well, lemme hear from you before you get married twice," and hung up. He heard afterward Scottie had started hitting the bottle. He guessed it must have been whisky talk, not knowing what other kind of talk it could have been. But she sure had been able to cuss good.

When the crash came, people said the bottom had dropped out; they did not expect things to get any worse. But two years later Son would say, everyone he knew was looking for money harder than ever. During these years, by five in the afternoon, the levee camps were jammed with salesmen—peddlers, the levee camp people called anybody selling anything; they came purposefully late, looking for free meals and a place to sleep. Will told Son he was tired of feeding folks; but some of them, if they didn't eat with him, wouldn't eat at all. Son had one meal in an unexpected place. He had left home so early one morning he did not even make Kate get up and fix his breakfast; he ate in a greasy spoon on the way and soon regretted it. Flying along a rutted back road, he got cramps. In sight was one Negro cabin and nothing else but cotton fields picked nearly clean with a sky reaching toward winter coming down close around them. He went up on the porch and saw a Negro woman inside, cooking. "Aunty," he said, "could I use your outhouse?"

"Yes suh, Cap'n," she said. When he came back, he stood at the screen door and said, "What you got cooking smells so good?"

"Menfolks' dinner," she said. "You want something to eat?"

"I'm not putting any more restaurant food in my stomach today," he said. He came inside. From the warming oven she took a plate already filled with food; while Son ate, she sat in the cabin's other room. Finished, he put a dollar under the plate and said, "I guess I'm going to live. Much obliged."

"Take care," she said and watched his car fly across the flat land, until he reached the horizon.

From a slight rise in the road, he came down toward camp feeling as always that flush of gladness as if he had come home. The blue misty look rose over green tents; there was the wood smoke smell and one of cooking; rain puddles still steaming dry in shady washed-out places caused a smell like flood, a crawfishy smell of something old, moist and mysterious. He went toward the commissary, filled as always with Negroes. They opened a path across the porch, speaking to him, and he spoke to them by name;

he knew everyone now. Inside, Martha and Carter were knee-deep in mail. "What's going on?" Son said.

"Sears catalogue day," Martha said. "They all come at the same time." Carter, struggling to move a pile of catalogues, said, "Why can't a few get catalogues and pass them around?"

"Lord, you got to have your own to read all fall or spring," Martha said and held up hers, gladly.

Son said, "Why in the dickens don't you get a road out to here?"

Carter said, "We did. The boys worked on it all week."

"Damn, if that's so," Son said. "I give that little old Ford buggy the gun saying, Go, and I give it the gun saying, Go, and it still like not to made it."

"Then she just don't have the stuff," Carter said. "Will's at the river. Trying to figure how to bring in the barge with the Caterpillar."

"I better get down there and see him then," Son said and left the commissary pleased: Caterpillars were the first good dirt haulers to come along, were strong, had a good motor; but they were expensive and had to be acquired slowly. The old mule system had almost disappeared; now the skinners drove tractors; work was getting ahead faster than he had ever dreamed it could. He crossed the last expanse between river and levee, seeing a crowd ahead, Will among them, his hair shiny as ice frozen hard by a winter's sun; he turned as Son came up. "I been looking for you," he said, shaking hands. "Frank, I'm sure in a mess. That barge can't land here with those willows growing right down in the water like they are. Can you blow them out?"

"I can sure try," Son said. Tangle-eye came close; he and Son studied the job. In an hour Son asked Tangle-eye to bring hip boots from his car, to get his own. Another Negro in a wagon would bring dynamite from the storage house. "Ditching dynamite, boy," Son said. "Can you read?"

"Yes suh, I can read some," the boy said.

"Well don't come back here with nothing but what says d-i-t-c-h-i-n-g on the box, you hear?"

163

"Yes suh." Raising the reins, the boy said, "Giddap," and was gone.

Water would give the blast an extra lift; he needed quick acting, fast shooting, sensitive dynamite. "You boys rustle me up some sticks," he said and Negroes went up and down the bank, looking. When Tangle-eye came back, he and Son waded into the water; with the biggest, stoutest stick, Son poked: found the bottom and tamped and tamped again; the depth to put the dynamite depended on the bottom's firmness; he had learned not to use this underwater method in sand. There were four ways he could place the dynamite. He chose a combination of two: studied the pattern of the trees and the river's flow. Water was swirling about his waist now. At least a cubic yard of material would be thrown out with each pound of ditching dynamite. The problem was not to have it all fall back and block up the landing as much as the trees had to start. It's got to all float down that river, he thought. A certain yardage of material, loosened, surrounding what he blasted, would have to wash away too; there was enough flow, volume to the river to wash it. If I shoot it right, he thought. Negroes were breaking open the boxes of dynamite. He had marked off an area twenty-five feet long for a test shot. He had decided on a line of loads spaced at equal intervals along a center line, with perpendicular cross rows located at every other hole. He notched a stick to measure each charge to the same depth in each hole; with the same notched stick he would space the holes uniformly; they had to be at an angle, not vertical. Gathering sticks from the Negroes he waded into the water and stuck them at intervals along the center line and loaded cartridges into the holes one above the other. He had to think about the depth to the top of the charge and the distances between and the number of pounds of dynamite every hundred feet. He cut off three feet of fuse, set it against the cap charge lightly, and crimped it with his teeth. Tangle-eye, having cut open a stick of dynamite, shook black powder into his hand, tossed it into his mouth and swallowed. Son said, "Tangle-eye, what in the name of Sam Hill are you doing?"

"I always eats me some powder, Boss," Tangle-eye said. "It keeps you from getting that headache."

For a moment, Son thought it might be worth trying. Then he said, "You better make tracks out of here," lit his cigarette and touched it to the fuse. It always seemed a second, yet he had climbed the river bank and walked fast across the clearing beyond, toward the levee, where the others waited, when the blast came. A hundred and fifty feet high a screen of water, mud, muck rose after the one great muffled-sounding roar that had set off, through concussion, all the charges in the line. It was a system he had devised himself; and he was proud of that. Everything that had risen fell again, the sound against earth like a hard hail storm, in the river, splashes; then it was quiet. People had hushed watching, birds had flown, mules, grabbing a chance to rest, stood still. Slowly everyone went toward the river, stood on the bank and looked at the gap in the trees, at the river itself, that a few minutes before had sprayed higher in the air than any of them standing there looking at it had ever been; wider across than any of them could swim, opaque, calm, muddy, old, the river had restored itself already to its steady and silent flow, the way a bug, momentarily deterred by a straw thrust before it, goes on again as immediately as the straw is removed, in the direction it had always been going. Only now the river carried with it the debris they wanted it to.

He repeated, lined up the sticks, and Tangle-eye followed making holes, filling them with dynamite. With one main blast the trees were cleared as Will wanted; the screen of water and debris rose, five hundred feet in length, leaving no spoil bank, nothing to be cleared up afterward. In his wet clothes, Son stood looking at the cleared place where eventually the barge would land; every job, he thought, was exciting, big and little; you never knew just exactly whether it was going to work or not. When it did, you alone had done it; it made a man feel proud to have done something he set out to do. Now why couldn't he shoot in a field under water? He bet himself he could make a ditch just as purty and straight as a dragline could do.

———

"Mister Boss, could we have us those empty dynamite boxes?"

"Sure," he said to the Negro women who asked. "You going to split you up some kindling?"

"Naw sir, we uses them as tables and stools in the tents." The women went away carrying the boxes. Son and Will followed them to camp. It was pay day and they had to push through a crowd of Negroes to enter the commissary. Carter sat behind a table full of pay envelopes, a forty-five prominently displayed; Will told Son they had it there always, to avoid lip-trouble as well as any other kind. Rent was fifty cents a week for a single tent, a dollar for a family's; most of the Negroes borrowed money to live on during shut-down time, mid-December to the end of January; what they owed was taken out of their pay a little each week. Son wondered if they had anything left. Will said, "They'll all be here at the beginning of the week to borrow some more. They like owing you money, you know. It makes a Negro feel he's got the best of you. If they run off owing you money, they really think they're even then."

As soon as the men got their pay, the women were waiting to spend it. They bought groceries, needed things, and as many luxuries as they could. Martha seemed to be trying to wait on everyone at once. Wine at a dollar a gallon went quickly. She glanced up once and said to Son, "Tell those boys not to drink up all that wine out there on my porch." Son repeated the message and the one passing the jug laughed. "Come on here, Sweet Thing," he said. The couple started away but Son saw Sweet Thing, and several other women stop, lift their skirts, and deposit money in the flat stomach pouches they wore suspended from a string about their waists. The women were in their brightest clothes and smelled of perfumes too enthusiastically imitating gardenias or violets. Couples headed out of camp in old wagons and cars; some walked the levee route, as in the old days, when the river bank was the shortest way anywhere, a place of meeting and one of promenade.

When Son went back inside, Martha, waiting on a middle-aged woman, said, "Sis Woman, don't go spending all your California money on the conjure woman again this week."

"No'm, I'm just going to try one more bottle of pills," Sis Woman said.

"I'm telling you there's not any pills going to get Tangle-eye to marry you," Martha said; she looked at Son. "Sis Woman's been trying to save enough money to visit her family in California as long as I can remember and keeps spending it on foolishness every week."

"No'm, this the last time, Old Miss," Sis Woman said, going out. When the commissary emptied, Martha told Son to walk down to the dining tent with her; from there he could see the conjure woman. In the middle of the Negro section a large black Packard was parked. Beside it stood a Negro man in chauffeur's cap and whipcord leggings. In the back seat a woman sat, barely high enough for Son to see; she was a light-skinned and freckled Negro, with cheeks naturally pink, and a nose more like an Indian's; she wore a purple turban and a gold rope twisted about her neck, higher and higher, ending in a snake's head with ruby-seeming eyes. Negroes were crowded about the car. Martha said they came to tell her their troubles; she sold them cures: charms to tie around a sick baby's stomach and make it well, pills to bring back a lover, little sacks of herbs, tiny pieces of wood nailed into strange shapes. Her specialty the Negroes called aspidistry bags: a small leather pouch of herbs to wear nestled against the throat hollow to keep away disease; and the conjure woman sold almanacs.

The day had promised rain and now there was a phosphorescent yellow-green glow to everything; mimosa trees shook as the wind rose, smelling of cool and dust. As Martha and Son went in to supper lightning blinked twice, the wind changed, and the rain came closer. "Huh," Emmie said; they stopped at the kitchen door. "That's the Lord for sho. You see yonder, Miss Martha. He sees Rosalita." Son had already asked about the line of men reaching half across the Negro camp; Rosalita, Martha said, was half-Spanish; every year she came back to live in camp with someone different; but on pay night she ran her own little business: twenty-five cents for a man to enter her tent.

Son said, "Emmie, who you fixing to shoot?"

"Anybody tries to steal from me, Mister Frank," she said. She told of her own pay night business; she sold homemade ice cream and sandwiches. On top of the freezer, Emmie had a revolver and now covered it with a clean dish towel. At supper, Martha said Emmie would shoot it too. From her business she collected at least a hundred dollars every week in small change, brought it to Will in a galvanized pail. He took it to the bank for her and exchanged it, at her insistence, for a hundred-dollar bill. She hid her money, trusted the revolver more than the bank, Martha said. Son liked these levee Negroes who worked and saved their money. Going out of the dining tent, he stopped and said to Emmie, "I'd like to hep you out selling them sandwiches. Wrap me up some."

Carrying them, going up the path to his tent, he could hear the Negroes laughing, calling among themselves, could hear their music, half-wailed and all about love: good or bad, true or false, jealous lovers, unfaithful women, hard times, the singer thought in the end to have had his baby at all was worth it. Son fell asleep listening to the singing and woke once to hear it raining hard.

Morning was not clear. If it rained again, he thought, he'd never get that little buggy of his out of camp. Having packed his grip, he went out. Carter called from the commissary: everyone had eaten and gone to the levee; tractor turned up a body. An old skeleton, Son thought. The levee had long been a place where Negroes and whites hid crimes: in the old days, Son knew, bodies were shovelled under twenty-five yards of dirt and never even reported.

At the levee, he made his way through the Negroes and unexpectedly saw the Negro, killed the night before. "Arkansas toothpick done that all right," Will said as Son came up. With a switchblade knife, the boy's throat had been slit from side to side. Above the terrible fresh wound was an old one, a necklace of healed cuts, raised bumps linked into one another like a chain. The sight made Son sick; to his surprise so did the thought of murder. All that singing going on while the boy was killed, buried alone out here in the rain and dark. Will was calm, steady before the Negroes; there was no time for grief. "Get back to work," he said. Son stuck trembling hands in his pockets; there was nowhere to look except at the body being stretched out on Skinner's tractor, at Greaser covering it with two crocker sacks. "Get back to work," Will said. Skinner turned the tractor toward camp; Cotton hopped on, would call the law. As terrible as the boy looked, Son, the others looked at him again. Tied to one exposed ankle was his dobie bag, a religious good luck medal; it hadn't done that boy much good, Son thought, but saw several of the other Negroes touch their own.

The familiar activity started; the tractors droned, the Negroes shouted, laughed; dirt was dug, hauled, dumped. Son walked to where Will stood giving directions. They shook hands, made a date for Son to come again and to play bridge in Delton soon with Martha and Kate. "Hope everything works out all right," he said.

Will said, "Formality. The law don't care what happens out here as long as my Negroes behave in town."

"I'll be seeing you then," Son said. He could not eat breakfast and went to his tent. As he started up the steps something moved beneath his foot; he jumped back as a moccasin slithered into the grass, dark beneath the tent. Inside he sat down still shaky, still feeling sick, told himself to laugh instead. He remembered Will saying you couldn't show fear of Negroes. Out here you couldn't show fear of anything. Kate was all the time saying he thought it was smart to be tough. You had to be, like everybody, to get along. He'd found that out in a hurry. Carrying his grip, he went to the car and drove away as rain began, fought that car out of camp, slipping in the muddy ruts, and laughed telling himself, if the snake had a bit him, if he had swole up and died, another dynamite peddler would have come along, same as on the levee they went on without that boy; he heard the tractors in the distance. You had to keep ahead. And it seemed there was always something following him.

That night he slept desperately. But all night Kate kept getting up, saying the baby was coughing. He said the baby would be there in the morning; didn't she understand about a man's rest? She kept on until he finally got up and tried to shut her mouth; he fell back to bed and she was still talking about him being the meanest man she'd ever seen; why did he come home? In the morning he asked why she had had the whisky out. She said a drink helped her to sleep. He said she better leave that stuff alone.

At the office, telling about the murder, he told mostly how the boy's pockets had been picked clean and his gold tooth gone. He, Holston and Buzz had a good laugh. He would tell them another thing, American Powder Company was going to give him a heavier car: he'd fought that little buggy out of camp like a baby mule that never had a bridle on.

It was a month before a representative from the company came south: then Son told him. The man said, "Our salesmen always have Fords, Mr. Wynn."

Son said, "I go places those other fellows couldn't dream up in a nightmare. Pushing that little car's too much like work. I'm in it a week at a time, sometimes more. I need something with more comfort and heavy, like a Buick. Something that when I say Scat, can scat."

"You'll have to drive a Ford," the man said. "Our other salesmen all have Fords. This isn't a time when the company can buy new cars, much less Buicks."

He was sitting on a straight chair in Son's office. Son was tilted back behind his desk in a swivel chair, his feet up. He looked at the man a long time out of eyes that narrowed. Slowly, he took his feet down, leaned forward to reach into his pocket, then threw the keys across the desk. With a wave of his hand, he indicated the man should take them.

The representative stood up, trying to laugh. "Now, Mr. Wynn," he said. "You're not going to quit."

"Naw," Son said. "I already have."

"Hot-head, you ain't got sense God give a flea," Buzz said when he heard. "This is a depression. Folks are out looking for jobs, not quitting good ones."

Kate cried, said they would be out selling apples too. Nobody in their right mind would quit their job to start their own business in the middle of a depression; was he crazy, like his mother?

You leave her out of this, Son said. The Sisters would no longer keep Cally; in a rage, she had flown at one of them brandishing her cane. Cecilia had a little girl, the house would be crowded, but she would take Cally. Son would pay her what he had paid the Sisters. Furious when her cane was taken, Cally had cut off her hair in a straight line around the top of her ears. Kate had knit a soft angora cap for Laurel; now she made one for Cally. All that winter she wore it, sitting on the edge of the front seat while Cecilia drove her around town. Cecilia said, I just get up in the morning, fill the tank with gasoline, and ride until it's empty. On the back seat little Cecilia sat patiently, her baby legs sticking straight before her. By spring, Cally's hair had grown, fuzzy and new, like a chick's. By summer Cecilia could comb it into the knot Cally had always worn. And by summer the sign across one half of Son's office read, Frank Wynn Incorporated. Inside on the door were the words, Representative, Illinois Powder Company. The afternoon he quit American, he had made an appointment with Illinois and went to Chicago two days later. Having learned you'd never make any money working for the other fellow, from here on out, he said, he was working for himself.

Illinois was a small company; he had picked it purposefully; they didn't have so much to lose, taking a chance on him. He was going to have his own company but he would sell Illinois's blasting supplies. In Chicago they said no other dynamite salesman in the country had a set-up like that. He already knew that. But he was going to have that kind. In a few years he would have run every competitor out of his territory too; if Illinois wanted to be the company left in there, take his offer before he took it some place else. Laughing afterward, Son would say, Those Yankees didn't have any idea in the world who I was walking in there. They thought I was just a country boy until they commenced looking at my sales figures. Before I left there that evening, I had everything signed up just the way I wanted it, just exactly.

Coming home, he thought it looked as if everything was going to be all right. Mr. Roosevelt, it seemed, was going to straighten the country out too. Over and over, he and the boys celebrated Mr. Roosevelt's election and never referred to him any other way. Not even at the height of revelry did they say FDR or Franklin. He was Mr. Roosevelt to the day of his death and beyond. Kate said it hadn't done any good for her to complain but, finally, all the wives were tired of Mr. Roosevelt being re-elected every Friday and Saturday night month after month. After one party, gigantic and final, Son staggered home saying, Well we shore elected Mr. Roosevelt. I shore hope the man appreciates it.

During the winter lay-off, when everyone was in town, he and the men found other reasons to celebrate: if someone got a job or to cheer up a man who did not. It was during this off season that Son maintained his closest customer contact; there was never any doubt in his mind or anyone else's that it was then he first began to pull ahead of his competitors. Every few days he went to every hotel in town and checked registers; men constantly checked in and out while their equipment was being overhauled or while trying to stall off creditors. As soon as Son saw a name he knew, he went to see the man, taking a bottle of whisky. As long as a man was in town, Son was ready to play cards, have him out to his house, sit in his hotel room if that was what the man wanted to do, take him out to dinner. To restaurants they had to take their own whisky and Son always said there was no sense lugging it back home; hell, if you couldn't drink up a fifth in an evening, why drink? No one drank cocktails; they drank to get drunk. Even when Prohibition was over, they drank whisky with something sweet as they had learned to do in the days when they had to kill its taste. Kate said about these years, Son never came home without bringing a bunch of men. She never knew how many people he would bring home to the dinner she had planned for three. And he never once warned her. On the other hand, half the time she had dinner ready and he didn't show up at all. Several years on his birthday she made a cake but he started celebrating at the office getting older and couldn't eat by the time he came home, if he came. She had added nothing else to the candy box but one of

Laurel's first shoes. Sometimes, Kate thought, she ought to put in all the scraps of paper with names and phone numbers she found or his shirts and handkerchiefs with lipstick.

When Son recalled these years, he said way on into '35 and '36 folks were still looking for money; he laughed about some of the ways he made it. Probably not many but those along the river ever knew that 1930 was the beginning of a decade in which over the whole country there were more floods and drought than in the preceding hundred years. One Saturday, he was sitting in the office with Holston. It had rained abnormally; that winter and spring every river and creek in Arkansas and Mississippi had been in flood at one time or another. A muddy Arkansas car stopped in front of the office and two men came inside. "What can I do for you?" Son said; they shook hands but he realized they did not give their names. They wore hats pulled in city-fashion over their eyes, but too far; he knew they were farmers. One said, "We want five sticks of dynamite."

Only recently, needing to sell dynamite any way he could, had Son broken open cases; the other salesmen would not, fearing they would never sell it off by the stick. In the shed behind the office, Son kept dynamite, against the law, but he worried more about not accommodating a customer than being arrested; if a customer wanted a few cases, he put them in the trunk of his car and drove them to him, threw the fuse in the back seat, and he wasn't never going to get out of jail if he got caught either, he said.

Hoping now for information from the strangers, he said, "I don't usually sell it but by the case."

The man said, "We don't want to buy but five sticks."

Son thought he better not lose even that little sale; if you accommodated a man he might come back for more. He said, "I reckon I could let you have them."

"We appreciate it," the man said. When Son brought the dynamite, wrapped in newspaper, the man paid in cash but in all denominations of change, like church collection. The men went away, having lifted neither their hats nor their eyes. Monday morning, Son came into the office already laughing, seeing Holston read-

---

ing the paper he had seen at breakfast. "Jesus Christ, Frank," Holston said. "You reckon if they catch those birds, you'll be in trouble too?"

"Hell, I'm just the peckerwood that peddles the dynamite. I don't ask a customer what he wants it for," Son said. They laughed later telling Buzz how the men came in the muddy Arkansas car, acted strange, paid cash in small change, and bought just enough dynamite to blow up the stretch of levee blown up over in Mississippi County, Arkansas, Sunday night. Water flooding property on one side of the river now flooded it on the opposite side below. It was a pattern repeated all winter and spring, even to the wadded-up bills and the change being spread out over his desk. He and Holston, having sold dynamite, would race to the paper the following morning to see where a piece of levee had been blown. The only time Son worried was the Sunday Mr. Ryder called at two A.M. saying two car loads of men at his house wanted ten boxes of dynamite. "Five hundred pounds a lot of powder," Son said. "They've got rifles and pistols," Mr. Ryder said. "Hell, if they want it that bad, sell it," Son said. Later, Mr. Ryder brought him the money, in two envelopes, even pennies, and dollar bills so old they were cracked and waxed-looking as if somebody had broken into what they had been saving a long time. The next day, Son thought that was a blast he'd like to have seen. A thousand sandbags piled on one side of a small intrastate river in Mississippi had caused flooding below but would no more.

In April, it was still raining. He and Kate went to Cecilia's for Easter. Kate had given Cally a new dress; sky-blue, the color of your eyes, she said, and Cally was pleased. She sat at her dressing table in the room she shared with her granddaughter. Cecilia had bought her a flowered straw hat and they left Cally dressing to help Laurel and little Cecilia find Easter eggs, hidden in the living room because of rain. When they were found, Son went to get Cally, having promised her a drive. "Mammy!" he said and could say no more. He turned around, calling Kate and Cecilia. "Mammy, why did you mess yourself up like that?" Cecilia said coming in. Cally turned toward them the face Son had seen, stark white, heavily and completely smeared with cold cream. "Mad because we didn't pay attention to her," Kate said. "Mammy, we were coming right back."

When Kate went back to the living room, Son had on his coat. He said, "I can't fool with her. I'll do everything in the world for her, but that."

Rain continued over most of the country. Floods were everywhere. In the northeast heavy snows, melting, added to them and the Delton paper predicted 1936 would rank as one of the major flood years of the twentieth century. Son guessed it was the time he felt sorriest in his life for Cally when they put her into the ground with water standing over it. He had a horror of water seeping in on him, dead.

After Christmas she had had a stroke and required constant care. The day they left the cemetery leaving her behind, he said, "I shouldn't say it, but this is the biggest relief in the world to us all." Kate said, "Why Frank, it's your mother." He did not say anything else; but he couldn't help the way he had felt; she had made him so nervous he just couldn't be in the room with her. More and more Cally had flown into rages, whipped her cane toward people who did not do what she wanted. She just wants to get her way to the end, he had said. Kate said, Everybody has to do what you want; you don't get along because you're just like her.

Cally never did rest, he saw that; at the end she was still worried, had a new idea every time he saw her about how he could help Joe make money, wanted him to take Joe into his business. Kate said, Humor her. But he couldn't; he just had to walk away. One night she called Kate to say the Sisters had stolen everything nice she had. She had to have a new nightgown, blue satin with brown lace. Kate searched every store. When she and Laurel arrived with the package, Cecilia had discovered Cally would never wake up from her nap. They buried her in the nightgown.

Son did not know how Cecilia, with two girls now and all she had to put up with, could be as broken up as she was; he got tired of her telling him Cally could not help the way she had been, that her mind had been affected by the last operations.

He had had a long drive home when Cally died and was tired. After the funeral he had a few drinks. Kate said, "Wait now," and hurried supper; but he did not want any. He just wanted to drink some whisky and sleep. He might not have wanted to be around her, he thought, but he had bought her everything in the world she needed; that was something he could do. Always he had known he would have to bury her and Poppa both; it was one reason he'd had to work as hard as he did; another was because nobody was going to take care of him, if he didn't. He had bought them good caskets to keep out rain. For a hundred dollars apiece, he had bought five lots in a cemetery opening up on the edge of town; he did not want Poppa left up yonder in Vicksville alone and would move him as soon as possible. The three other lots were for himself, Kate, Laurel. That was one worry off his mind. Still he could not sleep.

He remembered the dark muddy ground opened up beneath the grey January day, the flowers arriving bright and fresh and quickly ruined, the colors of the ribbons running in the misty day. He got up and went into the dark house, stumbled his way until he found a light. Kate was sleeping with Laurel. In the doorway, he said, "I feel sorry for Mammy all alone out there in the rain."

Kate said, "Frank, it's two o'clock in the morning. Go back to bed."

He said, "Don't you?"

She said, "You've waked Laurel. She's afraid."

"Well, she'll get over it before she's married twice," he said and went back to bed. What the hell did either of them have to be afraid about? They had somebody putting a roof over their heads. Hell, there ought to be somebody to talk to. He thought of old Winston Taylor; he sure 'nough could drink up whisky. Suddenly he called out "Will —Ohhh, Mister Will!"

"Frank, will you hush," Kate said from the doorway. He told her what she could do with herself. She went away saying, "Why do you come home. I wish you'd just stay gone."

He called, "Why don't you get out?"

"Because you wouldn't let another woman leave you, and you

know it," she said. "But I feel sorry for Laurel." She shut the door.

In the morning, he would have left town, gone down to see old Winston, but he could not. He had to have another drink: could not make it. He had to have some more. He kept on until he was sick and weak as a kitten. Then one morning he got up and got dressed, ate what he could and went to the office. Buzz and Holston were there. Having no pretenses all his life, Son walked in and said, "What's been going on while I was laid up drunk a week?"

"Rain," Holston said.

Buzz told how it was; he had just come back from up yonder. Ohio, Illinois, Kentucky. The Ohio River its whole length, Pittsburgh to Cairo, was at flood stage and the crest not in sight. All that water was pouring into the Mississippi, already bursting its seams. Son thought of old Red's long-ago warning: some day all rivers might flood at the same time. Jesus, he thought, suppose the time is now?

Above and below Delton every river in Tennessee, Missouri, Arkansas and Mississippi was swelling the big river. It was a test of the work he, Will, and the contractors had been concentrating on the past ten years. The past six, Will, others had been constructing cut-offs in the middle reach of the Mississippi to speed flood waters to the Gulf. If they work, Will had told Son, it's a whole new phase in flood control engineering. If they don't, it'll prove true what the most engineers have believed for two hundred years. Cut-offs are the worse way possible to treat flood control.

The uncompleted levees along the Mississippi had so far held the water; the Ohio was the threat. Opposite Cairo, where the two rivers came together, the fuse plug levee had been built on the Missouri side. From the time when it had been commissioned, under the act in 1928, Son had tried to make sure he understood it. When water reached a certain height, the plugs would be released; water, let out, would cover a floodway behind the levee; the Mississippi would be lowered. He said, "Suppose they ever release the plugs in that levee below Cairo. What'll happen to the folks living in the floodway?"

"They got to get out. The Government bought the land but it's rich and folks stayed, hoping it'd never have to be used as a floodway," Buzz said. "But folks up that way are running like jack rabbits from high water. I drove up to one filling station and the owner was boarding her up. Said he had to get his mother-in-law to high ground. Then his family come out the back of the station where they lived, all dressed up. Turned out they was stewing about getting the old lady to high ground to bury her!"

It was Saturday and Son went home early; the paper boy had just thrown the afternoon paper. Plucking it from the shrubbery Son went inside reading. Sixty were known dead in the flood and fifty thousand were homeless. At the Kentucky State Reformatory fifteen convicts were killed rioting when water seeped into their cell blocks, but they were not counted as flood victims.

He entered the house, sheepish about that week at home. After supper he said he would take Laurel and Kate to the picture show. What did they want to see?

"Mr. Deeds Goes to Town," Kate said.

"What's that all about?" he said.

"Jean Arthur's in it, Daddy," Laurel said.

"Hell, get your hat," he said.

ITT HAD RAINED, AS NEAR AS HE COULD FIGURE, FOR TWENTY-nine days and nights. In his seventy-five years, Samuel Beggs could not remember so much rain. Now, here toward the end of January, it had begun to snow and sleet; he told everyone neither could he remember a Missouri winter so cold. But it was no usual winter; floods were everywhere. The Ohio, just down the road, over the levee, threatened them all. He could not remember when that river had acted so bad and it pleased him he had so much to remember.

The wind drove sleet like needles, but he looked ahead at a small cemetery neatly defined into a square by four white posts at its corners. From the road, three steps of the same white stone led up to it. Carved into the top riser, in the script Pap had wanted, was their name: BEGGS. To read the gravestones was a story Samuel often read to himself. His Pap and Mam lay under one large stone, Amos and Mary; their dates could barely be read. Pap had settled here, worked his way from the east to Cincinnati, stayed briefly, then moved to Cairo; but the rich land in the shadow of the Mississippi and Ohio drew him across the river, into Missouri. He bought fifty acres cheap and later fifty more. Now the Beggs' owned close to a thousand.

Beside the large white stone were four small ones, straight, like soldiers' graves; Infant Daughter, Infant Son . . . He, Samuel, had been the only one of five children of Amos and Mary to survive. That, he believed, had taken Pap and Mam both to early graves. His own first child lay here, born dead; beside it the mother who had not lived much longer. He had known Sally so short a time, he remembered her most as the girl he had courted. Next to her plot was his; beyond that lay Mary Lee, a second wife fifteen years younger whom he had not expected to outlive. Burying her five years ago, Samuel had knelt, praying not to outlive any more of his own people.

His past was in the cemetery, his future down the road from where he had just come. Before he left the neat house there, his three grandsons had clamored to ride Huck. Aggie, his daughter-in-law, had said, Not in this weather! Grandpap, you don't have any business out in it either. He and the boys had been disappointed but he had said, Mind your Mam, and rode away sitting straight, knowing they watched. In the barn his son had been pitching hay and waved; he gave the boy a salute in return. From the road, he looked on one side at his cattle huddled, gazing out of faces that were frosty. On the other side were acres of fruit trees carefully pruned, branched against the grey-white sky as if etched in charcoal. When flood danger was over, Samuel thought, he, his son, the boys had to think of fertilizing. His face was full of sleet but he rode thinking of spring when he and Huck roamed his acreage. In far fields he never saw in winter he put cotton, corn and beans. His family urged: Pap, get you a little secondhand car and oversee everything comfortable.

He said, Old folks don't have any business out driving automobiles. He might make a mistake; Huck wouldn't.

This year his son had said Huck might not be able to help slipping on the road. But Samuel had said they had to get outdoors. He had been told snow on the levee was a foot deep but here in the floodway behind the levee, he did not believe it was so high. He and Huck went slowly; the roads were slippery but also the wind was unbearably cold, going fast. Passing the cemetery he had looked through frozen eyelashes as if through tears. Huck snorted; his breath shot ahead like the puffs of a cannon; his hoofs went delicately as if to avoid contact with the frozen road. The animal needed no rein, turned opposite into the driveway, toward the house where the wide front verandah overlooked the cemetery and the orchard around it. Often he sat on his big porch, overlooking his people and his land. When he was buried, his son would have the house; they would have to build two more. There was plenty of land and plenty of Beggs' to work it, and that was a piece of satisfaction to a old man, Samuel thought, arriving home.

It was that moment the airplane became visible. He was aware then he had heard it for some time, like a giant mosquito in the clouds, annoying the quiet. It seemed insect-sized, came out of the east, dipped a wing and flew so close his heart caught; he thought it would crash. Equal to that astonishment was his difficulty in handling his own horse; for the first time ever, Huck tried to rear. The airplane righted, flew off over his roof, leaving in the air a flurry as thick as snow of falling white papers. Nothing else moved, only the falling papers and the plane itself circling in the distance to fly over his son's house. Dismounting, Samuel picked up a paper. Without his reading glasses, he could make out only the large heading: WARNING. His hand trembled holding the paper and he led the horse to the barn. As he had expected, when he returned, the telephone was ringing. He wasn't going to answer any more than he was going to read that paper, he thought. Not even realizing it, he had crumpled the paper but could not make himself throw it away. All over his yard they lay, mud-splattered, wet, or blowing away in the wind. He had had on his mind a whole lot to tell and now here was another thing, if he just knew who to tell. Somebody ought to know it was against the law to fly over folks' property dropping trash.

The telephone rang off and on. He did not answer, knowing his son would come when his chores were done. He was eating a little bit of early supper when the car stopped outside. He listened with pleasure to the familiar footsteps crossing the old wooden porch. He was eating when his son came in. "Pap, we got

---

181

to go this time. They been fair, waited as long as they could. They let us keep them from it twice. This time is it," his son said, nodding toward the crumpled paper, not knowing it was unread.

Samuel broke corn bread into his glass of buttermilk and ate it with a spoon. His son sat opposite. He had not turned on lights when he came from the barn; they saw one another by the late grey twilight where snow twirled. Samuel's eyes watered, fixing on his boy, veins were apparent. The son thought, Pap's old and I'm not young enough to start over again either. He ran a hand over a face warm despite the day saying he just wondered how things would turn out.

Samuel said, "Whose fault is this? Who's to blame?"

His son said, "Nobody. Unless you want to call the Ohio rising God's fault."

"No, I ain't blaming nothing on God," Samuel said.

"Well then," the boy said.

"You eat supper?" Samuel said.

"Aggie's waiting it on me," the son said.

"Well I ain't going," Samuel said.

"You got to or be flooded out," the son said. "And neither me or the U.S. Engineers are fixing to let that happen. We got to fill the wagon and the car and the truck, drive what cattle we can and hope to keep them. People been driving cattle over the levee all week and leaving them." Out the back window, squinting, they could make out the dark shape of the secondline levee. Between it and the frontline one, along the Mississippi itself, was a narrow flat area with a few houses and a general store.

Samuel clattered his spoon into his empty glass. "It's somebody's fault," he said. "Who decided? Mr. Roosevelt?" If so, disappointed in the man, he regretted the two times he had cast votes for him.

"The Engineers in Cairo decided," the son said. "And they take orders from Delton. Not anybody you know decided." He said he had to go home and eat supper and start packing. Pap would have to go, he thought, if they had to chloroform him.

———

182

They went out on the porch and saw the first, going: some were headed to Cairo, some to Kentucky, but most to camp on the narrow strip of land between the Mississippi and the secondline levee.

"They going so soon?" Samuel said.

"Soon!" his son said. "It's the next day or so."

Then Samuel sat down like something the air had been let out of, knowing he was not going. Next month, maybe even next week, but not in the next day or two. You don't pick up and move off the land you had lived on always that quick, he said.

"Pap, it ain't quick," his son said. "They been talking about dynamiting the levee, letting the water in the floodway, almost since this time last Saturday. Some folks left then. We decided to wait and see, now we seen."

"They'll never do it," Samuel said.

"Nobody believed they would," the son said.

Cold, Samuel knew the boy was cold too but he could not stop watching his neighbors turn their heads and wave as they passed, leaving. He thought of when the Government had bought the land as a floodway, paid everyone a hundred and twenty-five dollars an acre. Mary Lee had said maybe they ought to leave then, like a lot of folks. Leave! he had said. He wouldn't sign anything; the Government condemned his land and paid him anyway. But he, nobody, had believed these ten years the Government would ever flood them out, no matter what the Mississippi River did. He said, "We held 'em off twice," and thought how they must have looked, a straggly bunch of farmers carrying anything that would shoot, wearing any kind of clothes to keep warm enough, marching toward the levee. The National Guard turned them back. But the local man going to shoot the dynamite had been afraid to and hardly anyone had left the floodway. He said again, "We held 'em off twice."

His son said, "The Ohio's still rising, Pap. All the lowlands have been evacuated. They say it's ghost towns everywhere."

It'll be one here, Samuel thought, watching them, still going. He saw those driving cattle had trouble; the cattle walked blindly, heads lowered into the wind; ice hung like beards on their faces and froze on their eyelashes. All to save Cairo, he thought, always the city folks.

"Hyar!" was a cry that came repeatedly from the road. Men on horseback, walking, drove the cattle; dogs ran barking at their hooves; the goal was to get over the secondline levee, into safety. The son blew on cold hands and said, "They been packed up since the first warning. We got a lot to do, Pap."

"I ain't going," he said.

Out of the line of cars passing, a small coupe turned and came up the driveway. That's why he was in the cold, the son thought. Samuel stood, held open the front door, as the men got out of the car, filed across the porch and came inside. This time he turned on lights, held his hands an instant over the globe for warmth, casting shadows. This time they were warmly and neatly dressed, not straggly looking at all, he thought.

A man named Chess said, "We figure to blow the frontline levee. If we let water into that strip between it and the secondline, maybe it'll lower the river enough; maybe they won't flood in here too."

"What about the folks on that strip, and the cattle pushed into there? Some of the folks out of here are there too," the son said.

Chess said, "They can climb the secondline levee back into here, stead of us doing it the other way round."

"They ain't going to just let you do it," Samuel said.

"We're going by dark, can blast once so they can start getting out before we blast again," another man said.

"Cattle might drown but cattle left behind's going to drown in here," a third man said.

"We got room in the car for one," Chess said. He left the statement in the air; the old man and his son would have to decide.

Samuel said, "Aggie's waiting supper on you. I've had mine."

The son said, "Pap, you ain't got any business . . ."

Samuel said, "It's my business if it's my land." He dressed warmly. They went out on the porch, having waited. It was full dark. The snow had stopped but the wind remained as cold as death. Beneath the cold pale moon the car, trees, housetops stood out covered with sleet. A moment, the car left exhaust hanging in the air like a ghost's vapor, then was gone. Samuel had said, "Have a good supper, boy," and the son had watched until the car was out of sight, then drove home. He knew Aggie and the boys were waiting supper as certainly as he knew that tomorrow he was taking them out of the floodway, as certainly as he knew something in the dark night would keep Pap, the others from flooding out folks of their own kind.

In the morning, Samuel told what it was. He had come to the conclusion, he said, there was a lot of things bigger than you. One thing was God and another was the night itself. Then, he said, there's the United States Gov'ment, the Mississippi River and the whole blasted National Guard from Missouri patrolling its banks!

It was Sunday, and they packed. The three grandsons said there was nothing they could take. The daughter-in-law, Aggie, said, "We got to pack food, clothes, and feed; there's not room for baseballs and mitts."

"Can't we play ball when spring comes?" the youngest said.

"Why, sugar," she said. Looking into his eight-year-old face, she saw he did not understand at all. "We'll be back 'way fore spring."

"I didn't think anything would be here," he said.

"I think the house'll be; that old tool shed upside the barn won't. We don't know what will and what won't, is the truth of it," Aggie said. "Besides mud." She looked around at the house she had kept clean twenty years thinking she might as well have been off gallivanting. She tightened windows as if it were going to rain. They had taken everything they could in boxes to the attic. The truck was loaded; a trailer attached to the car was piled high with corn. The car was full, the windows up, the cat inside. Shep barked, herding cattle and pigs. Aggie sighed. "We've got everything," she said, "except Pap."

All morning, as they packed, people from back in the floodway stopped to ask where he was. "He won't go," she or the son said;

the people went on, nodding, as if it were right. Wagons, trucks, cars passed, many with crates of chickens tied on. Freezing rain fell and again everything was white. The road was slick; cattle, mules, horses stumbled slipped slid were fearful and balky picking a path. Everywhere dogs ran, barking. For a moment, Aggie opened the car window; the cat, terrified, escaped. The youngest cried out. "We can't go back for it; we can't," she said. They saw it, its fur electrified-looking, running with humped back toward their barn. "If it stays in the loft, it might be safe," she said.

The son drove the truck; the other two boys were on horseback, driving cattle. It was a good thing cars had to crawl, Aggie thought, or somebody would slip off the road. They passed the cemetery and she looked toward the house. Pap must be watching, she thought. The boy said, "Suppose Grandpap don't come."

"He has to," she said.

"He says he ain't," he said.

"All I know is they got them Engineers on the levee, and we wouldn't have gone unless we knew they'd make Pap leave." But how? she wondered.

"I bet he don't leave because the Engineers want him to," the boy said. Cattle plodded beside them with bent heads; men walked, carrying tow sacks on their backs with pigs inside. Aggie predicted those in the open would take sick. By night, flu that would turn into an epidemic had begun.

At the levee people stood pushing over dogs, driving over cattle. All week, they had come pushing animals into safety; now they would find them, thin, hopelessly cold. In lost hungry packs dogs had run about until the woman at the general store fed them. Now, many were reclaimed. By the time people went back over the levee, not a stray would be left.

In the floodway, only Samuel was left. The son had argued all he could, then said he was taking his family out and would come back and get him. "I ain't going," Samuel had said.

In five states schoolhouses were filled with refugees. People were camped in empty box cars and on cotton weighing stations, with blankets strung around the sides. The son had brought a tent but the first night Aggie and the boys would sleep in the truck. The youngest wanted to go back with him; at the last minute the son said he could. Going against the exodus was hard going. It was late when they got back. On the way they heard the news. Walking in, the son said first thing, "Pap! water's lapping over the roadway of the Southern-Illinois."

"That high?" Samuel said.

When the Mississippi worked its way under a levee and bubbled to the surface the leaks were called sand boils. Early, the gaps had to be circled with sandbags or the levee was eaten away deep in its bowels. Men patrolled the levee looking for leaks; more were sent to wall them in when they were found. A thousand men had built a three-foot bulkhead atop the sixty-foot seawall at Cairo. But the Ohio had risen to fifty-nine feet. In Delton, Engineers told the Cairo office on Tuesday to wait for relief. On Saturday the plane flew over. On Sunday the Delton office sent word the levee would be blown on Monday. "Who's going to do it?" they said in Cairo. "Nobody here will try again?"

At eight o'clock that Sunday night Son's phone rang; how much dynamite did he have in his magazine? an Engineer asked. Son told and the Engineer said could he get more? Son said he could get all he wanted directly out of Illinois. Could he leave for Cairo by ten? The National Guard would drive him, the Engineer said.

What the hell's it all about? Son said.

The Engineer told everything except about the straggly line of farmers. He only said the trip was secret and Son had to go by night. Would his wife keep quiet? Son said he guessed she could keep quiet about that much, thinking, mainly because she won't think it's worth telling. They hung up, but the phone rang again and the same Engineer said, Mr. Wynn, be sure you put on some warm clothes.

I always do, Son said.

This time put on more, the man said, hanging up again.

When he told Mr. Ryder, Son laughed: You reckon he don't think we read the newspaper, don't know anything about those farmers? He said put all the dynamite in the magazine in the truck; the National Guard would escort it; he told the intersection where they would meet. The man says there'll be two trucks, one to go ahead, one behind.

It's that bad? Mr. Ryder said.

I reckon they want to kill the fellow bringing the dynamite as much as they want to kill the one going to shoot it off, Son said. But the fellow said not to worry; the boys got guns. You reckon there's anything else you need to know?

No sir, Mr. Ryder said.

Son said he'd see him in Cairo then.

There were two wide streets to the city, deserted now and slick with ice. It was almost dawn but there was little discernible change from the dark night hours during which freezing rain had fallen, turning the countryside white. Wary, Son looked out. But there was nothing to see except the sad, ineffectual light of the street lamps still burning and empty stores. A darkened marquee read, *Mr. Deeds Goes to Town*. Son said he had seen it the other night. Had anyone else? No one had. They were silent as they had been for most of the trip, hearing only their own sound, the splat splat splat of tires on slick wet pavement, until they came to the river. A barge was waiting at the base of the bridge, less visible from the opposite bank: the *Mark Twain*. Son made out the tarnished brass letters as he slipped down the bank of mud, mush and old snow. "What's all that?" he said. Below the bridge he saw lamps glimmer and fires. "Folks that come out of the floodway today, camped," the barge captain said.

It was colder on the river. They crossed hearing the thumping engine and the bow splatting against the choppy water. Above the bridge, on the levee itself, the Engineers were camped. On the road leading to the bridge, between the two camps, the others waited. The barge captain told him, They've got all kinds of rifles and shotguns. That's why we brung you by the water.

Son was in his own tent and it was not much warmer; but he

could change his socks; he put his feet back into wet boots and said, "How'd they know when we were coming?"

The Colonel had been sent from Washington to oversee blowing of the fuse plug levee at the Birds Point-New Madrid Floodway; he said, "They don't. There's just been one bunch or another patrolling ever since the first man was going to shoot the dynamite and they kept him from it. Yesterday, they even tried to blast the frontline levee. We figure they won't come all the way to Delton to kill you."

"If you get me back?" Son said. "And my truck and my driver too."

"That's right," the Colonel said.

"How you figuring on getting the truck out on the levee?" Son said.

"Outnumbering them," the Colonel said. "We got Guardsmen two and three deep lining the road where it's coming, with machine guns and orders to use them."

Then it was later, though still not daylight; even with machine guns, they would not have risked daylight. Son, from the higher vantage point of the levee, saw about as much as those lining the road, saw the tops of the two National Guard trucks racing through the near dawn, the red dynamite truck between, and heard later how when the shotguns were raised the machine guns were raised opposite; then, he supposed, they only stood as he had watching the almost gold-looking warning lights of the dynamite truck bobbing as it tore along the top of the levee itself. He said, "The dynamite's here, let's get to work."

"We can't," the Colonel said. "There's an old man still out in the floodway."

Son could not leave the Engineers camp. The Colonel told him how it went: he used every argument he could think of. Mr. Beggs, he said, there's water standing in the business district of Louisville, eleven feet in a hotel lobby in Paducah. People everywhere have had to leave home.

I ain't going, the old man said.

The Government had paid him for his land; he had known they had the right, might some day flood it, the Colonel said. The old man said he never thought they would. I even told him about you, the Colonel said, told him you were waiting, had come all the way from Delton, weren't about to go home without blowing the levee. What'd he say? Son said. What do you think? The Colonel said. His son was there and a grandson, a little tow-headed fellow who said, Why won't you go, Grandpap?

There won't be nothing to come home to, Samuel said.

I said he'd have more to come home to now than if he let the river keep rising, the Colonel said. His house and barn might be left, even his gravestones across the road.

Shoot, the old man said, you could knock some of them over with a feather right now, they're so old.

His son said, Pap, it don't matter about the gravestones; you've got to go.

The little fellow said, Anyway, Grandma'd still be in the ground.

That's so, the old man said.

It seemed he hadn't thought of that. After awhile, he said he would go. But he was going in his own way. But how . . . ? I said, after being shoved toward the door by the son who answered, Because he said he would.

Next, Son told how all that time they had stood on the levee watching and how those camped below the bridge had stood watching too. First, they had seen the Colonel's little khaki-colored car come shooting along the road like the floodway was opening up behind him, Son said, laughing. Next they saw the coupe with the man and boy in it alone; they had craned their necks to see. Then the Colonel arrived and told them and they kept watching. It didn't take as long as he expected, Son thought, even though the roads were slippy and the sleet slanted toward them. The old man wore a wide hat and kept his head lowered. As he came closer, Son saw the brim filled with sleet and occasionally spilled over onto the horse's neck.

It was a long cold trip and a long cold time everyone waited. When the old man was safe, Son set up the dynamite. It was late afternoon when the blast came. He was told later windows in the newspaper office in Cairo rattled; a farmer's wife, having a long delivery, told reporters it made her push and at last, a son was born. Window shades, everywhere, flew to the ceiling. But what Son never forgot was the sound of the first great swoosh as the water broke. Through two gaps and thirteen natural breaks it went, racing over the land, carrying livestock and farm buildings as if they were toys floated by children, flooding more than a hundred thousand acres. For days everyone had watched the two rivers of raging muddy water and now it seemed as if the whole world were only that, except for the levee where they stood and the little strip of land behind it where the floodway people were camped. All they could do now was go back there, Son thought.

The next morning, the water was calmer, lay like a great muddy lake, full of floating objects. One Engineer retrieved a trunk and found the clothes in it still to be dry. Son saw a hen floating on a nest; reaching land, the hen flew away and the nest full of eggs went on alone. All day they watched fowl flying from one object to another to reach dry land; they could see dogs stranded on the tops of houses and barns. That afternoon, the first people rowed out. It was late when Son saw a man rowing back in, with a cow. Cattle were found safe in lofts. Daily, people had to row out to feed and water them. It would be three weeks in all. By Thursday, sure no more blasting would be needed, the Engineers allowed Son to leave. Mr. Ryder had already gone, with an escort all the way. Son was taken the same way, by night, by barge, driven home in the same guarded car. Again gazing out at the wide dark streets of the city, he noted the picture show had changed. A whole lot had changed for those folks, he thought. He would remember always the old man coming out of the spillway and the old Negro who approached the levee guards with a question, pulling a large child's wagon; like a corpse, something humped was in it covered by a clean white cloth. The Colonel was summoned; he had killed four hogs, the Negro said; in his camp someone would steal the meat; could he leave it on the levee, come out and salt it down every day? The Colonel could not say no; it was the old man's meat for a long time to come; only he, except for those connected to the project and a few reporters came on the levee at all. About Cairo, Son had the same indefinable feeling of contribution toward something he could not name he had had when he shipped the dynamite to New Orleans and farmers there were flooded, long ago.

As bad as things had been when the water was high, he heard they were worse when it lowered and the thaw came. People, going back to the floodway after three weeks, drove ahead cattle through mud that reached the animals' chests. Some people had nothing to return to and went elsewhere, bitter. Everyone was bitter. He heard from the Colonel men hung around the levee road for days before they would believe the dynamite man was gone. They swore he better never show up around there again and Son knew he never would. The Colonel said he had gone to see the old man once. Several of the gravestones had been knocked down, broken and chipped, but the old man had repaired them; despite his family's protests, he was on the roof hammering and nailing, patching and painting; from there he could see the levee and on brightest days a sparkle, faint and quick, brief as a mirror's flash. It was the blew hole where the greatest force of the blast had come, through which the water had first rushed. It was great and round and deep. Water never left it.

At first, no one went near. Then little boys and Negroes crept there. Old people went next who usually held their grudges but the spring and summer days were long and there was little to do. Word spread. Finally everyone went except Samuel; he never did, never had cared about fishing anyway and the blew hole had the finest fishing anywhere. Always would, Son said.

The next week he was sent a copy of a St. Louis paper, the blast featured in the Sunday supplement, a reporter having taken pictures from a plane. *Life* Magazine had a picture as he was about to set off the blast, a picture of the blast itself, Son a tiny figure in the foreground walking away. It tickled him to death, even if you couldn't tell who he was.

He received a business-like letter from the head of Illinois telling him the company was proud. He was proud of that. He showed the letter to Holston saying, "That's some berries, ain't it?" While Holston read, he opened another company letter that had come in the same mail. From the first sentence he began to laugh. The letter was an enraged personal scrawl from the head of the company calling him every name in the world for a fool. On and on the man wrote about how the company tried to promote safety with explosives; then their own representative appears in a national magazine about to light his fuse, a cigarette dangling in his mouth. Suppose he had blown off a hand, fingers, his head? Did he use it to light the fuse too!

Tears ran down Son's face. With a yelp, he finally stopped laughing. He carried the letter around for weeks, showed it to everyone, then framed it. He had never thought of lighting a fuse any other way since the golf course job. But when you came down to it, he had to admit, he was the only bird he knew of who fooled with explosives as much as he did who hadn't lost at least a thumb.

That spring Joe and Cecilia moved down in Mississippi; another baby was expected and Joe felt the money would stretch farther in the country. That spring water stood over fields everywhere. Waking one morning, Son knew it was the exact time to start out promoting what he had thought about so long: ditch digging with dynamite. A selling point now was how long it would be before the ground was dry enough for a dragline to make one. After a struggle, he wrote an ad. FARM DITCHING: Dynamite was the easiest, quickest and cheapest way to make a drainage ditch. No spoil banks, nothing to clear away afterward. Frank Wynn would furnish supplies and do the blasting. Call day or night. He gave his home and office numbers. Afterward he told Laurel what they said about advertising was true: it paid. His telephone rang day and night. Having set up a week's itinerary, he got up at six o'clock the next Monday morning. Over and over he had to yell before he got Kate up to fix his breakfast and had to hear about it all the time she was cooking, until he set out with his juices churning. It was the same every Monday morning, he thought, as Laurel, awakened, thought too. He drove for miles, smoked half a dozen cigarettes before he could calm himself down, thinking of Kate's last words. He didn't show any interest in the world in her or Laurel, cared only about his business. What was he working himself to death for? he said.

She said, Because he liked to work.

He hit the Delta highway and forgot, thinking of it as his highway, would bet he could drive it blindfolded, he had driven it plenty. This week the other side of his business opened up; this week he began to teach the state of Mississippi everything there was in the world to know about dynamiting ditches. Farmers provided Negroes to carry boxes and Son taught them to punch holes and string fuses; but few wanted to stay around when he started handling the dynamite itself. He met one Negro not afraid and so interested, he told him to come on up to Delton, he'd teach him the whole business. All week he waded out of one field and into another, stayed over the week-end to shoot thirty miles of ditches on one man's plantation. He was as proud of that thirty miles as anything he had ever done and though he was about as tired afterward as he had ever been, he went on that Saturday night to see May. All these years, whenever he was in her part of the Delta he had seen May; she never had married. Then on Sunday night he checked into a hotel in Clarksdale. The first person he saw in the lobby was old man Woods' oldest son, Eddie. As far as he was concerned, he never had had any quarrel with Eddie, had eaten alone all week and would not mind some company. Would Eddie ride the train with him and eat? Hesitating less than a minute, Eddie said he would. His little boy, eight years old, was with him and he was expecting two dragline operators and left word he would be in Son's room. Having drinks, Son said, "Whew! This feels like the first time I've set down in a week."

Eddie looked into his glass and over at his boy playing with dice Son had given him, then said, "Dynamite, I'm going to tell you something you'll know soon anyway. We're pulling out selling powder. Just going to sell equipment from here on out."

He looked up to see if Son was going to ask why, saw he was not: he knew. Eddie had to grin himself watching Son's spread. Meeting him in the lobby he had noticed Son's eyes pale with tiredness; now they gleamed like a cat's. Dynamite was a rough, coarse son-of-a-bitch sometimes, Eddie thought, but you couldn't help liking him. He thought how he and Bull had started out in their old man's business; Dynamite, he understood, hadn't had a plug nickel. Another time Bull might beat him in a fight. It was the stuff inside driving Dynamite you couldn't beat. He had run them out fair and square. Eddie admired him for it.

Two down, two to go, Son thought. Raising his eyebrows, he had said, "Sho nuff? Well, we got to ride the train on that," thinking, Two down, two to go. Michigan was pulling out, American had not put in another man when he left, only the big boys were left.

Eddie's friends came bringing a bottle and wanted to shoot craps. The men pitched in change and bought the dice back from Eddie's little boy. The game went smoothly until one of Eddie's friends accused the other of cheating. Picking him up by the collar, he stood the man on his feet saying they were going to fight. The man denied cheating, said he wouldn't fight, didn't like to, and didn't know how. Eddie and Son did not think he had cheated. Still the first man insisted on fighting and the second insisted he could not.

Standing, Son said, "Hell, I'll fight him for you."

No one believed he would until he took off his shirt and started. All around the room they went, overturning furniture, broke a lamp. Once a porter opened the door and hastily closed it. Exhausted, they quit: stood opposite one another cursing, breathing heavily, and shortly started again; repeated the whole process several times, fought, rested, started again. "Just like two roosters," Eddie said.

Son sent the man sprawling across the bed, breaking the springs; slats clattered to the floor. The little boy, clambering to the headboard, braced himself, and continued to watch until they quit. Washed, dressed, Son said, "You've fought a lot before."

"I didn't get this nose drinking buttermilk," the man said.

There were no hard feelings; they would go down and eat. The elevator boy, having heard from the porter, cast a wary eye sliding open the door. But he reported later the two who had been fighting went down peaceful to the dining room late at night followed by a little boy, not at all sleepy, jingling a pocketful of change.

The story reached Delton a week before Son. It was the wide-eyed little boy, running into his house, who told it first. All over town, having heard, men said it was just like him. Kate thought, it was all right for them to laugh; they didn't have to live with a roughneck. Buzz, Will, Winston Taylor were as nice as any people she ever wanted to know; they not only didn't act like Son, they didn't go around with the people who did. He was always saying you had to be rough. But you didn't have to be rough the way he was; he didn't understand differences. And an idea he got about her was because of Lillian. Kate told him she didn't care about joining the Country Club, knew they never could, didn't care about society people, only about nice people who knew how to do things. When she put candles on the table, he turned on the overhead lights: said he had to see what he was eating. Did he think she was trying to poison him?

She fixed fancy things, beans and almonds. Peanuts and beans! he said, made her take the dish off the table. Kate said finally the only thing there was to say, I just give up.

Others kept telling her how funny Frank was. Using his phrase, she thought, Funny as a crutch. Others said he was generous and she said generous to his customers but she could not get a penny out of him, bought her clothes often in the basements of stores. Though she would say one thing, when he bought something, he bought the best; if they went somewhere he did everything right. He had nothing to do with anything secondhand or second class; in some ways it was like his fear of the sort of food she put on the table; he had to have a lot and would eat nothing left-over. No matter how much money he made he raised the roof about bills. Out of her weekly grocery money, she managed music lessons and payments for braces for Laurel's teeth. Braces! He said it was the biggest waste of money he ever heard. But Laurel's front teeth had a space between them and Kate was determined they would not.

The morning after the fight, Son woke sore but started out into a day just begun. He drove to see Winston, arrived at his house late in the afternoon, hoped to convince him to clean out all the county's ditches, done every ten years, with dynamite. Winston, his wife, Leila, a retired doctor, Doc Barker, now a planter, were in the kitchen where Leila was making pimento cheese, grating half a hoop. She had pickled tomatoes all day; jars of them were cooling about the room. The men talked, drank, as she worked: discussed drainage ditches, the best breeding ground in the world for mosquitoes, and the Delta's need to improve ditches, to have more. Through Winston, Son had an ear to the ground around the Delta. Talking now, Son was aware of dusk creeping toward the house across the flat land, moving almost visibly across a vacant field opposite; cars passing mingled with the sudden dark, obscuring everything until they passed, and he waited for the sky to reappear. Over the Delta it seemed huge, possible to touch the stars appearing. The steamy feel of cooking, the smells of the tomatoes and cheese made him feel a boy again, back in Cally's kitchen. If he hadn't found out about peddling dynamite being a farmer in the Delta was what he would like to have been; farming was hard but the life here was easy, the people the nicest he had ever known. Having killed almost two fifths, they decided to eat. Leila got up to put the tops on the tomato jars. Son offered to help, went about the room and tightened the tops on them all. Winston telephoned a restaurant: "I'm bringing over a big dynamite man and a big planter, put me on the biggest steaks you got!" Already, Doc and Son argued over who would pay the bill.

"You all act like a bunch of kids," Leila said as hilariously they went into the spring evening. Insect sounds that would continue until frost came shrilly from all directions. The moon, huge and bright, looked at them with a face quite cockeyed, the way they felt, and the sidewalks were wavery, white. They sped along gravel roads toward the paved one through town. Driving, Winston said, "That steamed-up kitchen give me the worse damn headache I ever had. Doc, what can I take?"

From the back seat, Doc said, "Take an aspirin."

"I already took one," Winston said.

"Take another," Doc said.

"I took up all we had."

"Hell, then swallow the bottle," Doc said, and whooping with laughter they entered the restaurant. Unlike hill country where Baptists ruled, Sheriffs ruled in the Delta and it was possible to buy a drink. Did the Sheriff still get his two-dollar kickback on each case? Son said and Winston said at least, same as with slot machines, which were supposed to be illegal but lined the walls of every filling station and restaurant. Now across a rear wall they saw smudge marks from a row of machines recently removed. Doc said because the Grand Jury was in session; everyone locked their machines out of sight out of respect to it. "We sho better drink to the Grand Jury," Son said.

Waiting for steaks, they had drinks, then Son ordered a second round; instead of the waitress returning, the proprietor came out, a fat Italian called Tiny, wearing a chef's hat. "I don't sell but one drink to a customer," he said.

"Well I want another drink," Son said.

"Just one to a customer," he said. "I run a eating establishment, not a bar."

"Well there's certainly not anybody going to tell me how many drinks I can have," Son said standing, thinking, certainly not no Dago; he took his hat from beneath his chair and said, "I'm going around the corner to that little Greek joint I saw."

As soon as he had gone, Winston said, "With that juice inside him he'll fight somebody yet that crosses him." They were willing to pay for the steaks without eating them to follow. In the Greek restaurant only beer was sold but at least he had two when he wanted them, Son said, indicating the bottles on his table. "But for

Christ's sake," he said, holding out the menu. "Look at the stuff on this. You reckon that Greek could just rustle me up some ham and eggs?"

He woke the following morning at Winston's, remembering only vaguely Leila had insisted he stay overnight. Doc, sleeping on the sofa, opened one eye to say weakly he hoped to see him when he was down in this part of the country again. After breakfast, Son went out to his car with Winston, opened the door and threw in his grip, caught the familiar smell of the car's interior, the worn and old leather smell of the grip itself, stale cigarette smoke, a permanent faint musty smell of dust, it was these that reassured him when he woke unexpectedly in strange hotel rooms, in strange towns, and wondered what the hell everything was all about. At dawn, starting out in search of strange roads and unfamiliar faces, he could answer when he entered the car. If he never had figured out anything else, he had figured that out: knew exactly who he was getting in this car, hitting these country roads, selling powder.

"You've drunk up all my whisky, I guess you ought to go," Winston said.

"Hell, come up to my house I'll give you some good drinking whisky," Son said. "You figured out yet whether you going to let me sell you dynamite to clean out them ditches?"

Winston said, "If you can spit past the end of the sidewalk I'll try to."

Aiming, Son shot saliva beyond and it landed on a blade of grass, sliding like a tear drop. They shook hands. Starting off, Son anticipated the wet smell of the early spring morning. Mist stood over fields and covered the emerging sun like dust. Chill bumps formed on his arm resting on the windowsill but the afternoon would be hot. He went on for several hours through little towns then thought, Here she comes, as abruptly the tires left smoothness and hit gravel. Up beneath the car it came like a great wash of water, in a rush, then singularly, chip chip chip beneath the fenders, against the axle and sometimes the windshield. He went unnoticeably up until grass-filled ditches and fields where geese weeded were below and he travelled a levee. Small wild prim-roses were tangled in the grass on either side and bobwhites and mourning doves called unseen; back and forth across the road small blue titmice flitted. Poplar leaves shook in the wind, dark then quickly silver, and he listened to the steady thump of his tires and the random cracking of twigs. Long before arriving in any levee camp, he heard the same familiar noise, the broken grind-ing rhythm of the tractors that rocked him more than the rising and falling feel of the car as he fought the road. *Lordy* was a joy-ous song he sang, coming near where the Negroes worked. He was heralded by dust and those along the road turned to see who came, leaned on shovels, touched hats. Dynamite man coming, someone called and others waved. He flew on, waving back.

He found Will at the water barrel rack where Skinner, several others were filling their tractors with water. To hear one another, he and Will moved away from the pump's noise. Son was to see about draining an old borrow pit that was full of water. Will wanted dirt from it again. They walked toward it. As many mules as once had been on the levee, they had all had names. Not so many were left, but Son heard the Negroes' same cry, Come on, Daisy, Mildred! Get on, Bucky! Having seen the borrow pit, he stayed on the levee with Will, talking to Tangle-eye and others who would help him. Men filled tractors for the following day and left them; the trudge back to camp was beginning, the sun going down. Men, quitting, came along the levee carrying shovels, passed saying, Evenin' Cap'n. Will nodded, still talking to Son. Then, suddenly, like a dog at point, he simply froze; stared straight ahead, not a muscle moving, and was silent. Son turned to look in the same direction, seeing the figures coming shadowed against the sky, saw nothing amiss, wondered. He was almost on them before Son took in the slight variations in one figure among them, that he was not sweating enough to have been working, wore a shirt fairly clean, and the overalls were dusty only to the knees as if from trudging. After all these years, at least ten, Son thought, it could not be the same hat, but it was similar and flopped as it always had, in time to his loping stride. He stopped before Will and removed it.

"I come home, Cap'n," he said.

"You want a job?" Will said.

"Yes suh," he said.

"Be here in the morning," Will said.

He walked on down the levee, now toward camp, his hat flopping and a little heavier, otherwise looking against the setting sun exactly as he had the day he had walked off down it. Son wondered if Will would ask questions, heard afterward he never did. Sho Nuff told only that he had worked his way as far as New Orleans; the Depression years were bad ones and he had been out of work and hungry. That was why he came back, Son guessed, then correcting himself used the words Sho Nuff had: Come home.

It was a time when the night seemed magical, silver-sprayed, the moon was high. Martha came to supper laughing. Carrie had said the moonlight was in her secret parts; someone else would care for the baby; she had gone to camp to find a man. When Son came from supper, Emmie was digging outside the tent. "What in the world you looking for?" he said.

"Plantin', Mr. Frank," she said. "You got to plant a garden when the moon's high or you don't get good roots."

Sis Woman, far away in California, knew longing. Martha showed Son a letter she had just received. Miss Martha, I want to be in the woods where it's calm, Sis Woman had written. And the buds is in the trees. It's funny how you can get lost and somebody else got to help you find yourself. Son thought the old Negro knew just the right words. One thing he regretted was that it was through Lillian he had found what he wanted to do; he always would be sorry about that. Never had he found the self he was when he was not working; it was another reason, he guessed, he worked so hard. Maybe if you'd had some education you didn't have this feeling of being lost, standing still.

In the morning, Will said, "Boy, if you don't get that hair cut I'm going to get the other niggers to hold you while I get the mule shears and do it." Tangle-eye, Son, the other Negroes who would help him laughed at the younger one. Then Son said, "I don't see but one way to do it." He descended the bank, and as he entered the borrow pit a moccasin with evil eye slid from a log into the muck; he went on, hoping the Negroes had not seen. Ahead of him he pushed an opened box of dynamite; the Negroes, following, did the same. Son called, "Stick one, lay one long." Plop, his box went ahead in the muck. Like echoes, the boxes of the Negroes made the same sounds, plop, plop, and afterward the sluicing sound of their bodies. "Stick one, lay one long," Son called again. To the boy behind him, he said, "Seems like you all had some winter here."

"Whoo-ee," the boy said. "This one winter I wished I lived three pairs of pants farther south."

Laughing, Son said, "That cold'll toughen you up now. It's good for you."

At last, like divers rising strangely from the sea, they came out, dripping and muddy. "Stick one, lay one long," a Negro said. "Whew." The work went on for days. Son blew a section; it drained; when it was dry enough the tractors moved out dirt. Steadily they droned until Son was ready to shoot and a shout carried warning of danger. "Dynamite!" the Negro nearest Son called; the next in line repeated the single word. "Dynamite!' went the shout until someone close enough to those on tractors could make them hear; everyone sought shelter before the blast. No matter how many times they had seen it, they felt awe when the dull roar came and the dirt sprang into the air. Every time Son's heart quickened. He had come a long way since the first time he had come out to Mister Will's, a peddler, since the time he'd talked him into using dynamite and together they had found ways. The job was done. He was leaving and had walked up to Will on the levee to say goodbye when Sho Nuff, his hat flying, came shouting, "Boss! We out of water, we out of water!"

Son would remember always that he was already too far behind Will, running, to ever catch up when Sho Nuff stopped shouting. Like shears, Will's long legs parted and were together, quick as clipping. The pump had quit and the water barrels were almost empty; if the tractors could not run, the job would shut down.

Tangle-eye was trying to fix the pump. In rage, Will shouted, "Where's the water brigade?"

"I ain't started one, Cap'n. I been trying to fix the pump," Tangle-eye said.

"Barrels going dry while you're fixing the pump. Get water started into the barrels then fix the pump," Will said and cursed Tangle-eye again.

From all directions men came, bringing anything that would hold water. Son, grabbing an empty oil can, joined the line that reached to Indian Lake, shining in the distance. Tangle-eye continued work on the pump and Will, helping, still cursed. At last the pump, having sputtered and died repeatedly, sputtered and caught; a relief as if it had been breath itself that had ceased and then begun. They faced one another, Tangle-eye's bottom lip protruding. Helplessly, like a chicken beheaded, he fluttered his arms, waist high and down, again and again, slapping his thighs, mute and furious. Will, as equally furious, put his hand flat against Tangle-eye's bottom lip and pushed it up, flap flap flap, saying, "If you want to cuss me, say it. But don't stick that lip out at me."

Tangle-eye stuck it in, flapped his arms again in frustrated fury and went silently away. After supper Will, Carter and a new salesman, out of Helena, came to Son's tent to play Pitch. Son said, "Suppose he had cussed you, would you let him?"

Will said, "I told him he could. I would have had to let him. I reckon he knew better. But I still rather have a Negro cuss me, than stick out that bottom lip."

Son disliked the new salesman at first only because his face was covered as thickly with pimples as with prickly heat. Then he asked to see the cards after Carter shuffled. Son and Will said nothing, did not lift their eyes, not for the rest of the game: endured him knowing it was the first and last time. Will won the money and Son and Carter paid, but the salesman, saying he did not have enough cash, gave a check. When he went to his own tent, Will held up the check to tear it in two, saying he didn't think it was worth the paper it was written on. "I don't think so either,"

Son said, "but I'm not going to let him get away with it. Sell it to me at face value. I'm going into Helena tomorrow, I'll see if it's good." The next afternoon, he went to all the banks in Helena and the man had no account. He drove as a last resort to a little country bank on the edge of town and found it there, scratched out the name of the bank printed on the check and wrote in the correct one and cashed it. He drove on to Helen's Isle to meet Buzz who was finishing up a job he had been on for months. Buzz was in a box car, overseeing his equipment being loaded on the train; he was staying there to escape the crowd of salesmen waiting for him. They knew he had just been paid off after months of work. "I told one fellow I'd buy some equipment from him if he'd get rid of all them other pests," Buzz said.

Son looked out of the box car. "What the hell they doing?" he said. The salesmen, in a circle, were shouting and laughing and looking at something on the ground. Son and Buzz came up and saw it was one of the salesmen, a little fellow from Magnolia, Arkansas, referred to as a hothouse flower; pale and delicate. The salesman whom Buzz had told to get rid of the others had started with the little fellow, telling him to leave or he'd whip him. To the amazement of all, the little fellow stretched out flat on the levee bank. Now the other salesman was walking around trying to make him get up. He circled him one way, then the other, occasionally nudging him with the toe of his shoe. "Get up, Goddamn it!" he shouted.

"Naw," the little man said, turning his head to look up, his cheek cradled in one palm. "If I get up you'll just knock me down."

He was still lying there when Son and Buzz started to Delton, laughing. Son guessed they laughed all the way. When he got home his sides ached. He tried to tell Kate about the little fellow, about cashing the man's check, about Mister Will standing there flapping that Negro's lip in. She didn't think any of it was funny; why did he think everything rough so funny? He guessed she didn't understand either when that fellow whose check he cashed called the next night to say if he ever came in his county again he'd beat him.

Son had been in bed reading a detective magazine. He put his feet to the floor and said he could start for Helena again right then. Kate, putting down her knitting, said, "Frank, are you crazy?"

He said into the phone, "Hell yeah, I like to fight. I'd fight a circle saw if I had the chance. My wife hasn't even unpacked my grip. Where am I going to meet you? Oh, you want to apologize?" He listened; then he slammed down the phone. "Hell," he said and got into bed, "he would have to change his mind."

Coming in, Laurel said, "Look, Daddy."

"What's that all about?" he said.

"My first evening dress," she said. "To play in my piano recital."

"Some other damn thing to spend money on," he said.

"Why, Frank," Kate said. "You ought to be ashamed." She got up and followed Laurel, who had gone. Well when he was twelve years old, he wasn't thinking up ways to spend money, he was out making some. And he didn't let up on Kate about bills, even though that summer his long-ago prediction came true; he looked back fifteen years to the night he had made it, sitting alone in that hotel room. For a long time now he thought he had seen it coming. All spring driving into dawn and at dusk up to some little hotel in some burg, he had thought: soon. Often he was so tired he hoped not to see anybody he knew, ate supper alone and went to bed. But coming into big places, Vicksburg, Helena, Little Rock, walking into a lobby, dropping his grip and registering, he always saw a familiar face or was called by a voice he knew, Hey, Dynamite! Many times, tired as he was, he was happy to break a long day's silence, to have something to listen to besides the radio, even to hear his own voice after hours of disuse, dry with that, with dust. But he would give nothing for those fifteen years, wanted to remember too the times he had thought he was too tired to make it, could barely drag that grip out of the car and across the hotel lobby or into his own house. There were compensations, travelling out of starry, insect-sounding southern nights and into the warmth of the little lobbies, smelling always of age and old magazines and carpets and polished wood and tobacco-stained old men who passed time greeting strangers; Hidy or Evening, they always said. And to himself he had said, Someday. Lately, he had said, Soon: because there was nowhere he could go they weren't expecting him, having thought when they thought of dynamite of Dynamite Wynn. If there was any business he wasn't getting, it must be so small he didn't even want it, knowing there was not any; he had it all. So that maybe he was not even surprised when, coming into Delton one evening, he stopped by Mr. Ryder's house and his wife came out in old felt bedroom slippers to greet him and behind her Mr. Ryder stood grinning shyly and said, "I don't have but the one telephone in my house any more, Mr. Wynn. They taken out the two others today."

"You mean I've finally run out the big boys too?" he said, simulating surprise.

Mr. Ryder seemed close to tears as if it were a long climb they had made together. Son stuck his nose into the glass of beer they had given him and for a moment could not look up. Mrs. Ryder said, "Could you take some supper with us, Mr. Wynn?"

"Much obliged," he said. "I hope you'll give me a rain check but I been gone two weeks and I promised to take my wife out when I got home." They never offered him a second beer; being Baptist, it was the only time Mr. Ryder drank at all. Mrs. Ryder kept two beers, in case Mr. Wynn came; when they were gone, she bought two more. He put down his empty glass and Mr. Ryder followed him to the car. Going out, Son thought back to when Mr. Ryder had met him with a team of mules and how this had been country; now it was part of Delton, just a street of little bungalows and street lamps at intervals; it could have been anywhere. As Delton had spread, he had twice had to move his dynamite magazine farther, by law having to have it so many miles from the city limits. Mr. Ryder bent to the car window; his voice seemed more frail, his eyes again seemed moist. Son thought the beer might have gotten to the old man, but he put his hand through the window and said, "Mr. Wynn, you been a fine fair man to work for all these years."

Son took his hand and himself felt the need to swallow. "Hell," he said. "If you'd a got shot up in Cai-ro, I might not have made it either. You've eat up as much dust as I have, I appreciate it."

Mr. Ryder let go of his hand and abruptly went into the house.

Coming into the living room after dinner, Kate twirled in her new dress.

"Damn, if you don't look like a dressed-up whore," he said.

"Frank, I swear, is that all you can say?" she said.

"Hell," he said, "that's a compliment."

They were meeting Will and Martha, Buzz and his wife and a few other couples. After taking Laurel to spend the night with a friend, they drove to a club at the edge of the city. Its name was spelled in blue lights that cast a dim and eerie glow over the parking lot. Inside it was almost as dark; above the dance floor a glass chandelier whirled, casting vari-colored light like flecks of rainbow. When he got ready to drink, Son peered closely at the bottles on the table. Will drank Scotch; he did not want to get hold of any of that stuff by mistake. He danced once around the floor, pushing Kate backward as if she were a carton he were moving, then danced no more. Kate said it was all right with her, announcing he couldn't tell the difference between Yankee Doodle and Dixie. Buzz's wife did not dance either. But Buzz once had won a contest proclaiming him "The Vernon Castle of Hernando County." Watching them, Son suddenly wondered why Kate had to buy that dress at all; she had some dresses. But he thought she was a good-looking woman still, had not started to fatten up on him like a lot of the wives; he never had liked a woman with too much meat on her.

It was toward midnight, coming back from the men's room, he saw a couple of fellows go out a side door and in a direction opposite from the parking lot, knew as well as he knew his own name where they were going. Buzz always said he could sniff out a game like a hound a coon; he guessed so. He gave a waiter a dollar, asking where it was, and the boy told. Taking his bottle, he went to the back of the building and into the basement. He did not have any idea how long he had been there when he quit, a winner, and came out as the night was ending; birds sang in the woods beyond as he stumbled along the path back to the eerie, blue-lit parking lot and finally found his car. He followed one narrow road from the club, through woods, until it ended at the highway back to Delton, almost a straight shoot to his front door. At this hour, free of traffic, the road was revealed beneath a pale grey, pre-dawn sky, and he drove slowly, knowing his condition. To the open sky and the open road ahead he said suddenly, I did it. Goddamn the big boys too! Inexplicably tears came to his eyes; he brushed the palm of his hand against them, turning too shortly into his drive, bumping one wheel over the curb and blaming the mistake on the amount of whisky he had drunk. Going into his own house, he shut the door hard, locking himself in, and shouted, "I got a right to get drunk if I want to," and waited for an answer that never came. "I got ever right in the world," he shouted loudly, thinking, any man had done what he had. Immediately, he fell into heavy sleep and the persistent shrill ringing of the door bell sometime later seemed part of that sleep until at last, opening his eyes, he heard the ringing consciously. A moment he lay looking at daylight on the ceiling, his brain twirling as the glass chandelier had, until he realized where he was. He went to a front window, opened it and yelled, "What the hell you doing waking me up this time of night?"

"What the hell you doing going off and leaving your wife?" Buzz yelled back.

"I don't even know what you're talking about," Son said.

"He's talking about me," Kate said. "Hush and open the door before you wake up the neighbors."

"I don't give any Goddamn about the neighbors."

"Open the door," Kate said.

"Open the door you old drunk," Buzz said.

"Who's drunk?" Son said.

"Open the door," Buzz said.

"Open the door," Kate said.

"Keep your shirt on," he said, turning the lock.

"You ought to have a punch in the nose," Buzz said.

"You want to try to give it to me," Son said.

"What'd you want to go off and leave Kate for?" Buzz said.

"Hell, I didn't leave her," he said. "I forgot she was there."

Kate slept in Laurel's room. He had to have a couple of drinks to fall asleep again and when he woke was starving. He waited for Kate to fix breakfast and had to have a couple of drinks because of the way he felt. Ahead was the open road and the white dawn and the best friend he had wanting to punch him in the nose; against Buzz he could not have defended himself and he cried, Buzz! Ohhh Buzz . . .

"Frank, will you hush," Kate said, opening the door. "You been in here drunk, hollering, four days."

He turned on the tumbled, whisky-smelling sheets and said, "I'm just waiting for my breakfast."

"I offered you breakfast two hours ago," she said. "You wouldn't eat any."

"What day is this?" he said.

"Thursday," she said.

"Hell, I thought it was Sunday," he said.

"It was Sunday after we came home from that nightclub and you haven't been out of here since." She went to the windows and let up shades, stabbing him with light. He felt as if he were on a merry-go-round; everything in the room went either up or down; in the bathroom he was sick. He looked into the mirror and saw his eyes were the same color, stared at a face he hardly recognized, covered with a beard he saw for the first time was tinged with grey. "Hell, I've got to be a ooo-ld man," he said. "I might have to have a drink to that."

"No, you're not," Kate said. He came back into the bedroom as she was changing his sheets. "You've got to get away from the house. Laurel and I are about to suffocate. I've had to keep the windows down so the neighbors won't think you've gone stark, raving mad. Laurel says she's going to run away from home and I wouldn't blame her."

He was so weak Kate had to help him dress. There was something the matter with his stomach he said; but he thought he could eat a steak. He went into the living room where Laurel was playing the piano. An instant he put his arms around her and tears rolled down his face. "Your mammy says you want to run away from home. You wouldn't leave me, would you?"

"No," she said. He went on out and Kate came saying, "He's really had the wind taken out of his sails, hasn't he?" Laurel watched them get into the car. It was the first time she could remember his ever letting Kate drive. He sat hunched and pale on the front seat; she watched them out of the drive, turned back to the house lonely and began to play again, thinking of the place she would go when she was grown where nothing would hurt.

I T WAS DONE. BY THE EARLY FORTIES THE LEVEE STRETCHED, unbroken, from Cairo to New Orleans. Son termed what began then "the second go-round." For the next ten years their work would be enlarging, rehabilitating, reinforcing work already done: clearing and grubbing, clearing borrow pits, making roads, draining swampland. The Engineers would widen, deepen and change the river's channels, making more cut-offs, until the Mississippi River would flow the way men wanted it to, not the way it was intended. They would need as much dynamite as ever, if not more, Son said.

Old Red Johnson warned still, the last time Son saw him, that the river could still win. No matter what we do, he said, the big flood can still come. A few days later, Shut-eye went to wake him and could not. Some years before he had moved back into the house but had kept the levee tent always. From all over the territory familiar to Son, men came to Red's funeral. He was old times gone, even to the young men. Negroes he had known stood behind his white friends; hats in hands, everyone looked freshly scrubbed. Walking away behind Will, Son noticed a pinched old man's look to the back of his neck, a faint hesitancy to his walk, and thought, We're the old timers; no work anyone here would do again would be as hard as the work they had already done. They had come a long way together and had not too much farther to go.

The final big section of work was to be let in Little Rock after Red's funeral; once only small jobs were left, people would not drive from all over the territory to lettings. But everyone had come to this because it was the last. Son saw even the hothouse flower. After supper, entering the hotel lobby, he got on the elevator with Son, Buzz, Winston and Will who were heading for a game on the top floor. No one wanted to when the elevator boy asked if they wanted to meet a girl, until the little fellow got off; then Winston gave the boy money, told him to send a girl to the little fellow's room; he had been too shy to ask. Son gave him another bill. "Get that big Rosie you got," he said describing roundly with his hands; the girls belonged to a chain of hotels spread across the state, moved from one to another, were known to all the men whether well or not. As they got off, a Little Rock contractor with a hotel girl went into the room next to theirs. Shortly after the game started, Buzz telephoned the room. "Desk Clerk, sir," he said. "Your wife got into the elevator and is on her way up." They listened to thumps in the next room as if people hurried; the door opened, heels crossed the doorsill, a woman brushed by. Laughing, they went back to the game. Son regretted these good times soon being over.

The next day it rained. Impatiently he waited in the lobby for the bids to be in. The major work being let was in East Tennessee, involved rock blasting and quarry work, things with which he was unfamiliar. A dynamite salesman from that part of the state had come to the letting, told Son he expected to get some of the business, his speciality. Son said that was mighty fine, wondering who he was going to get it from; but having a little competition made him feel like a young man again, he said. From the way Buzz burst into the lobby, Son knew he had won the big job which put him in the big time. Everyone said so, congratulating Buzz, began to woo him buying drinks. Son, having a bar in his room, had little time to circulate. It was almost daylight when the crowd thinned out and Winston, coming in, said he heard Buzz had bought some dynamite from the other salesman. What motivated him, Son called his juice; he felt it boil. "Boy, don't come in here with no tales," he said.

"That's just what I heard," Winston said. "I carry rumors too."

Everywhere Son went looking for Buzz, he heard it was true. People tried to tell him Buzz was too drunk to know. Son said it didn't make any difference; even full of bug juice he didn't expect his best friend to do him thataway. He was madder than ever, circling back, to find Buzz in his own room. He had already made plans, had ordered a hundred pounds of crushed ice dumped into his bathtub. He stripped Buzz to his underwear and put him in. Before Buzz could yell, before he could even flail ice, Son had him face up under the running faucet, ducked him under again and again. Struggling, now flailing ice everywhere, Buzz realized in a deep layer of consciousness he was truly about to drown; only as he began to lose consciousness did Son let him out. Shivering, Buzz said, "Jesus Christ, you like to drowned me."

"You ought to," Son said. Dried, wrapped in a towel, Buzz went into his connecting room to bed; all night he sank gloriously into darkness, told at breakfast he had had the most beautiful, wonderful dreams he had ever had in his life, in color; then, in amazement said again, "That old man really like to drowned me."

Two things happened after the letting. On his way home, a salesman Son knew had a heart attack, pulled to the side of the road and was found by a stranger. What Son remembered most was that after lettings the old man toured cemeteries copying names off gravestones to put on his expense account. Son had a drink to him feeling sorry about the old man dying out on the road like that, just a salesman all his life.

Secondly, he received a letter from Shut-eye who had told him at Red's funeral he was coming to the letting. The letter said he had started out but could not make it: the roads were tore to pieces. But I would like to have see your loving face. I got stalded on the road. My heart got full and I feel like I want to shout. Be a good man till I sees you again if life lastes. In one corner it was signed with an x; in the opposite corner it read, Dictated but not read over. Son thought someday he was going to stop over in East Delton and see the old man; he lived there in his own house, well provided for by Red's will.

Still it rained and still he rose with dawn and was on the road when daylight came. He crossed Tennessee to Buzz's job, going through gutted red hills and on into pretty mountainous country thick with trees. As if it were a gift, he carried the joyful news that he had been invited to join the Shriners, something he had long wanted; it gave him a good feeling, belonging. He wanted as quickly as possible to buy a diamond lapel pin of the Shriners' symbol, to put Buzz up for membership. The white men on Buzz's job were staying at the same motel. For three days while it rained, they played cards, at night ate in the nearest town's one cafe. There was a waitress there Son got to know pretty quick.

The fourth morning was a grey still day, cool for the time of year. Everyone came to breakfast in tight pants and boots to their knees. Would the Negroes show up? Buzz said, "I told them to the first morning it quit raining if it went on forty days and nights." As the men went to work, the sun came out, at first like a winter sun in some far north place, wispy and moon-white, its edges mingled fuzzily into the pearlized sky. Meeting, the workers spoke unconsciously in lowered voices, realizing only when the sun grew stronger they had felt themselves in someplace mysterious. They were used to heat, trusted it; as the sun grew stronger, the dirt warmed and the smell of ragweed drying overpowered the smell of everything else green and growing. With fifteen Negroes, Son started across a field single file, each man with a box of dynamite on his shoulders. At an old drainage ditch, now full of water, they could not cross, set down their boxes to search until someone found a log long enough to reach, and they started across, one by one. Halfway Son slipped, felt the dynamite box glance off his leg, falling behind him. He came up cursing, waded out pushing the box and laughing, not at himself but at sight of those dark faces and widened eyes peering down at him, the Negroes afraid to laugh until he did. They helped him; one carried the dynamite box and another said, "I seen one foot slip, I know Cap'n going," another said, "Splash." Along the line laughter passed again; they went on and Son spent most of the day working in damp clothes.

The following morning they began blasting. One of the hardest things he found about rock blasting was the white silt afterward.

214

More than anyone, he seemed choked by dust as if his lungs could not get enough air. Dusted white, all the men stared out of round-looking eyes. Even in Son's ears the word rang excessively all day long; others said afterward they hardly remembered anything else about the day: Dynamite! Hardly had the sound of the blast receded, the smoke cleared when the word came again and then again, Dynamite! Dynamite! Dynamite!

At six o'clock that evening the Negroes gathered about him, quit. "You boys know how much powder we shot up today?" Son said. "Two tons and a hun'ert pounds. Eighty-two cases. That's the most dynamite I ever shot in a single day and I been shooting it a long time." Everyone went home talking of the large amount. At the motel Son told them to wash up; he was buying everybody a steak. He had to celebrate. They had gathered back in his room, having changed, and had started celebrating when a knock came at the door. Over the noise no one heard it until it had come again and again; then Buzz, the closest, threw open the door, about to shout greetings, and hushed instead. They all hushed seeing the white-haired woman in the doorway, one arm in a huge bandage. "Who's the fellow shooting that dynamite off that's blowed windows out all over town?" she said.

"Phew," Son said, sinking to the bed, his head fell forward but he could not help laughing, on top of whatever was to come; those eighty-two empty cases had put him there. The woman held up her arm. "I reached up to pull down my window shade and the whole glass fell out on me. I been at the doctor's hours getting splinters picked out. He's sending you the bill."

Son stood. "I was in the limits of the law where I was doing that blasting at," he said. "If the concussion got carried into town, that's the wind, and I'm not about to be responsible for the wind."

"All I know is, the bank's wall got a crack and more windows than mine fell out," she said.

Son said he reckoned he'd be seeing her in court. He took everyone out to eat steak anyway, the only difference being he did not ask the waitress to go out afterward, his mind on business now. He stayed on in East Tennessee until the case came to court. An Act of God, the wind, was responsible. Having won, he came out of court to tell the woman he was sorry as could be about what had happened, and he'd pay half her doctor's bill.

All the way back to Delton the sun was in his eyes. At home, Kate put drops in them and fixed cold compresses. Why in the world didn't he wear sunglasses? she said. He never had thought about it, he said; hell, when he was twenty-five years old the sun didn't bother his eyes. She said, Frank, I swear. Several days later he faced the sun again starting out to Will's, stopped and bought dark glasses, though it seemed as if he were giving in to something he should not be. His way of thinking had always been if you were cold, you were supposed to be, if you were hot stay that way, if the sun was in your eyes, make the best of it. But the glasses helped. Driving into Will's new camp he noticed it was set up in a grove of trees which Martha had long begged for; but Will chose a spot closest to the road, not for comfort. "The old man getting weak in his old age?" Son said, walking into the commissary. "How'd you talk him into settin' up in the shade?" Martha laughed. "Luck. This pecan grove just happened to be close enough to the road to get in and out when the weather's bad."

Word had reached Delton of Greaser's death. Son said, "I sure was surprised to hear about that big strong buck just dying that-away."

"Frank, it like to killed Will. He hardly spoke to anybody for three days. Greaser had been with him always; we didn't even know he had any other family but we located a sister down in Mississippi and took him all the way down there to be buried. Will just sat rigid during the funeral. I knew he wanted to bawl. Greaser was driving his tractor. Will said he pulled up to him, started to say something, then just fell off dead. The doctor said his heart must have been bad a long time; not even Greaser knew it."

"Forty-six years old too," Son said. It brought death closer. "I reckon it could happen to any of us." Several Negro women waiting said in wonder and agreement, Um-*mmm*. A crowd of Negroes entered to shop and Son went out as Tangle-eye passed. "Boy, I finally remembered to bring you them shirts I promised," he said, handing him a sackful.

Tangle-eye, removing his hat, grinned. "I thank you," he said. Looking inside, he brought out a white shirt with whiter stripes. "I'm going to wear this here one to get married."

"Tangle-eye, you ain't gettin' no married," Son said.

"Yes suh, Sis Woman come back from California and ketch me." Proudly, he took from his pocket a round metal disc and handed it to Son. "What's that all about?" Son said.

"I got the license," Tangle-eye said. "Preacher sells 'em to us for a dollar and it's two up at the co'thouse."

Giving it back, Son said, "Well, that's mighty fine."

"Yes suh." Tangle-eye, clapping on his hat, went away.

At supper, Son said, "How long that preacher been selling them old dog licenses to get married on?"

"Long as I can remember," Will said. "He buys them up at the end of every year. Gets by with it as long as the Negroes can't read."

Son dared speak of Greaser. "Did cocaine kill him?"

"No sir," Will said, and Son felt that sudden rigidity too; Will's hands lay perfectly still on the table; then, as if deciding he would someday have to speak his friend's name, he said, "Almost all the boys I've known on the levee take cocaine but I've never known a one become an addict; they work too hard, sweat too much, I believe. Greaser had a packet on him when he died, like the doctor out in town sells them; but it's half ground-up chalk. It's white powder, that's all the Negroes know."

It was time for him to start trying to catch up on his rest, Son said then. He was going to do a lot of advising, let the contractors have their own men do the actual work. For the second year, he and Will had tried to stabilize a bank where the river curved; each time after the June rise, it began to wash away. "Think it will again next year?" Will said as Son was leaving the next day.

"Well, if it does, I'll be back," Son said. "There it'nt anything we haven't figured out yet, Mr. Will." He drove home hurriedly, two things on his mind. A teacher had suggested Laurel be sent to a private school; she could continue music for which she had a talent and she had made a high grade on some kind of test—he didn't know what that was all about—but she needed a smaller place; she was so quiet, shy, even fearful, the teacher thought. He guessed he never had paid much attention to Laurel; he had left her bringing up to Kate and maybe that had been a mistake. He thought Laurel was going to turn out exactly like her; all the time she had her nose stuck in some book. She had been a pretty little girl and he thought her still pretty, though she just stood around too much biting her fingernails; he told Kate so and she said well, they both had inferiority complexes and she guessed Laurel did too. If anybody had asked him he probably would have said Laurel looked just like her mother. Many people thought so but just as many thought she looked like Son; somehow she was an exact cross between the two; her skin was not as dark as his but darker than Kate's; when she wore certain colors her eyes looked blue but at other times they were hazel, closer to Kate's dark eyes; sometimes they seemed even to have flecks of yellow. Her hair had never been the color of sunlight, like Kate's, but it was blonde, almost as dark as Son's. Something about the smallness of her face helped to make her seem so shy.

Driving, he decided she could go to the school. He didn't mind putting his money out for education: maybe it would keep her from making any mistakes. The second thing on his mind was buying a house. He had always been going to buy a big pretty house when he could. For the past several Sundays the three of them had driven around looking. For the first time, he felt he knew the city as well as he knew the country roads surrounding it. He liked a large one-story house set at the end of a circular drive, out from the city. Kate said they would never see anybody living way out there; he said he saw enough folks. When he decided to buy the house, Kate said she hoped he'd have the gravel drive paved; it would ruin the tires and every pair of shoes she had. He said he wanted it gravel, to remind himself of all the country roads he'd been over. To celebrate buying the house, they went downtown to eat and to see a picture show. It was a war picture with a long printed explanation of what all the shooting was about; whispering, he said, Why didn't they make the writing in picture shows big enough to read? They do, Kate said. Can't you read it? He shook his head and she said he needed glasses.

That was something to think about the rest of the show. Monday morning he went to see Willard Owens who had grown up in Mill's Landing and gotten to be big stuff as an eye doctor, Kate said; she saw his name in the newspaper all the time. Son found him about the same. Sitting in the dark cubicle, the pinpoint of light probing his eyes, he and Willard talked about how far they had come, to have started out country boys. Willard's mother still lived near Mill's Landing; occasionally he went back. The mill had burned fifteen years ago and now the Rankins farmed the land; the two rows of houses and the commissary stood, for the tenants.

Willard said Son did need glasses, mostly for seeing at a distance. Since Son was on the road so much, Willard prescribed a pair slightly tinted. On another floor Son picked out rimless gold frames, then crossing the building's lobby, on impulse, went into a photographer's studio where he was fitted in without an appointment. His proofs would be ready the same day as his glasses, and he kept the pictures a secret. From then on he divided his life into two parts, before he wore glasses and after. When he arrived at home in them, the proofs in a brown envelope, Kate exclaimed over both; they were the best pictures she had ever seen anyone have taken. She had one enlarged and put in a heavy gold frame. Eventually, in the new house, she put it on a long table in the entrance hall. When anyone came, Son would say, "See that. That was taken when I was still a young man, before I put on spectacles and got old." He would laugh, explaining. If he wore the glasses for a long stretch of time, they left a red mark across his nose. Kate finally accepted that mark as part of him; a long time she urged him to have the glasses readjusted; he said it wasn't worth bothering the man about.

He told Kate he didn't know a thing in this world about what you needed to make a house look pretty but get what she needed, within reason, and don't ask him any questions; he'd pay the bills. On moving day Kate was awakened at six o'clock and looking out saw two Negro boys directing Mr. Ryder up the driveway in the dynamite truck. "Ye Gods and little fishes," she said as Son got up, "is that how we're going to move?" He hadn't seen any sense hiring a truck when he had one, he said. What's the matter?

Didn't he know anything about the way other people did things? she said. He didn't care what the other fellow did, he said, he did the way he wanted to.

That's just the trouble, Kate said.

Loaded, the truck pulled away from the house about noon. He followed in his car and Kate and Laurel in hers, piled high with things Kate had been afraid for the Negroes to touch. He told her she looked like an okie pulling up; he could always get her goat telling her she looked as if she had just come from the country; she couldn't get over the fact that once she had.

Kate said she never had expected to have such a pretty house, and thought maybe in it, things would be different. She had an opportunity to buy some of the nice things she had always wanted; but having to make so many decisions alone made her nervous. Only a drink made her able to face painters, rug salesmen, furniture stores without qualms. On New Year's Eve they invited almost everyone they knew to a party, to see the new house. Ever since they had been married, he had started celebrating New Year's Eve and Christmas Eve at the office; they always went to parties on those nights and always came home in an argument; the holidays had long been ones Laurel dreaded. This year Kate begged him not to start celebrating until the party began. He did not mean to. He had had only a couple of drinks and was leaving for home when the phone rang. It was two contractors he had kept in business, lending them money during the Depression. Mr. Will, nobody else liked him doing it; they thought these two were unreliable, dishonest and gave contracting a bad name; to Son it had been a business deal. But he liked the fellows too, thought others didn't because they had both started at the bottom, way down, driving bulldozers. They had gone to Oklahoma some years ago, told him when he met them down at the Andrew Johnson, they had become millionaires. He tried to tell Kate that, arriving home. She only burst into tears and said he had ruined the night again. She went into the kitchen and had a drink herself, thinking that was one way she could get back at him, match him. And it would help her to relax, face the party alone; he had to go to bed and slept halfway through it.

220

That night Kate slept in the extra bedroom again. It had always been her habit to go there when she could not sleep, when she was mad; she had begun to leave things there, her night cream, hair net, a night gown and robe in the closet. Gradually she moved altogether. His snoring kept her awake, she said.

The time was longer each year before Mr. Wynn came back after the holidays, Mr. Ryder told his wife. This year was the longest of all.

The war had begun but would change little about Son's business. Government work continued on the levee and farmers were more important than ever. He had a "C" card, as much gas as he wanted, did not travel as much because he no longer intended to. He had always been working toward the time when he did not have to work so hard. And that time had come. But for the third year he went back to Will's river curve. Will added cement to the dirt, having no more clay, the binder; they built a dike of dirt out in the river itself and had no more trouble. It was pay day when they came back to camp. Son saw Carter sitting outside at a table with a ledger. Negroes, coming out of the back of the commissary, stopped beside him.

Before Son could ask, Will said, "Mrs. Roosevelt again." Since she had started seeing about the underprivileged Negroes in the South, he had become a Republican. The law passed the contractors called Eleanor's: a boss could no longer take what a Negro owed out of his pay; he had to receive his salary in full in a sealed envelope. Will pointed out the Army Engineer corpsman in camp to see the law was followed. Son said, "You mean the Negroes walk in the front door, get their pay, walk out the back, open it and pay Carter?"

"That's right," Will said. "What would you do?"

"Lord, the same," Son said. Their eyes met and they laughed; there seemed always a comical side, despite everything.

By the war's end, Negroes working on the levee were making from eighty to a hundred and fifty dollars a week. Commissary prices were high but tent prices remained always the same; electricity costs were fifty cents a month for each appliance; everything that could be kept low was and medicine that most of the Negroes needed was free; regularly the mobile unit arrived, preceded by individual cards of notification. Always, Martha would exclaim in exhaustion, putting up mail, they come the same day as the Sears catalogues! Son urged the Negroes he knew to save; they were making good money now, he said. Still every Monday, after pay day on Friday, there was a line of Negroes at the commissary wanting to borrow money and Will always lent it.

In the South there was no labor union for levee workers. "Union country," Will described it, "is past the mouth of the Ohio." But the labor leaders were working south slowly. Son was in Cape Girardeau when men came on the levee, trying to force Negroes to join; when they refused, the men, having rifles, ran them off the job. Many Negroes stayed away, many came further south to safety. These days, Martha told Son, they were wary of strangers, though there was one kind you could always recognize. If a man in a black suit, carrying a suitcase, got off a train and asked for the Unity Church, you knew he was in town to teach the Negroes Communism. Mind over matter, the church taught. Its motto: The Brotherhood of Man over Fatherhood. It was some time after Son returned from Cape Girardeau before the labor leaders got to his part of the country. In a town near Will's camp there was a meeting at the Labor Temple; afterward several of the leaders were drinking in a cafe and talking about going to the levee camp and taking over, having had no cooperation. The cafe's owner telephoned Will and told him they were on their way. When the car drove into camp with three strange men Will knew exactly who it was. He made Son wait in his tent; he was close enough to hear, to come if Will needed him. Will said he was scared but he was going to have to run their bluff. Again, it struck Son: you couldn't afford fear. A man getting out of the car told Will they had come to take over camp. Son saw Will pull himself to his tallest. "You better bring more than three if you want to take over," he said.

"I'm telling you again, Carrothers, if your Negroes aren't going to join our union, you've got to hire our union men," the man said.

"I've got all the men I need," Will said.

"You got to get rid of them."

"Are your men trained?" Will said.

"You bet your boots."

"Your union men are all Northerners. Are they all white men?" Will said.

"Yes sir, they're all white men," the man said.

"So," Will said. "You want me to hire your white men. And you want me to fire my Negroes." He stuck his hands in his pockets and put his face close to the man's. "Mister," he said, "if you don't clear out of here, I'm going to wire Mrs. Roosevelt."

The man got back in his car and slammed the door so hard, Son thought he heard glass crack. After a final curse, a threat of return, he drove away fast and only an instant Son and Will saw the red tail light bobbing away. "You reckon he'll be back?" Son said.

"I don't think it's likely. They've found out we down here don't scare," Will said.

Son drove home, his scorn for Yankees deepened. But something underlay that, a sense of age. Often now, driving along, he thought back, something he had never expected to do, and it seemed he had a lot to look back over; everywhere now he saw boys in uniform, about to go off to war, who looked like kids. He wished there was something he could do for them. He had been kidded to death about something that happened in the grill at the Andrew Johnson; a table full of young sailors had asked him to buy them a beer. For several hours he was there eating and ordered round after round; the boys came to his table and picked up the bottles. Leaving, he was happy to pay the bill, almost fifteen dollars. He stopped to say goodbye and the boys pressed money on him, explaining. They had plenty of money but were not old enough to order beer. Son laughed at himself and waved their money away. It was something he could do.

During the second year of the war, Mr. Ryder had a heart attack. Mrs. Ryder phoned to say he was hospitalized though it did not seem serious. But he had a truck load of dynamite to drive in the morning; twenty-four hours' notice had to be given to ship by train, a box car specially inspected and placed in the middle. Son saw nothing to do but drive the order himself, said he guessed he wasn't ever going to get any rest. At daybreak, he left his car at Mr. Ryder's and picked up the truck. The way to the magazine was the same, though now the highway was lined with motels and ice cream stands and, leaving pavement, he travelled a smoothed gravel road. The Negro cabin still stood, though long abandoned; he thought of all the years the little boy had greeted him, swung wide on the gate, how he had raised him to a dime each way. Having closed the gate, he drove on through the silent winding country, remembering the first time Mr. Ryder brought him, with a team of mules, to see a stick of dynamite. He sure had learned a lot about business since that time; the business had changed and he wondered if he had.

Negroes met him to load the truck; he filled an empty case with sawdust and buried in it several boxes of caps and fuse wrapped in newspaper, placed it on the floor of the cab and covered it with an old piece of tarpaulin. Frequently, this way, they managed to have their caps and fuse arrive with the dynamite, and when he drove boxes of dynamite in the trunk of his car, he still threw caps and fuse in the back seat. If the truck was stopped for any reason, no one thought of looking for anything under the old piece of floor covering.

Sitting forward, his arms hugging the wheel, his foot to the accelerator, grinning through the windshield of his big red truck, he sped off down the highway. Past lunchtime he found a restaurant where he could stop, away from any congested area. It turned out to have the best barley soup he had ever eaten; he had two bowlfuls and drove on he guessed too full and happy because he drove through the next town when he was supposed to always go around them. Arrested, he was told to come to the courthouse and pay his fine. He would have to have the dynamite unloaded first; the policeman followed him where he was going. The man he was to meet and his Negroes were not there. Son said, "Well, if you want me to pay that fine it looks like you're going to have to unload the truck. I'm sure not going to."

The policeman, though young, was still winded when they came out of the courthouse some time later. "Much obliged," Son said again, touching his hat, and drove away.

The farmer he met had been told by the Drainage Engineers what kind of ditch he had to have, how wide and deep. He said, "Mr. Wynn, do I need a ditch that big?"

Son said, "You going to pay for it or the county?"

"I am," the old man said.

"All of it?"

"Yes, sir," he said.

"Hell naw, you don't need a ditch that big." Son shot it the way he saw it, saving the man a lot of money. A few days later, as he had expected, he received a letter from the Engineers' design department saying it was the last Government work he'd have in that county. Tearing up the letter, Son said he never had been in the position of making money off an old man who didn't have any and the ditch he gave him would do the job.

He had felt good about the ditch when he drove off that day; he stopped for lunch at Cecilia's and was glad to see her but the house was too full of women for him; there were four girls now. Early and comfortably, Cecilia had slipped into middle-age. As a young woman she had been gaunt, but having filled out now, she had begun to resemble Cally. Her hair had long been grey and she wore it the same way Cally had, skinned back as Lillian had always said, and in a knot at the nape of her neck. Kate said her hair would look so pretty with a blue rinse but Cecilia said she had always been plain and was used to it; she could not imagine trying to fancy herself up. But when she smiled, Son thought, she actually looked pretty; she had the same dark skin that he did and though she wore no make-up she did not look sallow, as Cally had. Soon after eating, Son drove on to Clay to meet Winston for supper. Walking into the restaurant, he sensed right away a game was going on in back; but Winston would not let him go near; said the Sheriff was playing and he was a plain artist with the dice; besides that, he was the only one who stayed sober and always cleaned up. Though drinks were sold people often had their own bottles; just trying to be a big shot,

Winston said about the Sheriff's deputy who came out of the back room and told them they couldn't have whisky on the table; he was going to have to confiscate it. With one accord, Son and Winston stood up. The fact that boy wanted the whisky for himself was plain as day and they told him if they couldn't have it, he wasn't: walked out of the restaurant and emptied two fifths into the gutter. Son said it was worth watching them two fifths of Old Granddad wasted just to see that boy's face, watching too. On the way to Winston's they bought more. Waking the next morning, Son knew the time had passed when he could go like he use to and get up in the morning. "I'm just not twenty-five years old anymore," he said.

Winston suggested hair of the dog but Son said he wasn't starting out on the road with whisky on his breath, even if his truck was empty. It was late afternoon when he drove into Mr. Ryder's. He had a funny feeling arriving without welcome, without Mrs. Ryder coming forward in her old felt slippers to meet him, Mr. Ryder trying to hide his pleasure. With age, Mr. Ryder's voice had become even softer, had a faint, far away sound. Son could hear now the way he said, Mr. Wynn, with a dropping of the final sound. The house was dark and he knew they were at the hospital. At home he would not take a drink, tired as he was, not wanting to visit the old man smelling of it. But when he and Kate went to the hospital Mr. Ryder was under sedation, had had a more serious attack in the hospital. Son did not think he looked good at all; there was something to the slack, pale face, a touch of old-age pink to his cheeks, that reminded him of Poppa's face the morning he had found him in a coma, near death; so that maybe he was already as prepared as he was ever going to get when Mr. Ryder's nephew phoned at seven o'clock the next morning to tell him the old man had passed away; slept on beyond them, Mrs. Ryder said.

He began to drink the afternoon before the funeral; when it was time, he could not go; Kate would have to. When he could, he went to see Mrs. Ryder. Hat in hand, he came into the living room and said, "Mrs. Ryder, I just couldn't make it to the funeral because . . ."

She said, "That's all right."

He said, "I couldn't make it."

She said, "That's all right."

He said, "I'm just as sorry as I can be."

"I know that," she said.

He was sorry about everything, sorry he had caused so much hell. The only way he got over it was that Kate took him to a sanatarium; then in half a day realizing it, he faced the four walls confining him and telephoned Laurel. "Are you going to let them keep me here? Are you?" he said.

"No," she said, beginning to cry. "Mother will come." She had been practicing the piano; she came back to it and began to tremble; her fingers slid from keys that gradually became wet. Having played the piano so long, there suddenly seemed no reason to. She got up. She was disappointed when he came home that he did not speak, went on by into his bedroom. She heard him get into bed. If it were only just him but it was both. Yesterday she had to thread a needle for Kate, too unsteady to. When her teacher telephoned, they knew she had stopped music. She had no reason. Well, I'd be ashamed to just quit, he said. She was not ashamed of that. He had come home once, staggered from the garage to the house; standing in the door she had said, Hurry, hurry, thinking the neighbors would see. He said, You're ashamed of *me!*

She said she was going to take up painting. He said she wasn't ever going to get anywhere painting pictures. He would not give her the money but remorseful coming from the sanatarium had given her and Kate fifty dollars each. For several years that money paid for classes at a local recreational center; then she gave up painting too.

He tapered off but stayed in bed reading detective magazines; finally said he guessed he would have to advertise for a driver; it meant he'd have to get out and teach the man the business. Kate said it would do him good; not travelling, he had nothing to do but sit in the office waiting for the telephone to ring. He said he was catching up on his rest as he had always intended.

Hauling dynamite paid more than hauling most things; a lot of men, not eligible for the army, answered his ad. He chose a middle-aged married man who seemed steady. When the man only delivered dynamite, Son stayed in the office. Other times he met the driver at his destination, gradually taught him to shoot ditches and stumps. Then, one of the toughest jobs he ever had to figure out came along, blasting for a road through a cypress slough. There was no bottom to the slough at all, only mush. Son stuck dynamite all through the bad dirt and shot it. The heavy, good dirt on top sank and the bad dirt on the bottom sluiced out the sides. He repeated this over and over until all the mush was gone and the good dirt solidly packed.

Finished, he grinned. "When you know how to do that, you know how to shoot off dynamite." A Negro standing by said, "Mr. Frank can shoot 'em. He can shoot 'em. He can sho shoot 'em." Sometimes, driving along, sitting alone at the office, Son would say the little phrase like a melody to himself: Mr. Frank can shoot 'em, he can shoot 'em, he can sho shoot 'em . . .

Toward the war's end, he sold a hundred and twenty-five thousand tons of dynamite to the Government for an airfield, cut out of solid rock. Directly from the front, men would be flown in and taken to a nearby veterans' hospital. There was a certain amount of luck to his life; it hadn't been all hard work. Whatever else had gone wrong, his business had gone right; he just happened to be the man where the airfield was going to be built. Most of the dynamite went by rail but several times he had to send the truck. Twice someone phoned to see when it would arrive; each time it already should have. The third time Son put down the phone, put on his hat and walked out of the office. He got in his car and started over the driver's route. He drove a hundred miles, stopping at every restaurant along the way where the driver could stop, had driven fifty more before he found the right place. There was a swarthy-faced blonde behind the counter he knew was the right one before he asked. Yes sir, she said, she had seen a dynamite truck parked outside sometimes, she believed. She didn't remember what the driver looked like, there were so many . . . He said something he didn't usually say to women and tell him one more thing, Did the driver drink beer while he was sitting here? She guessed so, she said, not seeing the connection. He arrived home long past dinner time, Kate not having had the faintest idea where he was. The next day he was in the office when the driver got back. As soon as he walked in, Son gave him his pay, plus two weeks; the only reason he gave him that was because he had kids and don't let him ever see his face around the office again. He'd spent twenty years building up a reputation no bogus sonofagun was going to tear down in six months. Get on out.

The next driver was young, not in the army because of asthma. The opportunity to start out someone young pleased Son. It certainly was an opportunity for the boy. If he tried, learned, he might end up taking over the whole business. Because now, Son was beginning to wonder who was.

Week after week he went out with the boy and succeeded only in teaching him how to shoot the simplest stump. It was a year before he could believe the truth; the boy didn't have the least ambition to do anything besides drive the truck. Son told Holston it was something he had known long before the year was up; had known but couldn't believe.

He had been working himself to the bone just when he ought to have been resting. And he couldn't go like he use to. He got to coughing too bad. When he drove very long his chest ached. Finally, he said, Boy, I've had niggers working for me wanted to work harder than you do. Somebody's going to push my truck down the road that wants to work. I can't stand folks around me that don't want to. Lazy, whew! he thought when the boy had gone. He put his feet on his desk thinking how glad he would have been to have had anything in the world offered to him when he was starting out and how nobody had ever offered him anything. Suddenly he put his feet down and picked up the telephone. Sweet and familiar her voice answered; he said, "Mrs. Ryder, I'm fixing to call up Mr. Ryder's nephew Mace and ask him to drive my dynamite truck."

She said, "Mace don't know anything about driving a truck."

"I'll learn him," he said.

"He don't know anything about dynamite either."

"Neither did I when I started out. I'll learn him that too."

229

"He's already got a good job," she said.

"Well I'm going to pay him so much he can quit it." Mace never had a chance, Holston would say. Dynamite had it in his head somebody with Mr. Ryder's blood could drive his truck, and Mace was going to drive it. Mace came because of the salary. He was twenty-three and had been a shipping clerk; his only qualification was he was used to lifting boxes. They started out, went east again toward Buzz's job, and Son showed Mace how to shoot the top surface of dirt off gravel so it could be picked up and hauled away for road building. Tishomingo! he called the gravel's name, shooting. He liked the names of a lot of things, sometimes said them over driving: Carolina Company, Snow Lake, Chickasaw Bluff. Going along the highway he ticked them off: Ouachita, Tallahatchie. He liked sections: South Miss'sippi, East Tenn a see, the Delta.

His section of the state had always lagged behind in road building because of politics. When the war was over, politicians long in power no longer were. The county began to catch up. With business booming, Son had what he had always wanted, one that ran itself. Orders came without his having to look for them. To make money, he only had to sit in the office and answer the telephone; he figured that was what Holston was paid to do.

At last he could sleep in the morning as long as he wanted. Waking, he would turn his pillow to the cool fresh side, close his eyes and lie thinking of all the spring summer and winter dawns he had started into, down some small highway in search of a gravel road or dusty path. Having daydreamed, he sometimes fell back to sleep. He got up when he wanted to, shaved, ate breakfast and went down to the office. He had all the time in the world to do anything he wanted; it seemed he did the same things he always had.

He sat around the office until time for a late lunch; sometimes people dropped in. After lunch he sat around the office until four-thirty and went home; or he went over to the Engineers office and played Pitch. He said he was really catching up on his rest. When he retired at sixty, had found someone to take over the business, then he was going to travel, do some of the things he had always put off doing.

———

230

When they moved into the new house, Kate had hired a maid named Sarah; he believed she was the best they ever had. She moved into a room off the garage. That summer Kate and Laurel took a short trip to look at colleges and Sarah was there to take care of the house and cook for him. Laurel did not like any of the colleges she saw. She wanted to go farther from home. He knew he didn't know a thing in the world about colleges; she had to make up her own mind. While they were gone, he had taken a few short trips with Mace and found him willing; he liked to tell about the first stump Mace shot alone; having lit the fuse, he ran and Son was so mad he almost knocked Mace down. Never, he told him, run away from a blast. If you stumble and fall you don't have a Chinaman's chance; walk, always walk away, as fast as you can. Never investigate a misfired shot before an hour's up was another piece of advice he gave. But Mace was left to find out alone, a long time later, there were proper ways to light a fuse. Mr. Wynn had always used the cigarette hanging out of his mouth, and Mace did.

Mace told that hard as the road was he travelled, he knew it had been smoothed. Doors stood open to him everywhere and Mr. Wynn had pounded them that way. He wondered if he was the only one who saw the toll it had taken. Mr. Wynn coughed so much he sometimes had to sit down afterward and breathe. Some places he went people said they wouldn't give anything in the world for the opportunity of having known Dynamite Wynn; he was a character if there ever was. Other places people called him all kinds of names. Folks that had got themselves in the position of owing him money didn't like him, Son said, laughing. Mr. Wynn, Mace said, took care of the people that worked for him though. Once he was sent in the truck to pick up dynamite a man had not paid for. When he walked into the man's office asking for it, the man said get out or he'd beat him. Mace went down the road and telephoned Son. What should he do?

"Go back," Son said.

"Go back?" Mace said. "Just go back?"

When he got back, Son already had the man on the telephone.

He told Mace afterward how it had gone. "If you touch that boy," he said, "I'm going to come up there and kill you."

"I didn't know the boy worked for you," the man said.

"He's in my truck, isn't he?" Son said.

"He just walked in here and asked for your dynamite, I never had seen him before," the man said.

"Well, you shore must have thought he was a brave son-of-a-bitch," Son said. "First, he steals my dynamite truck, then he tries to steal my dynamite."

Mace marvelled over the way Son, sitting in his office, could give him exact instructions about where he was going. He never needed a road map, Mace said. He kept a lavender comb in his shirt pocket. Listening, he sat combing his hair. Son would put his feet on his desk, lean back, and say, You take the Delta highway for thirty miles and turn off right at a filling station called Cottonmouth Corners. Run on a couple of miles past a long stretch of Johnson grass and a bobbed-wire fence. You'll see a old Negro cabin with some tall sunflowers upside it. Turn left past that cabin and go on to you hit a big dip in the road. Just beyond there's a little bitty dirt road just wide enough for the truck. Turn left. Take that to the end, you'll be at the landing where they want the dynamite. He'd follow Mr. Wynn's directions: there'd be the Johnson grass and the bobbed-wire fence and the cabin and sunflowers; everything always exactly as he said. Mr. Wynn knew every fork in the road, Mace said, every rough place to watch out for. He knew every cotton patch. Every creek. He knew every dirt road to get down to go out to the levee. He knew the countryside like the back of your hand.

Laurel decided on a college in New York City and he let Kate fly up there with her, sightsee for a week-end before school began. He thought it would do her some good, but when she came home she was worse. For the first time he spoke of it; not even he and Laurel had mentioned Kate's drinking. Now he told Buzz it was about to worry him to death. Buzz said with Laurel gone he wouldn't expect things to get better; for the first time in his life Son felt his hands were tied. She didn't even play bridge much anymore. During the war she had been a USO volunteer, had been happy doing things for the boys. When that was over she had time on her hands. She met with a group of women to knit, then decided she was allergic to wool.

These were the years when what he called "the second go-round" was ending, the final years of enlargements, clearing, making use of old borrow pits, the years when those who had built the levee assured themselves it was as stable as they could make it. Will told Son that after all these years as an engineer, he had come to believe that changing the river and making it stay that way was an art, more than a science.

When Laurel was home in the summer, Kate was all right. Cecilia came for a visit and the vacation seemed short. That fall, Laurel switched to another college in New York City; the cost was the same and that was all he knew about it. He just thought she ought to stick to something for a change. He made a few short trips, left at four every morning and was home for supper at six. Whupped too; by dark, he was in bed. It seemed to him like Kate made all the noise in the house she could, to keep him awake. He told Holston he was going to make her get up and fix breakfast at the hours he left; then she'd be ready to go to bed when he did. Did it work? Holston asked afterward.

Hell no, Son said. She fixed breakfast but I heard them bed springs squeaking again before I got out of the driveway good.

Daily he went to Arkansas on a final difficult job. Two borrow pits with a road between had to be drained into the river. Son had the road punched full of holes and shot a ditch through it; then the first pit drained into the second and the latter on into the river itself. When the job was finished, he went to the World Series with Winston. Buzz came from East Tennessee to meet them; just about all the boys were there and Son felt good, like old times. They even had a big crap game one night; he couldn't remember how long it had been since he had that old feeling of excitement. He was in the game long past midnight when Buzz had gone to bed. Buzz told afterward Son woke him at some nearly daylight hour wanting money; he was out, Son said. Having emptied his pockets, Buzz fell back to sleep. Next, at six o'clock Son was shaking him awake, thrusting money at him. Hell, couldn't he have waited, Buzz said, sleepy. Naw, Son said.

When he was home again, an engineer called from south Mississippi wanting a ditch blown beneath a bridge. Could he do it without blowing up the bridge itself? He hadn't been going to take on any more tough ones, Son said. But damn if he didn't want to see if he couldn't figure that one out. He had just come back from a trip and had to rest up, though. He told the man he had a lot of resting up to do to catch up on a lot he had missed. When he could he went, solved the problem by shooting the lower side and then the upper, leaving fifteen feet not blown at all. The water cut itself on through.

That was the highlight of the fall. Things were quiet the rest of the time; then Laurel came home for Christmas and everytime he came into the house there was a bunch of boys in it. Kate would say he had to go sit in the bedroom. He never had expected not to be able to sit down in his own living room when he wanted; but it had been this way all through high school too. He said who were all those lugs? Kate said boys from some of the nicest families in Delton; she had always been glad about the people Laurel had known going to that country day school. He didn't care who their families were; he just wanted to know why they didn't have any more to do, great big grown boys, than sit around somebody's living room. He talked to them about sports, then did not know anything else to say to college boys. That Christmas, the following summer when she was home, Laurel was in several weddings. He told Kate it looked to him like she ought to be thinking about one of her own. Kate said, "She's got plenty of time to be married. Let her have a good time."

For her final two years of college she went to California. Maybe that was having a good time, jumping all around, he thought. He had said do what she wanted to, but it seemed like she was doing a lot of jumping around. She did not seem to listen. Also, he wondered why she always had to pick out the colleges farthest from home she could find.

That winter Buzz stayed in town as much as he could and also Will and Martha; he guessed everybody was getting to the age they had to rest up. They played bridge or canasta every week-end, went out to eat often. He went along with as many plans as he could; Kate was better when other people were around. He had put a lock on the liquor closet and had the only key. But it seemed that was one of the reasons she did what she did; she could buy her own and he couldn't do anything about it.

Kate thought of that winter and spring as the time she began her walks. He had never talked to her about anything but business, not been interested in anything she did, and the house's silence finally drove her outdoors. That Christmas Laurel had bought a poodle she saw in a pet store window. Now almost every afternoon and as the days got longer, sometimes after supper, Kate and the poodle, Tippy, set out. She followed one side or the other of the circular drive, alternating days; it gave her something to think about. She listened resentfully to the gravel crunching beneath her shoes, knew she should have had sense enough to tell him not to pave the driveway, then he would have. She turned one way or another, alternate times, down the narrow sidewalk put in only recently by the city. But the neighborhood was as serene still as countryside; she saw rabbits and quail, heard nothing. She went as far as a boulevard to watch the changing of traffic lights, people passing in cars, entered stores to browse. She returned home thinking only there was nothing to go for; often she looked back on all those weeks, Monday to Friday, when she had been alone, would think how gradually even when he was home on week-ends, she still felt alone. She had never learned a thing in the world in Bess, North Carolina. When she left home, she had not known exactly what to turn to either. But one thing she knew was that people who didn't worry, lived on credit, were a lot better off than they were; people who went places, did things and had fun. She wondered if he ever was going to stop worrying about spending money.

One night, entering the house from a walk, she found him in a rage about a two-hundred-dollar department store bill. It was a mistake. Someone had used their charge account. Look at the sales slips, Kate said. Nothing would even fit me. Ladies shoes size nine. Probably one of your girl friends charging, Frank.

Hell! I never had no girl friend with big feet, he said. If it was

---

235

a bra now, it might be a different thing. For once, he and Kate laughed together.

That same spring he began renovating the office, said it was time they had room to cuss a cat in. He wrote Laurel how pretty it was; she'd have to come home now and take over the dynamite business. Sealing the letter, he glanced at pictures of blasts on the wall; all of them purty, he thought.

Suddenly he rummaged in a bottom drawer. On his desk were hammer and nails he had used to put up the photographs. Calling Holston, he gave him two more things saying, "Boy, do me a favor, will you? I'm too tired to move. Hang these up there on the wall for me?"

Holston read the fancy gold lettering, "Handy, Colorado. Where in the world is that?" he said.

"Hell, I don't know whether there ever was such a place. There never were such gold mines," Son said. "Put those certificates up on the wall. I want to sit here and remind myself it's possible to make mistakes."

While Holston hammered, Son told about buying the stocks, laughing. "I shore thought I had it made when I bought those," he said, seeing back to that beautiful fall day exactly, himself going down to the bank happily, in the sunshine, his coattails flying.

When Laurel graduated from college, he agreed to go to California by train, couldn't make that haul across Texas in June. Since he had been a stock boy in all those jewelry stores, long ago, he had dreamed of going to San Francisco. There was one particular big firm he had done business with he had always wanted to see. Kate said, Well here we are. What is there to see?

It was a grey stone building on a crowded narrow street. But he was thrilled, thought of the dreaming boy he had been who had never had any idea in the world whether he would make it out here or not. All that time as a boy, he had worked among all those beautiful things, not able to have a single one and had promised himself someday he would be able to buy what he wanted. That day had come. He took his wife and daughter inside, having said how much they could spend. Kate could hardly believe it; everything he had done on the trip had been in the best way; she had never expected to own jewelry too. She chose pearls and Laurel a watch. He said, "I'd like to have something inscribed on the back." Laurel said she would too. What did she have in mind? She said, "From Daddy."

"That's what I had in mind too," he said. The salesman suggested they add the date; they agreed and he wrote, June 1951. Then Son did what gave him one of the biggest kicks of his life: paid the man in cash. "You should have seen that peckerwood's eyes bugged out," he told at home. "He thought we were country folks walking in there, but changed his mind quick!" He would throw back his head and roar, then sober, a little unsure. "Miss Kate now," he would say, "was em-*barrassed*. She can't see why I don't pull out a check and pay like everybody else." He told her, You're all the time telling me I don't know anything. It's you don't know anything. You know how many people there are would like to be able to pull that much money out of their pockets? Half those peckerwoods at that Country Club you and Laurel think are so hot never have seen that much cash. I know that for a fact. Take that fellow I buy my car from, always having his picture on the front page. He sees me on the street and acts like he don't know who I am when I been buying cars from him twenty years and paying for them. Everybody in Delton knows he runs his business on credit. One time he was down in the hole just about as far as a man can get. I walked in there and paid for a new car in cash, pulled the money out of my pocket and said, Here, I thought I'd hep you out some.

"I still don't see why you couldn't have paid by check," Kate said.

"Oh hell," he said.

He went down to the hotel bar and had several Gibsons; he'd just found out about those. He thought of the time Kate had run up a hundred-dollar bill in a neighborhood shop. He gave her a single bill and told her to go pay it. Every bill he got he paid the day it came in, did not wait even for a month's worth to accumulate. Whoever sent him a bill had his money the next day. Kate came back embarrassed, said the saleslady had been so excited, run all about the shop saying she'd never seen a hundred dollar bill before.

I don't reckon she was embarrassed to take it, he had said. He couldn't understand anybody being embarrassed to walk in somewhere with money to pay a bill they owed. If there was any woman he never was going to understand, it was Kate.

"Boy, I better have another one of those with a onion," he said. After several drinks the boy Laurel brought along to supper looked a lot better. There wasn't anything the matter with George; he had graduated from college with Laurel and was a nice enough boy, way over six feet tall and sandy-haired, though he wore horn-rimmed glasses which he took off when he spoke and put back on to hear what you were going to say; it was just that he did not seem to know what he was going to do, now that he had been to college, any more than Laurel did. Laurel said he was going to go to school some more. He said, Whew. Kate wondered if Laurel was going to marry George. He said he'd like to know what they were going to live on if she did. He certainly wasn't going to support some big hunk of boy too lazy to get out and start learning a business when he was twenty-one years old and was still going to school, Jesus Christ. The next day, Laurel and Kate went to ride the trolley car. It wore him out walking up and down all those hills. He said he had to wait for the mail, see if there was anything Holston wanted to know about. But there was only a short letter from him saying everything was running along fine without him, stay as long as he wanted. There was a post card from Sarah, saying the house and Tippy were fine but she got lonesome at night with no lights on. All those onions had kept him awake. In the night he had decided what he was going to do and now did it. He was back in the hotel when Laurel and Kate came back, sitting in the room, looking like the cat that ate the canary, Kate said.

"What've you done?" she asked. "Bought me a light," he said.

"A light?" she said. "What are you talking about?"

He stuck his hand straight before him, wearing a heavy ring with a diamond center. "When I was a boy I worked around all those pretty things and couldn't have any of them. I promised myself some day I was going to buy me a diamond ring. Now I have."

"Frank, I swear to my soul, men don't wear diamond rings," Kate said.

"What the hell they make 'em for if men don't wear them," he said. "You don't know what you're talking about. I've known plenty men wore them. Lots of men on the levees wore 'em so they could scratch up another fellow's face if they got in a fight."

"That's just what I'm talking about," she said. "It's tacky."

"Tacky my foot," he said. Just because nobody in that wide place in the road she came from could afford a diamond ring she thought men didn't wear them. He told Laurel later, Your mother doesn't have any sense, never has had. Laurel only thought, Even now, even at my graduation, they couldn't stop.

Back in Delton, he went to the doctor about his cough, told him he didn't have the breath to get up and down a one of those hills in San Francisco. The doctor found nothing wrong, said it was probably a cigarette cough, to cut down on smoking. Not too much was going on in the office during the hot weather and he stayed home a lot the rest of the summer, getting up when he wanted to. One morning he was eating a late breakfast while Laurel ate lunch; he noted her fingernails were bitten to the quick, as always; and she had gotten too thin out at that school, he thought. Her hair had always hung straight to her shoulders but in San Francisco she had had it cut short; it swung against her cheeks, just covering her ears, and he thought she looked even more like Kate. He said, "Now what are you going to do?"

"Today?" she said.

"I'm talking about from now on," he said.

"Oh," she said. "I don't know. I've been to all the employment agencies. There aren't any jobs."

He had been cutting up two fried eggs, crisscrossing his knife and fork rapidly across the center of his plate. He stopped, reared back, his wrists settled to the table edge and his silverware stood upright. "That's the silliest damn statement I ever heard in my life," he said. "I told you I could get you a job down yonder to the bank. That's one place in this town somebody knows who I am."

The table was beside the window; they had to squint to bear the day. His eyes, blue, seemed to reflect the bright late summer sky. "I took out all the loans I ever took out for my business down at that bank. And I met all the notes early. I did that on purpose, to establish my credit. I took them all out through Mr. Gordon sits there in that first desk in the lobby. I could walk in there today and get any kind of loan I wanted in a minute. I believe if I asked Mr. Gordon he'd get you a job as one of those messenger girls they have there in the lobby."

"But, Daddy, I don't want a job as a bank's messenger girl," she said. "I want a job that has something to do with what I majored in at college, English."

"English?" he said. "Whew! Did you have to go to college for four years to learn English?" He sucked a bite of egg from his fork thinking how he had wanted her to go to college. She hadn't been interested in getting married and he figured the more education a woman had, the less likely she was to make mistakes. He had wanted her to learn how to make something of herself, remembered telling her when she left, Now, see if you can find out some of the things I never could. But he didn't believe she had. And what got his goat was, she didn't seem to have learned one damn thing to help her get out in the world and earn a living. He ate some more, wondering what all that money had gone for. Stacking his cup and saucer into his plate, he pushed them away, lit a cigarette, but began as soon as he inhaled to cough.

Laurel said, "I thought the doctor told you to quit smoking."

Taking out his handkerchief, he blew his nose with a hard blaring sound. His mouth cocked into its crooked, tough, still handsome grin. "That's what the man said," he said.

"Then why don't you?" she said.

His eyes opened wider, in astonishment. "Because," he said, "not a man alive's going to tell me when to smoke and when not to." He looked at her expectantly, laughing. When she did not laugh, he stopped. He stood up, narrowing his eyes against smoke twisting toward him. It was Sarah's day off. He picked up dishes and carried them to the kitchen as Kate came in the back door, her heels making mice-like squeaks across the polished linoleum floor. With two thuds, a sigh of relief, she set down grocery bags. Laurel, having picked up her dishes, came into the kitchen too. Son was backing rear first from the ice box holding a large container of ice water. He put it to his mouth and drank in long gulps, his Adam's apple jumping. Kate, taking things from the grocery sacks, turned in disgust. "That's supposed to be for everybody to use," she said.

Without answering, he returned the bottle almost empty.

Kate said, "I hope you had a nice sleep while I was off at the grocery and lugging in these heavy sacks."

Laurel said, "I would have helped, I didn't know what you were doing."

"I bet," Kate said.

Son crossed the room, belched and looked relieved. "She's too lazy to even get a job," he said.

"You talk about lazy when you sleep till noon every day," Kate said.

"Kate, are you trying to run my business again?" he said.

"You don't have any to run," she said. "That's what's the matter."

A long moment, he stood staring; then he said, "I worked thirty years so I wouldn't have any business to tend to, so I could sleep late in the mornings if I wanted. And nobody's going to tell me any different, you hear?"

"I hear," she said.

He stared at her out of eyes turned white. Skin sagged like jowls along his face. "I don't want to have anything to do," he said.

"Uh-huh," Kate said. Her back to them, she kept sorting groceries.

He stared as if she faced him, once would have hit her, now only looked as if he would like to. Too much juice, he thought, had gone out of him. Laurel wondered why Kate, who so often had wanted him to change, intentionally antagonized him now that he had.

241

Kate crossed the room, storing things. He said, "I told her I could get her a job as a messenger girl down yonder at the bank. But she can't start at the bottom. She's been to college."

"She doesn't have to know what she wants to do yet," Kate said. "She's only been home a month."

He pressed a hand against his chest and caught his breath, as if needing to store it to say what he wanted. "She's got stock in her name in that bank," he said. "She'll appreciate that some day. That bank's going to be one of the biggest in this part of the country, the way Delton is growing."

"Oh, Frank, that's not the point," Kate said.

"Well, I don't know what the point is then," he said.

He dug a toothpick from the breast pocket of his bathrobe and picked at a back tooth. The pick bobbed up and down; he sucked occasionally, keeping it in place and said, "That stock split two for one not long ago." For the first time he spoke directly to Laurel. "Do you realize that?"

"No," she said. She was washing lettuce and had no idea what a stock split meant. Her stomach had knotted resentfully at the way they had spoken about her as if she were not there.

"Two for one!" he said happily. His grin returned; his eyes were full of delight. Sucking juicily at the toothpick, he shifted it across his mouth. "All I know is," he said, "I'd have been a happy son-of-a-bitch to have had somebody offer to help me out when I was starting out, fourteen years old, to look for work. She'll find out what earning a living's like someday." At the back door, Tippy whined to get in. Son opened the door. Shimmying his rear in delight, Tippy came through. Son said, "It was a booger, boy. A booger."

Kate said, "Frank, are you going to stay here again all day without even getting dressed?"

He said, "Kate, I told you not to try to run my business." Turning, he went out and down the long hall slowly, to his room at the end. He would get dressed, though he had not been going to until Kate started in on him.

Laurel said, "Mother, all those girls do at the bank is stand all day in the lobby until someone has a message to deliver."

"I know it," Kate said. "But I don't know what you are going to do."

When he came back dressed, they were silent. "I bought that stock at twenty-nine, too," he said, coming in. "Now it's worth sixty-one." Neither Kate nor Laurel understood stocks and said nothing. He said, "I guess I'll have to go on down and get me a haircut and see about what's going on at the office."

He went out and down the back steps and slowly across the yard toward the garage. Kate said, "Will you tell me what he's going to do the rest of his life, sit here and me sit here and watch him?" She threw a bunch of celery at the drainboard and suddenly crushed a paper sack so hard her knuckles stood out white and separate. "Oh, you don't know what it's like having everything turn out wrong. Him just sitting here and a daughter who's the only one of her crowd not married, a home you never want to come home to."

Laurel thought, Why does she think I want to stay here? I've always been going to find a place where everything is different. Silent, she watched him out the back window; from the rear he looked like an old man; the back of his neck was narrow, his shoulders went forward and his clothes hung on him as if they were a larger man's; the sleeves seemed empty. Stopping at the garage, he held one hand against a door post.

In the car, he stared ahead at the wall where garden tools hung, smelled the cool damp smell of the concrete floor, listened to himself breathe. You never gave a thought to something like breathing until you couldn't do it so good anymore, he thought. The time was almost here to do some of the things he had put off, to have some fun with his money Kate said they never had had. He didn't know exactly what he wanted to do. But he knew one thing, he had to get to feeling better before he did it.

He went to the office off and on until Christmas; during January when Buzz was in town, he went every day. On the first, Buzz had looked at him in surprise. "Ain't you lost some weight, boy?" he said.

"I ain't doing a damn bit of good," Son said.

"Probably your damn meanness coming out," Buzz said.

"Hell, I ain't even mean anymore," Son said. "Until I fell off the wagon Christmas, I hadn't even had a drink in six months."

"You are sick," Buzz said. They were laughing, then suddenly Buzz was not. He sat down and said, "Old man," and his voice had no inflection; it was as if he were trying to hold it on one straight note. "I've gone broke, busted, on that job up there."

Son tilted back; one leg crossed the other; his hands gripped hard the arms of his chair. "Whew," he said.

Buzz said, "Every red cent I had was tied up in that job. First my machinery broke down and it rained four days out of every seven. Naw. First I underbid the job."

"Whew," Son said again. "Last thing I knew you was a millionaire, now you're broke. Don't you have no money put away anywhere for a rainy day?"

"You know I never have been able to save nothing," Buzz said.

"Old man, it looks to me like you're in a hell of a mess. I thought when you took on that job you was getting to be a pretty big operator. I can't imagine any grown up man not having money put away. Miss Kate now, she's always been on me about putting everything I made into stocks. But the way I feel, what if I had to be out on the road still, trying to make a living?"

"What's the matter with you?" Buzz said.

"Damn if I know. I'm not suppose to know anything except how to sell powder. And the doctor-fellow can't find anything the matter with me either. I have a bad cough. What's going to happen now?" Son said.

"My creditors are fixing to take my machinery," Buzz said. "If they do, I ain't got a snowball's chance in June. Would you lend me some money?"

Son said, "It looks to me like I'm going to have to bail you out this time."

They discussed the amount and Son's terms. "I'll go down to the bank this afternoon and get a bond," Buzz said.

"I don't want no bond," Son said. "I take your word."

"Not even for that amount?" Buzz said. "That's a lot of money."

"I couldn't stand to see no old man go to jail," Son said. With a little effort, he rose; they shook hands. "This is enough, for all that?"

"It's enough," Son said.

"Old man, you ain't as tight with your money as they say you are," Buzz said, laughing almost in his old way.

"I can be," Son said.

"How's Miss Kate and Laurel doing?" Buzz said.

"They're both about to worry me to death," he said. "I think sometimes that's what makes me feel so bad. Miss Kate is just the same. Laurel don't seem to be able to settle down. She's had two or three little jobs around Delton, and quits them. She's not doing anything right now but she's talking about going up yonder to New York to work."

"Can't you make Kate quit that," Buzz said.

Son said, "I thought she'd quit when Laurel came. I just don't know what to do."

In February when Buzz went back to East Tennessee, Son thought he missed the old soandso like he had missed few people; still he would not lend him money a second time. You could make a mistake once. There had been only a few old boys in town that winter staying around at the hotels, nothing like it used to be. He got around to seeing everybody, had them out to the house, shot craps once, not like it used to be either. That spring, Buzz called from his job. "Cliffs," he said. "Just solid rock two hundred feet straight up. I got to get the side shot off, to flatten it out wide enough for a roadbed. Frank, nobody can do it but you. Come on up here. It'll do you some good."

He started out a few days later for the Smokies. Kate said, "Thank goodness, he's got something to do." Maybe it was something to do, he thought; maybe it would do him some good; but what nobody could see was he just didn't have the stuff anymore. "I'm wore out," he told Buzz when he got there. "I'm going to have to rest up before I even look at the job." One problem was to get tractors up the cliff. When they figured a way, Son knew it was a sight he would never forget; they hooked a pulley to a tree and the tractors to the end of the rope and pulled them two hundred feet straight up the side of the cliff, before Son shot the side off.

It was the middle of a sunny afternoon when he got back home, but he could not wait to get to bed. As he crossed the back yard, Sarah came to the door of her room off the garage and said, "Mrs. Wynn's gone to play cards. She'll be back at six."

"Sarah, I'm about to starve to death," he said. "Can you rustle me up something to eat?"

"Yes sir," she said. She came inside and fixed him a sandwich and after he ate he went to bed. He tried to read a new detective magazine but he could not concentrate. He could not sleep either. Closing his eyes the road swept beneath him and he travelled again the mountainous curves; the wheel had seemed heavy, had rubbed red places on hands not used to gripping one. Mile had lengthened into mile, the way ahead had grown until he thought he could not push that buggy home. He had thought of stopping in a motel fifty miles out of town, then would not let himself do it, had pushed on. He had a drink and finally slept, heavily he knew, because when the phone rang, it was a long time before he could bring himself up out of the dark.

Holston said, "I thought you were coming back this evening. What are you up to?"

"Hell, I'm trying to get some rest but there don't look like there's any place you can go to get some," he said.

Holston said he was wanted way down in south Mississippi by a county to do some muck shooting; they hadn't been able to find anybody else who could shoot the stuff.

"Jesus Christ," Son said, laughing. "You mean there still ain't anybody that knows anything about shooting dynamite but me? I thought somebody else would have learned something by now."

Holston said, "Can I tell them you're coming?"

Son said, "Hell, I'm in the bed."

"Well get out of the bed," Holston said.

He said, "I'll have to see. I'll call you tomorrow."

All the way down to his toes his legs ached; he could not make it. No one seemed to understand; nobody seemed to know what it was like now or what it had ever been like. He got up and took another drink, looked at himself in the bathroom mirror and thought, I'm wore out. Only Sarah was in the house and it was dark except for a crack of light around the closed kitchen door. He smelled supper cooking and it made him hungry and suddenly it made him angry too: why wasn't Kate here seeing his supper got on the table? What time was it anyway? Angrily, he grabbed the clock to look closely in the twilight. It was only five and he had another drink and went back to bed. He woke when Laurel said, "Daddy, are you asleep? Some woman wants you on the telephone." He came up out of the darkness again and said, "Hello," gruffly.

"That's not any nice way to greet an old friend," a voice said.

"Who the hell is this?" he said.

"You know who the hell it is," the voice said and laughed. Of course, he knew then. He guessed that was the very first thing he had ever noticed about her. All those years he had seen her whenever he was down in her part of the Delta, a lot had changed, but her laugh never did. Then this past year or so he had not gotten down her way; but of all the women he had been out with, she was the only one he had ever cared anything about. "What the hell you doing in Delton, May?" he said.

"Got a ride up with a friend," she said. "Told her I had a friend I wanted to look up I hadn't seen in a long time." As she spoke, he thought what a long time it had been, looked all the way back to the time he gave her the teddies. May said, "We got a couple of rooms down here at the Andrew Johnson. Where you been so long?"

"Minding my own business I guess," he said.

"We're fixing to have a little party. Can't you come on down? We got some good drinking whisky that'll still be here if you get here soon enough."

He thought how it used to be: all night, any time; and the next morning too. He'd never needed anything but whisky to keep him going. Looking back, he thought of all the laughing he and May

---

247

had done; it seemed it had all been a whole lot of laughing; why wasn't it anymore? If anybody understood him, he guessed she came the closest. She had said, "Mr. Will now, some of the others seem satisfied. You've made your money, got your business, but it don't seem like you're happy. Seems like there's always something eating at you still."

He had said, "I hate to say it but the older I get it seems like I get more like my mammy every day."

"What do you mean?"

"I'm impatient," he had said. "I know it and I can't hep it. She was like that too. She was always worrying after something and some of it she didn't really want, but she had to worry. It don't look like I'm ever free of worrying. I worry all the time. I got my money but suppose I don't keep it. That's one thing I worry about." Then he had stopped. There were more things he worried about he had no name for; nameless, they were in the dark when he closed his eyes.

He said, "Naw, I don't guess I can make it down to the ho-tel tonight, May."

"Why not?" she said.

"I don't get around anymore," he said. "I've got wore out."

"Come on a little while," she said. "I'll tell you whether you're wore out or not."

"Naw, you'll have to go peddle your papers someplace else," he said. "I don't mean that kind of wore out. I mean too wore out to get dressed and drive the car downtown."

"Well, if you're that wore out, you are too wore out," she said and slammed down the phone.

"Go————yourself," he said and slammed down the phone too. For a minute he thought of getting up and going down there and showing her whether he was wore out or not; then he thought, Hell he was wore out; it wasn't worth the drive. He got up and went into the bathroom and seeing the bottle on the floor took another drink. Then he came into the hall and yelled, "Kate, are you ever going to get my supper on the table?"

"It's ready now," she said from the dining room.

He came to the table, saying, "Buzz's job was a booger," but no one said anything. He sat down. "What's this?"

"Lima bean casserole," Kate said.

"Well get it off the table," he said. "I give you money to buy groceries, not to put scraps on the table. Get me something to eat."

Kate said, "Just because it's in a casserole, doesn't mean it's leftovers. Sarah just fixed it."

Laurel said, "Can I be excused?"

"Go on," Kate said. Sarah had to open a can of hominy for him. Kate told her to pitch the casserole into the back yard. They ate in silence. Finished, he said, "I may have to go down yonder to south Miss'sippi to do some muck shooting can't nobody else do. Whew." Kate did not say anything. He stood and went away from the table in a slow shuffle, as if he were ready to be an old man, she thought.

That night he slept deeply, then woke. A long part of the night had passed, but there was still a long part to go. He had dreamed he and May and Buzz were on a merry-go-round laughing, whirling about, with colored lights brightly reflecting in mirrors above them. He wanted Kate and got up and went into her room; but she was sleeping slantwise across the bed; her hair was darker though she kept it still blonde and she wore it much as she always had, very short and with the two deep waves coming forward across her cheeks; she had always had very pale skin and would never go in the sun; she looked very tired sleeping; her hands were beneath one cheek and she was snoring lightly. After a moment, he turned around and went into the bathroom and had a drink instead. He sat in the bedroom chair, trying not to think about whether he was going to south Mississippi or not. He said, "Pheww." He had been sweating, asleep, and now shivered in his damp pajamas, ran his hands through his hair and let them remain pressing the back of his skull, his head down.

When he woke next, it was the middle of the afternoon. Kate brought food on a tray. "Now get dressed," she said, "and go on down to the office. Holston's called several times. Don't start all this again."

"Don't start trying to tell me what to do," he said.

"Well if you don't get something to do," she said, "I don't know what any of us are going to do."

He started up, and she went out. Presently, he heard her drive away. He took a hot bath and afterward felt so weak he put on his robe and lay on the bed again. He called May. "I just wanted to see if you were still there?" he said.

"I am," she said. "But I thought you were too wore out to do anything about it."

"I was," he said. "But Old Granddad's got me not so wore out anymore."

"Oh," she said. "Is that a fact."

"Yeah, you want to make something out of it?"

"Nothing," she said.

"I just wanted to see whether you were still there or not."

"Well, I am," she said.

"Well I might be down to see you," he said.

"Come on then," she said.

"I don't know whether I can make it or not," he said and hung up.

In a little while he put his pajamas back on. He went to the kitchen and said, "Sarah, if anybody from my office—if anybody calls me, tell them I'm not home and you don't know where I'm at or when I'll be back." He read through several detective magazines again and slept fitfully. He was lying in bed, having listened to the ball game and then to the six o'clock news when Laurel passed the door and he said, "Laurel."

She had been out walking and came to the door wearing a turtleneck sweater, her hair blown about her face, making it appear even smaller; but she was tanned and he noticed for the first time that she had freckles. She said, "Yes?"

"How old are you?" he said.

"Twenty-two," she said. "Why?"

"Jesus Christ," he said, then said nothing else and Laurel went on to her room; he heard her close the door. He got up and closed his. That made an old man out of him if he hadn't been one before, he thought. Twenty-two years old. Why the hell didn't she know any more than she did for two thousand dollars a year for four years? Wasn't that the answer either? Mammy had always said everything would be all right if she had gone to school like her sisters did; but school didn't seem to have done Laurel any good and it hadn't done Cecilia any good; she had married Joe, had the four girls, and lived out from a little hole in the road down in Mississippi with just enough to live on, if they had that. What was wrong with Cecilia was, she was too good. She had always just been content with whatever she had.

He guessed they were never going to give him any supper; he never got anything to eat around here without making a big fuss about it. Standing to go to the bathroom, he found he was drunker than he had thought. Opening the door, he heard them eating and closed it again. He came from the bathroom and lay on the bed. He'd starve to death, he thought, and Kate would let him; that was just how grateful she was. He had worked himself to death and was this what it had all been for: not to have the strength to get up and go to the bathroom without thinking about it twice? "Wheww," he said. Suddenly he threw back the covers and got out of bed and threw open the door so hard the knob chipped paint on the wall. He went into the hall and shouted, "Kate! There's going to be a murder around here!"

Kate and Laurel were just crossing the hall and they stopped and stared. It was dark and Kate turned on the light. "Frank, hush," she said. "You're drunk. Go back to bed."

"I'm going to murder somebody around here," he said again. He turned and went into his room and picked up the telephone.

"Mother, what is he going to do?" Laurel said.

"I don't know, but I can't do anything about it," she said.

He said to the operator, "You better get the po-lice."

Laurel began to cry and went into her room and shut the door.

"Po-lice department," he said. "You better get somebody over here. I'm fixing to kill somebody." He gave his name and address and hung up. Then he got back in bed. Shortly, they were at the door and he listened to them come down the hall, Kate following, talking in a voice that trailed away as she went into her own room. One policeman, at the door, said, "What's going on? You don't look to me like you're fixing to kill nobody laying up in the bed."

"Hell," Son said. "Turn off the light."

The policeman turned off the ceiling light he had switched on, entering. They saw by the light from the hall. "What are you trying to do? Scare your wife some, cause some excitement?" he said.

"Naw, I just had a drink or two," he said. "Where'd you boys come from? How'd you get here so quick?"

"We was just cruising around," the second policeman said.

"You ought to be ashamed of yourself," the older one said. "Scaring everybody. What are you going to do now?"

"Get me some sleep, I reckon," he said.

"Well don't bother nobody else," the policeman said. "We don't want to have to worry about you."

"Hell, don't anybody have to worry about me. I get along all right." He sat up.

The policeman said, "You better get back in the bed now."

He said, "Don't anybody tell me when to get up and when to go to bed in my own house."

"Oh," the policeman said. "You going to get tough."

"Tough," he said. "You want to talk about tough. You ought to have been around here fifteen-twenty years ago you wanted to see somebody tough."

"Is that right?" the policeman said.

The doorbell rang. Son said, "Who the hell's that? How many boys you got to send to keep one man from committing a murder?"

"We two are enough to handle you," the policeman said.

Kate, having answered the bell, passed the door again. Buzz came behind her and stopped. He looked in. "What the hell you doing off the wagon, old man?" he said.

Son, in delight, swung his feet to the floor. "Where'd you come from?" he said.

"I got in today and called you and now next thing I know Miss

Kate's calling back saying I got to come over here and calm you down."

"I reckon he's about calm now," the policeman said. "We'll leave him to you." He and the other one started to go.

Son got out of bed. "I better give you something to take along for your trouble," he said. From his cabinet, he took two fifths of whisky and gave one to each. "Much obliged," he said.

The policemen touched their hats, thanked him and were gone. Buzz said, "What you want to scare the fire out of Laurel and Kate for?"

"Oh hell," he said. "You don't know what it's like living in the house with two worthless women." Son grinned, and Buzz threw back his head and bellowed, shaking all over. "Old man, there's not another woman in the United States would have put up with you as long as Kate has," he said.

"Well, I've sure put up with a lot," Son said. "I had a load to carry. I might have to have a drink to all I've put up with."

"You don't need a drink. Get back in the bed," Buzz said, holding the covers open.

"Oh are you going to start telling me what to do now?" Son said. "If I want a drink, I'm going to take it."

"Don't gimme no trouble. I'll get those boys with the billy clubs back to take care of you."

Son swung his feet under the covers and pulled them up. "There was a time when it would have taken the three of you to do it too," he said.

"Yeah, but them times are over," Buzz said. "You've done got to be a old man, like me." He pulled up a chair and sat beside Son's bed.

The telephone rang, and Laurel opened her door and went down the hall to answer the one there. Light from her room fell across Buzz's face and turning, Son saw him closely and thought: you don't know how old you are until you look at the other fellow. Buzz had paid back some of the money he had borrowed; but he was working like a fool still to get ahead again; he saw how tired Buzz was, for a moment felt glad he never had to get that tired again; in the next moment, he envied Buzz, starting out all over again, as he was finished. He wondered which of them was better off. They had hoed some tough roads together. He said, "Buzz, remember that letting over in Little Rock when we sent the woman up to the room of that little fellow from Magnolia?"

"Yeah!" Buzz said.

"Last I heard, he hadn't stopped running yet!" Son said. They laughed until Son had to blow his nose afterward; then he said, "I got to thinking about all those days here not long ago; looks like I can't stop. That was when you got the big one wasn't it? Who got the bid on the sodding that time?"

"That's going back some," Buzz said. "Was it that fellow from up in St. Mary's, Missoury."

"I believe it was," Son said. "What was that old fellow's name?"

"Squint?" Buzz said. "Wasn't that the one they called Squint McBride."

"That's him," Son said. "Whatever happened to that old peckerwood?"

"I haven't heard about him in years," Buzz said.

"Whatever happened to old J. J. Lawrence from up in Dyersburg way?" Son said. "I got to thinking about him not long ago."

"I heard he made a lot of money up thataway doing gravel work," Buzz said. "He was a tough customer."

"He wasn't no tougher than Dynamite, was he?"

"Naw, he wasn't no tougher than you, old man," Buzz said. They were laughing when Laurel passed along the hall again; she went into Kate's room and closed the door. Son thought he had a couple of fifty-dollar bills in his wallet; he'd have to give them each one tomorrow. "You want to know somebody else was tough," he said. "That old fellow that was at all the lettings named Roseamond."

"Yeah, he was tough too," Buzz said. He told something he remembered about Roseamond. He was still talking when Laurel opened the door to Kate's room and they heard the last of what she was saying, "—paper."

Kate said, "Go on to the party. There's not going to be anything in the paper about it. He's nobody."

When Laurel closed the door they saw each other by the lesser light of the hall. Son said, " '27, '28, '29. I'll never forget those years. I was starting out in my own powder business and everybody said I was crazy to do it. But it turned out all right." He told Buzz about the first little bungalow he lived in on Oak Street, about his mammy's and pappy's little bungalow, about buying his present house. "This house," he said, "is right across the street from a house where my mother did some catering for a big fancy society party one time. When she got there, they asked her to go around to the back door. Some of that family still lives over yonder and when I moved in here, it like to tickled me to death."

Buzz said, "I don't reckon you've told me all that before."

"I don't reckon I've told anybody," he said.

"Is that so?" Buzz said.

"I started out working when I was fourteen years old," he said. "I never have known how to do anything but work." He had never had time to develop any hobby, the way Kate was all the time telling him he ought to have a hobby. He considered stocks and bonds his hobby. He said, "I never knew there was anything else to do but work."

"There's not anything that's any better for a man," Buzz said. He thought everything was going to be all right; he hadn't mentioned a drink again; if he'd go to sleep now, he'd be all right tomorrow.

Son stared ahead at a mirror on the wall. He could see part of the hall reflected, a pretty light fixture hanging from the ceiling. This was a pretty house, he knew that. They had clothes enough in the closet to wear and money enough to spend. It didn't seem like there was anything else in the world they could want, but they didn't seem to understand what he had tried to do; Kate never had been interested in his business. He said, "I certainly thought I had done everything in the world a man could do."

"You have," Buzz said. "Did it all alone too."

.   .   .

255

It was a week before he felt any good at all, but he went down to the office for parts of every day. Buzz was having his side of the office painted and Son wanted to see how it was coming along. He had an idea about what to do with his business and thought about it a lot, sitting there. Holston said they still wanted him down in south Mississippi; finally he said it looked like he would have to go. The following Monday, he went, saw Winston several times while he was there, found the old bug juice had hold of him bad too. When he got back, he asked Laurel to come down to the office and see how it looked. All winter she had been helping out mornings in a nursery school and came down after lunch.

He showed her around the office and told her the plan that had been on his mind for some time. "You aren't ever going to make any money or get ahead any in this world teaching school, that I can see," he said. "I've got this business I've worked like a booger to build up, and it's going to go out the window. I just don't see any reason in the world why you can't take it over. It just runs itself. All anybody's got to do to rake in the money is just sit here and answer the telephone. You could come and go as you please, have your own hours: take as long as you want for lunch, get off any time you've got anything else to do. You just got to show up enough to justify your salary to Uncle Sam."

"Why Daddy," Laurel said, surprised, "I couldn't take over the dynamite business. I don't know anything about business. I wouldn't be able to travel, go out to levee camps, do all the things you've done."

"You don't have to," he said. "Mace does all that. All you got to do is sit and answer the telephone and draw a salary."

"I just don't see how I could," she said.

"Well come down for a while and see what it's all about before you make up your mind," he said and she agreed. He had worked all his life, though, not to have to get up in the morning until he wanted and they would go down when he got ready. The times varied. Each morning Laurel waited. Kate had said it was the silliest thing she ever heard of, only he would think a young girl would want to sit down at that office, cut off from town, and run a dynamite business. He said it wasn't silly; she was silly; she was the silliest woman he'd ever known. Laurel had said to Kate, Mother, even if I wanted to do it, I couldn't. I don't have any head for figures. I wouldn't know how to deal with all those kind of men he knows.

I know that, Kate said. Nobody but him would think you could. But you'll never make him understand.

If they went early enough for lunch, he took Laurel across the street to the Dixieland Café where, he said, they had the best barley soup he had ever eaten, except for one time down in the Delta. He told her about the time he had driven the dynamite truck and made a policeman who arrested him unload the truck before he'd pay the fine. He laughed a long time, telling.

He showed her the new filing cabinet, opened all the drawers, explained if they got a letter from Mr. Brown it was filed under B. Letters from U.S. Army Engineers, they had decided to file under E. If anything like that came up she couldn't decide, ask Holston; he knew more about the system. Happily, Son held up some letters. "Here's some correspondence from old Winston Taylor down in Clay. We write each other ever once in a while."

Each morning after Holston had answered Son's mail, he gave Laurel the letters to file; there were seldom more than three or four. Afterward she sat in her office, filed her nails, read, wrote to George.

In his office, Son sat. Infrequently, his telephone rang. He answered abruptly, as if busy. Holston's continual typing filled the day's silence; Laurel found when the phone rang she tried to will it into being for Son. When he could sit no longer, he suggested they go home. Laurel went once to get cigarettes for him. Coming back, she met Holston in the parking lot. "Why isn't there anything to do?" she said.

Holston said, "It's mostly been done. And people don't use dynamite as much. There are cheaper substitutes. But if Frank felt like it, he'd be out beating the bushes finding other ways, wouldn't let the business shrink. As it is, he doesn't want to let go what's here." They glanced up at his name across the building.

One day she filed a letter from Winston Taylor. Big 'un, it began, are you selling any dynamite? I hope to get through Christmas sober then will be conductor on water wagon. The letter went on to give an order for dynamite. Clipped to it was a letter Son had been writing when the order arrived. He had written: Skinny, I hear you been on a milk diet. I told you what the old rot gut would do. Why don't you get smart and lay off like me. Are you buying any stock? Do you ever get all your money counted? Are you making any money digging ditches? Has the thing been stiff lately? Don't you need some dynamite? We got plenty . . . Laurel slipped the letter into the file wondering how her father had thought she could take his place. More and more, she saw the differences in their lives. It struck her deeply, with sadness, that it was his struggle and the money he had made to provide her with an education that had helped to make them.

Sometimes after she waited all morning, Son would decide not to go to the office. One morning, after a month, the phone rang as they were about to leave. Having spoken, he hung up to say there was a Pitch game downtown somebody wanted him to join; she did not have to go to the office that day. On the next he slept until noon and never dressed. He never again mentioned her going to the office; neither did she.

He was always at home, sitting in his room, lying on the bed. Passing his door she would see him, but having grown up accustomed to silence there was nothing she could think of to say. She spent time in her room. Infrequently they met in the hall, often passed without speaking. Once, getting up from the bed, he said he had been lying there trying to think what she was going to do; didn't she want a job? There was nothing to do in Delton, she said, unable to admit or even explain the wavering inside herself. What was the point of a degree in English? To be a receptionist, the only sort of job ever offered her? Several times he offered money for her to take friends to lunch at the Andrew Johnson. She had to decline, could not explain that to him, either: when she was thirteen and fourteen, she and her friends had spent Saturday afternoon that way, not since. She had gone to New York and stayed a month but whatever she had expected to happen had not and, impatient, she had come home, trying to think of the next place to try. She and George still wrote; how could they see each other again? For her to go to California seemed the only way. Even if she had not been planning to go she would have said No to Son's next suggestion. "I never have cared about any such thing myself," he said, "but I was thinking maybe you would like to join the Country Club. I'll pay for it."

"No, I don't want to," she said.

Kate got to the truth saying, "Frank, young girls just don't go join the Country Club by themselves."

"I don't see why not," he said and sat down to the phone. For a moment, he looked off, grinning. "Did you know I cleared all that land out yonder for their golf course?" He thought, he might not want to run around with society people but Laurel could.

She said, "Daddy, I don't want to join the Country Club." He was going to find out about it. Kate sighed.

He spoke to the admissions secretary who said he would have to have a sponsor; did he know any of their board members? He didn't know whether he did or not; she read the names slowly and he had to answer after each one. At first, he said, No. Then he said, Ummm. Finally he said, Now I've heard of him of course. He said, Much obliged, and was about to hang up. Then he said, I knew a Mr. Rollins once was the manager out there. Mr. Rollins had not been there for some years, she said and he said again, Much obliged. He sat a long moment, his hand on the phone, then got up and went slowly down the hall, having thought all it took was money.

Before Christmas Laurel told him she wanted to go back to California to get a Master's; she had applied to the graduate school some time ago and been accepted.

"A what?" he said

"Another degree like George was going to get, you remember?" she said. She told him she had decided to teach and would be able to get a better job. He said he hated to think of her ending up a old maid school teacher and he didn't think she had any business in the world going back out there; then he said nothing else.

———

259

Kate told her to plan on going; he seldom stopped what she wanted to do, just didn't understand any of it.

He had never observed wedding anniversaries or birthdays, had observed Christmas in his own way. He paid the bills, he had always said; that was his presents. This Christmas, Laurel came into the living room wondering if Christmas morning was ever sad to others. The house, decorated, seemed to wait for a party no one would ever attend, the tree by daylight was as melancholy as aging ladies overladen.

He had always slept late on Christmas morning. The trappings of childhood she had had, Kate had given her alone, and Laurel was grateful to her for it. Sometimes he had not even opened his presents; after a few days Kate did and put them away.

This morning, Laurel looked about the room at everything in order, before noticing an envelope pinned to the tree. She was moved not so much by what she suspected the envelope contained before taking it down and finding it did as by his having come into the living room secretly to put it there. It was a check for her tuition in a Christmas envelope from a bank. Opening it, she thought he had had to get it with her in mind. This was the closest thing to a present selected, wrapped for her, he had ever given her. She held the envelope close abruptly, suddenly wondering whether to go to California after all. But how could she backtrack? Changes that were coming were coming too late; he had even gone quietly about his holiday pursuits, was already tapering off three days after Christmas when she woke him at daylight to say she was leaving. Kate was backing the car from the garage.

"Why didn't you tell me?" he said, turning on the whisky-smelling and rumpled sheets.

"But I did, Daddy," she said.

He said, "All I know I've learned is, a rolling stone gathers no moss," and he turned back into the dark he sought, though she touched his shoulder and said, "I love you, Daddy," doing away with fear to say it; it was the first time she ever had. She wondered if it made up for her going away, knew she might not if she stopped to think; but she had tried to stay and nothing ever changed. When she had found what she had to, someplace else, she would come back. She did not mean to leave them for good, thought less than briefly of his final words: "Let me know if you need anything. I want to hep somebody."

On New Year's Eve, Winston came, Leila having refused because he would not let her drive. Son said, "It don't look like we can go anywhere with the shape he's in."

Kate said, " I stopped expecting things a long time ago. I'm not disappointed."

Son thought the only way to humor the old man was have some drinks with him, yet after a few Winston broke down. They were in Son's room. Closing the door, he got Winston to bed. He continued to sob and Son lay in the dark beside him, tugged covers close. "All right, old man," he said. "All right." Winston told of financial problems. Son gave him the best advice he could. Winston talked on, without control. Son told him he wanted to help him if he could, stayed on the bed beside him talking, keeping Winston covered and warm. Winston said he could not help himself, had been like this too long. Son got him to agree to go to a sanatarium, not only drove him there, but stayed all night.

Before midnight Laurel called. "What are you doing?" she said.

"Sitting here by myself looking at television, getting ready to go to bed," Kate said.

Laurel was at a party and there was noise. "With Daddy?" she said. Kate explained and Laurel said, "But you're all by yourself on New Year's Eve!"

Kate said, "His customers come first, and to me it's just another night." Sensitive to every nuance in Kate's voice, Laurel knew she had not been drinking and was flooded with pity. At midnight in California balloons fell, church bells rang and George kissed her. The next moment, alone in a strange room with people she did not know, in a part of the country to which she did not belong, she thought of Kate, moved to the window and looked out, said

261

against the cold glass, Happy New Year, Mother, thought of the incomprehensible thing he had done and wondered why so much always had been.

Kate, taking decorations from the top of the tree, handed them to Sarah. "I hate for Laurel to go away—the telephone never rings," she said.

"It sho is quiet," Sarah said.

He went sooner than would have been expected to the office for a few hours a day. On the way down, he stopped at the bank to redeposit money withdrawn from all his accounts prior to January first. On that date, the state collected taxes on personal assets and every year Son withdrew his money, carried it around in cashier's checks, and put it back in the bank when the tax period was over.

He stopped at the main post office downtown, bought a hundred post cards, wrote one and mailed it. There was a man in Hill, Mississippi, who had bought dynamite and never paid for it; Son had written, phoned, threatened. Now he was going to send him a post card every day asking for his money. He figured in a town that size, the postmaster would soon notice, read them and start talking. He would see just how many post cards it would take to embarrass that soandso into paying him.

At the office, Holston said, "That fellow in West Delton you talked to finally gave us a big order."

"Is that so?" Son said. "I'm sure glad to know something goes on around here when I'm not here."

"Oh, old man, we get along all right without you," Holston said.

"Well, I'm sure surprised to hear it," Son said.

They looked at one another a long moment, Son not trying to hide his loneliness. Holston went back to work; ping ping ping, only his typing broke the silence. Son put his feet up and stared at the pictures on the wall, tilted back in his chair. Then he put his feet down, swung around and stared out at the road. Nothing happening out there either. Swinging back, he took paper and envelopes from his desk and from his breast pocket a fountain pen and looked at it; his name was on it in tiny fourteen-carat-gold letters. It had been his habit for many years to send his best customers a poinsettia every Christmas; one year the pen had come back in return. This year he had sent only a few plants but had received a tie from the wife of a good customer down in Batesville. It wasn't one he would ever wear, but he was as proud as he could be she had thought enough of him to send it. It hung in his closet where he liked to see it, opening the door. He wrote her now and thanked her, tried to think of other letters to write but there were none. Proud that he knew how, he folded the letter correctly as he had been taught long ago in night business school, the bottom up first, the top half over that. He crossed over to tell Holston he had to mail a letter, might as well go on home afterward. "How you fixed for towels?"

Holston said, "I believe we're doing all right in that department. Don't you want to stop fooling with that? I could send them out from here."

"It's not enough to have a fellow stop," he said. "I got to come down and see what's going on anyway. It's easy to take them home, let Kate put them in with our laundry."

"Suit yourself," Holston said.

"Take it easy," Son said.

"You do the same. We'll see you, Frank," Holston said. His typing resumed as Son turned slowly and went out to his car. He mailed the letter and drove home slowly, trying to think of other errands to do. In his mind he ran through the things in the medicine cabinet. Did he need tooth paste, shaving cream, razors? He decided he needed a new laxative. The one he was using didn't do him a damn bit of good. He always had had trouble going to the bathroom; Kate said it was because he had rushed out every morning to get on the road and never given himself a chance. At the drug store, having discussed all the laxatives he had tried, he asked for another one; the druggist suggested a new one called Magic. He bought a box of Whitman's candy and several packages of gum. Outside an old man was in a wagon selling produce; Son bought apples, feeling sorry for the old man out in this weather trying to make a living. In the car, he rubbed an apple along his pants leg, then bit into it; juice ran down his wrists, up his shirt sleeve, but he did not mind. He liked driving along with it cold outside, warm in, the winter sun coming through the windshield, the almost sour taste of the apple in his mouth.

Magic was the most successful laxative he ever had; later he sent Laurel a box telling her if she ever needed one it was the best he had found. He told about sending sixty post cards to a fellow who finally paid some money he owed. He wrote that it was windy but bright and pretty every day; he was going to the office as much as he could but didn't feel any better at all. He knew it hadn't been much time since she left, but if she'd like to come home for Easter he'd be glad to send her the money to.

At the office he began to clean out things, told himself it was only spring cleaning long overdue. Going through the files he found the personal letter from Winston Laurel had put there and threw it away. He found other things it seemed nobody had any business seeing, threw away wastebaskets full, to Holston's astonishment. Son had always kept receipts, bank statements, cancelled checks for years back; now he kept them only for a year. He could not have explained a feeling of urgency about getting everything in order. He went through an old photograph album, mostly pictures of blasts; but there were some of him and Betty Sue swimming in the bayou in Mill's Landing. He threw those away thinking they sure didn't mean anything to anybody in the world but him.

He found in the files another man who owed him two dollars for a roll of fuse, started sending post cards to him.

In the summer Laurel was home briefly and went back to summer school. What he had said had taken root; she was going to stay in one place until something did happen. Occasionally Son played Pitch at the Engineers office, came home at four-thirty when it closed, waited until the paper came and read it until supper. He looked at television until he went to bed but seldom slept well. It was because he hadn't done enough during the day to be tired, Kate said. When he fell asleep it was late, then he slept late the next morning and could not sleep again at night; he could not break the circle. Often he lay in bed all morning not really asleep, his knees drawn toward his chin. One morning, struggling up, he said he always had wanted to go back and see Pike's Peak; they would drive to Colorado and perhaps see Laurel. He went to the doctor to see if he ought to make the trip. This time the doctor sent him to a specialist, Dr. Phillips. He came home trying to tell Kate what the specialist said he had; he couldn't remember how to pronounce it. But it was something they were just finding out about and even the doctor-fellows didn't know too much about it. He held up his hands the way Dr. Phillips had done, showing the size his lungs ought to be and the size they were.

"Well, what can they do about it?" Kate said.

"Nothing," he said. "There isn't any medicine, there isn't anything. You just got to live with it the man said." He could do what he felt like doing and would go ahead with the trip. The day before they were to leave he took towels to Holston. He wrote post cards, dating them ahead, for Holston to mail while he was gone. Sitting alone in the office thinking, he knew it was foolish to start out on a drive across the country without a will. But he wasn't going to pay any shyster lawyer to draw up one; he'd write it himself. When he had, it didn't look like much on paper for thirty years' work; there ought to be some way you could put down what it had been like scraping around for every dime. Maybe Laurel would appreciate more all those shares of old A.T.&T. if she knew what he had been through to get them. His pen hesitated over the paper a moment, but having disposed of his stocks, house, car, he wrote only that his diamond ring was for Buzz. He guessed that was all else of value he had. Mace and Holston were witnesses.

"Well," Kate said when they started off at noon the next day, "I never thought I'd live to see the day we didn't start out on a trip at the crack of dawn."

"Hell," he said, settling to the wheel, "I never thought I'd see the time when I couldn't sleep at night either."

They stayed in New Mexico for a week. For the first time in years, Son bought a bathing suit, sat beside the motel's pool, said he believed the sun helped his chest. Kate said he just wanted to look at those little airline stewardesses staying the week-end. He wanted her to buy a bathing suit; she would not, had never been swimming in her life. Where she grew up there had been no place to learn, except in muddy ponds with snakes, and afterward she had been too timid. She did not want to be wrinkled (more, she said) by the sun. She sat in shade near him. In the afternoons he rested and Kate took walks, visited places where Indian carvings were sold, began a collection. It was the first thing he had ever seen her interested in; he was glad.

They drove on. By the end of each day, he was too tired to lift the suitcases to carry inside a motel, would have changed all their reservations ahead to hotels but Kate carried the bags. He never had expected to be in this kind of shape, he said. It was night when they reached Colorado Springs. The porter, showing their room, pulled aside the window curtain to say the lighter section of sky in the distance was from a light atop the Peak. Son turned toward it, embarrassed by his own grin of pleasure. Next morning, as early as he could make it, they started. Driving the winding route to the top and down, he knew just how long ago it all had been, thinking that once he had walked it. The next day, they went in search of the lumber camp and the ways he took were wrong. He drove through forests until Kate made him stop at a filling station where an old man sat on a bench in front and answered that the camp had not been in operation over fifteen years; long ago everyone had lost contact with the couple who had run it. Bent forward—he said he could breathe easier that way—Son stared into the distance, raced the motor once. Then, turning, he said expectantly, "I worked out to that camp when I was just a boy."

The old man spit into the road. Kate said, "Frank, that was more than forty years ago. It couldn't be the same. Those people probably aren't even alive."

He said nothing until a few moments later that he was too tired to drive. Having exchanged places, Kate released the handbrake; they moved. "Much obliged," he called back to the old man, driving away, again through trees, then facing forward said, "I thought I saw some things I recognized."

At the end of the week, Laurel came, George with her. They had been married the week before. Son thought he had to be glad she was settled at last; taken care of, he hoped. He had been fooling himself all this time thinking she would come back. Buzz had tried to tell him when she went the last time she probably never would be, had told him not to worry; but as long as she was alone, he had. He never would understand why she left home. He had thought she had everything in the world to make her happy.

Not understanding how things had gone wrong, he knew he had to make the best of them, told the hotel clerk he had a bride and groom on his hands, fix up the bridal suite. He treated them to it as long as they could stay. When they had to leave, he gave George a thousand dollars, said he figured they had saved him at least that much running off to get married. Couldn't they stay longer?

George had to get back to teach, Laurel to classes. He told her, Any time you want to come home, I'll be glad to send you the money. She said they would come at Thanksgiving and she could stay for a long visit. Afterward she got on the plane with George, not wanting to. She had let happen what had, never stood still to think, knew now she did not want not to be going back to Delton either.

They were gone and he said, Did Kate think George would ever amount to a hill of beans? Kate said he already did. Because he didn't work with his hands, sweat to make a living the way Son had, didn't mean he didn't *work*. He said at least he wasn't a Jew or a Catholic or a shoe salesman, he had something to be grateful about. Kate liked George, was glad Laurel was married, like everybody else's daughter. The house had been empty so long, she thought she was used to it.

But it seemed more quiet, more empty after they had been travelling, had someone in the motels always to talk to. And before it had not seemed Laurel was really gone. For a few days Kate had to unpack, had things to go over with Sarah. Then when everything was put away, clean, she began to stretch out on the bed for long parts of the day, closed her eyes but was not asleep. By suppertime her cheeks had a faint red flush, her eyes a look of wandering.

He had to rest. As much as he might want to do something about Kate, there was nothing he could do. And he had to rest. He sat, resting and worrying about Kate, elbows on his knees, his head hung almost between them, rubbing his hands back and forth over his scalp, watching dandruff fall.

Kate went to the grocery store, occasionally played bridge. He searched the house, once asked Sarah to help him lift her mattress but found nothing. Sarah said she didn't know where Mrs. Wynn hid them but she for a long time had been the one carrying out empty pints in the trash.

"Pints! What kind of whisky is it?" he said.

"Southern Lady," Sarah said.

"Je-sus Christ." If that wasn't just like that woman. Nobody but Negroes bought Southern Lady or whisky by the pint either. That night, slapping a twenty-dollar bill on the table, he said if she was going to sneak whisky into his house stop sneaking in that cheap stuff. Get some good whisky and get it by the fifth. Taking the money, Kate said he had lost his mind.

Whew! He lay awake nights wondering what was going to happen to Kate if anything happened to him. Often, still awake in the middle of the night, he would get up and sit in a chair, look out at the nighttime trees and the black yard and the even blacker street where there was nothing to see but occasional cars going by, their lights mellowing the lonesome night, their tires making sounds like *thump* as they passed the house. He thought of her reasons for drinking when she could not deny she did: to get back at him for all the drinking he had done, for the times he had hit her, for the women he had known. He waited as expectantly for sleep as if it were a guest coming to the door, wondered all the time now what had happened, where he had made his mistake.

He did not see how things were going to get any better and thought of the times she had said she would leave him if she hadn't known he wouldn't let two women do it without scandal and mess. She had tried to save Laurel that. He thought one midnight, Laurel was gone, let Kate go too; he could get along all right. He wrote to Cecilia and told her when she came, he had decided to get a divorce. What he thought was, he would buy a big house down there in the Delta, have only a small part, and Joe and Cecilia could have the rest if she would run it for him. Cecilia said, "Brother, Joe's managed to finish paying on that little house we have. The girls are grown and married. We're set for the first time. I can't ask Joe to give up what he's worked for so long to live in a house you buy. And what's going to happen to Kate?"

"That's what's about to worry me to death," he said. "Now that Laurel's settled, it seems like I could stop worrying if I just knew what's going to happen to Kate if anything happens to me."

Cecilia promised to come as often as she could. The last morning she walked through the silent orderly house where everything gleamed, was waxed, polished, dusted. Kate had made the house beautiful and seen it was kept that way; why couldn't they have been happy in it? Cecilia wondered: knew how Brother had been but knew if Kate had been different, he might have been different too.

However it ended, she prayed it was in peace, had always done so. Hearing him come slowly down the hall, she picked up her suitcase. She had said as much to Buzz once; he had said no matter what, they had stayed together and there had to be a reason for it.

Kate had opened her eyes to say Goodbye, then closed them. He passed Cecilia, went out the back door, the car keys catching the sun to gleam. Following, Cecilia stopped, turned back to the kitchen where Sarah ironed. They stared a moment, hearing the car start, sharing the same knowledge. Cecilia tried to find words then did not need them. "I'll do the best I can," Sarah said.

"Thank you," Cecilia said.

In the car, she said, "Brother, can't you see again if that doctor can't do something about that cough?" He was having another check-up tomorrow. He let her out, did not have breath to park and walk back to the station with her. Standing on the curb, Cecilia said, "What are you going to do now?" As long as he was dressed, he'd go on down to the office. She said again she would come back more often. Then she stood holding the suitcase he could not carry, watching him drive away.

Holston said, "Boy, I thought you'd decided to let the dynamite business go down the drain."

He just hadn't felt like dressing and coming down. "What's been going on?" Holston threw a check for two dollars on the desk and Son laughed. "So he finally paid off?" Only Holston compared how much he had spent on post cards to the cost of the fuse. "One more," Son said. "That doctor-fellow down in Grenada owes me for four hundred pounds. I've written him all I'm going to. I'm going to call him on the phone and get rough when I get rested."

Mace, coming in from a trip, said Mister Will had sent word he would be home as much as possible this winter, would see Son soon. "How's the old man getting along?" Son said.

"Mrs. Carrothers finally was able to talk him into driving around the levee. He just couldn't walk from one place to another. How old is that old man?"

"Lord, past seventy," Son said.

"Tangle-eye, Sho Nuff, the old boys are still with him," Mace said, but there were differences. Contractors usually rented houses in the nearest towns for their help; even all the Negroes had cars and roads were good; easier to have them drive back and forth than to set up a big camp. The owner, the foremen, a few who had never lived anywhere but in a levee camp still had their tents. Even if he felt like travelling, Son thought, it wouldn't be the same. But he felt so good after talking to Mace he called the doctor in Grenada, told him what was going to happen to him if he didn't pay off. He drove home feeling better than in a long time, admitted maybe there was some truth to what Kate said, getting out and seeing folks did him some good.

When he came into the house, he said to Kate lying on the bed,

"You know some of these nights I've been sitting up thinking, I was thinking that if I could get to feeling better, I wouldn't mind going over there and seeing what It-ly looks like."

Kate said, "It's too late to go on a trip like that now and you know it."

He stood a moment, then turned around and went out, guessed he had known it but had not been sure anyone else did. In the living room he sat down to wait for supper. The afternoon paper came and he read it. Turning on television at random, he called, "Groucho's on!" but no one answered and no one came. Tippy's toenails clicked across the kitchen floor and he whistled. Tippy came and he watched the program, occasionally rumpling the dog's ear, saying Boy, ooold boy . . .

After supper, he felt tired; having had more activity than usual he thought he would sleep. He watched television as long as possible, until he felt sleepy, and went to bed thinking he would sleep. Then he lay staring into the dark, wondering when.

It seemed a long time until Thanksgiving but George and Laurel came. Kissing him, Laurel thought how much smaller he seemed. Her arms went around him; she felt the larger. She spoke of it to Kate who said, "People always shrink up when they get old."

"But he's not old. He's not even sixty."

"Well I'll be glad when he is so he can stop talking about it," Kate said. "It seems to worry him. He can't get over being almost sixty."

For the few days George was there, they talked. Laurel asked about what. "Football, baseball, money, his business," George said. "He told me about going to Cairo and having to be protected by the militia. About men with wads of small bills and change buying sticks of dynamite to blow up levees and flood other people; how he knew it but had to sell dynamite any way he could during the Depression. He just needs somebody to talk to, to listen."

"Yes, but a man," she said. "Mother says that's another sad thing about men having to stay home. They never see anyone but women. For so many years, he paid no attention, never talked to me, that now I don't know anything to say to him. I don't know anything he knows and vice versa."

"He's easier to talk to than Kate," George said. "She's got a wall a mile thick around her. I tried to talk about Frank's being an invalid, said she had to start planning the house around that."

"He's not an invalid!"

"That's just what Kate said, in just that way."

"Well he's not," she said.

"He's the next thing to it, Laurel," he said. "He will be."

"No, he couldn't be an invalid. If he had more to think about, he might be better. And he told mother what to do all those years, she can't just start telling him."

"She's going to have to."

"She can't. He wouldn't let her anyway. You don't know the way it was."

George was on the plane and she thought him still wrong, thought everything would be all right. Maybe he wouldn't get better, but he wouldn't get worse. And her baby would be a boy, to make up for her not having been. He would "toughen the little sucker up," make him a man. She did not know how when she was in California; in her dreams, she never was. She knew of positions in southern universities she thought would be better for George; she would somehow get him to move. She had thought of coming back to Delton, then she would see again that semi-dark early morning room where the sheets smelled of whisky and were rumpled as he turned to give her the only piece of advice he ever had, about a rolling stone. Because of that she had had to stay with George. But if he came to Delton, everything would be fine.

George had said, When will you be home? and she had answered, Two weeks, knowing that when the time was up she would extend it.

Regularly now he went to the doctor, one morning asked Laurel to drive him. Having spoken and before she could reply, he began to cough. Smoke from the cigarette he had inhaled, spit back, tumbled through the air on gusts of his breath. He seemed about to strangle. Having stood, he held to the back of the chair and shook like a mechanical toy, coughing, short, hard, sharp, so relentlessly he could not catch his breath between. Saliva appeared at the corners of his mouth. He stopped, exhausted, his eyes apologized, his face was pale. He sank his weight to one leg and slurped, recovering the saliva, then took out his handkerchief and blew his nose with a hard, blaring sound. Slowly his face regained color but seemed deflated; the skin hung in soft folds, like something punctured. He seemed a concave standing, his chest in, shoulders bowed. Staring at the floor, he quieted. Then in an attitude that missed being defiant, he threw back his head and his eyes held defeat.

"I believe it's going to kill me," he said.

Everything was still, they, the house, the outdoors. He moved a hand slowly to his chest and held it there flat. Following the movement, Laurel thought his hands seemed smaller too and they had always been so large and strong. Kate often had said, Like paws. With those big thumbs, he can't do a thing in this world with them, and he would look apologetic. From all his years in the open, his hands were permanently tanned to the wrists where his shirt cuffs had ended, as if he wore mittens. His nails were shiny and well-shaped; a thin gold hair, fine as a duckling's, lay along the back of his hands and they always seemed freshly scrubbed, to smell of soap, felt cool to the touch, like the hidden ends of grass. It was only a moment they were silent, but she thought too, I've got to remember everything about him, memorize it; thought, still, she did not believe he would die soon. She said, "That's not what the doctor said. You're just going to have to give up smoking, that's all."

He did not answer and went down the long hall. Halfway, he had placed a slender chair to rest in and stopped now. Then they were at the doctor's and Son said, "I want to do everything I can to hep myself." Dr. Phillips suggested a therapeutic girdle. Laurel drove him to the shop, waited in the room of portentous things, oxygen tanks, iron lungs, braces, crutches, supports, while he was fitted. He wore the girdle home and after dinner went away from

273

the table holding his stomach saying, "Wheww." In his room, he took the girdle off, put it in his underwear drawer and never took it out again. "That thing like to cut me in two," he said coming back.

Laurel was irritated that he gave it up so quickly. She wanted to will into him her own feeling of hope, wanted him not to sit for hours his head hung, seeming to have given in. Sometimes, passing his door as he sat, she was unable to think of anything to say, went on by. It was the relationship he had established the years he was busy; she thought of it resentfully. But she softened, thinking he had been the way he had because he had not known better. He had mellowed with age, like most rough men, had begun to sense mistakes, too late. She was gone, Kate was beyond reach. It seemed he had put all his eggs in one basket; now it was empty. She wrote George saying so and he wrote back he had seen it happen to many self-made men when they reached the top. It was as if they had hammered at one door all their lives and when it finally opened, no one was there.

To bring the house alive, she made as much noise as she could, talked along the center hall to Sarah or Kate, let doors slam, called loudly to Tippy. She thought Dr. Phillips, knowing more, could make him wear the girdle and went to see him. "Young lady, I found out in a short time I couldn't tell your daddy what to do," he said laughing, to her surprise, in admiration.

She protested and he cut her off. "It's only to make him more comfortable. He's the judge of whether it does. It's not going to cure him, Laurel."

She thought, driving home, that he was the braver after all. Simple and country maybe but without pretense. Her college-educated friends would have clapped the girdle on telling themselves it would do some good. She urged him to try the Mayo Clinic, a doctor in New York, another climate. He said he was better off at home, Dr. Phillips knew as much as those birds, she was like his mammy, always wanting to jump around.

The things she had come home for had been sent to California and arrived. George wanted to know when she was coming. She had to go. Having told about the baby, she said she would come back after it was born and from the plane window stared out thinking how many times she had, with the same regret: it was too late to turn back. He leaned against a post, one hand to his chest. Kate stood off alone; her voice had broken saying goodbye and Laurel had gone to the plane unable to look back, until now.

When the doctor in Grenada ordered another four hundred pounds Son told Holston to send it, sure he would pay off after that telephone call. Several times in the next month he went to the office and wrote the doctor each time. It was the only fellow who ever got the better of him that way. He hated to let the business go with even that one debt outstanding; but there was no reason to hang on anymore, the shape he was in, not even another year until he was sixty. In his best years he had averaged selling about a hundred and thirty-nine thousand pounds of powder a month. When he started in the business, if he sold a thousand he was doing good. That record was one thing he didn't have to be sorry about.

He wound up everything the first of the year, got on the plane and flew to Illinois. Leaning toward the man behind the desk he said, "Fifty thousand dollars. That's my price," living through now what had been so long a dream. If some things hadn't worked out, this was. The man had said they wanted to buy use of his name, wouldn't do as much business in that part of the country without it. Son said, Sho nuff?

Selling of property and fixed assets had been agreed on without trouble; his name was the last point and the man had to argue. Son thought, Hell, he had waited all these years, he could wait some more, hoping they would give him a watch with an inscription, For Thirty-five Years Service.

But they did not. They shook his hand all around, took him out to dinner and put him on the plane the next morning fifty thousand dollars richer. He hadn't budged a inch, he told later. The plane rose over the unfamiliar cold country, went into clouds threatening snow, and he felt it right to be hidden, suspended, nowhere, because suddenly with his business lifted off him he didn't feel any-

where. I'm retired, just a old broken down retired powder peddler, he thought. A crowd of men had gotten on the plane, feeling good, wearing ten-gallon hats. Oil men, he thought, because
from Delton the plane went on to Houston. He felt like standing
up and saying, O.K., big shot, how much's anybody ever going to
pay you for your name? Not that oil you bring up out of the ground.
Your name.

For most of the trip he slept dreaming about the watch, woke
thinking maybe he'd buy himself one with an inscription that read,
To A Tough Customer.

As little, Kate said, as he had had to think about that business,
what was he going to think about now? He ought to have had a
hobby.

He hadn't had time to have a hobby, he said. He said stocks and
bonds were his hobby. He had financial magazines coming in the
mail and read those. He ordered stationery with his home address,
set up a desk in his room, wrote checks, attended to what business
he had to there. Clipping his first coupon, he wrote Laurel and
Winston to tell them. Regularly now he wrote them, took rides
about the city to find mail boxes he could reach from the car.
One day, making a left turn, his fender was struck by an on-coming car. No one was hurt; he contended it was the other fellow's
fault and the case came to court. Once he would have had the
juice to argue, now stood holding the rail, heard himself judged in
the wrong. It was the first wreck he had ever had. He worried,
knowing his reflexes and judgment had slowed down. Writing
letters, he had to think a long time.

Still, all that spring he ventured on his afternoon rides, up and
down highways and seeking back roads. Buzz was in town and
came to see him. Son told him, "Hell, I get so lonesome sitting here
I get out and ride. Look for gravel roads. I bet I've found ever
gravel road left in Delton County. I get on it and just ride up and
down, to remind myself what it use to be like."

Buzz had come with news but for some moments could not say
anything. Then he said that all these long months since Son had

last been in East Tennessee he had been taking out that waitress. He was going to get a divorce and marry her.

If there was anything that could make him forget how lonely he was, for the time being stop trying to figure out things, that was it: his best friend about to make the biggest fool in the world of himself; he told him so. Jesus Christ, that woman had been out with every contractor and peddler that had ever been up thataway: nobody had been going to marry her. Whew! You didn't give up the kind of woman he had for that kind. He had been out with aplenty women; there wasn't any two ways about that. But, hell, he never had been going to marry any of them. What does she want to marry a old man for anyway? he said.

I ain't that old, Buzz said.

You're old enough to know better, Son said. If you're going to marry her, get on out. I don't even want to see you anymore.

What should he do? Buzz said.

Take your wife back up there with you and don't let her come home again to you do, Son said.

It was a mild winter and at the beginning of March forsythia buds opened in the warm afternoons. He started again rides he had stopped while Buzz and Will were in town. He had thought for the first time of investing money in real estate, drove about looking at lots advertised in the morning paper. He always took Tippy, sometimes drove to the edge of woods and let Tippy run there, after birds and things he never saw that disappeared down holes. He laughed telling Kate and Sarah, Tippy was going to catch himself something some day too. Driving along, he thought of all the dogs they had had, mostly plain dog, the kind he liked. His favorite had been a black and tan named Sam. He had seen it following a Negro boy down a country road, stopped and said, "Boy, how much you take for that dog?" The boy had said four bits. He gave him a dollar and brought the dog on home. After he was run over, Laurel had gone fancy and bought this pedigreed poodle that looked more like a monkey than a dog, stayed under a chair and peed if you spoke to it. He had not liked Tippy until they started taking rides. Now he guessed he was one of the smartest dogs he had ever seen. Almost every day after his late breakfast, he started out with Tippy, sometimes to look at property, sometimes without aim. Sometimes he stopped by the office for a few minutes, other times went on by into Mississippi, just to travel the flat open road.

This morning the anticipation of spring drove him out earlier than usual. He could not find Tippy, went alone, the radio on for company. He always turned to the Negro station. Aside from music, they had a fellow talking in a conversational way, announcing dogs that were lost and jobs open. Today the State Employment Office was looking for fieldhands, seamstresses and dishwashers. A record was played that seemed like a lot of hollering to him before the announcer said, On the Main and Elm Street bus today —bus number five—Mrs. Lettie Sue Jackson of 4-0-3 First Street lef' her wallet; telephone 227-0717. Anybody finding it please call Mrs. Jackson. Son said aloud, She won't see that wallet again, losing it on the bus.

After another record, the announcer said, Billy Roy Brown has lef' home. Billy Roy, he said, call your Momma. Billy Roy, call your Momma, let her know where you're at or come on home.

Thinking of Billy Roy roaming the city, Son laughed, knowing no such plea would have brought him back when he was fourteen years old and ran away. Settling to the highway he knew suddenly where he was going, kept straight on until he pulled into the parking lot some time past the usual lunch hour. He went inside slowly. The restaurant was empty except for a waitress cleaning up behind a counter and a hostess who came forward carrying a menu and said, "How do. Can I give you a table or you want the counter?"

He found breath to say, "How bout over yonder at the table by the window?"

"That'll be fine," she said, going ahead and pulling out a chair. He sat down and the sun through the plate glass window made the white starched tablecloth bluish like water through heat. The hostess was large and soft, blonde except for an inch of hair close to the roots. "What can we do for you today?" she said.

Holding the menu, not reading, he said, "Can you rustle me up a bowl of barley soup?"

"Sure can," she said.

He sank over his arms folded on the table and said, "I drove near bout a hundred miles to get me a bowl of that soup."

She had been turning toward the kitchen, stopped and said, "You don't mean it."

He tapped a foot, grinning. "I passed here, Lord, I don't know how many years ago, and had me some barley soup. I been meaning to get back ever since."

"I declare," she said and called to the waitress. "Alice Jean, this gentleman's driven near bout a hundred miles to get some of our barley soup. Can you beat it?"

Alice Jean stopped wiping to stare but said nothing. The hostess said, "Cook's gone for a rest. I'll get it. Anything else?"

He looked at the table, trying to think; breakfast had been a short while ago. Looking up, he said, "I'll have to let you know."

"Take your time," she said, turning away. He watched her go, wide hips rocking like boats at sea, not even thinking about them. With a sound of expiring, the kitchen door fell to; the room was quiet. Alice Jean sat reading now, her head barely visible. One of his arms lay in a half-circle across the table; he moved the other to meet it; his fingertips, touching, raced one another. He looked forward to the soup. Time passed and he had to think about something else, watched a fly trapped inside a transparent cake box, hit again and again and finally settle, still. On the highway cars passed, chromium glinting like foil shining. He watched each car; one turned into the filling station next door; an overalled attendant ran out, bent to the window, put in gas. Hanging up the hose, the boy took money and leapt on long legs back to the station. Son thought, It must have been the right change. Heat made the day dance beyond the window; thin streams of rain seemed to fall in the shimmer.

The hostess's face filled the round porthole window in the

swinging door before she pushed through carrying a tray steam rose above. He smelled the soup as she approached. It was as he remembered, thick with barley and diced carrots. He said, "Looks like I'll have to have a glass of sweet milk after all."

She called, "Alice Jean, a cow juice," and laughed, exposing gold fillings. "We seen it ordered that way in a picture show," she said. Alice Jean brought the milk foamy from the spigot and went away without speaking.

He blew on the soup and tasted it tentatively, after a spoonful said, "Not bad."

She smiled. "I'm glad it's not no disappointment when you've come so far. Sometimes, things aren't like what you remember."

"Last time I had two bowls and I remember driving away feeling full as a tick.'

"I declare," she said.

"You got the same cook?"

"To tell the truth, I'm not sure. I haven't been here too long myself."

He was glad she was not busy. He said, "I didn't think you was here before. Seems like there was a tall woman with a thin neck. Friendly and nice as she could be though."

"Always had a bow or a bunch of flowers under here?" Raising her chin, the hostess cupped her small puffy hands beneath it.

"I don't know now. I was only here the one time."

"Miss Selma, bound to be," she said. "She up and left without a minute's notice, to get married. Figured she better grab the chanct while she had it, I reckon. Lucky for me. I got the job. Before I was a waitress and didn't care for waitress work."

"Hard on your feet," he said.

"Huh, hard on a lots of things you don't know nothing about," she said, looking down at his bowl. "Want another one this time?"

His arms circled the bowl as if the warmth were precious. He took them away. "I don't believe I could make it," he said.

"You could stand some weight," she said.

He looked down at himself. "I can't get a ounce on me. I got my wife putting me half a pint of heavy cream on oatmeal and bananas every morning. It don't do a bit of good."

———

"If that's not always the way." She lowered her chin and looked over her bosom. "If I drink a glass of water it puts a pound on me even standing and working like I do."

"If you're fat you want to get thin, if you're thin you want to get fat," he said. "Do you smoke?"

She pulled out a chair, sat down and said, "No, I've never cared for the taste of tobacco."

"That's one thing the doc says keeps weight off me," he said. "But I don't know whether he knows what he's talking about or not. I tried to give up smoking but I got so nervous I liked to jumped out of my skin."

"I guess I'm lucky about tobacco. I know everybody says I am."

"It don't do you any good but if there's one thing I enjoy, it's cigarettes."

She nodded at his bowl. "How bout some pie or cake?"

Thinking of the fly, he shook his head. "No mam. I might do with some plain vanilla ice cream, though."

She called, "Alice Jean, bring the gentleman a dish of cream. Vanilla."

"The thing the doc wants me to stop smoking for is my cough," he said. He coughed lightly to show. "I got a cough that's a booger."

"I said to myself when you come in, he looks kind of peaked. You better take care. A cold can fool you."

"No mam, it's not a cold. It's a cough. I keep it all year round. It's something to do with down here." He indicated the hand he held hard and flat against his chest.

"Well, I'm sure sorry to hear it," she said. Alice Jean brought the ice cream. Puckering her lips, blowing upward, the hostess said, "I got heated up when the soup did. Alice Jean, I could do with some cream, but not that much." When Alice Jean brought it, the hostess ate several bites with quick tongue flicks, then sat back to say, "What business you in?"

Very deliberately he put down his spoon, leaned back and said, "I'm a old wore out powder peddler."

She had her spoon halfway to her mouth, her mouth open, stopped the spoon and said, "A what?"

"Powder peddler," he said.

"You mean face powder, cosmetics, so on?"

He was laughing before she finished, having led her up to it carefully. It always gave him a kick. "Blasting powder!" he said. "Caps, fuses, dynamite, explosives."

As breathless as if she had been running, she said, "You don't mean to tell me."

"Ain't you ever known any old wore out dynamite peddlers before?" he said, grinning.

"I have not," she said and called, "Alice Jean, want to buy some dynamite? This gentleman sells it."

Low, he said, "She needs a stick of it under her." The hostess threw back her head and laughed in a holler. Alice Jean had stood to look with interest across the room of empty tables. "What does anybody want dynamite for?" she said.

"Farmers. Road builders. And how you think the levee got here?" he said. "I blasted for levee work from Cai-ro, Illinois, to Vicksburg and back. It was a booger but we made her. I cleared a thousand acres of land for old man P. J. Willson near here."

"I know Mr. Willson," the hostess said. "That's where I was a waitress at, in Willsonville. He'd come into the cafe."

He said, "Old man P. J. Willson started out like the rest of us, without one dime in our pockets to rub against another."

"I declare, I thought he had always had his money."

"No mam, that old man made it; you got to hand it to him too. During the Depression, he was just starting out to farm all that land when I was starting my own dynamite company. It took me awhile to do it, but I run ever competitor I had out of this territory. Once they started running, they kep' on too, just as far-rr as they could run." He looked at her triumphantly, sat back and laughed until tears came. Her eyes held vicariously his delight. "Everybody said I was crazy to start out when I did and I had to work myself almost to death now. But I did what I said I was going to. I made it."

"That's something for a man to be able to say, to me," she said.

"Yes mam, that's what it seems like to me too," he said. "But to some folks it seems like it it'nt anything."

"You never know what's going to happen," she said. "My husband left me. Died of a heart attack when he was forty years old. You can't look ahead to those things, can you?"

"No mam, and that's why I've always believed you had to save for a rainy day. My wife says what's the use of making money if you never spend it and have a good time, but I promised myself a long time ago I wasn't ever going to get caught short of cash again."

"I got enough to get by, as long as my health holds," she said.

"There's some women not happy or satisfied no matter what you do for them," he said.

"You only make yourself unhappy wanting all the time," she said. "I got me a nice son, lives down in Florida in a little house him and his wife has fixed up as nice as can be. I go down there every onct in a while and they come here come Christmastime." She looked at him expectantly.

He said, "What I started out to tell you was, when old man P. J. and me started, we had a falling out because I wouldn't extend him credit."

"You don't mean it?" she said, her mouth opening as if something hot were in it.

"Shoot, I couldn't extend credit to nobody. I was scraping around trying to eat like the next fellow. I didn't know the old man was going to hit the jackpot."

"If I don't kid Mr. Willson if I see him again!"

"We got back together. He was one of my biggest customers around here for thirty years. Last time I saw him, four, five, I don't know how many years ago, we got to laughing about it then." He pushed his chair back and sat, one hand to his chest. "I guess I've eat up about all I can. How much I owe you?"

She looked at his dishes, whispering inaudibly, then said, "Sixty-five ought to do it."

He stood, sinking his weight onto one leg, dug deeply into a pocket full of change and brought up a handful. He extricated a quarter for Alice Jean and gave the rest to the hostess. Going ahead, she rang up the money. He took a toothpick from beside the register and his hat from a peg by the door, opened it, and stood aside as she came forward and went out behind her. They stood squinting, then walked to his car, shining like a squat black beetle in the sun. She took her hand from shading her eyes and offered it. "It sure has been a pleasure, Mr . . ."

"Wynn," he said, shaking hands. He touched his hat with the other. "Dynamite Wynn."

"Stop in again when you're travelling this way," she said.

He said, "I don't do any travelling any more. I retired here not too long ago."

"Why that's nice," she said, "when a man don't have to work so hard, can take it kind of easy."

He was in the car, had started the motor, sat humming it. "That's the way I always had it figured," he said. "I'd catch up on my rest, then me and my wife would do some of the things I'd always put off. I'm about caught up on my rest but it don't seem like I can get to feeling like doing the other things."

"Well, take care of yourself, hear?"

"I intend to," he said. "Pleased to meet you." He touched his hat again, the car was moving. "Tell old man P. J. if you see him you saw Dynamite. He'll know who you mean."

"I'll do it," she said, calling as he drove away, "I'm Iris!"

At the edge of the highway, he stopped, saw her in the rearview mirror turning back to the restaurant; he knew he could not make it this far again but she was the kind of woman he liked, like Scottie, one who knew what it was to get out in the world and turn a nickel. Having looked, he drove quickly onto the highway to avoid being caught behind a truck which came ponderous and slow like some antiquated animal; he watched it fall behind, the driver a tiny figure bouncing in the cab, thought of the time he drove the dynamite truck, knew he wouldn't want to have pushed one down the road for a living. Belching, he tasted the soup and something cold, reminiscent of the ice cream. He searched the toothpick from his breast pocket and picked at the back tooth that always worried him after eating. He drove with the pick in his mouth, sucking at it occasionally. The highway stretched ahead as long as the rest of the afternoon. On either side wide flat fields rushed away full of cotton plants now no higher than mushrooms. From an unadorned shack in the center of a field three tow-headed children ran to the road, stood at its crumbling edge and waved as he passed, their pale eyes vivid an instant in flushed faces. In return, he waved and went on, thinking they would never amount to more than their pappy, thinking of his own rise. He settled with his old feeling of familiarity to the wheel and the road, flying along past countryside eroded into gullies filled with old cars and tin cans rusted almost beyond recognition, the earth's color the same as the Mississippi. He viewed with a sense of change kudzu vine planted to stop erosion, growing so thickly roadside, trees and telephone poles were choked and rushed on through a tangled, jungle-seeming world of greenery. Around the squares of little towns he went, remembering the mornings with the old Negroes coming to town, how he liked listening to their conversations; now benches were empty because of the chill afternoon. Close to the city, he was aware of changes that had come since he had started out peddling dynamite; the countryside lost its particularity, was the same as he had seen coming close to cities across the country and back; there were shopping centers crowded with automobiles as dazzling in the day as mirrors. Gay as carnivals, the shopping centers were hung with triangular banners and bunting and smelled, as far as the road, of yellow-greased almost stale popcorn. They were filled with people stopping to stare, ponder and move on. Now, on what had been countryside when he started out, row after row of small houses were set on treeless plots of land, but there was a vacant feel, different from the first little street where he and Lillian had lived, though here too the yards were littered with riderless tricycles and corroded toys. Behind him the highway rushed backward as quickly as the years; the years fell before his mind like pieces in a puzzle. He thought of the things he had told Iris about starting out, thought how hard it had been and good because it was, how on the levee he had learned you couldn't be afraid and it had given him the courage to quit his job the way he had, start his own company; he thought on back to Mammy and Poppa, those years, of Mill's Landing and Old Deal, knowing now he was the same as that old man had been, always talking and thinking about the past, what had already been, because not much else was going to go on. All that time he had been working he had thought he was working toward this time, maybe had not been after all. At least he had found the business he wanted to be in; maybe that was all you could ask. Some men didn't have even that much to be grateful about. Over and over he thought about Laurel, that the mistake he had made was letting her go off in the first place or to California or out there the last time; maybe that had been his mistake. If he could go back, whatever he had to do to keep her at home, he would have. He had the baby to look forward to, even if Laurel was far away. Leaving behind road, fields, gutted, vine-covered countryside and people who had turned to watch him go, he went on, pursued by the sun emblazoned above him like a medal and by memory.

"Do you know why your wife does this?" the doctor said, filling out a form.

He sat forward, able to breathe easier, and said, "She says to worry me to death."

The doctor gave him a steady look. "From the looks of you it looks like she's about done it," he said.

"She says she's getting back at me for a lot of hell I use to raise," he said. He looked down a moment, one hand flat against his chest, then raised his eyes. "I guess I did. I guess I made some mistakes. But I didn't know I was."

"I see she's never been in a sanatarium before or had psychiatric help. If you leave her long enough, maybe we can help."

"Hell, keep her," he said.

"At least a week," the doctor said.

He was in touch with Cecilia but said he could stay alone with Sarah to cook. When the week was up, the telephone rang one night and it was Laurel saying the baby was born. "Well that's mighty fine," he said. "What kind of baby is it?"

"A boy," she said.

"We needed some more boys in the Wynn family," he said. "How are you?"

"I'm fine," she said. "Is mother there?"

"She's gone to the drug store to get me a prescription. She'll call you first thing in the morning."

"Daddy, he already has big hands that are going to be strong like yours," she said.

He said, "Well I hope he finds out some more things than I ever could."

When he could get up the next morning, he went to get Kate. She was on a sun porch playing cards and came toward him smiling, looking better, he thought, than she had in a long time. He believed the place had done her some good. From many rooms along the hall people came to tell her goodbye. Leaving, she said she had liked it; there were people around to talk to all the time and something to do. She was full of conversation, he knew that. She said how nice the doctor had been, but quickly, "It wasn't really like seeing a psychiatrist. He just talked to me. Said he knew I drank to give myself a lift, feel happy. I told him I was the most miserable person in the world when I was drinking."

When he could get a word in edgewise, he told about the baby.

"Why, it's more than a month early," Kate said. "Did Laurel say anything about that?"

"No," he said. "And neither did I." But he had sat up half the night thinking about it, had always thought that if a woman had all that education she could avoid making mistakes. And if that wasn't the answer, he wondered what was. "I'm just going to think about it like a stock dividend. We got two for one," he said. But it was not so easy telling his friends.

When the baby was six weeks old, Laurel came home. Her hair had grown and she wore it pulled back and in a large knot on top of her head. Kate said right away be sure she didn't skin it back tight like Cecilia; but it was softly waved about her face. He was glad to see she had gained some weight and later asked her when she was going to stop biting her fingernails. Never, I guess, she said. At the airport, he peeped into the blue blanket and said, "Shoot, that's a pretty baby," and held him all the way home. Laurel carried the baby into the house, then he held him some more. During the month she was there for the first time in his life he realized just how helpless a little baby was.

Laurel came again when the baby was four months old and he had even more pleasure. The time in-between had been spent waiting for the baby to come again. He said, "What in the world you been feeding this baby? He's popped out like a bull frog. I'm going to call him Roll-o. No little baby ever wanted to be called George."

Each morning, waking earlier now, he called at the top of his voice. "Roll-o! Hey, Roll-o, what are they doing to you?" When he could get up, he went to where the baby was. "Roll-o," he would say, "we've got a load to carry being in a house full of women. What's that stuff they're feeding you, phew. You need a steak." One evening each week he watched prize fights between young Negroes and whites. He sat the baby on his lap to watch too. "Roll-o, tell him hit that nigger again," he would say. Sometimes when he lay in bed, Laurel put the baby beside him. He drew the baby close, covered him, put his arms around him. One night Kate said, "Frank, I swear, you're going to smother that baby yet." He withdrew, looking sheepish with need.

In the long twilight hours before dinner when he had finished reading the afternoon paper and usually sat waiting for supper, now he began to talk to Laurel. One afternoon he told her to get paper and pencil. "Write this down," he said. "Maybe you'll never need it but it's information that's only in my head. You have three hundred shares in the Delton County Bank and Trust Company . . ." Impatiently, she wrote stock numbers, dates bought, prices paid, wondering why it had to be done this minute. No, he had said, it could not wait until morning. But she was convinced there was plenty of time. Moments before, groping for words, he had tried to impart some idea of what it had all been about, building a levee, said it had begun with men with wheelbarrows trying to fight floods, how had they had the nerve? And a hundred years later there was one safe secure line, unless the big flood came; did she realize that? No, she had said, thinking it was interesting, that she would listen later. She was staring in a mirror trying to decide if she had gained weight since the baby. Dr. Phillips had not said the disease would kill him and she held fast to her dream. Roll-o would grow up and he would be here to see him.

One evening he exclaimed sharply, holding up the paper. "I see here where Lillian's died." It had always surprised him, he said, that living in the same town they had never run into each other but once; he told Laurel about that time, told about the time he came home and found his furniture gone. "I made up my mind then wasn't anybody ever going to do me like that again and nobody ever has." He told about the bills she had left and how ever since he could, he had paid every bill he got the day it came in, did not wait for a month's worth to accumulate. In a moment he said, "I'd be a widow-man now." He tried to imagine that, tried to imagine Lillian old and Lillian dead, but he could picture only the young woman he had last seen. The paper said she had died after a short illness; he wondered what it was, wondered if she had ever thought of him again. All he knew about her was that shortly after marrying that old man he had lost a lot of money speculating in grain. He sure had been glad to hear it.

He said, "I can't pick up the paper anymore without seeing somebody I use to know has died." He leaned back, his hand against his chest. "You know a lot of folks for a long time, then suddenly it seems like you don't know a damn soul. I mean it."

One night he told about an old man who had cut the price of dynamite and how he had broken his son's nose. "See these knuckles? They never did grow back just exactly right." Long afterward the old man had blackballed him for a club he had wanted to join; he had been sorry about that. Another time he told about running away from home and of the trip to see Pike's Peak again. A moment he seemed to confront a long empty corridor, then said, "I guess I should have known it couldn't be the same." Then his eyes were full as they must have been long ago with merriment. "I worked out there with a bunch of Mexicans, learned to talk some Mexican. *Frijoles, frijoles, frijoles,*" he said, fast. "Beans! That's the way they talked holding out pans for food. *Zapato, zapato.* Shoes!" Laurel waited expectantly. He looked sadder. "That's all I remember," he said. "But I use to know some more."

One morning he got up with a desire to eat hot cakes; several mornings in a row they went out to have brunch. Sarah could make hot cakes better, Kate said; but it gave him a reason to go out. He took Laurel into Mississippi to see a marker where the levee began, one day asked if she would drive to Mill's Landing.

The shelves of the commissary, a store now, were sparsely filled, only a few of the twelve houses still standing were occupied, but the cottonwoods shaded the road. Waving a hand toward empty countryside, he told where the mill and Niggertown had been. Laurel gave such a start, he laughed. "Well that's what we called it back in those days," he said without apology.

The road to the highway was little more than tracks through dirt. He had Laurel stop at a small unpainted store, a gas pump in front. Inside, an old lady pulled an overhead string unlocking the pump. She came out and gave them gas. He asked if she had known a man who long ago ran the store and had a daughter named Betty Sue. Remembering, the old lady said Betty Sue had married a man who bought an orange grove in Florida; she thought he had done all right. Pulling away, Son told that Betty Sue had been his first gal.

Another day, driving, he decided to find Shut-eye. Laurel, having read his letter to Son, wanted to meet him too. They questioned Negroes in East Delton until they found the old man, his eyes covered with a film nearly blue. His mind was clear. He and Son, in the living room, talked of old times. The floor held patterned linoleum hardly distinguishable from a rug. Crocheted doilies were on the wall as decorations, along with two framed placards. Son read, Is My Name In the Book of Life? and Give Me My Flowers While I Live.

Shut-eye's niece, Laurel's age, was cooking. Shut-eye asked them to eat and Son agreed. Laurel was embarrassed to find only two places set, could not look at the niece who did not look at her, went to sit in the living room with Shut-eye while they ate. Afterward, Son took a toothpick from a little glass in the center of the table and left several dollars under the rim of his plate. Going home, Laurel said, "Couldn't we have asked them to eat with us?"

"Shut-eye don't want to eat with me," he said. "Wouldn't if I had asked him."

She bet he would, Laurel thought, thinking of the niece; nothing would make him think ways he had treated Negroes in the past were wrong; why argue? The future was important and she was sorry but he would have no influence on that. It was impossible to understand why it outraged him to see Negro entertainers on television (is that another nigger they got on there?), though he enjoyed being with Negroes and had been more than anyone she knew except those who lived in levee camps: had risked safety for them: had told her all the time he drove Greaser looking for Booker T. his flesh had prickled wondering if that big Negro on the back seat would lose control, turn on him. He seemed to sense disapproval by her silence, suddenly told about Mister Will taking Emmie's galvanized pail of change to the bank every week to get a hundred-dollar bill. Did she know any Yankees who would have? He had known men who had Negro gal friends, too, if she wanted to know that, because they liked them. Yankees ran off at the mouth, thought they knew everything, tried to run everybody's business, but when it came to taking care of Negroes they never had or would. They sped through countryside where once he had gotten out of his car, knocked on a cabin door, asked a Negro woman to use her outhouse; she had fed him too; he guessed none of it could happen anymore; it was too bad. Laurel asked if the woman had come to his house would he have let her use his bathroom? He said a four-letter word and they sped on, he knowing one thing, it had been a mistake sending her up there to that college in New York. He was silent; she thought her words had sunk in. He knew there was no sense telling about Sho Nuff coming back up the levee saying he had come home, wanting a job, and Will saying nothing after ten years but, Go back to work then.

Kate said he had changed. He would eat and do things he never would before. An Italian restaurant opened and they went over and over to eat a special salad. Wop salad, he called it. Kate said, "I never thought I'd see the day you ate garlic, green peppers and ripe olives."

He smiled, suddenly shy. Remembering the Gibsons in California he told Kate to invite Martha and Will to dinner, he was going to fix some at home. In the afternoon he went for a haircut and came home with a bottle of wine. Kate lit candles and he said nothing at all about turning on the overhead fixture too. Afterward she said it was the nicest party they had ever had.

Will walking in gave Son a start; white-haired, fragile, old, he seemed Red Johnson coming all over again, until Son looked in the mirror at himself, thought how young he had been when the old man taught him to figure, marvelled at the time passed since, wondered looking at Laurel where he had been all the years she was growing up? Mister Will was determined despite bad health to have the last camp on the river; there were only a few and Son hoped he made it. After dinner Martha said, "Frank, we had been thinking about you. First thing when we came home we were going to call but you beat us to it. Is there a single scrap of old times we haven't talked about tonight?"

"Not any I can think of," he said. They had taken turns recalling. Son remembered Tangle-eye eating powder before he shot dynamite, had always meant to try it. Once more, they would all like to be in camp on a pay day, the way it had been. Remember the conjure woman? Emmie with her pains leaping here and there? I could even put up with trying to sell Mrs. Riley some good food to cook for all those kids she had, Martha said, laughing. I'd even like all those old fly-bitten mules around. I'd like every boy back in those old floppy straws and pinned-up overalls. "What would you like, Mister Will?" Son had said.

"Shoot," Will said, his way quiet and hesitant. "I'd just like to have it all to do over again."

Son knew that was what it came down to: it had been more fun making his money than having it. Once more he would like to fly down a dusty road, have Negro boys turn to call, Dynamite man coming! He recalled the eighty-two cases he had shot up in a day, could not tell how the single cry shook him like love: Dynamite! Dynamite! Dynamite! He heard it mutely in his long and silent days and nights.

Leaving, Will shook hands, turned to shake Laurel's and said what she had not wanted anyone to: unsaid it might not be true. "When are you leaving, Laurel?"

"Day after tomorrow. But we'll be back Christmas," she said.

"I know your momma and daddy hate to see that baby go," Martha said. They were gone and only her words remained. The three left said nothing, avoided one another's eyes and went silently to bed.

Then it was that morning and Laurel felt it was a dream saying, "Tell Grandpa you'll see him Christmas." She took the baby from Son who had held him wordlessly to the airport. He could not walk to the plane and back, would wait in the car until Kate returned. Laurel leaned through the open door. "Christmas. Take care of yourself till then."

"I'll do what I can," he said. "The doc says he's going to try me on some oxygen. Maybe that'll fix me up."

Kate said, "Laurel, they're calling your plane," took the baby's bulging diaper bag and hurried inside.

He sat forward in his characteristic bent way, looking at nothing; she stood on the curb. Behind were years of silence and ahead was understanding; but what words made any difference now that she was leaving?

He said, "Do you need any money?"

"No, I have plenty," she said. "Thank you."

Kate called from the doorway; even the porter returned to hurry her. She took one step backward and closed the car door. "Goodbye," she said. "We'll see you."

He said nothing. A loudspeaker called her name. In a rush she turned and ran in the direction she did not want to. Strapped into the plane, she was breathing heavily, her arms ached; she realized how far she had run, up steps, through the terminal, down a long ramp, carrying the baby unaware, the weight inside her was so much greater. She held the bag Kate had thrust, whose face had been cold and moist. Kissing her, Laurel had smelled the particular sweet smell she always associated with Kate. "You all come to see us," she had said. The stewardess had urged her on, someone barely looked at her ticket, hurried her through a turnstile; she had been running frantically again as if she might outrun Kate's answer, "He can't go anywhere."

How many times had she looked out from a plane window in exactly this way? This time Kate did not even wave. She stood in a grey dress hardly distinguishable against the grey building, except for her lonely and still lovely face, was obscured when the plane moved. Laurel held the baby so tightly she wondered he did not cry and told herself not to: he would be here and they would be back. The stewardess approached with gum. Laurel concentrated on the rhythm of chewing rather than on the scene she had left, could not look a last time at the flat brown land and the river in the distance, looked instead at the baby, wondering what he had thought jounced along in his running mother's arms. Kate had said, He'll probably throw up. She brought the clean diapers closer, wondering if George would have bought anything for dinner, if he would cook, whether she would have to, whether the baby would sleep on the trip, thinking, Now they'll be home; they'll have come into the silent house and tomorrow when he gets up it will be quiet too; he won't yell Roll-o!

Sarah had said, I'm going to take down his bed and playpen and have everything in the basement before they even get back.

She had gone away to college and he had said, Now maybe you can find out some of the things I never could. But the older she got she did not have answers, she had more questions.

The baby slept and she tried to. Closing her eyes, she saw him. She had told herself to memorize him and found she had, in detail. She saw exactly the way his hands had rested on the chair as he watched television, how he had sat resting halfway down the long hall, head hung, cigarette smoke curling about him, rubbing his hands through his hair, remembered how suddenly one day he had stood as straight as ever he had showing how Mister Will had flapped Tangle-eye's lip shut saying don't stick it out at him, then dropped back into his chair laughing until he whooped, happy the rest of the day, remembering.

Holston, she told George, had said he did not believe her father would ever have retired if he had not gotten sick, even though the business had shrunk, even though he had always planned to. Did George think he would have? Who knows, George said.

After Laurel left, there was a heat wave. The oxygen tank was placed in his bedroom and he spent a little time using that. But he had to get out and bought air conditioning for his car. Then he began again, travelling roads old and new. He realized one afternoon that he turned toward home each day as the fieldhands did. In Arkansas, shady pecan groves alternated with open cotton fields and by four o'clock every afternoon clouds were so low in the distance over the flat land it seemed you could touch them. Early the Negroes were like scarecrows in a bunch in the fields. But by four-thirty, coming from them, they were silhouettes against the horizon. He saw a man coming as if crucified against the sunset, a hoe across his shoulders, his arms stretched wide on either side holding it. Maybe that set him to thinking about the Bible he won as a boy for perfect Sunday School attendance; at home, he found it. He began to read it, was embarrassed to tell even Kate, afraid she would laugh. Sometimes he did not understand what it was all about and laughed telling himself, Well, that was why he was reading it, because he didn't know what things were all about. He got enough comfort to keep reading. The hot summer was abundant with wild hollyhocks and petunias swinging in pans on the porches of houses and cabins. Wherever he drove, people sitting on porches watched him go. Often he was caught by a quick southern rainstorm; one moment the day was beautiful and the next the windshield was splattered with rain, causing him to jump. Bright clouds would be replaced by dark ones as quickly as a scenery shift. Rain came swiftly, hard on a rising wind, pelting the car as once gravel had. He would have to slow, wipers could not keep up, peer, would hear the ceaseless flap of his tires on the pavement. Always there was jagged lightning and a moment later thunder, as if something had fallen and rolled on and on into the distance. With lessening rain he would enter the city, the whop whop whop of the wipers louder as his speed reduced, the sound a rhythm in his brain. As suddenly as it had begun the rain would stop; the sun would shine, jubilant against the sky only a short time before it set, giving a similar ocher glow to wet magnolias and city streets. Steam rose from pavement and as if the rain had never been, heat settled over the city again. The last thing in the world he would have told anybody was that in the days when he travelled most, driving along, he used to think up stories. But you had had to think about something mile after mile; after awhile you hadn't heard the radio anymore, got burned out thinking about the things you passed, though you had had to be constantly alert, particularly if caught by dark. Down in his part of the country, there had always been farmers and Negroes out in some old vehicle without good lights or any at all. Crossing the bridge into Delton once, he had come smack up on a wagonload of Negroes sitting with their legs dangling out the back, completely covering a little lantern they had tied on as a tail light. Whew! he thought, if he hadn't stopped just in time, they'd still be scraping up nigger off that pavement. He had always wanted to write a story about a cowboy, once had begun and threw it away. He had felt silly thinking up a name but had wanted something plain like Sam. He (Sam) went out of the bunkhouse and saw a horse to rope. He walked over and got a rope . . . The story had begun that way but now he didn't have what it took to think up any more. Laurel once had wanted to be a writer; maybe she'd get it all down some day.

That summer Buzz was in town for several weeks. They took the wives out to dinner and played cards. Afternoons when he did not feel like doing much, Buzz sat with him. They talked about old times. Buzz asked what advice he'd give a young boy starting out as he had. Son said, Don't. He'd hate to see any young boy starting out to stay on the road the way he had. Then I'd tell him one thing I learned quick. Don't ever order any kind of egg out on the road but a fried one; and don't eat it unless it'll stand up and

---

look at you. They talked of things they were proud of. Son said one thing was thinking up the way to set off a whole line of charges with one cap. He sat back, laughing so hard he had to have a whiff of oxygen afterward. Once he had been shooting such a charge, a ditch in a farmer's pasture. At the last minute the man said he had his prize Black Angus bull in there; but it was too late. As the charge went off the bull straddled it, was lifted straight up; he came down tail first and lit out, unhurt, running. That farmer told me, Son said, reaching for the oxygen again, he didn't find that bull for three days!

Buzz left, saying he'd see him Christmas. O.K., old man, Son said. Take it easy, thinking, Roll-o would be here too.

In the fall he crawled behind decrepit leaning school buses over-loaded with cotton pickers, a water barrel strapped to the rear, Jesus Saves scrawled along the side. With cool weather people were inside and only dogs stood at doors. The foliage was gone, the countryside was bare, and he had covered every road he could find more than once and began to stay at home. One day he thought about a steak and a butcher shop across town where they would cut a good one. Kate had gone out. He asked Sarah to come with him. She exchanged working shoes for her Sunday pumps, put on a brown wool tam, doubled a shiny velveteen ascot across her neck. They bought steak and pork sausage the butcher made the way, they both said, their Mammy had. What did she need to make a cherry pie? He bought those things. He bought dog candy on display and peppermint sticks for himself and Sarah. While Tippy ate on the back seat, they ate. He drove Sarah to see the first little bunga-low he had ever owned and Sarah told about her sister who wanted to buy a house. He told things her sister ought to know before she did. Another time, having bought another steak and more candy, he drove Sarah out from the city to see his office. He told how he had come to have it, how he had gotten into the dynamite business, some about good times and bad, and about the redecorating he had done. He gave her more advice for her sister, who was negotiating about the house, and told what it had been like giving up his business.

Regularly they went to buy food that struck his whimsy, Sarah in her Sunday clothes. They bought pecans from a friend of hers who had a good crop and was selling them cheap. A week, he sat by the gas logs shelling pecans. Later Kate was to say it was then he began talking to her in a way he never had, even asking questions about things she did, people she saw.

One morning a dozen roses arrived. Coming from the door in amazement, holding the card that read Happy Birthday from Frank, Kate entered his room and bent anxiously to the bed. He lay so still, so pale, and it was unusually late. But he was breathing. She waited a long while until he woke. He had had to take a pill, toward dawn. He struggled up and she motioned to the flowers she had set in the room. "Frank, I never have been so surprised," she said. He grinned and she said, "How did you know it was my birthday?"

He said, "Hell, you've talked about it for a week."

She said, "I've talked about it thirty years and I never got anything before."

He said, "I was too busy selling powder to listen. How old are you?"

"Fifty-five," she said. "And you don't have to put it in the newspaper either."

"Whew. Pretty soon I'm going to be sixty years old. Goddamn," he said. He got up and went to eat and talked to Sarah about problems her sister was having with her mortgage. Kate went into the kitchen, having decided to make herself a birthday cake. Once she came out to say she was making the kind Cally had. When the doorbell rang, he got up and went into the living room to see the man Sarah let in. Holding his hat, the man said, "Dynamite, you remember me?"

Son said, "Damn, if I know."

He introduced himself. He was one of the salesmen Son had run out of the territory. He had been out ever since, selling equipment in the southeastern part of the state: retired, he had come to live with his son. They talked until the man said he had to go home, his daughter-in-law was expecting him. "I was driving by and saw your name on the mailbox and I got to thinking about old times. I didn't see what difference it all made now. I just thought I'd like to see old Dynamite."

"I'm mighty glad you stopped in," Son said.

"This being retired now ain't what it's cracked up to be, is it?"

"Naw," Son said. "I guess all us old peckerwoods were any good for was work. We worked too, didn't we?"

"You can say that," he said, shaking hands. Son said stop in again when he had a chance and the man said he would. Son stood at the door a long time, having watched him go, breathing in. Then from the closet he took an old leather jacket he had worn to shoot ditches in the fall.

Kate had closed the oven door when Sarah, wide-eyed, tip-toed in, saying in a whisper for no reason except from surprise, "Mrs. Wynn, come quick and look." They stood together at the front window in astonishment. He was halfway down the driveway in slow but certain steps. At the end, he stood, hands in his pockets, looking both ways. Shortly, he returned. Kate said, "Sarah, I swear he's been taking more oxygen lately. I think he's getting better."

"He been looking better to me too," she said. "I pray so."

He came inside saying he had just thought he could make it; and he had. "I got to have my wind up if I'm going to start teaching Roll-o to fight when he comes."

In the kitchen Kate struggled with herself and won. The rum flavoring she did not put into the cake, she returned to the shelf. She had acknowledged long ago it was the first drink in the morning she had to get past; if she did, she was all right the rest of the day. She had finished the icing when he came in and said, "Tippy's about to run me crazy to go for a ride. I reckon I'll go out and get a hair-cut."

"This late," she said.

He said, "We'll be back just at suppertime."

Through the cold smoke-colored afternoon he drove over streets where long-abandoned street car tracks were still imbedded, that once he had travelled on his way to meet Poppa, to work. He was able to park in front of the shop and when he went inside Tippy scrabbled to the car window to watch. He decided on a shave and longer than necessary the barber held a hot towel to his face, bringing a color good to see. When he said so, Son said he had been to Hot Springs since he was sick and the attendants there said they never had seen anybody the baths did so much good. They talked about horse racing at Hot Springs. He hadn't done any gambling in years, Son said, but use to like to throw his money in. The street lights came on; he looked out at cold, scurrying people, glad to be in the warm shop among the familiar masculine smells. Running a satisfied hand over smooth cheeks, he climbed from the chair as the barber shook out his white towel; he whisked a broom across Son's shoulders. "Much obliged," he said, paying.

The barber, holding the coat that seemed too big, too heavy, said, "Come back to see us." Son put two pennies into a peanut machine and with a handful of nuts got into the car, Tippy greeting him. Again, he followed abandoned tracks until they disappeared, alternated eating peanuts and feeding them to Tippy. The smell of the cake, like Cally's, had been with him when he left home and had made him think of some of the better times he had had as a boy. The peanuts reminded him of eating hot roasted ones at ball games on Sunday afternoons; that made him think back to all the steaks he had eaten and whisky he had drunk with all the old boys. It had been good seeing Buzz, that other dynamite fellow this afternoon; recently Holston and a couple of others had phoned to say they had been thinking of him. Things seemed to be getting a little better. He was proud as he could be of that walk down the driveway today, wondered if he could beat this thing yet. He looked forward to warmer weather, spring, thought of all the mornings he had started out into one to shoot ditches, could not help grinning as he turned into the driveway thinking of the ways he had invented to do it. He drove fast down the driveway to splay gravel, hear it hit the underside of the car, as he always did. Winter made him think of the times he had worked wet, of the bad case of flu he had had years ago; he always would believe those things had weakened his chest, made him get sick the way he had. He sat in the garage, a hand against his chest before, aware of the effort it

took, he climbed from the car and entered the kitchen at ten
minutes after six.

Kate had let Sarah go home; they were only having cake and
soup for supper. She put two bowls, full, on the table and by the
time it cooled and they had eaten it was six-thirty. There were some
wrestling matches on he had hoped to see. She said go on, she'd
bring the cake in the living room. Was she going to watch too?

She said she might as well. She put the soup bowls into the sink
and had cut one piece of cake, was cutting the other when she
thought she heard him call. She went to the living room. He was
sitting in his chair, one hand flat against his chest. The television
was on but there was neither picture nor sound. Turning his head
as she entered, he said, "Kate, I never have felt like this before."

As she started to reply, his head went back, his mouth opened
and his eyes closed.

Over and over she would tell those who wanted to know, Laurel,
Cecilia, Sarah, how it had been; she thought he had called her but
she was not sure. She had gone to the living room at that instant,
maybe just to continue the conversation it had taken them thirty
years to start. Afterward, when the walls enclosed her and bars at
the window, she would wake to hear again her own inadequate
scream. She would tell the doctor how much time she had lost looking for an ambulance's number before she dropped the book and
called the operator instead. Taking her hands, he would say, "No,
Mrs. Wynn, the ambulance was there at six forty-five. You held
the book only an instant before you called the operator and told
her to call Dr. Phillips too."

"Oh did I do everything right?" she said.

"Everything," he said.

"They put him on a stretcher and I kept telling them Frank
took oxygen and begged them over and over to give him some
oxygen. Then we were in the ambulance and the intern looked up
and said, 'But mam, we are,' and he wouldn't tell me anything. I
waited in the corridor by myself, then Dr. Phillips came out of the
emergency room carrying Frank's wallet and a big ring of keys he

---

carried even after he sold his business and his diamond ring. He opened my pocketbook and put them inside and I said, 'Is Frank breathing?'

"And he said, 'No, he isn't.' "

It rained the morning of the funeral and Laurel, waking in her old bed, thought, He never saw Roll-o again; don't let it rain too.

The baby slept in his crib and George beside her. For thirty-seven hours her suitcases had remained in the middle of the floor and she could neither unpack nor move them. They held all her clothes; it had been her intent, packing, never to see California again, as if everything had been that place's fault. She heard Kate pass, breathing and a rustle of taffeta robe, down the dark hall. In the kitchen tap water ran and a glass was replaced. Kate cleared her throat passing along the hall again, into her bedroom. Laurel spoke to herself so clearly it might have been aloud, glancing once at George as she left the room. Entering Son's, she woke Cecilia sleeping in a voluminous white gown, only her face visible against the white sheets. Afterward Laurel would think Cecilia had not even questioned, had merely gotten up in the dark hour to help, and would sense again what it meant to have left her family. She said, "Aunt Cecilia, I'm determined about one thing more than I've ever been in my life. She's coming to the funeral sober or not at all."

"What should we do?" Cecilia said.

"We've got to throw it all away," Laurel said. Finding the cabinet open, she thought how it must have been for Kate, in possession of the keys at last. They emptied the bottles into the bathroom sink. The last fifth, full, went slowly, the fumes in the room overpowering, and Laurel could not help smiling, heard him say clearly, Phew! if that's not the biggest waste of good whisky I've ever seen. She should have hidden the bottles or at least given them away. In raincoat and boots, she took them across the yard to the alley, tumbled them breaking into the trash and looked up to see Sarah watching. She came through the gate and closed it and around to Sarah's door, which stood open. Fire in the stove made the room hot. Sarah, holding her robe close, said, "Dr. Phillips come and get me that night and I stayed in the house with her. She kep' on getting up and opening that cabinet all night. I tried to tell her. I said the house going to be full of folks in the morning. She going to see the baby soon. She say, 'He been looking forward all this time to that baby coming and now he going to be here and so what?' Seem like she don't care about nothing no more, Miss Laurel."

Not about doing one final thing for him, with dignity and with love, Laurel thought. She said, "She's not coming to the funeral if she's been drinking."

"No'm," Sarah said.

The rain had dwindled to sea spray, a mist; against the window, a final moment, there were drops the size of tears. Kindling settled, making the fire spurt, fade, and shadows loomed on the ceiling, life-sized. It had been dark in the house that night too; he had said, I'm going to murder somebody around here! and she had been embarrassed after the fear, once he had turned like a rumpled mistaken animal back to its lair. Now she was embarrassed about that, having known compassion too late. Standing in Sarah's small room, she swore she would never make that mistake again. She turned a face that was wiser toward the other who said, "I guess he was about the most lonesomest person I've ever seen," and she thought, I'll bear it because I have to: I can't run anymore. She would restrain Kate however she had to, publicly or by law. She had glanced once around the room and Sarah said, "You remember this?" From her rocking chair, she took a large stuffed dog.

Laurel said, "I think so." Against her face the false fur smelled like dust; she held it, looking at two incongruous rhinestone buttons glittering, for eyes.

"She was fixing to throw it away cleaning out the attic," Sarah said. "It didn't have no eyes and one leg tore up. I carried it home and sewed it, bought it those eyes."

Laurel would like it for the baby, had not known where it was; so many times the animal had been comfort she wondered it had fur she had matted it so with tears. Sarah said, "You want it?"

I couldn't take away the eyes you shopped for, Laurel thought and said, "No." She opened the door on a day the wind no longer disturbed saying, "I think it's going to clear." The roses were rain-stripped; the bereft garden smelled of their final sweet scent but that smell soon would be obscured by the musky one of the leaves dead and beginning to fall. The funeral parlor had had the same sweet cold scent, only of flowers from the refrigerator. Laurel said, "Are you coming to the funeral?"

"Miss Cecilia going to carry me to view him this morning, then seem like I rather stay home with Roll-o," Sarah said. She closed the door to dress as Laurel ran with the empty wastebasket across the sodden yard.

The Bible was small and thin. Without reason she had removed it from his room and put it in her own; an old hand had written the inscription; the thin ornate script was shaky: Frank Wynn for Perfect Sunday School Attendance. Now another church of the same denomination had supplied, after a search by Cecilia, a young minister who had never seen Son but stood speaking of his loss and his life to come. Amen, he said. Laurel raised her head to look once again about the room crowded with everyone he would have wanted to see, except Roll-o and Sarah; we're here because he's gone, not because we could do him some good, Laurel thought a numberless time.

The room's entrance was rounded and coming into it for the first time she had unexpectedly faced the casket seeing, above its rim, his profile; not meaning to, she had called to him aloud and gone slowly forward. His look had been perfect, his grin askew, as if he had played a giant trick: gone off and left them without saying he was. Why did you? she had said.

From their various distances, as quickly as possible, they had come, Martha and Will, Buzz and his wife, Mace, Holston, a woman named Scottie she had never seen who said, Honey, your daddy had the key to the sweetest music, B natural. Each, hugging her, communicated sorrow, and differences in their ages had perma-nently disappeared. Buzz's wife smelling of many sweet things like Kate said, Buzz said he knew if he had lost his own brother he couldn't have lost more. Buzz told Laurel, One night soon after we moved into the office together I was home and the phone rang. Frank said, What the hell are you doing? I said, I'm reading the paper. He said, Why the hell aren't you down here in Room 1403 of the Andrew Johnson? I didn't ask any questions. I just put on my coat and went. I knew somebody was there I would get a lot of business from. Frank always had his ear to the ground. He never stopped thinking of business. Then Buzz's eyes filled with tears; he went away and Laurel thought how strange it was the things people remembered to remember.

Kate had lifted the veiling, cupped her hand too late about his face. Laurel had put her hand out to touch him too and George had put out his as if to stop her. Why? she had said, having touched his shoulder before Kate put back the veiling. He said, I've never seen anything like this, it's barbaric.

It's southern, she had said. It's better than shoving people into furnaces, being afraid to look.

Holston gripped her arm too hard: That old rascal, not a day'll go by we don't miss him. People are always stopping in the office, seeing his picture, asking about Frank.

Will gave the reason: When God made him, He threw away the mold; there'll never be another like him.

Mace said, He was a ditch-digging genius.

The night had ended and they had taken pills to forget it. In the morning it had rained. She had run from the sodden yard into the house with the empty wastebasket, passing Kate who said nothing. In the dining room, Cecilia fed Roll-o. Does she know? Yes, I heard her go in there and come out as soon as I left the room, Cecilia said. I found the one hidden in the ice box and threw it away too.

They had lunch. Winston, Leila and Joe came. They crowded to the table where he was absent. Leila said, One time Frank came to our house and he and Winston and old Doc Barker drank up two fifths of whisky. I had been pickling tomatoes and Frank screwed on the tops of the jars. That winter, I started getting out jars of

---

305

tomatoes and I couldn't, nobody could get the tops off. She laughed. I had to throw away almost my whole afternoon's work. I never did tell Frank that. He had the strongest hands I've ever seen.

Kate seemed to eat what was bitter, her face dour. Laurel thought, Tomorrow she'll be all right. Afterward they stared into closets that were full saying they had nothing to wear, then dressed appropriately. George sped them through a day dazzled by the sun, where no wind soughed, and cold was barely insistent, past heartless strangers who turned blank faces, not acknowledging their grief. Laurel wanted to cry, This day's not like another. A particular man has died and the world will never again be exactly the same. But the world went unheedingly about its afternoon pursuits. In a car next to them, briefly stopped, teenagers entwined and she told them through silent lips it was not a day for love.

The minister had said, Amen, and she raised her head. He shook their hands and Kate gave him the envelope with the amount over which she had worried. Grave and on silent feet, the funeral director drew a curtain which even the minister waited beyond. Laurel knew what was in George's mind but the rest of the family were not horrified at all: he and Joe stood behind. Cecilia said, I always thought Brother such a handsome man, and turned away with Joe. Laurel said, Was he cold? knowing he was; she only wanted something to say. Kate said, Of course, and went away too. Laurel thought, When I turn, they'll close the casket. I'll never see my father again. George's hand insisted at her elbow and this time she went, without choice.

It was heavy for old Mr. Will and drooped slightly at his corner. He spoke over it to Buzz who looked back and smiled. Aren't they going to grieve either? she thought. They bore him on who had seen him through so much else, shaking the blanket of roses, buds tight-curled against the day. Mace and Holston stepped carefully over the uneven way. Winston's face was flushed from the weight and he looked only at the ground. Joe, with regret, saw the path ahead lay over the edge of Cally's grave.

They were alone for the first time. Coming into the living room, Laurel said, "George's plane is about halfway there."

"The night you were born," Kate said, "I couldn't find him. I called his hotel all night. He never would tell me where he was."

Plaintive and unanswered the question was in the room as urgent as ever it had been; being women, they still wanted to know. "Cecilia was there and Joe. The doctor and the nurses. They all knew and there wasn't anything I could do." As pliant and soft as once it had been young, Kate's face held the same dismay until she said, "After that, I didn't look for him anymore. I didn't care where he was."

They sat at the table and Sarah circled the empty chair and left dessert, crying. The back door slapped sharply shut behind her. I'll never make that mistake again, she had promised herself in Sarah's own room. She got up. Sarah's shoulders were soft and quite round. "Sarah, you didn't know him before. He was so strong and rough. It was terrible to see him this way and Dr. Phillips said there was nothing ahead but what was worse."

Sarah said, "I know. But he set there that last morning so long telling me things about my sister buying her house."

Cedars were slender spires against a sky the moon revealed full of clouds and the stars were glimmerless speckles, faint and far. Kate had come into the kitchen, seen them on the back steps and turned abruptly away. She doesn't feel anything anymore; she doesn't even understand, Laurel thought; as badly off as he had been, Kate was worse. Laurel thought how long ago it all had been; that if he had lied a moment thirty years ago, everything that had happened since might have been different. She and Sarah were cold and came inside.

This morning, no one she knew was beyond the plane's window. Staring from a taxi it had seemed beyond belief; in her life she had never ridden in a taxi in Delton before. Friends could have driven her but she would have had to tell them why and she could not explain in part. She would have had to tell it all.

Kate had said, "I want to tell you one thing. He ran my life, now you're not going to. Put all those bottles back."

"I threw them away," she had said.

She had planned to stay a month; Kate would have begun to adjust. She had always said she wanted to be free; now she was, and Laurel thought she would stop because the reason she had always said was the reason was gone. But she had not; she was worse. Dr. Phillips came and the house was filled with the smell of paraldehyde, like a smell of serious illness, of hospitals and operations. Kate lay in a darkened room and Laurel and Sarah unintentionally tip-toed. Even when Kate was walking again the smell clung; she went about without expression, like a corpse, and it was like the smell of death inside her. "What are you going to do?" Laurel said.

She said, "I'll be all right."

"But you won't be," Laurel had said. Yet they went about their days as if she would, not knowing what else to do. They shopped, bought black dresses and new shoes for the baby; friends came and they went out to lunch. Laurel waited, knowing it must be the way he had waited; it had been his problem, now was hers. She wanted him to know she had accepted it. Dr. Phillips said he had brought something from the hospital. Thinking of Kate, Laurel had not asked what. She had wandered into the empty bedroom and on the bed saw a rumpled brown paper sack, curious, opened it. She was too horrified even to cry. Mutely, the contents seemed to say: this is the sum, and she arranged them on the bed, shoes together, sleeveless undershirt, undershorts, very lightly stained, he had worn the night he died. She stuffed them suddenly back into the sack and left it. That moment, going quickly from the room, she swore her own life would come to something more. He had sat seeing nothing ahead, done nothing about it, but she would not. His other clothes Kate sent to the sisters in North Carolina to be distributed among husbands, sons, fieldhands. Laurel mentioned only these, said how strange it was to have your clothes outlast you: remembered the day he had come home proud of the suit he was buried in, never dreaming he would be. Another day, going into the bathroom, she saw his toothbrush and threw it away.

A young Negro came for the oxygen tank; Laurel had seen him

when he came to refill it. Carrying it crosswise, he stopped at the door. "Where Mr. Wynn at?" he said.

She stuttered to begin and said, "He passed away."

Abruptly, he went down the long hall and out the front door, fast. Laurel followed wondering why she had said, "passed away," an expression she had never used before in her life, wanted to correct herself, to say, I mean, he died. He turned not to see her, storing the tank. She had made a mistake but there was no way to turn back. He got into the truck, his eyes sliding past her. She said, "Were you the one who always came?"

"Yes." He started the motor, not wanting to talk. "Mr. Wynn sho was a nice man," he said, and backed out before she could reply.

She had wanted him to say it had not been the way she knew it was: his bringing the tank the most important interruption in a day of silence. She had wanted to hear every detail of the times he had come but could not have asked. She would never forget the look on the young Negro's face, wondered how long he would remember. She felt separate from everything, turned back to the house, lonely, remembered he had always tipped the boy a quarter, wished she had.

They should not have gone out to dinner but Kate would not let her refuse. Offered cocktails, surely she would refuse; but she did not. By the following evening, Sarah said, "There's one hid in the lettuce leaves."

Laurel wondered who she was hiding it from. On Sunday, Kate woke and there was no more in the house. In the middle of the morning, she called. She sat in bed in disarray, one hand to her throat. Laurel came in and she said, "You'll have to do something. I'm sick. I'm so sick."

"What's the matter?" Laurel said.

"I drank my perfume," Kate said.

Laurel felt as dispassionate as if it were happening to someone else. As if panicked, she moved; but she was not. Beneath the surface of things she did, telephone, pour out the news, she felt only outrage at being in such a position, brought to this. Dr. Phillips said to take her to the emergency room and Laurel said, "Get dressed."

Kate said, "I'm so sick."

"Get dressed," Laurel said. She put on her coat knowing she was past guilt, not responsible if Kate ruined the rest of her life. She was no longer the girl who had shilly-shallied from one thing to another: could set a course and follow it: had been able to from the moment she determined Kate was not going to the funeral if she had been drinking. "Get dressed," she said.

In the emergency room where he had been declared dead she said, "This lady drank perfume."

The nurse, taking information, said, "Why did you do that?"

A summoned intern having come said, "It's alcohol, isn't it?"

None of it touched Kate who only sat, looking sick. The intern said there was nothing to do, take her home, and went away. Laurel stared furiously at his retreating back, wanted to tell the nurse she was a fool for having had to ask. She was outraged that she had to pay five dollars for having entered the room, only to be insulted. Twice she had to tell Kate to come on, who seemed not to understand nothing was going to happen. Walking out, Laurel understood why he had come so close to defeat. Going along the corridor, past the lounging intern who gave them a knowing smile, she drew on a strength she knew she had inherited. Tough, she thought. Hell, you had to be.

In the parking lot, she sat holding the wheel, not looking at Kate. Instead she stared ahead at an old man in blue-striped pajamas looking out of the hospital window and said, "Mother, I'm going to have another baby."

Kate had sat in this same parking lot with Dr. Phillips trying to comfort her. For the first time since, she cried.

Laurel said, "I was going to stay through Christmas and George was going to come here. Now I don't know what to do."

Dr. Phillips said, "She won't be all right by Christmas. No sense having yours ruined. Why don't you go home?"

Her mind leapt ahead to all she had to do, at home. "What about her?" she said.

310

"She asked to go to the sanatarium. I asked her to promise to stay until your baby was born and then to come out to you. She said you had asked her."

"Will she be all right?" Laurel said.

Kate said she would be; this time she said, "Don't worry." They were in her room and Laurel was helping her to pack. Her clothes, her room smelled of the scent that made Laurel always think of her as young. The suitcase was closed and they went down the long hall; Dr. Phillips was waiting. Kate said again, "Don't worry," kissing Laurel, the baby, Sarah. Then she was gone abruptly, not to cry.

It was the last afternoon and she and Sarah went to the cemetery. She said, "What are you going to do now, Sarah?" Sarah said she was going to take a rest. "Miss Laurel, I'm fifty-five years old and I been doing housework since I was twelve. The first family I worked for went to Paris, France, for a year and wanted me to go and nurse the baby. But I was afraid to cross all that water. I wish I had that chance now."

"I've learned a lot too late too," Laurel said, thinking no one was without regrets.

They left the car and walked between mimosas, down a slope of dry, winter-short grass, the only immediate sound the snapping of acorns beneath their feet. Beyond guarding hedges in the distance, traffic was an intermittent sound; an airplane went overhead and a young dog barked and hushed. They stood looking at three small headstones. Cally, Laurel read, and Henry. She wondered what her grandparents had been like. Beyond his grave were the boundaries for two more. Forcefully, she knew she never wanted to be buried in California as long as she lived there. Someday her children would stand here in this exact spot and look down at five headstones in a row, as he had planned. Pleased, he had told her once, I paid a hundred dollars a piece for those plots when the cemetery opened and now they're worth almost a thousand!

Around an oak a bench was built. She and Sarah sat down; holding on, the baby stood. Sarah said, "Mr. Buzz's wife ask me to work for her, anytime. But if Mrs. Wynn wants me when she comes back, I'll stay with her. She was always good to me, Miss Laurel, even when she was not at herself. And she never did go to do the way she did."

"No, she never did," Laurel said, anymore than I ever meant to be settled away from home. How did life happen? Things she had been going to listen to, she would never hear; things that had been going to happen, never would.

"There's an old dynamite box in the basement. Could I have that?" Sarah said.

"Of course," Laurel said. "But don't you want something else from the house?"

"No'm," Sarah said. "That's the most thing like him. I can use it as a stool."

Then it was the morning the taxi was waiting. Laurel watched the driver store her suitcases. She had already kissed Sarah and started away, then ran back up the front steps. "Sarah, I'll be coming back as long as mother is here. But even if she moves to California, I'll always come back. I don't know how or even where I would stay. But I know I'll always come."

"Yes 'm," Sarah said. "I'll sho always be glad to see you."

Then she was in the taxi staring in a different way at streets she had always known and at strangers from the plane's window. But she was learning to accept differences. He was gone and she had moved up a generation. Instead of being taken care of, she took care of others, tightly held the baby as the plane began to move. It lifted over wide flat fields. Distantly she saw the river in careful curves, the levees beyond. He had always said he came along at the right time in the right place, seen the business there when he was. Beyond fame, the mark he had left on the countryside would last. So would his mark on her, she thought. Directions her life would take would be because of him. She had even begun to believe she would find out some of the things he never could. She would not make exactly his mistakes. In turn her children would know more than she. It made everything all right. She wished she could tell him.